For Pam and Bev

I0628740

By Andrew J. Luther

Tales of the Undying Empire

Undying Empire: Rebellion

Acknowledgements: I want to thank the following people for all their help and feedback.

Pam, for all the big and little things she does to make this process easy for me, and to make the book so much better.

Dan for his invaluable help smoothing out all the rough edges and filling in the holes in the plot.

Bev for her great feedback and constant moral support.

And I want to thank everyone who purchased The Tower of Dust. I cannot express how great it was to receive your comments, congratulations, and support. I hope you enjoy this one even more than the last.

TALES OF THE UNDYING EMPIRE

The Severed Oath

ANDREW J. LUTHER

VANISHING GOBLIN

www.vanishing-goblin.com

The Severed Oath

© 2013 by Andrew J. Luther

All rights reserved.

ISBN: 9780993650284

Vanishing Goblin Inc.
www.vanishing-goblin.com

Chapter One

L EYNDRA WAS WALKING TOWARDS OSHO'S OFFICE WHEN she heard the scream. Her fist tightened on the hilt of her sword, and she had to stop herself from breaking into a run. She slowed her pace and looked for somewhere to hide.

Tyina's voice continued from the scream directly into a tirade of verbal abuse without pausing for breath.

How does that woman do it? Doesn't she ever need to stop for air?

Leyndra stepped into the doorway of a small storage room off the main hallway and hoped the shadows would keep her out of Tyina's direct view.

"I *told* you I would be heading out to the country estate! How could you forget such a thing? How *stupid* can one person *be*?"

There was a blessed pause in the noise. Apparently, Tyina was giving Osho a chance to answer her questions this time. His voice, when it came, was remarkably calm. He was well used to Tyina's outbursts.

"It is not a matter of forgetting, my wife. I informed you at the time that work was scheduled to begin on the house, and you would have to change your plans—"

"That's ridiculous!" she shouted. "I don't remember you saying anything of the sort. I would remember something like that!"

"Only if you were inclined to listen in the first place," he retorted.

"How! ... Dare! ... You!" Tyina was nearly speechless with rage.

"Tyina, that's enough." Osho was still calm, but there was an edge in his voice that Leyndra knew well. His patience had just run out. "You want to go out to the country estate. You cannot. I am sure your disappointment could fill the entire Bay of Ythis. Regardless, you must find some other way to amuse yourself, and I must prepare for a meeting. I will see you at dinner."

Tyina had no intention of letting Osho off so easily. But Leyndra understood her cue and proceeded toward the door of his office.

"If you want to get rid of me, you'll fix things so I can go to the estate! Then I won't have to see your fat face for the next month, and you can pretend you have a wife who doesn't hate your guts!"

Leyndra stepped into the doorway. As she looked over Osho's wife, she was once again struck by the horrid mismatch between Tyina's appearance and her manner. She was a beautiful woman with long, golden hair and an almost translucent complexion. She wore a tight, dark gown that accentuated her curves and contrasted with her bright hair and skin.

Leyndra knew Osho had desired Tyina purely on her appearance, never spending the time to discover what her personality was really like until it was much too late to do anything about it. If only Leyndra had been working for Osho back then, she might have guided him away from such a terrible woman. In her role as Osho's protector, Leyndra always regretted that she was unable to do anything to protect him from his own poor choice of wife.

Osho was still seated at his huge desk, the dark wood matching the panels on each of the walls. His great-grandfather stared down at him from an old painting mounted high behind the desk, stern and disapproving. The large window let in the early afternoon sunlight, illuminating the heap of papers on Osho's desk.

The man himself was imposing—tall and big-boned but not, despite Tyina's accusation, truly fat. He carried a quiet demeanor that belied the iron core within. His sparse golden hair had touches of grey at the temples and his eyes were a deep blue, set into a not unattractive face.

Leyndra noticed, not for the first time, that he would still be quite a catch if Tyina didn't exist. Not that Leyndra herself had any interest. She genuinely liked Osho, but had never entertained any romantic thoughts. Her oath bound her to him in some ways that were more intimate than what he had with Tyina, but it also separated her from Osho in other ways that were definite and final.

She didn't regret it. She had a job to do, and was content being the professional who kept Osho alive.

He noticed Leyndra enter, and his glance caused Tyina to turn and see who was interrupting her stream of vitriol.

"Oh, I guess the *other woman* is here to get rid of me."

Tyina had never hid the fact that she thought Leyndra and Osho were lovers, despite the assurances from the Guild that such a situation was extremely unlikely if not genuinely impossible. For her part, Leyndra tried to remain professionally detached when it came to Osho's wife. Her oath did not extend to anyone other than Osho, and she knew this was another point of contention where she was concerned.

But the truth was, if the Idaphos family's lives were threatened, Leyndra's sole duty was to save Osho. She would pull him out of harm with not a second thought for Tyina or anyone else he cared about. It wouldn't even be a choice on her part—her training had made it instinct.

But with no immediate threat from which to protect Osho, Leyndra had to accept Tyina as a fact of life. She had long ago learned not to confront Tyina directly, as that only exacerbated matters. So, she stepped into the room and looked only at Osho.

"Master Yusku and Master Beddral have arrived. They are being shown to the conference room."

Osho nodded and stood up. Instantly, the power dynamic in the room changed, and Tyina closed her mouth and stepped back. Osho had never been violent with his wife or anyone else, but he was an intimidating figure when he stood over a person, and Tyina wasn't about to try his patience when she was visibly reminded how easily he could break her if his calm ever shattered.

Glaring at Osho and then Leyndra, Tyina strode from the room as if she had just won a complete victory over the two of them. Osho looked at Leyndra and shrugged, and she was forced to suppress a chuckle.

"What am I going to do, Leyndra?"

"It's not my place to say."

He nodded, but made no move to head towards the door.

"There are times I wish I had never married her."

He paused, considering his words. "But I did. I accepted that responsibility and I cannot just abandon it, as much as I might wish to sometimes."

Leyndra knew what he was trying to say without stating it outright. Osho was feeling trapped by his bad decision, was looking at many more unpleasant years in Tyina's company. She would never leave—his money and holdings were too important to her. But she would make the rest of his days miserable.

Osho wanted out, and yet he was trapped by his own sense of responsibility.

Leyndra didn't know what to say. She genuinely admired Osho, but also saw the truth of Tyina's life. The woman was starved for attention and excitement, a break from the boredom of being married to a nobleman who spent more time with his businesses than he did with his family. Leyndra imagined that Tyina had once considered herself extremely lucky to find a rich, handsome, nice man who wanted her, and it must have come as a terrible disappointment to find that her life as a noblewoman was not filled with lavish parties and exotic entertainments.

"If there is anything within my power that I can do to help—" she began, but he waved her off.

"No. Tyina's tirades are not enough reason for me to banish her from my life. It would mean the end of her, and I cannot do that. I'm responsible for the greater portion of our unhappy marriage, after all. I will think on it some more, and see what I might do to improve things."

Leyndra nodded, sure that it was probably too late to salvage anything of their relationship.

"Do you think she is unhappy enough to do anything...?" Leyndra searched for the right word, but couldn't settle on anything inoffensive.

"Drastic?" he asked.

She nodded again.

"No." His voice was firm and his face deadly serious. "I do not believe she has it in her to take real action against me."

Leyndra considered—as she had many times—the possibility of Tyina becoming a potential threat to Osho. She had to be careful that her familiarity with the woman didn't dull her sense of danger and make her complacent. Was Tyina capable of harming Osho directly? Did she have it in her to act on her anger and strike out at him in anything but a symbolic way?

Osho was right, though. Leyndra had to admit that, as unpleasant as the woman was, there was no real danger there. She was all noise and bluster, but very little edge.

Osho heaved a great sigh and grabbed his papers. Motioning for Leyndra to move ahead of him, they left his office and proceeded to his meeting.

She moved through the mansion, always alert for any threat to the man she was oath-bound to protect with her own life, if it ever came down to that.

Leyndra was glad Osho lived a mostly boring life. She spent long hours honing her instincts and reflexes, practicing her deadly talents, examining ways that Osho might find himself in mortal danger. And yet, she hoped never to use any of those skills in a truly dangerous situation.

Those who craved danger and excitement didn't make it through the training, and were never taken into the Guild. No, Leyndra understood that if she had to act directly to save Osho from some kind of attack, then she had already failed at her job.

She stepped into the conference room and gave the two guests one more quick examination with her eyes. Neither man set off any warning signals in her gut, so she stepped to one side as Osho entered.

As she watched him greet the two merchants and sit down to discuss business, Leyndra knew she had Osho's safety well in hand.

*　　　　*　　　　*

"GOODNIGHT, LEYNDRA."

Osho closed the door to his bedchamber and Leyndra stretched her arms over her head to work out the slight stiffness that had crept into her shoulders during the long meeting, the tension-filled dinner, and the evening of standing watch over Osho while he spent yet more time in his office. It was almost time for her to sleep, but she had her routine to perform before she could do so safely.

The small room outside Osho's bedchamber had three doors. The first, Osho had just closed. The second led out to the hallway, and Leyndra closed and locked this one herself. She then proceeded through the third, into her own room.

It had been almost a year since Osho had last brought Tyina into his bed, and he did not keep any mistresses, so Leyndra was confident of his safety as she sat on the edge of her own bed and ran the first sequence of words through her mind. Breathing deeply, she felt her senses expanding and eventually, as she reached the end of the sequence, she felt Osho's heartbeat in the palm of her left hand.

Leyndra turned and lay back on the bed, continuing to inhale and exhale in a deep, regular rhythm. Once she was fully reclined, she began to recite the second sequence of words in her mind. This time, her skin began to tingle as her muscles relaxed, and she felt her conscious mind untether itself from her body. She completed the second sequence and knew that her body had entered the resting state that allowed her to awaken feeling fully refreshed and instantly ready to react to any danger.

She prepared to begin the third and final sequence. Once begun, she would—essentially—be unconscious. Her mind would gain the benefits of a full night's rest, and she would awaken an instant before Osho, ready to face another day. Her only dream would be the sequence of words in her mind, though the Guild trainers had told her she would still dream normally—she just would never be able to remember them.

She began the sequence and was instantly asleep.

And then Leyndra found herself at the door to her bedchamber with her sword in her hand before her mind could fully comprehend what had triggered her awakening. She yanked it open and lunged for the door to Osho's room as she realized it was still the middle of the night. It was as she was shoving his door open that she first consciously noted his rapidly beating pulse in her left hand.

The room was dark and full of shifting shadows as Leyndra ran to the bedside where Osho was sitting up, staring out at the heaving darkness.

"What—?" he managed to croak out as one of the shadows detached itself from the wall into a humanoid shape and dove at him.

Leyndra reacted by instinct, slicing through the shadow and meeting no resistance. The creature dissipated into normal darkness with a low hiss. Leyndra couldn't tell if she had killed it—whatever it was—or if it had simply merged back into the rest of the darkness. Its dissolution, however, seemed to be some kind of signal to the other shadows filling the corners of the room. In an instant, a dozen figures were lunging at Leyndra and Osho, outstretched hands forming into jagged claws.

Leyndra grabbed Osho with one hand and yanked him off the bed onto the floor behind her. Despite his size, she had no trouble handling him as one might a child. All of her skills, all of her abilities, were engaged in this moment. She could perform superhuman acts of strength and agility and would only feel the damage to her body later.

Aware of Osho at her feet, she flowed into a fighting stance that would allow her free movement of her blade without danger of striking him by accident. The first three shadows to come within range of her sword were struck—and dissolved—before the rest could react. Three more shadows engaged her directly, trying to strike her while avoiding her quicksilver blade.

Another three tried to approach from the side, and she shifted to put herself between them and Osho. At the same time, she bellowed for the guards who protected the rest of the estate. There were too many of these things, and even with her abilities, it would only be a matter of time before one of them got past her.

She realized as she yelled that she was probably dooming most of the guards to a horrific death, but her oath was to Osho. If they provided a distraction for the shadows, that was enough for her, regardless of whether they lived or died.

As she fought, her conscious mind tried to analyze what she was seeing. She had never encountered anything like this before, had never even *heard* of anything like this before. What *were* these things? How many were in this room? How many were on the grounds of the estate?

She considered that everyone else on the grounds might already be dead.

The hairs on the back of Leyndra's neck tingled, and she knew an attack was coming from another quarter. She looked up to see three more shadows on the ceiling, about to drop on her and Osho. Still battling the shadows in front of her, she reached down with her other hand to grab Osho and fling him out of the way.

She felt a bundle of blankets at her feet, but didn't find Osho. How could she have lost him?

Leyndra lunged forwards and managed to eliminate two more shadows, before reversing direction. The creatures on the ceiling dropped down as she moved forward, but she had intended to lure them into attacking on her terms. Spinning around so that she could locate Osho—she saw him curled up in the very corner of the room—she swiped her sword through one of the shadows and then thrust through another shadow that had landed beside her.

This time, her blade stabbed into something solid.

The pulse in her left hand sputtered and spasmed.

And then the shadows melted away into nothingness, and she saw that her blade was embedded in Osho's chest. In his heart. He looked at her, his eyes wide and glassy, and then his legs gave way. He fell to the floor, taking her blade out of her hand, and in her other hand she felt his pulse stop.

Leyndra could feel something welling up inside her, anguish too large to keep contained in a human body. Confused, she looked over to where she had seen Osho curled up in the corner. There was nothing there.

She knelt down beside Osho's body, her mind reeling. How could she have not seen it was Osho beside her? But it *hadn't* been Osho. She had seen it drop down from the ceiling, and she had stabbed it, because Osho had been *over there*.

But it had all been shadows.

She heard the running footsteps of the guards, and the first man to enter charged into the room, nearly tripping over Osho's body. Leyndra could still feel the eruption building inside her, and it was getting ever closer to the surface. She didn't know what would happen when it broke through. She vaguely hoped she wouldn't survive it.

She felt a burning sensation on her cheeks and wondered if tears were running down her face.

The guards stopped and stared at Osho's body, and then at her. They were all staring at her face. She couldn't talk, knew her voice wouldn't work right. The lanterns they carried were too bright and cast long shadows on the walls. She vaguely wondered if these shadows would attack, too. Some part of her mind told her she was in shock. It wasn't going to be enough.

One of the guards stepped forward and held up his lantern, looking closely at her face. No, he was looking at something on her cheeks. In the very pit of her soul, she knew what was on her face, what the burning feeling had meant. She couldn't acknowledge it, though, or that would trigger the eruption *right now*.

It was coming anyway. It was inevitable.

The guard's fist smashed into the side of her head and flung her sideways onto the floor.

She heard one of the other guards yell "Hey, what are you doing?"

Leyndra was barely holding onto consciousness. She knew she should defend herself, but she forced her limbs to remain still. She had to let them stop her before the rage took over.

"You see what's on her face? Give me those manacles *now*, before she decides to fight back."

Leyndra knew what he was saying. The other guards didn't seem to understand. But *he* did. She continued to float on the edge of unconsciousness, the wave inside her getting closer and closer to the surface. If he didn't hit her again, or get those manacles on her right away, all these men were going to die.

"She's an oath-breaker! That's what happens when a member of the Guild kills the person she's supposed to protect. It tells everyone what she is."

He was standing over her, but the manacles were still not on.

"It means *she* killed Master Idaphos. She broke her oath and killed him."

Leyndra could feel her blood go cold and her muscles tense up. He had waited too long, and now she was going to snap.

But then the toe of his boot connected with the side of her head where he had already punched her and a swirling blackness reached out and grabbed her, sucking her down into an even deeper darkness.

Chapter Two

L EYNDRA REGAINED CONSCIOUSNESS WITH A STEADY pounding behind her eyes. She could tell she was slumped over on a cold, hard floor. Booted feet moved around her, and voices were raised in command and heated discussion. She figured from the echoes that she was in the mansion's foyer.

She forced herself to breathe deeply and smoothly, and examined all the sensations she was experiencing. Something hard and metal encased her wrists, pinning them behind her back. The guardsmen had managed to get the manacles onto her, after all. She could feel a matching set around her ankles, and knew they would all be attached to each other with strong chains.

And then the thought hit her like a kick to the belly once more. Osho was dead.

I killed him myself, with my own sword.

Leyndra waited for that wave of grief and anger—of power—to begin welling within her again, but nothing happened. It had been so close to erupting before she was knocked out that perhaps it had passed through her and dissipated without taking effect.

She couldn't help but breathe a sigh of relief at that thought. Such an effect was of no use to her right now. She couldn't exactly expend that energy on destroying Osho's killer. All she could do was hurt more innocent people.

"She's awake."

The man's voice cut through the babble of noise, and she knew someone had taken charge here. She opened her eyes and saw a man standing just out of her reach—or what would have been her reach if she wasn't bound in iron.

Smart, she thought. *He's not taking any chances.*

The man was big, with a layer of fat over what Leyndra could tell was a great deal of muscle. The bursting seams on his uniform told her that this was a man who had once been truly tough, but had recently begun to let himself go. His bald head shone with sweat in the light of the lamps, and he frowned down at her as if she had personally insulted his mother.

She noted the crest on his uniform and realized the City Watch had arrived while she had been unconscious. The murder of Osho had brought a sergeant out to the estate. And she knew sergeants hated having to leave the Watchhouse. This man was going to make things even more difficult for her.

"I'm only going to tell you this once, Oath-breaker, so you'd better listen."

His voice carried the tone of a man who was used to giving orders and expecting them to be obeyed. Leyndra remained silent.

"We're gonna take you out to a wagon and bring you back to the Watchhouse. You've been checked over for weapons, but I know what you can do with your bare hands. So, let me make this clear to you—if you so much as twitch in a way I don't like, I'm going to have three of my best sharpshooters put a bunch of quarrels into you. No one will come at you with a sword and give you a weapon to use against us. We'll just shoot you down in the street, and that'll be that."

He paused, waiting for some kind of response from Leyndra. She looked him in the eye and gave a wordless nod. He seemed satisfied.

As he turned away to speak to his men, Leyndra's mind began to race.

She had killed Osho. She had made the worst mistake someone of her profession could ever make. She had lost track of his position in the room somehow, and in her defense of the man she had accidentally attacked him. She was an oath-breaker now and there was nothing to prove it had not been intentional.

She knew this numbness was not going to last much longer. She had liked Osho, perhaps even loved him, if only in a sisterly way.

She had been lucky to be hired to such a man, one who treated her with respect and compassion. And she had failed to protect him from....

What, exactly, had attacked him in his room? Leyndra had never heard of these shadow creatures. There had been so many of them and she still didn't know if she had truly managed to slay any of them, or if they had merely been toying with her.

Were they even real? What if the creatures had been a trick of some sort? What if they were an illusion designed to confuse her senses and cause her to attack the wrong target? How would she ever find out the truth?

And she finally faced the truth of her own situation. The estate guards obviously thought she had deliberately killed Osho. The City Watch was probably inclined to believe them. Osho was a nobleman, and Leyndra was nothing, an oath-breaker.

They were going to try her for Osho's murder. They would find her guilty. They would make an example of her. She would be executed for her crime, and perhaps be tortured first.

And there was no way out.

"They was screwing behind the Lady's back, but she figured it out."

One of the estate guardsmen was talking to the sergeant. The watchman looked down at the smaller man without expression.

"Really?" Leyndra heard the scorn dripping from the sergeant's voice, but the guard was oblivious to it.

"Yeah. He must'a broken it off and she killed him for it. You know how women are."

The sergeant leaned down over the guardsman, who took a nervous step back.

"I thought she wasn't just a bodyguard. You told me she came from the *Guild.*"

The guardsman became even less sure of himself.

"W-w-well, yeah. That's why we had to knock her out and chain her up. I've heard about the Wardens and what they can do. You c-can't take any chances."

The sergeant ran his beefy hand over the top of his head.

"You don't know the first thing about the Guild. Or much else, from the looks of it. If she's Guild-trained and was protecting the nobleman, then he couldn't have been nailing her. Besides, Wardens are a hell of lot more professional than you lot."

He shook his head and turned away from the guardsman, who just stood there looking dumbfounded.

Two watchmen entered the foyer carrying long poles with loops of leather at one end. The sergeant met them near the door and spoke to each in a low voice, and Leyndra couldn't make out the words.

She didn't need to hear him. She knew what the poles were for. The watchmen would place the loops around her neck and force her to walk to the carriage while preventing her from getting too close to either of them. This sergeant was being extra careful with her.

It would probably save his life.

Leyndra knew that she would have to escape, somehow. Even with the death of Osho, she knew she still had some of her special abilities. And all her training, of course, wouldn't just disappear into nothingness. But over time, she knew, anything special would fade away.

She would just have to make the most of what she had as soon as she was given the opportunity.

Leyndra considered what her options would be once she was free and felt despair well up in her again. *Someone* had brought those shadow creatures to Osho's bedchamber. *Someone* had set this chain of events in motion. *Someone* had wanted Osho dead and had tricked her into doing it for them.

But Leyndra had no idea how she could possibly discover the identity of the real attacker. She doubted there was any evidence left behind, and once she escaped, she would be hunted with every available resource and would have no opportunity to return to this house ever again.

It was an impossible task. She would be better off leaving Ythis and going on the run. With her skills, she could easily leave the Empire and make her way in the kingdoms to the south. They wouldn't care about the symbols burned into her cheeks, as long as she could prove her worth.

But then she thought about Morit and his family. She couldn't just leave him to his fate. Her brother was not like Leyndra. He couldn't protect himself *or* his family. And he would be a target as soon as she escaped.

No, Leyndra wouldn't do that to her brother. He was the only family she had.

She would have to stick it out and do whatever she could to solve Osho's murder.

The two watchmen approached her and, one-by-one, they slipped the leather loops over her head and around her throat.

The sergeant returned and once again stopped at a safe distance from her.

"Okay, it's time to go. I don't care if you live or die, so don't try anything with me."

Leyndra finally found her voice.

"You're going to kill me anyway."

The sergeant looked taken aback.

"You must be crazy. Killing you in self-defense is one thing. But I ain't about to kill you unless I've got a reason. The Emperor will want you to face the Magistrates, all public so the people can see what he does to oath-breakers like you. So, I'm just taking you to the Watchhouse to ask you a few questions. What happens after that isn't my business."

Leyndra was suddenly struck by the oddity of the City Watch taking her out of the estate.

"The Imperial Guard isn't here. Shouldn't *they* be the ones taking me into custody?"

The sergeant, surprisingly, smiled at her.

"Screw 'em," he replied.

*   *   *

"WHY DID YOU KILL HIM?"

The sergeant had leaned in close to Leyndra and his breath—a mixture of tobacco, whiskey, and whatever he'd eaten for dinner—threatened to suffocate her. She tried turning her face away, but the

15

metal collar around her neck bit into the underside of her chin and stopped her.

She was surprised at how well she had been treated so far, relatively speaking. They had been so very careful around her, which translated into what was probably the gentlest escort these men had ever conducted. Now she was chained up in one of the holding cells, her arms, legs, waist and neck securely fastened to the stone walls.

Leyndra was exhausted, but the taut chains prevented her from sitting on the floor. So, she remained standing, wishing for a seat, for some water, for some relief. She knew there was no relief coming. Once the Imperial Guard showed up to take her away from the City Watch, everything would be much worse for her.

It was only a matter of time before she went from interrogation to torture.

"Yeah, I don't really need to know," continued the sergeant, stepping back. She had heard someone shout his last name—Lumayth—at some point, and she idly wondered what kind of man he was outside of this place. She knew his type, so very rough around the edges but not unkind. He came across as a man who embraced the corruption in his job, but she thought she could detect a core of professional pride in him.

"I just really want to throw it in the faces of the Imperial Guard when they get here, to tell the truth. Bunch of bastards, always thinking they're better than us. Doesn't help that they get the best equipment, the best training, the best recruits."

Leyndra knew he was trying to draw her out, get her to make a comment. Once she started talking, it would be much easier for him to lead the discussion around to what he wanted to know. Leyndra wasn't sure she should say anything to him, and was still weighing the benefits of remaining silent over telling him everything.

"They'll be here soon enough. I don't envy what you're going to go through once they get you back to the fortress."

He snorted.

"Look at me, showing pity to an oath-breaker like you. Ah, screw it."

He ordered two of the men of the Watch to come back in from the hallway and take up positions on either side of the door.

"I've got a couple of things to do before those pricks from the Guard get here. If you decide you want to talk, one of these men will come get me. Otherwise, I doubt I'll see you again, except maybe from the crowd on your execution day."

He walked out and closed and locked the door.

The two watchmen stood on either side of the room for a few minutes, waiting for the sergeant to get out of earshot. And then one of them stepped over to her. When the blow came, Leyndra was ready for it.

The watchman's fist still drove the wind out of her, despite her tensed muscles. The guy was thin, wiry, and much stronger than he looked. He leaned in towards her face, but not close enough to give her any kind of opportunity.

"The sergeant left us in here with you because he knows we can get answers. He's not coming back until you tell us what we want to know, and he can delay the Imperial Guard for a long time."

Leyndra was confused. Why would these watchmen be so concerned about getting a confession out of her? It wasn't as if they could do anything with that information. And she couldn't believe she had been so wrong about Sergeant Lumayth. Her gut feelings about people were very rarely this far off.

"Your master was a rich man. Probably had lots of mistresses, didn't he? He'd need a stash of money to buy them gifts that his wife didn't know about, right? Tell us where we can find a decent haul and we'll leave you alone."

Leyndra almost laughed out loud. These guys were petty thieves, nothing more. She remained silent, however. She was in no position to taunt them.

"Just because you have to be alive when the Guard gets here, doesn't mean you have to be in one piece."

The watchman pulled a long knife from his boot and waved it in front of her face.

"Just imagine what it'll be like, going through the trial, waiting for the execution, all in darkness. No one's going to care if I take your eyes out of your skull."

Leyndra didn't move, didn't say anything, just kept her eyes on the floor. The longer she could drag this out, the greater the likelihood the Guard soldiers would arrive. Not that their arrival would be much of a rescue.

She saw it coming, but couldn't turn her head in time and the watchman's fist hammered solidly into the middle of her face. She felt—and heard—her nose shatter. Her vision immediately went blurry as her eyes began watering uncontrollably, and she forced her head forward as the rush of blood came. Over it all, she could hear the watchman chuckling at his strike.

"You weren't a beauty before, but now you're going to die *ugly*. Do you want to die ugly and *blind*?"

His fist hammered into her stomach again. He shifted around beside her and planted another shot in her left kidney. She had nothing left, no way to block the pain. Still, her training had prepared her well and she didn't cry out.

That just made him angry.

She caught a glimpse of the other watchman leaning against the wall, staring at her with bored, dead eyes. And then the fists began hitting her again, all over her body. She couldn't curl up and protect herself, couldn't lash out, and couldn't let herself scream.

As suddenly as it had started, the beating stopped.

"Okay, you're a tough bitch. But you don't believe I'm going to cut you open or take your eyes. And you're a little bit right. I'm not going to start with your eyes. First I'm going to do *this*."

His knife slashed across her check and she felt nothing at first, and then the cut began to burn as her blood started flowing from this new wound. He grabbed her by the hair and lifted her face up. She could feel the blood running down her face and under the collar around her neck.

"You see? I'm not playing around here."

He pointed the tip of his knife at her right eye.

"Now start talking, or I take the eye."

Leyndra steeled herself for the pain she knew was about to come.

And then the door opened and Sergeant Lumayth stepped back into the room. The watchman who had her by the hair gave a guilty start and let go of her.

"What in the abyss are you doing?"

The sergeant's voice was low and Leyndra could feel his anger radiating from him. This had not been his doing.

"I was just trying to help you out, Sergeant. I thought maybe I could soften her up for y—"

The sergeant's hand shot out and wrapped around the watchman's neck. His other hand grabbed the wrist of the hand holding the knife and jerked. The sound of this man's bone breaking was even more unexpected than hers had been.

The watchman started to scream as his partner stepped toward Sergeant Lumayth. The sergeant let go of the watchman's wrist and backhanded the other man across the face, sending him bouncing off the wall of the cell. With his other hand he squeezed, and the smaller watchman's scream was choked off.

Then Sergeant Lumayth pulled the watchman over to the door and heaved him out of the cell. Leyndra could hear the little man land hard on the stone floor of the hallway. His partner, dazed by the strike to his head, scrambled on all fours out of the cell after him.

"Th-thank you," Leyndra managed.

"*Don't* thank me. We're all a bunch of thieves and cutthroats, and the city would be better off without the lot of us."

Leyndra could tell he was furious. Not because he cared what happened to her in particular, but rather because she figured he kept getting reminded that men of honor weren't to be found in the Watch. And she was willing to bet Sergeant Lumayth was a man of honor.

"Why did you come back here?"

"I'm stubborn. I had decided I was going to get you to tell me why you killed him. I don't just give up when I've decided I'm going to do something."

Leyndra considered for a moment and then blurted out "It was a trap."

The words were out of her mouth before she even intended to say them. The sergeant looked at her, confused. She had apparently decided to tell him what little she knew. Deep down, a tiny voice suggested that maybe the sergeant *had* orchestrated this little drama after all. Leyndra ignored it and continued.

"Something appeared to be attacking Osh...Master Idaphos. It was real enough that it triggered my defensive response, but now I wonder if it would have been able to harm him directly."

"What attacked him?"

"Shadows. With teeth and claws. But I've been replaying it in my mind, and I think they may not even have been anything more than illusions. They made me think Osho was out of the range of my blade, but when I attacked one of them, I hit him instead."

"We didn't find anything in the room with you." She could hear the skepticism in his voice.

"No, when I hit them, they had no substance and just faded away."

He looked at her evenly.

"Yeah, mighty convenient. I can't prove I didn't kill him on purpose, and it makes no difference anyway. We all know the only...beings...in Ythis who could have done what I describe are beyond the law. And *someone* has to pay for Osho's death."

The sergeant considered this and was about to speak when another watchman entered the cell.

"Sergeant Lumayth," the man said, his rapid breathing indicating that he had run all the way down here. "The Guard just showed up."

Chapter Three

ORIT ROLLED OFF HIS SLEEPING PALLET AND GRABBED the wooden club that lay on the floor beside him. Hathi was already sitting upright, her eyes wide as they darted around the room. The pounding on the front door stopped for a few seconds and then started up again.

Morit put his hand on Hathi's shoulder and gently shook her.

"Get the kids to the back window. Be ready to run."

She looked at him without seeing him for a moment. Then she was up and moving into the other room to scoop up their two children, who were starting to wake up from the noise.

Morit moved over to one side of the door and paused, trying to clear the cobwebs from his head. He could now tell the pounding on his front door wasn't an attempt to break in. Someone out there was in a hurry and wanted him awake.

"What do you want?" he shouted over the sound of a fist or boot on his door. The noise abruptly ceased, and the muffled voice of Nayect answered.

"Morit, I need to speak to you right away!"

Morit shook his head. What could have brought his friend to his home in the middle of the night? He lifted the wooden bar from its brackets and pulled open the door.

Nayect was practically dancing from foot to foot on the small wooden landing outside the door to Morit's and Hathi's rooms.

"Morit! I have something to tell you!"

Ice water ran down Morit's spine. He dumbly nodded and stepped back as Nayect pushed his way into the room and shoved the door closed. He couldn't tell if Nayect needed help with something terrible in his own life, or if he brought ill tidings for Morit.

"Where's your wife and children?" asked Nayect looking around.

Morit didn't answer him. He turned and called out to Hathi.

"It's safe, Hathi. Stay with the children."

He could hear his young son whimpering with fright, but forced it out his mind. It was Hathi's job to keep them quiet and get them back to sleep.

"What's happened, Nayect? It's the middle of the night and I get little enough sleep as it is." He couldn't keep his irritation out of his voice, but he was glad it was masking the fear that filled his belly.

"I was delivering food to the Watchhouse when the message came in. I couldn't believe it at first, so I followed the men when they went out to the estate. They didn't care—many of them are friends to me, so they told me what happened, though of course I couldn't go in."

"WHAT happened?" Morit realized his fists were clenched—one of his hands still wrapped around the club—not out of anger or frustration but to keep them from shaking. He was beginning to prepare himself for the news that Leyndra had died protecting the nobleman. Why else would Nayect come to tell Morit about the Watch being called out to an estate?

"It's your sister, Morit. The nobleman is dead." He paused, as if waiting for a reaction.

Now a flush of heat replaced the ice. She had finally done it, finally gotten herself killed and abandoned her family for good. He wanted to curse her name, and yet also felt tears beginning to sting his eyes at the same time.

"How...how did she die?"

Nayect looked confused for a moment and then shook his head and looked at the floor.

"She's not dead," he said in a low voice. And then, quieter still, "Better for both you and her if she had."

The shock of that statement caused Morit to flinch and he dropped the club to the floor. That caused Nayect to cringe backwards, as if he thought Morit might hit him. Tonight, anything seemed possible.

"Nayect," he said, trying to keep his voice calm. "Tell me what happened. Where is Leyndra?"

"She has been arrested, my friend. She was taken to the Watchhouse, but the Imperial Guard will soon go get her and take her into the fortress. As I said, the nobleman is dead."

Morit felt his legs were on the verge of giving out. He grabbed one of the small, wooden chairs scattered around their table and slowly lowered himself into it. He was grateful he didn't fall.

"Why was Leyndra arrested? Did she do something wrong? I don't understand."

Nayect stood near the door, no longer shifting from foot to foot, but still clearly agitated. He kept glancing at the door, as if expecting someone to suddenly start knocking.

"Your sister killed the nobleman. According to the watchmen who saw her, she now wears the mark of the oath-breaker on her cheeks. The estate guardsmen found her with the nobleman, his blood on her sword, and watched the marks appear on her face."

Morit was stunned into silence. He couldn't wrap his mind around the idea that Leyndra had murdered the man she was sworn to protect.

"Morit, you have to go."

Nayect's statement cut through the fog and brought a fresh stab of fear into Morit's belly.

"Why? What does any of this have to do with me?"

Nayect grabbed another chair and sat in front of Morit. He leaned in and spoke in a low voice. Morit realized he was trying to prevent Hathi from hearing his next words.

"Morit, a nobleman was killed by your sister. Her face proves her guilt. There will be no way out for her. The Emperor won't be satisfied with just her head, though. He'll want to make an example of her. He'll want to destroy her and everything connected to her, everything she loved. The Imperial Guard knows this. They'll come for you as soon as they have her in their possession."

He leaned in only inches from Morit's face and looked him in the eyes.

"You *have* to leave. You have to take your family and leave Ythis.

Now."

"Won't that make me look guilty? Like I know something about what happened?"

"It doesn't *matter* how it makes you look. Your life, and the lives of your wife and children, will be forfeit if you don't get out of Ythis right away."

Morit sat there, his mind racing. He didn't have any money to arrange travel. Even if they grabbed what food they had and left right this minute, the Guard wouldn't let them pass the city gates before dawn. And by then the Guard would be searching for him. They'd never make it.

"I can't, Nayect. I don't know what to do. I can't pay anyone to help me and *I don't know what to do!*"

Nayect put his hand on Morit's arm.

"I will help you, my friend. I have many friends in this city, and some are good at hiding. I will call in a favor someone owes me, and you and your family will be quietly put on a ship that will head out before dawn."

Morit wondered if that would be enough. There weren't many ships in the harbor these days, the result of a huge beast that had moved into the bay and had destroyed two ships, killing a hundred men. The Church had driven the beast away from Ythis a few days ago, and news hadn't spread yet that it was safe for watercraft to return to the city.

It wouldn't take very long for the Guard to search what ships were still there.

But then, Morit didn't have any other options. He had to trust Nayect and let him manage his escape. In any other circumstances, it would have been Leyndra telling him what do and how to do it. Sometimes her controlling nature drove him crazy.

And then the tears did start rolling down his face. Leyndra was lost to him forever. She would be executed for her crime, and he would probably never know why she had done it. And Morit couldn't help her the way she always helped him.

The only thing he could do was run.

He stood up and went into the other room to find Hathi sitting between their two young children, one hand on each. They were already starting to drift back off to sleep. Hathi looked up at him with a calm face, but he could see the fear in her eyes.

"I'm sorry, Hathi. We have to leave Ythis. Leyn—" he paused, unable to speak around the lump in his throat. He swallowed and managed to continue.

"Leyndra has been arrested for the murder of the nobleman she was protecting." He continued over Hathi's gasp of shock. "The Imperial Guard will come for me and you and the children. We have to leave Ythis tonight... right now."

Hathi stood and spoke in a low whisper.

"Where can we go? We'll need food—"

"Nayect is taking care of that," he interrupted. "Get the children ready to leave, but keep them quiet. We need to get out of here as soon as we can."

He stepped back into the main room just as something smashed into the front door and broke it entirely off one of the hinges. An armed and armored man shoved the broken door aside and stepped into the room.

Morit was paralyzed with fear and could do nothing but watch. Nayect had picked up the wooden club Morit had dropped earlier, and he turned as the door was kicked asunder. The huge man in the armor of the Imperial Guard stepped toward Nayect, and the smaller man raised his hands as he cringed. As the club came up towards the soldier's face, the soldier raised his shield to block it, and lunged forward with the short sword in his other hand.

Standing behind Nayect, Morit watched the point of the soldier's blade emerge from his friend's back. The Guard soldier withdrew the blade and knocked Nayect to one side with a swipe of his shield. Nayect collapsed against the wall and didn't move.

Morit felt his bladder release as the soldier moved up and pointed the blade at his chest.

"STAY WHERE YOU ARE!" he shouted in Morit's face.

This time, Morit's legs did give way, and he slowly collapsed onto his knees. He couldn't take his eyes off the point of that blade, dark with his friend's blood. Behind him, he could hear his son start to cry, and at the edge of his vision he saw more members of the Imperial Guard entering his home.

Morit could only stare at the bloodied blade.

*　　　　*　　　　*

LEYNDRA SLOWLY DREW HERSELF UP UNTIL SHE WAS SITTING WITH her back to the cold, stone wall. She knew she would start shivering soon, but right now the chill helped clear her head and she needed to be able to think when her visitor inevitably showed up.

The small amount of dirty straw barely covered the floor and wasn't worth collecting into a mat to sit upon. Her bare flesh was scratched and bruised from her rough treatment—the Guard soldiers had stripped her naked before she was thrown into the cell, of course. They wouldn't risk leaving her with a weapon or other useful item, and they had not been surprised to find another two blades and a set of lock picks hidden in her clothes, all missed by the men of the City Watch in their own search last night.

The Guard soldiers, male and female both, were tough, hard soldiers with iron discipline. Leyndra had been handled roughly, but had not been unduly abused during her trip from the Watchhouse to the Imperial Fortress. That would change when the Inquisitor arrived.

Leyndra breathed deeply and tried to settle her emotions. Her cheek ached horribly, and she knew she would have a terrible scar across her face if she lived long enough for the wound to fully heal. One of the Guard soldiers had pushed the cut closed and smeared some grease that smelled of rotten eggs across her cheek. It had not lessened the pain, though the grease had kept the cut closed and prevented further bleeding. It was the bare minimum they would do to keep her alive and healthy long enough to face trial.

She figured it must be dawn by now, though no windows or other sources of light penetrated into her cell, deep under the Fortress. Not for the first time in the last couple of hours, she thought about Morit. What would happen to him and his family? She didn't want to consider the possibility the Imperial Guard had rounded them up because of their connection to her. She didn't want to be responsible for their deaths.

The clang of the door brought her out of her musings as the large metal bolt on the far side was drawn back. The metal slab swung outward and a flood of lamplight filled the room. Leyndra shut her eyes tight against the glare and slowly pushed herself up. She could hear booted feet enter the room and stop a few paces from her.

Leyndra opened her eyes and saw a large man in the breastplate and greaves of a Guard soldier standing in front of her. His eyes were dark, and he wore a short beard, but the rest of his face and head was obscured by the cheek plates of his helmet. Another soldier stood just outside the door, holding the lantern. The man in front of her didn't appear to be armed, but she had little doubt he'd be able to beat her if she tried anything. His muscles were smooth, not bulky—she expected he was as fast as she was. This wasn't going to be an opportunity for escape.

"Leyndra Jirau, you are hereby formally charged with the murder of Osho Idaphos, scion of the House of Idaphos. You will remain in the custody of the Imperial Guard until such time as you can appear before an Imperial Magistrate for trial. Your cooperation in our investigation will improve your chances for mercy from the Court."

He stopped and stood there, looking at her face. Leyndra stood as straight and proud as she could, despite her nakedness. She noted that his glance never dropped—another example of the Imperial Guard discipline.

"As the primary investigator, I have questions for you. Are you willing to answer?"

Leyndra knew he wasn't really asking a question. If she refused to talk now, he would simply send for the Inquisitor and eventually she would tell them anything they wanted to know. Even her training wouldn't be of any help once the Inquisitor got his hands on her.

"I will," she replied.

The man nodded once and a third soldier brought in a small, wooden stool and placed it on the floor beside Leyndra. As soon as he had stepped back out of the room, the man in front of her said

"You may sit."

This was a minor reward for agreeing to talk, she knew. As long as she continued to answer questions, she would be able to sit on something other than the cold stone. Despite her knowledge, she still felt grateful for the small mercy. She sank onto the stool and rested her forearms on her thighs. The soldier continued to stand.

"I am Investigator Chamirra. I will ask the questions, and you will answer them to the best of your ability, or this interrogation will be suspended pending the arrival of an Imperial Inquisitor. Is that clear?"

Leyndra nodded without speaking.

"Are you a Guild-trained Warden?"

"Yes."

"Did you take an oath to serve Osho Idaphos as a Warden?"

"Yes."

"Did you kill Osho Idaphos with your own blade?"

She swallowed around a lump in her throat.

"Yes."

"Why did you murder the man whom you had taken an oath to protect with your own life?"

Leyndra shook her head.

"I—I didn't murder him. His death was an accident. I was tricked into attacking him while I was trying to save his life."

Investigator Chamirra paused, and then said "Explain."

Leyndra repeated everything that had happened from the moment she had awakened with her sword in her hand, to the moment the estate guards had entered the room. She told him every detail she could remember, leaving nothing out. When she was done, the man moved to the door and whispered something to one of the other soldiers. Then he returned to stand in front of her.

"Are you aware of the branding on your face?"

Leyndra looked at the floor.

"Yes."

"Does the brand not mark you as an oath-breaker?"

"You know it does," she replied sarcastically. He ignored her tone.

"Does the mark appear in the case of a purely accidental death?"

She couldn't tell if he was asking because he didn't already know the answer, or if he was trying to trap her. She decided to keep to her plan of telling him everything.

"In my training, I was told that a true accident that resulted in the death of the subject would not trigger the branding. As I said, this was no accident. This was a deliberate attack by some outside force. My ability to always know Osho's exact location was suppressed somehow. His death was not accidental."

"Who do you believe trapped you?"

This was the question Leyndra had been dreading. What had happened wasn't something simple, like an ambush in a dark alley. Whoever had tricked her had a great deal of unnatural power. That meant it was someone in the Church, or a sorcerer, one of the Five. But Osho had never had any dealings with either of those groups. She could not guess why someone with such power wanted him dead.

"I don't know. If what I saw was just an illusion, then someone was deliberately manipulating me into accidentally killing Osho. That would have to be someone with power outside of my understanding. To my knowledge, Osho never dealt with anyone who had that kind of power."

Investigator Chamirra asked if there was anything else she wanted to tell him, and she just shook her head. She doubted any of this would make a difference. If Osho had been murdered by the Church *or* the Five, that knowledge would never be allowed to pass outside of this building. The city's delicate balance couldn't afford such a revelation. The noble families would cry for the Emperor to do something to protect them, and there was no way he'd be able to take on either the Church or the sorcerers and come out on top.

The Chamirria stepped back and the other soldier came in to remove the stool. Leyndra stood and let him take it—fighting for the stool wouldn't make anything any easier for her. In another minute, the Guard soldiers had left, taking their light with them. When the sound of the metal bolt sliding back into place had faded, Leyndra felt her way to the wall and slid down to the floor.

She didn't doubt that Investigator Chamirra would look into her story. He would go over every inch of Osho's bedroom, searching for any piece of evidence that either supported or disproved her claims. She just didn't believe it would make any difference. Even if he found something, the political implications were too large to investigate any further. The best she could hope for would be the mercy of a quick death instead of the torture she would undoubtedly endure if all evidence pointed to her deliberately killing Osho.

Not much comfort, really.

Leyndra sat on the floor and leaned against the wall, and as the cold seeped into her bones, she started to shiver.

Chapter Four

SERGEANT FLASEK LUMAYTH HEAVED A HUGE SIGH AS HE signed his name at the bottom of the report. Gathering the sheaf of papers that contained the reports from the rest of his squad, he silently cursed his luck. What had he been thinking, getting involved in the murder of a nobleman? He had slowly worked his way up to the position of sergeant so that he could *avoid* situations like that.

And yet, here he was, completing *reports.* The other sergeants were going to have quite the laugh at his expense, and his own men were grumbling about responding to the murder. This wasn't how the Watch was supposed to operate.

If there was no profit to be found in it, there was no reason to get involved.

Flasek tried to tell himself that he didn't know why he had grabbed his squad and raced to the estate when the report came in last night. But he couldn't deny the truth—he wanted to show up the Imperial Guard and solve the case before they arrived.

Only there hadn't been much to solve. A Warden had gone crazy and killed the man she was sworn to protect. Her own face held the evidence of her betrayal.

So why had Flasek found himself believing her when she told him her story? It was crazy and unbelievable and, what's worse, most likely not provable even if true. And he didn't really want to consider the implications if evidence to support her claim *was* found.

Flasek had heard stories about the sorcerers of Ythis. They had mostly come from a friend of Flasek's named Borolt Zale, who really worked for one of the Five. What the woman, Leyndra, had described sounded like something a sorcerer could pull off without breaking a sweat. And that was assuming it *was* one of the Five. It could just as well have been the Church for all anyone knew.

Regardless, Flasek was done. The reports of his men were complete, and his own summary report was finished. He would drop it off upstairs for the lieutenant to see once he arrived, and then it was out of his hands. He needed sleep.

Well, he needed alcohol, and *then* sleep. Either way, he wouldn't spend more than another few minutes in this building if he could help it.

He was on his way back downstairs to the main entrance when one of the newer recruits saw him and came running over. Flasek interrupted him before he could say a word.

"No, no, no. Oh, and no. I'm not interested in anythin' you've got to say, grunt." He always called the recruits "grunt" until they had lasted at least three months. "I've done what I had to do and I'm leavin'."

He turned towards the door and the recruit stammered out "S-s-sir, there's someone here to see you."

"Don't care!" Flasek kept walking.

"It's the Imperial Guard!" called the recruit.

Flasek almost paused. Almost. But he'd had enough for one night and it's not like they could arrest him for leaving at the end of his shift.

He stepped through the doors onto the street and stopped. Four men in the armor of the Imperial Guard stood ranged around the doorway. One of them put up his hand as Flasek emerged.

"Stop and identify yourself," the soldier demanded.

"By the hairy balls of the Abyss!" cursed Flasek. "By what right do you dare challenge watchmen as we leave our own headquarters?"

"By order of the commander of the Imperial Guard. Identify yourself... *now.*"

Flasek was about to tell the man what he could do to his own mother when a new voice cut in from behind him.

"Stand down, soldier. I will vouch for the identity of Sergeant Lumayth."

Flasek cursed silently this time. He knew that voice. Though dawn had already well and truly broken, he knew his entire night had just gotten a lot worse. He turned and faced the man behind him.

"Well, if it isn't Beyus Chamirra, the man who was too good for the Watch. What brings *you* down to the slums this morning?"

Beyus stood straight and tall in his polished armor, looking like he had just stepped out of a painting of the First Guard. As usual, he ignored Flasek's verbal barb and kept to business.

"You know why I am here, Sergeant. We must talk about what happened at the Idaphos estate last night."

"You're in luck, then. I just dropped my report on the lieutenant's desk. Get one of the grunts to run up and grab it for you and you'll get all the detail you need. As for me, I'm off duty now. You remember what that's like, bein' off duty?"

"I do not intend to take up much of your time, Sergeant."

"You'll not take *any* more of my time, Beyus. See ya'."

Flasek turned and began to walk away, but the other four soldiers moved to block his way. His hand went to the truncheon at his belt, and their hands went to the hilts of their swords.

"I said STAND DOWN!"

The soldiers jumped as if the commander of the Imperial Guard himself had just given them an order and immediately obeyed Beyus Chamirra. They stepped to one side, leaving the street open for him to leave.

"Please accept my apologies, Sergeant. This has been a...difficult night for all of us."

Flasek turned back to Beyus and nodded at him.

"That it has. But I'm well and truly done now. So, if you don't mind...."

Once again he moved to leave when Beyus' voice stopped him in his tracks.

"Of course, Sergeant. It was my mistake to assume you would be interested in the story our prisoner told about the murder. It is beyond the scope of anything a *watchman* would be interested in, of course."

Flasek knew Beyus was trying to get under his skin, to attack his pride and make him stay to answer questions. It was an obvious and clumsy attempt, and Flasek knew better than to let it get to him. There was no place in the Watch for honor and pride. And nothing he could tell the man would matter anyway.

"You're right," he said without turning back to face him. "Well beyond my scope."

"Have a good morning, then Sergeant. Next time I need any of your assistance, I'll try to remember to bring my coin purse."

Flasek hadn't removed his hand from his truncheon, and it was out of his belt loop before he could think. He spun to find Beyus Chamirra moving inside his swing. His arm was blocked and twisted around behind his back with disturbing ease. Beyus leaned in close and spoke in a low voice.

"I knew the fire hadn't completely gone out yet, Flasek. There's still something of a real watchman in that flabby body, isn't there?"

"You're a right bastard, Beyus."

As he spoke, he tried to shift his weight and break free of the other man's grasp, but Beyus' grip on his wrist was like iron.

"I am when I have to be. I know she told you a story about what happened in that room. She told me a story, too. I don't believe it, but then I'm just a bunch of muscle in a suit of polished armor according to you, right? You got there first, you took her into custody, and you questioned her. All before the Imperial Guard could respond. You won the battle you wanted to win, but this isn't over yet and I'm offering you a chance to be involved."

Beyus let that sink in for a moment. "If you want me to believe the same man who took his squad out to that estate last night suddenly doesn't care about this investigation, then you must think I'm the head idiot in an army of idiots."

Beyus let go of Flasek's wrist and stepped back. Flasek just stood there, not sure what to do. Beyus knew him too well, knew how much he wanted to be involved. But Flasek was a sergeant in the Watch, and there were only so many disappointments a man could take. He couldn't let himself hope that he might make a difference, not in this city.

Finally, he turned to face the other man.

"Okay, we can talk about what happened last night. I'm not going to stick my neck out for you *or* your investigation. That broad is probably insane, and I won't put myself to all kinds of trouble just to have you shove me aside at the moment of truth. Like you did last time."

For the first time since Flasek had known the man, Beyus' face showed an instant of shame. He looked down at the ground for a few seconds, and when he raised his head all traces of emotion had been wiped from his face.

"Fair enough, Sergeant. We'll just talk about last night."

Flasek turned away and began to walk down the street again, away from the Watchhouse.

"Good! You're buying."

He heard Beyus following him.

"We cannot meet in a tavern and talk about this while you get drunk, Sergeant. I'm an Imperial Guard soldier. I have to maintain certain standards."

Flasek glanced back over his shoulder but kept walking.

"Tough shit," he replied. "You'll get over it."

*　　　　*　　　　*

ALONE IN THE DARK, LEYNDRA HAD NO WAY TO MARK THE PASSAGE of time. Eventually, despite the hardness of the floor, exhaustion drove her to sleep. When she awoke, she couldn't tell if she had slept for one hour or ten.

Her muscles screamed as she pulled herself up into a sitting position. The cold had seeped into her bones and she shivered uncontrollably. With some effort, she managed to stand and began stretching out her muscles.

By the time she had finished her stretching exercises, she was no longer shivering. She felt like practicing the movements she had been taught to keep herself in fighting trim, but she knew it was more important to conserve her energy. Now that she had warmed herself up enough to avoid the worst effects of the cold cell, she planned to only expend enough energy to keep her body at a reasonable temperature.

Sometime later, the metal slot in the bottom of the cell's door slid open and something was pushed through. She carefully felt her way over to the door and found a thin wooden bowl with something warm and mushy inside. She sniffed and found it to be some kind of gruel. Despite her expectations, it was thick and still retained its heat.

She paced herself as she ate it, making sure not to gorge and make herself sick. By the time she was finished, she was surprised to feel that she was in fairly good shape. Her cheek still hurt, but when she tentatively touched it, she found that the wound had completely scabbed over. Whatever the grease was that they had spread on the cut, it had done its job.

She wondered how long she had been in here. It may only have been part of a day, or it could have been a couple of days. She was sure it wasn't more than two nights past the night of Osho's death, but that was about as far she as had confidence to predict.

Again, time passed in utter darkness and she alternated between standing and sitting so as to keep warm, but also conserve her strength. She knew as long as she was in this cell her chances of escape were non-existent. But she had to be ready for when they took her to stand before the magistrates.

Opportunities would be few and far between, and her remaining life could probably be measured in days at this point.

Eventually, the metal bolt on the door was pulled back and the portal swung open once more. This time, she had already squeezed her eyes shut to avoid the pain of the sudden light. It was still dazzlingly bright through her eyelids.

When the voice came, she figured it was the same man who had questioned her the last time, Investigator Chamirra.

"Leyndra Jirau, I have further questions for you. Are you willing to answer?"

"Yes."

She managed to open her eyes slightly and saw the second soldier bring in the stool once again. She sat and waited for Chamirra to proceed.

"Were you in a carnal relationship with Osho Idaphos?"

The question stunned her. She was expecting more questions about the shadow creatures, or about anyone who might have wanted Osho dead. This was...absurd.

"Of...of course not. I am a Warden and was sworn to him."

"Why does that matter?"

Again, she wasn't sure if he already knew the answer and was testing her, or if he honestly didn't know.

"It's part of the oath, part of the bond. There is no...lust...possible between the Warden and her charge. It just doesn't happen. Anything resembling love is like that between brother and sister."

He waited for her to add more, and she realized he did know.

"At least, that's the way it usually is. There are a very few rare cases where it happens anyway. The bond doesn't suppress it the way it's supposed to. But those are extremely unusual situations."

"Were you one of the rare cases?"

"No. I admired Osho. I enjoyed his company. He was a good man, a nice person. He treated me with respect and consideration, and I was glad I had been chosen by someone I could respect as well. But there was no lust there."

The investigator stayed silent again.

"Why are you asking me this?"

"I will ask the questions. Your parents died when you were young. Is this true?"

"Yes. What do my parents—"

"You were destitute before you managed to gain admittance to the Guild, correct?"

"Yes, I was. Are you suggesting I killed Osho because I wanted his money? How in the world would I get my hands on any of his money if he died?"

She saw him set his jaw and knew his patience was running out.

"Leyndra Jirau. You will answer my questions to the best of your ability and refrain from asking anything else, or this interrogation is over. Is that clear?"

She knew what that meant. Instead of sitting on a stool, she'd be placed in the hands of an Inquisitor. Then she'd learn what real pain felt like.

"Yes. I'm sorry. Please proceed."

He waited a moment more before speaking again.

"Did Osho give you any special gifts before he died?"

Leyndra was well and truly confused now. These questions didn't make any sense to her, not after she had told this man everything that had happened.

"Um, no. Nothing special. I was given a horse to use as my own when I joined the estate, but it doesn't really belong to me. Same with the rooms where I stayed."

"How do you explain the large sum of money found hidden in your room?"

Leyndra felt her gut clench. Whoever had set her up had done a thorough job.

"I was not aware of any large sums of money hidden in my room. But I never went searching for any, so it may have been there a long time. Or it was planted afterwards."

"Lady Idaphos has accused you of having carnal relations with Lord Idaphos. She told me he admitted the affair to her, and said you were trying to extort money from him. How do you answer these accusations?"

Leyndra didn't know what to say. This made even less sense. Tyina couldn't have arranged for the attack on Osho by the shadow creatures—she was as terrified of the Five as any other citizen of Ythis, and she had no love for the Church. None of the noble families did. And yet, she was trying to pin the blame for Osho's death on Leyndra.

If she wasn't involved somehow, she should be afraid of someone attacking her as the temporary head of the family. Not throwing out false accusations.

"Lady Idaphos was jealous of my position in the household. She assumed the worst because she didn't want any other women near Osh—Lord Idaphos. It was never true. As for why she is trying to make it seem like I wanted him dead, I cannot speak to her motives.

All I can say is that she lies."

Leyndra knew the futility of her words. Of course, she would not be believed over the words of the Lady Idaphos.

Investigator Chamirra was not yet finished with his questions or revelations.

"We found the remains of the letter in your fireplace. Most of it burned, but enough remained for us to give to the alchemists. They managed to pull most of the writing from it, despite its state."

"What letter?" Leyndra asked, forgetting her earlier agreement not to ask any questions. She was fortunate in that the investigator did not end the interrogation just yet.

"Who hired you to kill Lord Osho Idaphos?"

Leyndra knew she was well and truly trapped. An incriminating letter, a large sum of money hidden in her rooms, the accusation of an affair with Osho and demands for payment, all added up to a foregone conclusion. She couldn't tell if this investigator was involved in the cover-up or if he was just doing his job.

She didn't care. She would pay the price for her failure to protect Osho by being accused, tried, tortured, and executed for his death.

"No one hired me. The letter is false. As are Tyina's accusations. Whoever wanted Osho dead wanted to ensure that the evidence would point to me. They've done a wonderful job. I just don't know how they managed to get someone with the power to summon those shadow creatures, or create the illusions of them, whichever it was."

"*Who* hired you to kill Lord Osho Idaphos?"

"I can't give you a name, because there isn't one. Tyina is obviously involved, but I do not know who her allies are. She most definitely didn't do it alone."

"This is your last chance to answer the question. When I leave, you will be given to the Inquisitor. The magistrates will show you mercy if you identify the persons who paid you to kill Lord Idaphos. You have nothing to gain by protecting them."

"I ask you to not let this drop. Whether you believe me or not, keep looking for the real killer, even after I'm dead. I swear to you, if you let this go once I have paid the price, the murderers will go free. If you care about justice, if you want to find the truth, *don't let this go."*

The investigator motioned for the other soldier to come in and remove the stool. As the men left her cell, Leyndra called out to them once more.

"Don't let my death stop your investigation!"

The door slammed shut and Leyndra was alone in the darkness once again.

Chapter Five

LORD PHIRAL NAJARE STEPPED OUT ONTO THE STONE walkway and shut the concealed door behind him. He carried no light and wore a heavy, dark cloak. Clouds obscured the moon and he could barely see five paces ahead of him.

At least I don't need to find some excuse to send the guards away tonight, he thought. It was getting harder to come up with methods to ensure the way to his secret meetings were clear.

He was sweating under the cloak, but didn't want to risk the glint of a belt buckle or metal button giving him away. It was the risk of doing this in the summertime. Of course, the rains would have presented their own difficulties, not the least of which was the obviously wet clothes he would have had to hide after his sojourns into the crypts.

In minutes, he reached the end of the path and stood before the stone door that protected the remains of the Najare family from tomb robbers and other mischief. Not that his ancestors needed such protection these days, he mused. Anyone entering the mausoleum was not likely to come back out.

Except me, he noted with some trepidation. Not for the first time he wondered if he had made a bad choice getting involved with the...being...that inhabited the Najare family crypts. He forced himself to move on—he didn't want to dwell on the fact that it was much, much too late to have second thoughts about this arrangement.

He pulled out the large iron key and slowly unlocked the doors, carefully trying to minimize any noise that might draw the attention of his estate guards. When he opened the portal, nothing but impenetrable blackness greeted him. Talking a nervous breath, he entered the mausoleum and pulled the door closed behind him.

Completely blind, he carefully reached down to his left and found the lantern and flint he had previously placed there. In moments, he succeeded in lighting the lantern. He found it easier to accomplish in the utter darkness each time he did it.

Phiral raised the lantern and took a quick look around the crypt entrance, as he always did. It remained a good idea to pay proper respect to one's ancestors, he believed. They did not always stay safely in the past.

He proceeded to the stairs along the back wall and held the light high as he descended. The last thing he needed was to fall and injure himself here. It wasn't as if his...associate...would be able to help him return to the mansion.

A few feet from the bottom of the stairs crouched a large stone gargoyle, intended to scare away evil spirits who might attempt to inhabit and animate the ancient remains of a Najare ancestor. Phiral smirked at the statue and its eldritch runes carved into the base. He couldn't imagine worrying about such a minor threat as a possessing spirit anymore.

Not when he was about to come face-to-face with something so much greater.

The chamber at the bottom of the stairs was shaped like a hexagon, with an open doorway piercing each wall. The crypts spread out from each of those portals, the most ancient inhabitants nearest the entrance and the recently dead at the farthest ends.

"Idaphos is dead."

Eothep's hollow, empty voice—right behind Phiral's left shoulder—shocked him to the point that he almost dropped the lantern. He spun around but the dancing shadows showed him nothing but flickering movements. Then he heard the slow, shuffling footsteps of his visitor coming from a doorway to his right.

Phiral turned and raised the lantern again and saw the shape of the necromancer approaching the doorway into the hexagonal chamber. The man was slender to the point of emaciation and moved with a slow deliberation usually only found in the most elderly. Phiral lowered his eyes to the floor as Eothep moved into the light of the lantern. He had no desire to look on that face again—the nightmares were too vivid.

"I-I don't see the point of trying to frighten me. We are supposed to be working together."

Eothep stopped just inside the room. As he spoke in his cold, dead voice, Phiral could faintly hear the creaking of old bones and the howls of the long dead echoing around his words.

"I speak through the shadows where they are...convenient. Your fears are for you to deal with."

Despite the chill in the crypts, Phiral realized he was sweating profusely.

"Yes, well, I come to bring you news." He belatedly realized Eothep already knew what he had been going to say. "H-how did you know—"

"The shade of Osho Idaphos was drawn to me before it moved on. It spoke to me as it passed."

The necromancer paused, and Phiral had the urge to look up at his face, but he managed to stop himself in time. He forced himself to wait until Eothep spoke again.

"It told me I had made a terrible mistake. I am trying to decipher if it was telling me my future, or making an empty threat."

Phiral closed his eyes and took a deep breath, but the scent of dust and decay filled his lungs and he instantly regretted it.

"This happened three nights ago. And you only bring me the news now."

Phiral swallowed nervously.

"Yes, well, I cannot always get away from my other duties. I have businesses to run, and your project often takes me off the estate. I only returned this afternoon."

Eothep was silent for a moment. When he spoke, Phiral was glad he did not pursue this line of questioning.

"Tell me of the Warden."

Oh, so you don't *know everything*, thought Phiral.

"Ah, okay, she was taken into custody by the City Watch. They managed to hold her long enough for the Imperial Guard to arrive and remove her to the Fortress. An investigator was named—one Beyus Chamirra—and he has been quite busy over the last two nights. He found the items we placed in the woman's room, and has called for an Inquisitor. Everything appears to be proceeding as we planned."

The light of the lantern began to dim, and Phiral checked it to see if he was out of oil. The flame appeared normal, but it was not giving off as much light as it should. Without thinking, Phiral turned and looked directly at Eothep.

The necromancer was shrouded in writhing, floating shadows. Only his face was visible, the papery skin stretched over his skull, the sunken cheeks on either side of his thin, bloodless lips. And then Phiral met his gaze, looking into utter pits of darkness, the pupils tiny points of unholy light.

Phiral wanted to scream as the light continued to fade, but found himself unable to move. Eothep moved closer, stopping within reach of the terrified nobleman. Phiral could see the shape of the man's skull clearly through his skin. And then that voice spoke again and Phiral felt his skin drying out as if he was stretched out in the early afternoon sun.

"You will continue to watch and report back to me. Should our pieces move in ways we do not wish, you must give me ample warning. There are those in this city who would hunt for me if they knew I had returned. I am not yet ready to face them. Not until I have what I seek."

Phiral wanted to agree, but could neither speak nor move his head. His mind was recoiling from the sight of the necromancer, and some small part of him knew the nightmares would be waiting for him, if he ever truly managed to fall asleep.

Eothep held his gaze a moment more, and then stepped back as the light returned to normal. Phiral wrenched his eyes from the sight of that ghastly face and began shivering uncontrollably. He was unable to speak for several minutes, and the necromancer just stood motionless—with the infinite patience of the dead—while Phiral regained his composure.

Finally, he was able to ask about his own plans.

"W-what about Tyina? When can I visit her? When can I begin taking control of the Idaphos' holdings?"

"You will wait for the Magistrates to hand down the woman's conviction for the murder of the nobleman. Claiming your prize too early may raise suspicion. Your mistress will have to be patient."

"But it's not just Tyina I need. It's the money. This expedition of yours is going to cost me a lot, especially doing it under such tight secrecy. The men I've hired do not come cheaply. I cannot finance the entire trip without new funds coming in."

The shadows in the room became agitated and began to flit and leap from wall to wall.

"You can, and you will," answered Eothep. "You vowed to help me in return for your prize. You will do what I require, or your prize will be placed forever out of your reach. The loss of some money should be the least of your concerns. Once the Warden is convicted and the investigation is over, you will be free to take the nobleman's wife and property. When I have what I seek, you will receive the immortality I promised you. Until then, you are my servant and will follow my commands."

Phiral wanted to argue. He *needed* to see Tyina, to possess her again. But he knew it would be futile.

He was terrified, but was also excited. Everything in life was a gamble, and one did not become truly powerful by avoiding risk. Phiral knew Eothep could slay him with little effort, but the necromancer needed his help. And in return, Phiral was going to receive a great deal of money and property, and two priceless gifts: immortality, and the only woman who had ever truly made him feel alive.

So Phiral swallowed his pride and bowed his head to the necromancer.

"I will do as you command. The preparations for your expedition are already underway, and I will do whatever is necessary to see it is successful. It will not be easy, but I will take the risk upon myself. Should anything new happen with the Imperial investigation, I will inform you immediately."

Eothep neither responded nor moved. Phiral remained silent,

with his head bowed. He knew the necromancer was deciding whether or not to believe his promises. Phiral hoped Eothep could tell he was being sincere. He was already risking everything—it would be madness to stop now.

Finally, Eothep turned and slowly shuffled back into the darkness of the crypts. He said nothing else, for nothing further *needed* to be said.

With a shaky breath, Phiral made his way back up the stairs. He had so much still to do.

*   *   *

THEY HAD POISONED HER.

By the time Leyndra realized her most recent meal had been compromised, she was already feeling too dizzy to stand. When the cramps hit her, she crawled to the cell's door and began hammering on it with her fists. She couldn't keep it up for long, as the pain forced her to curl up with her knees to her chest.

This was like facing the shadows in Osho's room—an enemy she couldn't fight. Whoever had poisoned her knew help would not come in time. She was going to die alone in the darkness of this cell underneath the Imperial Fortress.

She screamed again, this time in anger and frustration. She wanted a chance to fight, to make her enemies pay for what they had done. She pictured Osho's face, his kindness, and gritted her teeth at the pain in her gut.

And then a warmth began to spread through her. At first, she thought the poison was beginning to shut down her body, but she refused to give into death. As the cramps began to lessen, she realized her focus on Osho was opening her up to *virtus*, a Warden's flow of power. She concentrated harder, imaging Osho alive and in danger, and the rush of warmth was enough to break her out in a hard sweat.

The pain in her stomach faded enough that she was able to stretch out and feel *virtus* flowing through her muscles. She reveled in the feeling, but couldn't believe it was happening. Her face carried the branding of an Oath-breaker. She should be cut off from this power forever.

And yet, despite her failure and Osho's death, it was still there. Difficult to reach and tenuous, but there, nonetheless.

The clang of the metal bolt being drawn back on the cell door brought her out of her reverie. She doubted she would need the ministrations of a doctor now. The poison had already done some damage to her, but she was sure the worst was over and she would heal on her own.

Her memory of Osho had saved her life.

The door opened and five Imperial Guard soldiers entered the room, with a sixth guarding the door and holding the lantern. They stood over her and Leyndra immediately noticed the manacles and chains in the hands of one of the Guard soldiers.

Investigator Chamirra looked down at her and spoke.

"Leyndra Jirau, you are hereby ordered to submit to the questions of an Imperial Inquisitor. You will lay face down and allow the manacles to be placed on you."

Leyndra wasn't quite sure she understood. They had not come to see if she was dying. They had come to take her to be tortured by an Inquisitor. She tried to sit up and the dizziness returned. Her mind was clear, but her body was nearly incapacitated.

She realized she hadn't been poisoned after all. She had been *drugged*.

Leyndra was on her feet in an instant and the soldiers moved in to grab her. She once again pictured Osho's face and felt the *virtus* just out of her reach. Even without her powers, however, she was far from helpless.

As the soldiers behind her attempted to grab her arm, she flung herself upwards and lashed out with a foot aimed directly between the cheek pieces of the helmet of another soldier in front of her. She would have crushed his nose and possibly killed him if her reflexes hadn't been slowed by the drugs. Her foot glanced off one side of his helmet, knocking him off balance but doing no actual damage.

A boot lashed out at her thigh and she managed to twist just enough to avoid a broken bone, but she was knocked down to her knees. Her speed was completely off, and the dizziness wouldn't go away. As she rose and elbowed one of the soldiers in the throat, she realized the fight was hopeless.

As good as she was, she was outnumbered five to one, and had also been drugged. Her head snapped back as she was tackled from behind. The weight of the man drove her into the stone floor with a powerful impact and she was surprised not to hear any of her bones break. The others rapidly pinned her arms and legs to the ground while the soldier who had tackled her used his weight to prevent her from rolling or twisting away.

When Leyndra was finally hauled back to her feet, she could no longer stand fully upright from the short, heavy chains that linked her ankles, knees, wrists, elbows and neck.

The soldier she had hit in the throat took a few minutes to recover from the blow and continued to hack and cough as she was marched down long hallways to where the Inquisitor waited for her. Surprisingly, he did not retaliate, nor did any of the other soldiers inflict any punishment on her for her attack.

It was small comfort as she was brought into the room where the Inquisitor was preparing his tools of torture. The man was neither particularly young nor notably old. He had dark hair cut short and a serious face. He did not look like a cruel man, a man who made it his job to torture people until they revealed every secret they could possibly remember. Somehow, that made it worse. It was just a job to him.

Leyndra was strapped down on a hard metal slab that resembled one of the cell doors. When she was completely secure, the soldiers began to leave the room.

The Inquisitor stopped Investigator Chamirra.

"You should stay, soldier."

He glanced at Leyndra and back to the Inquisitor. "She will not get free, I assure you."

"No, no, it's not that," answered the Inquisitor. "I require a witness to everything she says. It's procedure."

Leyndra could see how uncomfortable the soldier became at the thought of watching her get tortured.

"You want me to witness the ... questioning?"

The Inquisitor nodded.

"Shouldn't someone else be the witness? I'm investigating the case."

"Actually, as the investigator, you are required to be here. You have not witnessed an Inquisitor work before." It was not a question.

"Well, no. It's never been necessary."

"It is necessary now, soldier. Just as it is necessary for you to witness it. You know this, because two days ago you signed the request for me to conduct this session."

Leyndra felt inexplicably betrayed by that. She had told Chamirra everything, and he had chosen to have her tortured. Leyndra figured he must have signed the request after questioning her about the evidence they found in her room. She was shocked to find it had been two days since that had happened.

The Inquisitor kept speaking.

"You have no doubt killed men with that sword you wear. I'm sure some of them died in extreme pain. She will not die today, but she *will* tell us everything we need to know. And her pain will open that locked door for us."

"I've already told him everything," Leyndra whispered. She had wanted to sound strong, but her voice could barely make a sound. "You don't have to torture me to get answers."

The Inquisitor turned to look at her.

"But your story does not fit the evidence. We have facts, and we have your words, and they do not match. Perhaps it is the evidence that is wrong and you who are right. But how are we to know for sure? I must be convinced that you are telling me the absolute truth, and there is only one reliable way to reach that point."

"After a while, I will tell you anything to stop the pain," she replied.

He shook his head and moved around Investigator Chamirra to close and lock the door to the room. The soldier stood rooted to the floor, his eyes on the metal slab upon which Leyndra was chained. The Inquisitor returned to his small table of implements.

"I am no butcher, Leyndra Jirau. No thug with knives and spikes to make you scream and beg for respite. I will not hurt you until you pass the point of no return and start babbling whatever you think I want to hear. I am one of the best in the Empire at getting to the *truth*. That is all I care about. And I know how to make you reveal the truth and nothing else. I have done this many, many times."

"You don't have to do this." Leyndra was disgusted by the fear in her voice. She wanted to be strong, but she was terrified. She had been in life-or-death situations before. She had felt real pain before. But something about this man, about this situation, was scaring her more than anything she could remember.

The Inquisitor turned back to her.

"Are you going to tell me the truth that fits with the evidence? With the facts we have? If so, we can avoid all of this. But it must be the truth, Leyndra Jirau. If you cannot tell me the truth and it makes sense with what we already know, then I *do* have to do this."

Leyndra tried to think of something to say, something he would believe. She wanted to tell him the truth, but it wouldn't stop him from torturing her. And she was even more terrified of telling him a lie and being punished for it.

He continued to look at her face, waiting for an answer, but she didn't have one to give. And so, he turned back to the table and picked up something that was just out of her sight.

And then the questioning began.

Chapter Six

ORIT WAS FLANKED BY TWO IMPERIAL GUARD soldiers as he was marched down the dark, stone corridor in the deepest reaches of the Fortress. Large metal doors were spaced at regular intervals, and Morit felt his blood run cold at the thought of being placed in one of those cells. It was made worse by his knowledge that he might still end up in such a situation despite his cooperation.

The soldiers stopped him near one of the portals—there was nothing noticeable to differentiate it from any of the others—and the large metal bolt was pulled back. The soldier with the lantern pulled the slab open and the other stepped into the doorway. He surveyed the cell for a moment and then stepped aside.

Morit didn't want to walk forward. They had told him Leyndra had been questioned by an Imperial Inquisitor the day before, and his stomach clenched at the thought of being tortured. He didn't want to see what they had done to his sister. He could be angry with her choices and overbearing attitude, but he still loved her and wanted her to be safe.

And now the soldiers were going to use him to get any final answers out of her.

One of the men placed his hand on Morit's shoulder and firmly guided him towards the doorway. Morit stepped into the cell and gasped.

Leyndra lay face-down on the stone floor of the cell, her entire body covered in small purple bruises, short cuts that were already beginning to scab over, and strange puckered holes that pierced her flesh. At first Morit thought she was dead, and he began to feel light-headed. Then he realized he could see her back slowly rising and falling and knew she was at least still breathing.

The soldier removed his hand from Morit's shoulder.

"The Inquisitor has said your sister answered his questions to the best of her ability. We do not feel you have done the same."

Morit shuddered. He wanted to rush over and cradle Leyndra, but was terrified of moving, of being beaten by the soldiers, of being locked in this cell or one like it.

"I-I swear I have told you everything I know. We didn't...we didn't talk much. I didn't like what she was doing."

There was no inflection in the man's voice as he asked, "What was she doing?"

Morit only realized as he answered that the soldier was looking for something specific.

"Her choice to be a Warden. I didn't like that. It wasn't right for our family for her to go off and dedicate her life to protecting some noble. Some *stranger*."

The soldiers stood in silence. It made Morit even more nervous.

"C-Can I help her somehow? Am I allowed to do anything?"

The men looked at him and didn't respond. Morit began to think they were getting ready to do something terrible. He found himself babbling at them to fill the silence and delay whatever it was they were thinking of doing.

"I know she did something terrible, but she's still my sister. Not that I would keep silent if I knew anything. No, I'm telling you everything I know, which isn't much but it's everything. I'm not going to make stuff up just to give you something to hear. I'm trying to cooperate with you, and if she murdered someone then I'm not going to throw my lot in with her. I have a family to take care of. That's why I didn't want her to be a Warden—I knew something bad would happen and put me and my family in danger. I told her to find a husband and settle down, but she's not like that and never listened to me anyway."

One of the soldiers looked at the other, who nodded. Morit wanted to curl up into a ball and hide in a corner. It wasn't fair that he would be punished for something Leyndra did.

"You may have five minutes to speak with your sister. You will not likely see her again."

It took a moment for the soldier's words to sink in. Morit finally understood they weren't going to beat him. He was being given a chance to say goodbye to Leyndra. He nodded at the man.

"Thank you! I—"

The Guard soldier turned and stepped out of the cell. Morit watched them, puzzled, and then realized too late what was happening. The cell door boomed shut and Morit was left in pitch darkness. He couldn't help letting out a yell and he threw himself at the door as he heard the metal bolt clang into place.

"Please! You don't have to close the door! You took the light and I can't see!"

He paused, but there was no sound from the hallway outside. A low whisper came from behind him and he spun around, putting his back to the metal slab, but in the utter darkness he could see nothing. It took him a moment to understand that Leyndra was trying to talk to him.

"Leyndra! I can't see you. They took the light and locked me in here!"

"Morit," whispered Leyndra. "Get down on your hands and knees and slowly crawl towards my voice."

Morit followed his sister's instructions, and soon his hand made contact with her side. She hissed in pain and he snatched his hand away.

"Oh, Leyndra. What have you done?"

She made a low noise and he realized she was laughing.

"Your faith in me is touching, Morit."

He could feel a flush of shame rush over his face and for an instant was glad of the darkness.

"What am I supposed to believe? They said you murdered the nobleman you were supposed to protect. They told me you wear the sign of an Oath-breaker. Why would you have that if you didn't do it?"

Leyndra took some time to answer.

"I did it, Morit. I killed him. That's no lie. But I was—"

She cut herself off and Morit was worried she had passed out. Or died. He reached out to touch her, but pulled his hand back, afraid to cause her more pain.

"Leyndra? Are you okay?"

"No, Morit. I'm not okay. They're going to execute me, and that will be that."

Morit felt like he had been punched in the stomach.

"You don't know that. When you go in front of the Magistrates, you have to tell them everything, admit your crime, beg for mercy. They might let you live."

"I killed a nobleman. I know what's going to happen to me. The question is what's going to happen to *you*?"

"What do you mean?"

"They will want to make an example of me. It might not be enough to just execute me. They might decide to do...more."

Morit didn't want to hear this. He had kept himself distant from Leyndra and her employer because he wanted to be safe. Now he was dragged into this terrible situation and Leyndra was telling him he might be punished for something she had done.

"Why didn't you listen to me? I told you being a Warden was a bad idea. I said it was dangerous, didn't I? But you wouldn't listen to me. You always think you know more than I do."

"Oh hush, Morit. You wanted your life, and I wanted mine. When our parents died, you were too young to take over as head of the family. But even when you got older, you lack their courage, their determination, and everything that made them people I admired. I provided for us, and you just became jealous. Well, it's a bit late for recriminations now, isn't it?"

Morit could feel the familiar anger welling up inside of him. Leyndra had always known how to push him over the edge.

"Are you calling me a coward? Because I want to be safe? You can only say that because you don't have a family. You're not responsible for anyone but yourself!"

"I understand responsibility only too well, Morit. It's a shame you'll never live up to it."

Morit could hear the pain in her voice, but he was too angry to let it stop him.

"I don't have to sit here and be insulted by a murderer! You have dragged me into your own folly, and I want no part of it. There were times when I regretted not having you closer to us. Now I see that I should have cut you out of my life completely. I am responsible for my family, and you, you're an Oath-breaker."

Morit pushed himself away from his sister and crawled back over to the door. He hammered on it a few times.

"Guard! My time is up! I have nothing more to say to this criminal!"

A moment later, he heard the bolt being pulled back and the door swung open. Morit squinted in the glare of the lantern.

"She admitted it. She told me she killed the nobleman."

The faces on the men were expressionless, but something in their eyes when they looked at him made Morit uncomfortable.

"We know. She's never denied that. Step out of the cell."

Morit realized that, had she not already admitted her crime, he would have condemned her with his words. Suddenly, he wanted to run back in and apologize. This really was the last time he was going to see his sister, and he didn't want to leave it like this.

He turned, but the door slammed shut once more. One man shoved the bolt home while the other grabbed his arm and pulled him down the hallway. They were considerably less gentle than they had been on the trip down here. He wondered if they thought less of him trying to sell out his sister for his own safety.

Silently, Morit wished he could take it all back. But it was too late for that. He had missed his last chance to say goodbye.

*　　　　　*　　　　　*

ONCE MORIT HAD LEFT, LEYNDRA RETURNED TO A HAZE OF darkness and pain. As she lay on the stone floor, she thought of her brother and their last words to each other.

Leyndra hadn't wanted to fight with him, but it had been necessary. She knew someone had been listening to their discussion, and she wanted to make it clear to any observer that she had not told her brother anything—that they were estranged to the point where hurting him wouldn't make any difference to her.

She only hoped it had worked. Perhaps Morit would one day understand what she had done, why she had said the things she did, and why it had to end like this. Though she didn't want to admit it to herself, she doubted he would ever figure it out.

Morit had never been one to feel real empathy for others. The truth was that he *was* a coward. He put himself first, and would possibly even give up his wife and children to save his own life. And what gave rise to his anger was that he knew this about himself, and tried to justify it instead of growing or changing.

Every so often, Leyndra would try to summon the image of Osho in her mind to see if she could feel the *virtus* once more, but she was too weak. She couldn't focus on his face, couldn't concentrate enough to feel anything but the pain of her wounds. And that brought her thoughts back to the Inquisitor and her time spent under his power.

She tried to shy away from those thoughts. Leyndra had told him everything, and had begged him to believe her. He had broken down any resistance she might have had and looked into her mind. And when he was finally satisfied that every word she had said was the truth, she had still been returned to this cell.

Leyndra held out no hope that she would be spared. No doubt there had been discussions between the Magistrates and the Emperor, decisions made on how to handle this entire matter. But ultimately, Leyndra knew she would be publicly tried and executed. No other option made any sense, at least not with what was at stake.

She could barely move, and yet she forced herself to eat when the bowl was shoved through the opening at the base of her cell door. It was important to build what little strength she could, to heal as much as possible, before it became too late to act. She had no intention of going calmly to her own death. No matter how grim her situation, she wasn't going to give up her fight.

Leyndra had tried to mark the passage of time by counting her meals, though she had no way of knowing if they were delivered regularly or not. By her reckoning, she had been tortured only yesterday, though it felt like it had been much longer. What she guessed was a few hours after her meal, the bolt on her cell door was thrown back and the metal slab swung open.

She had already covered her eyes, though the light seeped between her fingers. She heard the booted feet of a single soldier enter the cell, so she slowly forced herself to sit up and let her eyes adjust to the light.

"Leyndra Jirau, you will now be escorted to the Imperial Court, to stand before an Imperial Magistrate where your case will be heard."

Leyndra squinted up at Investigator Chamirra.

"Like this?" She gestured at her nakedness.

He motioned to the door and another soldier stepped in and handed him a simple robe of coarse fabric. Leyndra knew it would be painful on her raw skin, but she didn't have any other choice. She slowly raised herself to her feet, grimacing at the deep aches from the bruises. Chamirra handed her the robe, and she carefully slid her arms into the sleeves, trying to avoid abrading her skin any further.

"Okay," she said, once she had tied the simple cloth belt. "What happens now?"

Chamirra looked down at the floor and then snapped his eyes back to her. She could see him set his jaw and figured he was mentally berating himself for dropping his guard with her, even if it was only for an instant.

"You will stand before the Magistrates who have reviewed the case. They will make a judgment. If you are found to be innocent...."

He trailed off.

Leyndra took a deep breath and let it out slowly.

"That's not going to happen, is it?"

He didn't answer.

"You know I'm telling the truth. So does the Inquisitor."

He swallowed and cleared his throat before speaking.

"What happened in that room—"

"*Don't* try to explain it to me! I was *there*, remember? I know what happened and what it means."

"Then you know how this is going to end."

Leyndra realized her fists were clenched and she forced herself to calm down.

"Do me a favor, Inspector Chamirra? Tell me you know who really caused Osho's death. Or at least, tell me you have an idea."

He paused for a moment before answering.

"I have a few ideas."

"And you've been told not to investigate any further, haven't you?"

He nodded, once.

"And I suppose you're going to obey those orders?"

"I am an Imperial Guard soldier. The orders come...from the Emperor himself."

Leyndra felt herself getting angry again, and wanted to lash out at Inspector Chamirra. Instead, she tried to focus on Osho's face, not to summon the power but to calm herself down.

"So, they'll declare me guilty of murder. What then?"

"I don't...I don't know. You will surely be sentenced to death, but I believe the Magistrates have been ordered to bypass adding any punishment before it happens, though they do not know why."

"Won't that make the people of Ythis suspicious?" asked Leyndra.

Investigator Chamirra didn't answer.

"You seem like a decent man. You know this is wrong. It doesn't have to happen this way. If I could—"

"NO!" Chamirra looked at her with horror on his face. "Do not ask me to help you! I cannot...I *will* not break my oath to my Emperor no matter how innocent you are. It is terrible that you were used as a weapon against the man you swore to protect. You already have my pity. I cannot give you anything more than that."

Leyndra smiled without humor.

"Your pity? I guess I should feel special, then. I should ignore the fact that you're willing to sacrifice my life to keep things peaceful, because at least I have your *pity*."

Leyndra expected him to get angry. Instead, he just stood there, staring at her face. She thought he wanted to say something, but he was holding back. Finally, he took a deep breath.

"You are smart enough to know what this attack means. Someone sent those shadows after Osho Idaphos, and there are very few who have that power. Whether it was done by a..."

He lowered his voice.

"...a priest or one of the Five, we must tread carefully. It was only a couple of weeks ago that the High Priest of the Church died under what most of us feel were suspicious circumstances. Now the head of a noble family is murdered. Are these two deaths related? Will there be more? They went to great pains to make us think you did it, alone. Our only advantage is to let them think they succeeded in their plan. Your innocence is known only to me, the Inquisitor, and the Emperor himself. It will have to stay that way."

"And I get to die for that secret."

She didn't want to admit to herself that Chamirra was not the real enemy. He obviously wanted a different outcome for her. Leyndra knew she was punishing him for the Emperor's decision to let her take the blame, and the punishment, for Osho's murder. But she just couldn't find it in herself to care about Chamirra's feelings. He represented the crushing weight of the Empire to her. And he would do nothing to help her, regardless of his personal feelings.

"As wonderful as our conversation is, Investigator Chamirra, I believe the Magistrates are waiting to sentence me to death. I'd hate to make a bad first impression by showing up late."

Leyndra stepped toward the door, and Chamirra moved to block her path. What she could only describe as a guilty looked crossed his face.

"Not yet. We must take precautions."

She raised her eyebrows at him as he motioned for another soldier to enter carrying manacles and heavy chains.

"I don't think I'm strong enough to carry all those this time. If it's a long walk, I'm not going to make it."

The investigator took a single manacle and placed it around her neck.

"We cannot bring you into the courts without at least one chain on you, so you'll have to wear this one. I don't believe we need the others this time."

He looked into Leyndra's eyes.

"Don't make me look stupid for taking pity on you."

She gave his look right back.

"Don't worry, Investigator. I cherish your pity. You'll get no trouble from me."

This time, she could see her words sting. Right now, it gave her a certain amount of satisfaction.

But Chamirra just nodded and handed the chain to another soldier. With one hand on the pommel of his sword, he nodded to the others and they stepped into position around Leyndra and escorted her out of the cell.

Chapter Seven

J EYRRA STEPPED FROM AROUND THE CORNER OF THE WALL and hammered her fist into the man's face. His nose broke with a satisfying crunch and he reeled backwards. Jeyrra followed and drove her foot into his groin. As he dropped his hands to his crotch from the shock of the kick, she swung her fist at his temple.

The man's eyes rolled up in his head and he dropped to the pavement at her feet. Jeyrra quickly got her bearings and made sure none of her boys needed any help in their own fights. She immediately spotted Qatee getting pinned against the alley wall by two thugs.

She charged the man on the left, driving her shoulder into the middle of his back. He was thrown forward, his forehead smacking off the wall. Jeyrra was already throwing punches into his kidneys, and he dropped to the ground in a mad scramble to get away. His howl of pain alerted his remaining allies that the tide of this battle had turned for the worst.

In a few moments, the rest of the thugs had fled the alley, leaving their unconscious fellows to the tender mercies of Jeyrra and her gang of cutthroats. As the last of her enemies beat a hasty retreat, she screamed after them.

"Tell Xyar to stay out of my neighborhood or I'll come for him myself!"

She turned to see her boys stripping the unconscious thugs of everything they had, including their clothes. She left them to their fun. She had important business to attend to.

Jeyrra stepped up to Qatee and shoved him back against the rough wall of the alley, in the same way the other two men had done. He winced as he hit the wall. She held him there, staring into his face.

"That's the second time I've had to rescue you, Qatee. Are you going to make this a habit?"

Qatee shook his head. "I had one of them, but his buddy jumped me from behind."

The slight whine in his voice did not improve Jeyrra's mood.

"That's only 'cuz you don't know how to fight properly. I need people I can trust to stand up for themselves and not need rescuing."

She felt a presence at her shoulder. "What do you want, Kabix?"

She felt the breath of Qatee's brother on the back of her neck as his deep voice rumbled, "I'll take care of him, Jeyrra."

Jeyrra let go of Qatee and spun to face the much larger man.

"But you *didn't* take care of him. You let him jump into the middle of the fray, and he doesn't have the skills to get himself back out again. So, who do I hold responsible, Kabix? You or him?"

Kabix narrowed his eyes at her.

Here it comes, she thought. *He's finally ready to challenge.*

"He's *my* brother, not yours. I was keeping an eye on him, but you jumped in where you weren't needed. You do that a lot."

Jeyrra looked him in the eye, though she had to tilt her head up to do so.

"If you don't think I'm needed, then it's time you do something about it."

She could hear the muttering of the others around them. Jeyrra knew the gang would lose members if Kabix managed to take control from her. They followed her because she was tough *and* smart. Kabix was missing that second part.

Still, the support of the rest of the gang didn't mean much if she couldn't stand up to the challenge. And, tough as she was, Jeyrra wasn't entirely sure she could take Kabix down. The man was huge, with slabs of muscle. Worse, he was fast for his size. Even if she won, she'd be hurting for weeks.

But Kabix hesitated. He could hear the mutterings as well as she could, and there was no point in being leader of a gang that had only two members. Kabix was perhaps not very smart, but he could tell his challenge wasn't welcome.

Still, he couldn't exactly back down now without losing a great deal of respect from the other boys. It was one thing to challenge and lose. But he was in too far to give up now. Jeyrra silently cursed herself for pushing him too quickly to this point. She had misjudged how ready he was.

Jeyrra considered the situation as Kabix looked down at her and seized on a way out.

"In fact, Kabix, you *are* going to do something about it. You don't want me rescuing your little brother, and neither do I. So, you're going to teach him how to fight ... *properly*. No covering for him, or pulling your punches. You'll put him through his paces and get him up to speed by doing whatever you need to do."

Kabix blinked at her. She was giving him orders as if it was all her idea to get into this argument in the first place. And then something subtle in his expression changed, and she knew he saw she was giving him an out.

It was all up to his pride, now. Some men would take such an offer as an insult and immediately ramp up the challenge. Jeyrra hoped Kabix was just smart enough to see that this fight wasn't good for anyone.

It was time for Jeyrra to slam the door shut.

"In fact, the next time we get in a scrap like this, if Qatee hasn't gotten any better, you and he will *both* be looking for a new gang."

She leaned in a tiny bit closer.

"Clear?"

"Jeyrra!"

A young woman bolted into the alley and was immediately surrounded by her gang.

Jeyrra turned her attention from Kabix and saw who it was.

"What are you doing here, Any?" Jeyrra couldn't keep the exasperation out of her voice.

Her boys parted and let Any approach their leader.

"I was looking for you. I wanted to make sure you had heard."

"I'm in the middle of business right now, Any. Heard what?"

"About Leyndra."

At those words, Jeyrra felt her shoulders slump and she didn't care that she looked weak. There could be only one reason why Any would come rushing to find her this late at night to tell her something about Leyndra. Her friend must be dead.

She focused on keeping her voice steady.

"What happened to Leyndra, Any?"

The young woman brushed her long, unkempt hair out of her eyes before answering. It was obvious Any was struggling to remain focused on what she had come to say. There were voices in her head, voices only she was able to hear, and they sometimes distracted her from the simplest of tasks.

"They say Leyndra killed him, the nobleman she was protecting. She was just found guilty and her execution is in three days."

Jeyrra stepped up to Any and took her hands.

"Who told you this?" It was always wise to confirm that the news Any was repeating was real and not just in her head.

"The announcement just went up at the Fortress. I was with a watchman and he told me all about it. He was there when they arrested Leyndra, but the Imperial Guard took her, and now she's going to die."

Any leaned forward and spoke in a low voice.

"They say she's innocent. The darkness made it happen, and when he finds it, he'll come back and throw down the Church and the Five and everything."

Now Jeyrra was confused.

"*Who* says she's innocent? Who are you talking about?"

Any's eyes became unfocused as she looked up and seemed to see something there. And then she came back.

"My friends say Leyndra was tricked. They'll kill her anyway."

Jeyrra knew that Any referred to the voices in her head as her 'friends.' She couldn't tell exactly which parts of Any's story were real and which were in her head, but it was obvious that Leyndra was in trouble but still alive, at least for the next three days.

"Thank you, Any. I'm glad you came to find me."

Jeyrra pulled out a few coins and pressed them into Any's hand. Any looked at them and then spun on her heel and skipped out of the alley into the street beyond.

Jeyrra would have to do something to help Leyndra. She owed her so much, and there was no way she would abandon her one true friend now. The first step was to find out exactly what had happened, and then work from there.

And then she remembered there was unfinished business here in the alley. She turned to face Kabix.

"You never answered my question. I gave you an order. You know what will happen if you fail. Is it clear?"

Kabix looked at her, momentarily surprised, and then slowly nodded.

"Yeah. Clear."

He shared a look with his little brother and then turned and left the alley. The rest of the boys breathed a collective sigh of relief and began to filter out behind him. Jeyrra glanced over her shoulder at Qatee and moved to leave.

"Hey," whined Qatee. "How come there's no fight?"

*   *   *

LEYNDRA LUNGED, THRUST, AND LASHED OUT WITH FIST AND FOOT, elbow and knee. She was sweating heavily, gasping for breath, and her body screamed out for rest. She forced herself to continue.

There was no way to know if any opportunity to escape would come, but she had to be ready if one did present itself. She was weaponless but far from helpless. Her body continued to heal, and she felt her strength coming back far faster than she had expected.

It was almost as if she was still a Warden.

She figured it had only been two days since she was tortured. She had been sentenced to death yesterday, or thereabouts.

Leyndra continued to train until her body was ready to give up entirely. Then she sat on the cold stone floor and practiced her breathing exercises. When her heart had stopped racing and she was no longer gasping for breath, she sat still and began her mental preparations.

Leyndra knew that Osho's death should have severed her from

her Warden abilities, but she could still feel the *virtus*, just tantaliz-ingly out of her reach. Nothing in her training had indicated such a thing was even possible. Especially since she wore the branding of an Oath-breaker on her face.

But then, nothing about her situation was normal.

She reached a calm state where her mind could float free of her body's sensations. She felt herself becoming a being of pure thought, unhindered by the anchor of her flesh. This was a ritual she had done countless times, and it always brought her peace and left her feeling refreshed.

She pictured Osho's eyes. Just his eyes, his gaze on her. There was such a mind behind those eyes, careful, thoughtful, intelligent. When she had fixed the image firmly in her mind, she began to imagine his face. His expression, his skin, how his beard looked, how his mouth moved when he spoke, all became parts of her mental picture.

A small part of her consciousness was aware of the *virtus* welling up inside her, but she knew she wasn't ready yet to try touching it.

She concentrated on his voice. The deepness and richness of it, the slightest Knirros accent and his unique way of pronouncing certain words, his laugh, the tone of his annoyance. It was almost as if he was here in the cell with her, speaking directly into her ear.

She imagined his hands. The ink stains on his fingers, the dark hair dusting the backs, the chewed fingernails he refused to have manicured, the strength of his grip, the ring that represented his house.

The *virtus* was almost a physical thing inside her now. She continued to tune out the sensations from her body, however. She had tried too many times over the last couple of days to access the power and felt it slip away into nothing. This time she would let it build until it erupted from her without conscious thought.

If it was possible, she would touch that power again.

Leyndra pictured Osho in his office at the estate. How he sat, how he moved around his home, the possessions that he kept close, and how he engaged others when in his personal space.

She could almost feel Osho there with her, standing beside her.

She was vaguely aware of a chill in the air of the cell, like a light breeze blowing across her skin. She ignored it and continued to concentrate.

Leyndra was so close to the *virtus* it was an ache in her mind, but she couldn't break past the barrier. She had conjured an image of Osho that felt as real as the man had been, but it wasn't enough. For just an instant, her concentration faltered, and she pictured the night of the attack.

The shadows slithered over the walls and ceiling, and she stood over Osho as his Warden, her sword in her hand, every sense alert to the threat to her charge.

And like a dam bursting, *virtus* flooded into her. She was on her feet instantly, her arms stretched out to her sides, her head thrown back. She felt like she would burst from the energy flowing through her body. She could feel her wounds healing, all aches and pains being swept away by the driving need to protect Osho.

In that moment, Osho was alive, in danger, and he needed her. Nothing else mattered but that she stand between him and any threat. She wouldn't stop, *couldn't* stop because her oath drove her on until there was nothing else left of her but her need to protect.

And then the flood began to subside, and the *virtus* slowly left her. She tried to hold onto it, but she didn't know how to stop it from draining away. In a few moments, it was nothing but a tiny trickle.

She waited, and then realized that faint touch was fading no further. It was nowhere near what she had been able to reach while Osho was alive, but it wasn't fully gone, either. She was no longer cut off from the power entirely.

Leyndra didn't know what this meant. Nothing in her training had prepared her for this situation. It was beyond anything her instructors at the Guild had covered, and she wondered if even they had ever encountered such a set of circumstances. It was possible she would never know the answer to this mystery.

She slowly ran her hands over her body and discovered that all her wounds were fully healed. Slowly, tentatively, she touched her face. On her left cheek, her flesh was raised in scars in the shape of the brand of an Oath-breaker. Her right cheek, however, was completely smooth.

The branding had been healed fully on one side of her face. There wasn't even a trace of the knife wound she had received from the watchman. But on the other side, the healing had left her with permanent scars. Again, she had no idea what this meant. She wished she had light by which to see, and a mirror. But this was foolish. If she was going to make wishes, there were more important things she needed.

Roughly a day had passed since her sentencing. Other than the delivery of meals through the slot in the door, there was no other contact with anyone. Her one chance for escape would likely only come on the way to her execution.

She didn't want to think about how difficult that might be. The Imperial Guard would expect her to try something, so she might end up fully chained and surrounded. She couldn't let that stop her, though. She would fight to the bitter end, if need be.

And she might just be able to use some of her Warden abilities, if the *virtus* was strong enough. She would have to practice constantly for the next couple of days.

The slot in the door slid open, and the wooden bowl was pushed through. She carefully moved over to the door, feeling in the dark for the food. As she picked up the bowl, she suddenly realized the metal plate had not been slid closed.

A whisper almost made her drop the bowl.

"Leyndra, can you hear me?"

She didn't recognize the voice. It was a man, older, perhaps one of the servants who took care of the food and waste. She carefully set the bowl aside and moved up to the small opening.

"Yes, I can. Who are you?"

"Just a friend of a friend. I bring a message for you from Jeyrra."

Despair welled up in Leyndra.

"Please tell me Jeyrra hasn't been taken by the Guard."

"No, no, she is safe and free out in the city."

Leyndra breathed a sigh of relief.

"She heard about your capture and wants to help. She is pulling what strings she can, trying to make arrangements so that you have a chance. She couldn't say when the chance will come, or what will happen. She just wanted you to be ready. She can't break you free, but she said she knows what you can do if the right moment comes. Watch for that moment."

Tears welled up in Leyndra's eyes. She wanted to tell this man to get Jeyrra to stay out of this situation, to stay safe. On the other hand, someone who cared was trying to save her. She couldn't turn away from that.

"Thank you so much for taking this chance."

"Don't thank me. I will do anything I can to help Jeyrra, and be glad to do so. I may be able to come back and tell you more tomorrow, but I cannot promise. If you do not hear from me again, be vigilant. It means I didn't have anything more to give you and it will all be up to you."

"Okay," she whispered, a lump in her throat.

The metal plate slid closed and Leyndra returned to her meal. She had to keep up her strength—there was much to practice and little time left to do so.

Chapter Eight

"S ERGEANT FLASEK LUMAYTH, OF THE CITY WATCH, TO SEE Tyina Idaphos."

The servant nodded at Flasek and stepped back to let him in. *I bet he'd bow if I was a noble*, thought the sergeant.

Flasek entered the large foyer and looked around. It was much quieter than the last time he'd been here, the night of the murder.

"This way please."

The servant led Flasek down a long hallway to a small sitting room.

"Please wait here. The Lady Tyina will join you at her convenience."

The servant left and Flasek grimaced at the door. He wasn't used to waiting on anyone's convenience. The people he usually dealt with knew not to keep him waiting. He wasn't a patient man.

Rather than sit as directed by the servant, Flasek moved over to the window and looked out at the grounds around the estate. The Idaphos family was quite wealthy, though very small, and the estate was well kept. Flasek idly wondered what the nobles did with themselves all day long, those who weren't directly involved in running the family.

They probably got into all sorts of mischief that he never heard about, but which wasn't that different from the kind of stuff he dealt with every day. People were people, no matter how much you dressed them up and gave them titles.

Clouds covered the sky, and he expected it would be raining by the time he left the estate. He hoped the rain would break the heat a bit, though he doubted it. Most likely the city would just become muggy and damp.

Eventually, the door opened, and the servant stepped in with a small tray of breads and cheeses, and a carafe of flavored water. He saw Flasek standing at the window and gave him a disapproving look before setting down the tray and leaving. A moment later, the door opened and Tyina Idaphos entered.

She wore a long black dress that hardly gave the impression of mourning, despite the lack of color. Her golden hair hung loose around her shoulders. Her attractiveness irritated Flasek. He wasn't here to look at pretty things.

"Sergeant Lumayth, I am the Lady Idaphos."

He stepped forward and took her hand. She began to lift her arm so that he could bring her hand to his lips, but he gave it one quick pump and let go.

"Thank you for meeting with me, ma'am. I will try not to take up too much of your time."

She frowned at his lack of etiquette as she watched him take a seat at the small table. He grabbed a piece of the bread and tossed some cheese on top, and then looked up her expectantly. With a small sigh, she seated herself across from him.

"I was informed that the Imperial Guard was taking over the investigation into my husband's murder. I have already met with—"

"Investigator Chamirra, right? Yeah, me and him are working together on this, since the Watch was the first to respond that night. He overlooked a couple of things when he spoke to you, so I'm following up."

Flasek stuffed the bread and cheese into his mouth and poured himself some water. Tyina did not touch the food.

"I thought Investigator Chamirra was most thorough. His men discovered the letter that proved that woman was hired to assassinate Osho."

Flasek swallowed and gave her a grin.

"Yeah. Convenient, that. Tell me, when did the affair begin between your husband and his Warden?"

Tyina's eyes went wide and she gasped at Flasek's question.

"You are being rather impertinent, Sergeant. There are better ways to approach such a subject than...blurting it out directly like that."

"I'm a direct person. I also hate to waste your time sneaking around a subject. Sorry if that shocked you. I don't deal with the nobility that often."

Tyina pushed back her chair as if she was about to stand up.

"Well, Investigator Chamirra does. I expect that is why he is in charge of the investigation. Perhaps he should have returned if he had further questions about my husband's indiscretions."

Flasek raised his palms in a placating gesture.

"I'm sure he would have preferred to come himself. But he's tied up with other things right now, and we need some of these questions answered to move forward."

Tyina wrinkled her brow.

"What do you mean by 'move forward?' The Magistrates found that woman guilty yesterday and I hear she will be executed. What difference does her relationship to my husband matter now?"

Flasek shrugged.

"Timing. Executions can sometimes be delayed until all the facts are out. I know the news of your husband's cheating will cause you embarrassment, and I'd like to avoid that if I can. But the truth is, your servants heard you accuse him of such behavior many times, and servants love to gossip. That news is already out there. It's how I heard about it. So, you're not going to be very successful keeping it a secret."

Flasek was trying to walk a fine line. He wanted to keep pushing Tyina to see what she might blurt out, but he couldn't get her so angry that she ended the interview. He had heard about her temper, so it was a real risk, but pushing people was how he got results.

He expected Tyina to be shocked at the news her servants were gossiping about her off the estate, but she surprised him by smiling. There was no humor in her expression, only a coldness that made him remember there was often a price for beauty like hers.

"Sergeant, I don't care who knows about the affair. I never made a secret of it when he was alive and I will put no effort into keeping it a secret now that he's dead."

She leaned forward and the smile disappeared.

"In fact, I already told Investigator Chamirra all about my husband's activities, and his concerns about the threats from that woman. So now I question whether you were really sent here by the investigator, or you are just sticking your nose in where it doesn't belong. If that is what's happening, Sergeant, then you have insulted me with your lies. I remember insults, Sergeant, and believe me when I tell you they usually come back to haunt those who make them."

"Then let me apologize, my Lady. I meant no insult—"

She waved off his apology.

"Your apology doesn't mean anything to me. You are out of your element here, Sergeant. The Watch is a joke, and so are you. You play at being an investigator, but you are little more than a petty thief, just like all the members of the Watch. I don't know what you think you were going to accomplish here, but you have failed."

She sat back in her chair.

"I think perhaps I should have you beaten and thrown off the grounds of the estate."

Flasek knew he had blown it. He had gambled and lost. There was no good reason for him to keep pursuing answers, but something in him wouldn't let it go. Now his goal was to get out of here without needing to fight his way out.

Flasek looked down at his boots. It was the reaction she would expect from a simple watchman, and he was good at giving people what they expected. It left him openings he could use later on when he needed them.

"I know the Watch is a joke, ma'am. That's why I came here. I wanted to do something real. I...I hate the Watch."

Tyina laughed in his face.

"And you really thought you would discover something the Guard missed? How pathetic. I think you wanted to be in the Imperial Guard when you were younger and you failed, didn't you?"

Flasek nodded, still looking at his boots.

"Perhaps I should hand you over to them."

Flasek looked up at her sharply. She was grinning again.

"I'm sure Investigator Chamirra would be interested to hear about a Watch sergeant bothering me, sticking his nose into the investigation, trying to make him look bad. What do you think he'd do to you?"

"P-please don't, my Lady. I will leave and never bother you again. I made a mistake, and for that I am deeply sorry."

She stood up and opened the door.

"You're sorry now that you're in trouble. You are here alone, and I doubt anyone knows you came here today. I could have my guards kill you and bury your body in the back end of the estate and no would ever know what happened to you. I could hand you over to the Guard, and they would toss you in a cell and forget about you."

She stopped and stared at him and he waited. He knew anything he said now would make the situation worse, so he kept silent.

"But you're not worth the effort. Get out of my home. If I ever see you again, I will have you killed."

She turned and left the room. The servant stood in the hallway, waiting to escort him to the door. Flasek quickly hurried out and left the grounds of the estate before Tyina could change her mind.

As he walked back towards the Watch building, he played the meeting over and over in his mind. He had years of experience dealing with the best liars in Ythis, and had developed a good knowledge of how people acted when they told the truth and when they were lying. He was sure Tyina was hiding something big.

This only reinforced the strange story Leyndra Jirau had told him the night he had taken her into custody. It was a story he had repeated to no one else except Beyus Chamirra. The fact that she had been convicted and sentenced to death told him Beyus hadn't believed her. It appeared the investigation was going to be closed, and once again Flasek was left out in the cold.

Flasek still wasn't sure what to make of all of this, but he was more and more convinced that she had been telling the truth, at least as she knew it. And it was obvious no one else was going to follow up on her story.

I should drop this before I get myself killed, he thought to himself. *I don't owe her anything.*

But by the time he reached the Watch building, he knew he was going to keep going. Flasek Lumayth had never been one to give up.

*   *   *

THE CLANG OF THE LOCK ON HER CELL DOOR BROUGHT LEYNDRA TO her feet. She didn't know what to expect, but she was ready to take advantage of any opportunity that came her way. She jumped to one side of the door in case she needed to fight her way out.

The metal slab was pulled open and the bright light from the lantern blinded her. She was forced to squeeze her eyes shut against the glare and she heard booted feet enter the room. Hands grabbed her arms and pulled her back from the doorway.

By the time she managed to open her eyes, she was surrounded by four Imperial Guard soldiers, one of whom was Investigator Chamirra. A cold dread filled the pit of her stomach. Had they overheard her message from Jeyrra yesterday? Were they even now hunting down her friend?

Chamirra looked angry. She could see him trying to control his expression, but it was clear something had set him off.

"What is your relationship to Sergeant Flasek?"

The question took her completely off guard.

"Who?"

"Sergeant Lumayth Flasek. What is your relationship to him?"

Leyndra shook her head.

"I don't know who you're talking about."

Investigator Chamirra raised his voice, and this fact alone shook Leyndra more than what he said. He was losing his professional cool, which meant he could do *anything*.

"You *do* know who he is! You admitted to telling him what happened the night of the murder. What else is he to you?"

Leyndra realized Sergeant Lumayth was the man who had taken her into custody that night, the man who had saved her from his own fellow watchmen. She had blurted out everything to him before she had been given time to think it all through. The Inquisitor had gotten that information from her, but she had never given the sergeant another thought.

"He's nothing to me. I already told you everything about him, while you were torturing—"

"I never tortured anyone!"

She had hit a nerve—he was obviously still uncomfortable with what the Inquisitor had done to her, at his request.

"Fine, the Inquisitor tortured me while you stood by and watched. It's hard to remember exactly who did what because I WAS BEING TORTURED!"

She screamed the last into his face.

He looked at her, shocked by her outburst, and took a step back. He inhaled deeply and let it back out slowly. Leyndra forcefully calmed herself down. His anger had given rise to her own, and she was tired of being a victim. She wanted out *now*, but it wasn't time yet. But soon, very soon, she would turn that around.

"Listen, you may see yourself as some dedicated soldier doing what's necessary for the Empire. But to me, you're the man who called in the Inquisitor, the man who heard that I was innocent, but still the man who took to me stand before the Magistrates and get sentenced to death. You may not see me as *your* enemy, but by the Abyss, you are certainly *mine*."

She wondered about her declarations of innocence in front of the other soldiers. It was impossible that one or more of them had not heard her argument with Chamirra the last time he was in the cell. They must know that the Inquisitor had confirmed she was not lying about the death of Osho.

Inspector Chamirra had told her that only the Emperor, the Inquisitor, and he himself knew the truth. But that wasn't correct. At least a few other soldiers had probably heard enough to figure it out.

Just how disciplined were they? Could they be trusted to know what the Emperor had chosen to keep secret from the Magistrates?

And then there was Sergeant Lumayth.

Investigator Chamirra eventually managed to get control of himself. He stood tall, his face impassive.

"Yesterday, the sergeant apparently took it upon himself to start conducting his own investigation at the Idaphos estate. There is no reason a member of the Watch would care about what happened at the estate that night, unless they were given *reason* to care. What did you hold back? You will tell me everything or—"

"You'll kill me? Have me tortured some more? You're running out of time to threaten me, investigator. Tomorrow is my execution, remember?"

She knew she was pushing him, but couldn't help herself. It felt good to make things difficult for him.

What's more, she had no idea what the sergeant had done, or why he was looking into her story. He hated the Imperial Guard—that much she knew—but was it enough for him to want to get involved in a situation like this?

"You're right."

When Chamirra spoke, Leyndra didn't know what he was saying at first.

"What?"

"You're right. There's nothing we can do to you, no reason for you to cooperate with us."

She could hear the resignation in his voice.

"So, I'm just going to tell you this. This sergeant is going to be told to forget about you, forget about Osho's murder, and forget about this entire ordeal. If he chooses not to do so, he will be seen as a threat to the peace of Ythis and will be dealt with accordingly. So if you have a relationship with him, if you have some message I can pass along to him to convince him to move on, believe me when I tell you it's in his own best interests that he drop this. Otherwise, he will gain attention that he *does not want*. I think I'm being clear."

Leyndra couldn't help but feel sorry for the sergeant. He seemed like a decent man. It was a shame that his curiosity and his refusal to give up would likely get him killed.

"You know as much about this sergeant as I do. I'd never met him before the night he arrested me, and I've not seen nor heard from him since. There's nothing else I can tell you, except that from what I saw of him, he wasn't the type to give up easily. Strong-arming him will likely get you the opposite result you want. I'd try a different tact."

Chamirra nodded.

"What happened to your face?"

His voice was mild, as if it had just occurred to him, as if he was only vaguely curious about the answer. Leyndra knew better. He had noticed almost immediately and was waiting for a moment to spring the question on her, to see her reaction. She was more than ready for it.

"I heal quickly. It's a Warden thing."

"I thought you weren't a Warden anymore. Your charge is dead. You said you had lost your abilities."

She looked down at the floor, defeated. At least, that's how she hoped she appeared to him.

"I *have* lost my abilities. If I was still a Warden, the four of you wouldn't be able to stop me from leaving this room. But the rituals that give a person the Warden abilities also change their body in ways that are permanent. Those changes don't require any power and don't go away no matter what happens."

He stood there, looking at her, not saying a word.

He doesn't believe me, she thought.

Leyndra considered acting right now. She didn't know if she could suddenly open herself to the *virtus* without preparing for it, but she hadn't lied about them not being able to stop her if she did. Of course, there was the huge risk that she would fail, and they would beat her down and likely chain her, thus eliminating any further opportunities.

Then again, this might be the opportunity she had been warned about. Perhaps Jeyrra had gotten to the sergeant, and he was stirring up trouble so that the cell door would get opened again. She thought about it for an instant and discarded the idea. Jeyrra didn't know Investigator Chamirra and couldn't plan for him to respond the way she wanted.

No, this visit was not related to her escape.

"Tomorrow," Chamirra suddenly continued, "I will ensure you are properly secured before we escort you from this cell. I understand your desire to escape, but I've sworn to the Emperor himself to see this through, and I will *not* fail in my duty. I wish your situation was different, but this is the path we must walk."

Leyndra gave him an even stare, and it was her turn to say nothing. This was the man who would try to stop her from escaping. This was the man she must beat, by guile, by luck, or by force.

He stepped back and motioned for the others to leave the cell.

"Don't do anything stupid," he said, and then followed them out.

As the door slammed closed, Leyndra shook her head. He still just didn't understand. Leyndra had nothing left to lose.

And then she thought of her brother, his wife, and their children. If she escaped, Morit would be used against her, as a hostage. He would likely be tortured for any information he could provide. Leyndra had tried to make it seem as if she had no ties to him, but they wouldn't take the chance she had been lying.

And then she decided Morit wasn't going to stop her, either. She was getting *out*.

Chapter Nine

PHIRAL NAJARE'S CARRIAGE STOPPED AT THE END OF an alley near the docks of Ythis. He quickly exited the carriage and, hood up over his face, proceeded down the alley to the exit on the next block over. There, another carriage waited for him, the windows secured against the night. He climbed in and settled into the seat beside the other passenger.

As the carriage began moving, Phiral lowered his hood and watched eagerly as Tyina did the same with hers. As always, he was struck by her cold beauty, a beauty he had wanted to possess for so long.

And now she was fully his.

He grabbed her and thrust his face forward, his lips puckered. She turned her head at the last instant and all he felt was her smooth cheek. She shoved him backward against the other side of the cabin.

"Stop pawing me, Phiral! We have time enough for that when we get to where we're going."

He looked down at his boots and nodded. They had been visiting the same inn for months now to spend evenings in each other's embrace. The place was very private, and the staff was *very* discreet.

"Sorry, my love. It's so hard to wait between the times we can be together."

She snorted.

"Of course it is. I'm sure you aren't banging your other mistresses on nights your wife won't let you touch her."

Phiral shook his head.

"Oh, no! I have no one else but you, my love. I have not tried to touch my wife in almost two years."

"Poor her," Tyina replied, and Phiral chose to believe the tone in her voice was not sarcasm.

She settled back in her seat, and when she spoke, she was all business.

"Listen, Osho's bodyguard dies tomorrow, and then the investigation officially closes."

Phiral frowned. "Actually, we don't want the case to be closed just yet."

"What are you talking about? We need to get this whole thing behind us as quickly as possible."

"There's still the matter of your brother-in-law, my dear. The bodyguard wasn't in it alone, remember? Someone hired her to kill your late husband. They got the assassin, but not the man behind the murder. As long as Wydo is alive, you don't get control of the family holdings. And without those resources, I can't keep up my end of the deal with Eothep."

Tyina pondered this, and then shrugged.

"I'm tired of all the waiting. This has been going on forever. When will the Guard take down Wydo?"

Phiral smiled. "They will receive the next piece of the puzzle shortly. It won't take long for Investigator Chamirra to resolve the situation in our favor."

Tyina closed her eyes and heaved a sigh.

"I got a visit from a sergeant of the Watch yesterday, the same one who was in charge the night of Osho's death. He pretended to be working with the investigator, only he was obviously clueless and doing it on his own."

Phiral turned to face her.

"What did he want?"

"He tried to ask me questions about the affair between Osho and that woman. I knew right away he wasn't working with Investigator Chamirra."

"What did you tell him?"

"I told him to get off the estate and not come back. I don't think I really answered any of his questions."

Phiral nodded.

"No one is going to listen to a sergeant of the Watch, my dear. I can have him killed if you wish it, but it may gain more attention than if we just ignore him."

She was still upset. Tyina wasn't the type of person to be easily reassured.

He considered the best way to get rid of the sergeant. The easiest way would be to pay one of his fellow watchmen a small fee to knife him in the kidneys while on patrol one night. Some of those cutthroats were masters at making murders on the streets look like accidents.

Of course, if he wasn't acting alone, then doing anything at this point was risky. There was too much going on, and it was easy to miss a detail and make a costly mistake.

"I think we need to wait this out. Tomorrow, the execution will take place, and the woman will no longer be a factor. You'll keep quiet and do nothing. And in a few days, your brother-in-law will become the main target of the Imperial Guard."

He didn't want to say the next words, but they were necessary.

"We shouldn't meet again until this is over. Once Wydo is removed and you are placed in charge of the holdings, then we can move forward."

Tyina still didn't look happy.

"What about your ... guest?"

"Once we purchase the object he needs, and pay for the expedition, he'll leave the city. Probably for good. If we need to tie up any loose ends, I'll take care of it."

Phiral couldn't help but smile. "We will still be rich, we'll be free, we'll be young again, and we'll be *immortal*."

Tyina didn't smile back.

"Come, my love. I know you want your beauty to last forever. And I was a much handsomer man ten years ago. There's nothing to be afraid of."

Tyina's face hardened. He had just made her angry, somehow.

"If you don't think there's anything to be afraid of, then you're a fool. You have made a deal with a *necromancer*, harbored him on your estate when you know what *they* would do to you if they ever found out. And now you trust him to fulfill his promise to us once he has what he needs?"

Phiral was shocked by her outburst, but a rush of warmth to his face quickly replaced it.

"You think I'm powerless? You think he's outsmarted me and holds all the cards? I'm not just some lackey doing the bidding of the two of you. One word to the wrong person and they will be hunting *him* down, not me."

Now it was Tyina's turn to be shocked. He had never spoken to her this way before.

"You, my love, are in this as deeply as I am. And the only way out lies on the other side of this path we've chosen together. You're ridiculous to suddenly worry about the danger now. It's been dangerous since the first day he contacted me."

He knew how much Tyina loved to hold a grudge, and he wondered how she was going to make him pay for his words, but he couldn't stop himself. He had been living with the stress of having that...man...on his estate for months, and now his shell was cracking and letting some of that stress out.

"I'm not stupid, Tyina. I've planned this out, and made certain assurances that he won't just betray me once he has what he wants. He knows this. The danger to him is just as great as it is to me. We are all in this together. He will get his object, and his expedition, and there will be no benefit to him to not give us what we have earned."

When she spoke, it was through a clenched jaw.

"You really think it'll be as easy as that, do you?"

"Of course not! It'll be difficult, and painful, and terrifying. But when it's over, we'll be young, and we won't have to worry about natural death anymore. And if you decide you don't want to go through with it, I won't force you. But once the chance is gone, it'll be gone forever. Just like, eventually, your beauty."

The carriage lurched to a stop and the coachman climbed down and opened the door. Phiral looked at Tyina and saw the cold expression on her face. He turned back to the coachman.

"It appears we won't be spending time here tonight, after all.

Please return me to where you picked me up."

"Very good, sir," said the coachmen, closing the door.

*   *   *

IN THE MORNING THEY WILL COME FOR ME, THOUGHT LEYNDRA. *I must be ready.*

She had been taking short naps throughout the day, interspersed with bouts of practice and meditation. She had no idea what Jeyrra might be able to arrange, but she wasn't going to let any opportunity pass her by. She was as prepared as she could possibly be.

In the timeless dark of the cell, she couldn't tell what time it was, or whether morning was near or still many hours off. She was still naked and without anything to use as a weapon. And she still didn't know for sure if her gifts would come to her when she needed them most or remain tantalizingly out of reach at a critical moment.

Still, she was not going to let them take her to her death without a fight. Her training was extensive, and she was dangerous even without her gifts. And the healing she had managed earlier had undone most of the effects of the harsh conditions in which she was kept.

Now it was simply a matter of time.

She could feel her concentration slipping as anticipation of the moment of truth kept intruding on her consciousness. With great effort, she tried to master her emotions once more.

And then the bolt on her door was pulled back.

Leyndra leaped to her feet and closed her eyes against any sudden glow of a lantern. She waited, but the door didn't open. She had an instant of further hesitation as she considered the possibilities, and then lunged for the door and shoved it open.

Stepping out into the dark corridor, she could make out a hunched figure scurrying away in the shadows at the far end. It could only be the old man who had brought her the message from Jeyrra.

He stopped and turned, and only her heightened senses allowed her to hear his hoarse whisper.

"Two blocks northwest, from northwest corner."

He turned and moved off, obviously wanting nothing further to do with her escape, so she let him go.

Looking up and down the corridor, she remembered that she had been taken to the right from her cell when she was brought to the Magistrates. But the old man had run down the corridor to the left. Would he have been going deeper into the fortress, or was that truly a better way out?

In an instant she had made her decision and was bolting up the corridor to the right. She couldn't afford to guess at any unknowns right now, and at least this way did eventually lead up to a possible escape route. A single lantern hung at the end of the corridor where a set of stone steps led upwards. Leyndra squeezed her eyes shut to keep her night vision intact and left the lantern where it was.

At the top of the second flight of the steps, two Imperial Guard soldiers stood in front of a doorway. Another lantern hung above them illuminating the landing, but the stairway was still mostly shadows. Her bare feet made no noticeable noise as she rushed up towards the two men, and they were caught unprepared as she leaped out of the shadows.

Her first attack was a sharp jab into the throats of both men, effectively cutting off any cries of alarm before they could be uttered. It gave her perhaps a few seconds of silence before they recovered, and she made good use of it. Dropping down, she swept the legs out from under one of the soldiers as the other began to draw his sword. Ripping the helmet off the downed man, she swung it up towards the face of the other guard as his short sword was freed of the scabbard.

He twisted his head to the side to avoid a crushed nose and Leyndra grabbed his wrist with her free hand. Spinning around, she tripped him and yanked his sword-arm down. His sword slid easily into the throat of the other soldier who was just sitting back up. She applied leverage on his wrist, which caused the short sword to drop from his fingers into her other hand.

An instant later, the blade had gone through his throat as well.

Leyndra didn't give herself any time to think about how quickly she had killed two fairly innocent soldiers. She was running on her Warden instinct, where it was kill or fail. She had no intention of failing.

She debated for an instant taking a cloak, but decided that her nakedness was really an advantage. Their armor was too large for her to wear effectively, so her speed and agility were her primary assets right now. She grabbed the second short-sword and carefully peered through the doorway.

A large hall greeted her, mostly stone columns and open space. Tiny windows along the top of each wall told her she was still below ground level, and that it was still night. A door at either end of the hall stood closed. She knew the door at one end led to the staircase that wound upwards to the prisoner entrance for the courts. There were no exits from that stairwell, and the courts were well above ground level, so she decided to try the other door.

Leyndra placed her ear to the heavy wooden door and listened for any sounds. Hearing nothing, she slowly pulled the panel open. Fortune was with her, as the hinges were well-maintained and did not creak. She held back her sigh of relief so as not to alert the dozen soldiers who stood ranged around this large room, guarding six doors spaced evenly along the walls.

She wasn't sure what do to. To retreat and go up the other staircase meant she would then need to find another way back down to ground level. And she had no idea how many guards would still be between her and freedom.

Going through this room meant twelve more soldiers would have die. Leyndra was fairly confident she could get through this room alive. Her concern was that there was no way for her to silence all the soldiers, and the fortress would be on alert by the time she made it out of this room.

Time was her enemy, but stealth was her friend. This one choice might make the difference between escape and death.

And then the choice was made for her. Behind her, at the other end of the large hall, she heard the door open and booted feet enter the room.

She was moving before the soldiers behind her could notice her in the shadows of the doorway. Shoving the door closed with her foot, she lunged out of the shadows into the smaller room and slew two of the soldiers in silence.

The remaining soldiers reacted to her silent and vicious attacks with varied results. The closest two soldiers reeled back from her blades, shouting in alarm. Four others, at the opposite end of the room, drew their swords and stepped into fighting formation. One yanked open a far door and ran out, obviously intending to alert the fortress. The remaining three stood in various stages of shock and surprise, unable to move for an instant.

Leyndra took advantage of this momentary lapse of discipline and reversed direction. As her blades slid into vital organs, she could see the knowledge in their eyes that they were going to die having done nothing to defend themselves. She had no time for remorse.

The four soldiers in formation closed with her and she back-pedaled. One of the two behind her drew his sword and lunged at her back. As he approached, she realized she could see him in her mind's eye, and then suddenly the *virtus* was flowing through her and she felt every inch of this room, every heartbeat, every intention.

As he came at her back, she sidestepped and impaled him on her own blade. She used his momentum to force him to stumble into the formation. The other soldiers broke ranks to avoid stabbing him further, and she dove among them.

In such close quarters, they had to be careful to avoid impaling each other on their swords. Leyndra had no such concern. One by one, the soldiers around her dropped, clutching their wounds.

The final two soldiers stood side-by-side with terrified expressions on their faces.

"Which door?" she asked them. They stood there, blinking at her. "*Which door gets me out?*"

The man on the left flinched as she shouted. He pointed to the door to the right of where one of the soldiers had disappeared moments ago. He might be lying, but she figured he was too shocked and scared to try an attempt at deceit.

As the she reached the door, a howl rose in the air. Leyndra hesitated for a second before realizing it was the horn that alerted the fortress to an escape attempt. She was through the door and climbing the stairs beyond before the soldiers behind her found their courage.

Leyndra emerged into the courtyard beside the stables. She could hear the shouts of soldiers on the walls of the fortress, and the main gates clanged shut as she crouched in the shadows. A platoon of Guard soldiers charged out of the main entrance and spread out, searching for her.

She moved quickly and quietly into the stables. A boy, no more than twelve years of age, stood just inside the entryway holding a dagger. His eyes took in her nakedness and then the bloody swords in her hands. Involuntarily, his eyes moved back to her body.

Leyndra lunged and knocked the dagger out of his hand. She stepped close and put one finger over her lips. His eyes nearly falling out of his skull, the boy nodded at her.

More soldiers boiled up out of the stairway beside the stables, and Leyndra threw her swords into the loft before leaping up and grabbing the edge. The boy watched her swing herself up and into the hay and shadows. He turned back to the door as the soldiers entered.

Leyndra could see between the wooden planks and cursed herself for gambling like this. The boy could easily point to her hiding place and run out. This was a spot she may not be able to easily escape.

Investigator Chamirra stepped into the low lantern light in the stables. He had at least a dozen soldiers with him. He put his hand on the boy's shoulder.

"Where is she?"

The other soldiers began to move into the stables to begin searching for her.

The boy raised his arm and pointed... at a large patch of shadow out in the courtyard at the base of the exterior wall.

Inspector Chamirra motioned with his arm.

"Go!"

The soldiers immediately left the stables and moved carefully towards the dark spot, holding their lanterns high. In a moment, the shadows would dissipate in the light and they would turn and come back to the stables. But Chamirra still stood at the door, his back to her.

Leyndra could easily drop behind him and cut him down where he stood. With him out of her way, she could climb to the roof of the stables and perhaps reach the top of the exterior wall. She grabbed her swords and jumped out of the loft.

And as she landed behind him, Chamirra moved out of the stables and toward his men. Before she could recover from her leap, he was out of her reach. She gave the boy a quick kiss on the lips and then spun around to the side of the stables.

She dropped the swords and began scaling the wooden framework. As she glanced over, she saw Investigator Chamirra turn back to the stables and look at the boy in the doorway. She froze, hoping the darkness of this corner concealed her from his gaze.

He stood there for a moment, staring at the building, and then one of the other soldiers called out to him to indicate Leyndra had not been hiding in the space the boy had pointed out. Chamirra called them back to search the inside of the stables from top to bottom.

It was only as Leyndra reached the roof of the stables did it occur to her that Investigator Chamirra had given her the opportunity to get out of the stables on purpose. That he had known she was there all along.

She shook her head. She couldn't really believe he had let her go, not after everything he had done. Besides, it was a moot point, anyway.

Leyndra still had to scale the outer wall, which had at least another couple dozen soldiers along the top. Her escape wasn't finished yet.

Chapter Ten

JEYRRA CROUCHED ON THE ROOF OF THE TAILOR'S SHOP, scanning the streets for any sign of her friend. The horn had been sounding for at least five minutes at this point. Eventually, the Watch would start to respond and begin clustering on the streets near the Fortress. It would make her own movements that much more difficult.

At least the Imperial Guard hadn't spilled out from the Fortress yet. They must believe Leyndra was still inside somewhere, or they had her trapped and were slowly closing in on her. Jeyrra didn't want to think about what would happen if her escape failed.

A low whistle from below brought Jeyrra's heart to her throat. She strained to see any movement, and then a figure stumbled from an alley across the street toward the corner where the tailor's shop sat.

Jeyrra immediately knew it was Leyndra, and could also tell she was injured. Jeyrra rushed over to the roof's edge and lowered herself down. Leyndra reached the corner and was immediately surrounded by Jeyrra's boys.

Jeyrra pushed them back and grabbed Leyndra in a fierce embrace. Her friend groaned and Jeyrra immediately let her go.

"She's wounded," reported one of her boys, and pointed out a puncture in Leyndra's side that was leaking blood.

Leyndra faintly shook her head.

"...s'okay...nothing...serious...."

Jeyrra nodded at her boys, who immediately wrapped Leyndra up in a blanket and began to carry her. Another block, and they reached a wagon, where they carefully placed the injured fugitive.

Jeyrra rode in back with Leyndra as they put as much distance between them and the Fortress as they could without jostling her friend too much.

"Leyndra, what am I dealing with here? What stabbed you?"

"...spear...not deep...be fine...."

Jeyrra opened a bag beside her and grabbed clean bandages. She pulled the blanket back and put direct pressure on the wound while one of her boys wrapped a strip of cloth around Leyndra's waist to hold it in place.

"Leyndra, you sure nothing vital was pierced? Tell me how serious this is."

Leyndra smiled.

"...I...did it...got away...and...my gifts...are back...when I...need them...."

"Well, you need 'em now, my friend. What do you need to do to heal yourself?"

"...nothing...I heal...fast...just need...rest...."

Jeyrra couldn't help being worried. She knew Leyndra's gifts could deal with some pretty severe wounds, but she wasn't sure how drained her friend was from her imprisonment. Not that there was much she could do about it.

Jeyrra considered taking Leyndra to a street surgeon, but she didn't want anyone outside of her gang to know Leyndra was with them. The Imperial Guard would start hunting her throughout the city shortly, and they would offer a good sum of money to anyone who turned her in. She didn't want to put that choice in front of anyone she didn't fully trust.

To Jeyrra, the ride seemed to take hours, but it couldn't have been more than thirty minutes before they reached the building her gang called home. The old, wooden walls were scarred and cracked, and the whole place gave off the sense that it was always a few minutes away from complete collapse, but it was a carefully maintained illusion. The gang had done extensive work on the inside, and it was far sturdier than it looked.

They carefully carried Leyndra through the front door and up to Jeyrra's room on the second floor. Once she had been settled on

Jeyrra's bed, they all left except for Zheemeng, the oldest of Jeyrra's gang and the one most skilled with tending the wounded.

Jeyrra looked down at the woman who was as close as a sister.

"Rest now, my friend. Zheemeng will take care of you."

Leyndra weakly shook her head.

"No...you can't keep me...here...the Guard will...search...."

"Later, yes. But it'll take some time, at least days, before anyone gets around to searching this place. You'll be much stronger by the time we have to move you."

Leyndra closed her eyes for a moment, and then snapped them open.

"Jeyrra...my brother...do you know what's happened...to him?"

"I'm sorry, no. I never gave him a thought. I was more worried about you."

Jeyrra saw Leyndra's fist clench. She knew what her friend was thinking. Morit would be in terrible danger now. The first place they would go would be Morit's home, and he would be taken into custody to use against his sister.

"I can try to get a message to him quickly."

"No...they already have him...and his family. There's nothing you...can do now."

Jeyrra swore and paced around the room. She had never liked Morit, but didn't want to see him in the hands of the Imperial Guard. And Leyndra cared for her brother and would take responsibility on herself for whatever happened to him.

"If you can think of anything I can do, just ask."

Leyndra smiled.

"You have done...so much already...you rescued me."

Jeyrra stopped pacing and knelt by the bed.

"No, you got yourself out. I just opened a door."

She saw Leyndra was about to protest and cut her off.

"You have to rest, no matter how fast you heal. In a few hours the whole city will know you escaped from the Fortress. The Guard will go crazy trying to find you—it'll be a matter of pride for them. You need your strength, or things will be harder for all of us."

Thankfully, Leyndra nodded.

"Tomorrow we'll discuss getting you out of Ythis. It won't be easy while they're hunting you, but I know someone who can probably do it."

Leyndra frowned at her.

"No...I can't leave Ythis...I have to find the...murderer...."

"Are you crazy? Tomorrow you, yourself, were going to be killed. Once the Guard announces the bounty on your head, the whole city will start hunting you. I'm sorry your noblemen got killed, but you can't stay here. Not if you want to live."

"I...didn't kill him."

Jeyrra laughed out loud.

"It never crossed my mind that you did. But I'm in the minority, here. As far as the rest of the city is concerned, you're the murderer of a nobleman, an escaped convict, and shortly to be worth a great deal of money. It doesn't matter that you're innocent."

"It's bigger...than that. There's...more to the story...."

"Leyndra, I'd be lying if I said I didn't want to hear about the entire thing, from start to finish. But you need your rest and I can wait 'til tomorrow, or the day after that, if I have to. No more talking, or I'll throw you out in the street again."

A small smile crept across Leyndra's mouth.

"You never...would."

She closed her eyes and was asleep in seconds.

Jeyrra nodded to Zheemeng and left the room. It was time to take care of other business. She returned to the ground floor and entered the large room in the back where her boys waited for her. A few of them looked up at her with questions on their faces, some looked worried, some were masters at hiding all emotion, and two looked resentful.

"She's going to be okay. By tomorrow she'll probably be able to move around a bit on her own."

"What about us?" asked Qatee. "Are we gonna be okay? The Guard'll have our heads if they find her here."

Jeyrra turned a hard stare on Qatee.

"Then they better not find her here, understand?"

Drulo stood up and took a deep breath. He wasn't generally one to talk much, and when he chose to speak, it was because he had been thinking things over carefully.

"There are lots of people who know you're friends with Leyndra. It's not a secret around here. It won't take as long as you think before someone tips off the Guard about you, and they'll come in force right away. And it won't matter if she's here or not. We'll all get taken into the Fortress in case we know something."

"Great!" yelled Qatee. "Jeyrra helps her friend escape and the Imperial Guard will come after all of us."

Jeyrra had hit her limit. Qatee needed to be put down hard so that he learned who was in charge. As Jeyrra took a step toward him she saw Kabix tense and knew that if she started beating on his brother, the big man would challenge her right now.

Drulo saved her the trouble.

"You're an idiot, Qatee. Leyndra would probably have escaped anyway."

Kabix rose to his full height.

"You don't talk to my brother that way, Drulo, or you answer to me."

This was the moment for Jeyrra to take back control.

"No, Kabix, you *all* answer to me. And I told you to get your brother under control and teach him about the way things are."

He looked at her as if he was about to give a retort, but held his words.

"You know what needs to be done, big man. So, *do* it."

Qatee looked from Jeyrra to Kabix.

"What's she talkin' about?"

"Be quiet," replied Kabix. Qatee looked at him, confused.

"Why? I think we all need to know—"

"SHUT UP!" Kabix' voice shook the room. No one had ever heard him yell before.

Jeyrra looked at Qatee, who appeared as if he was about to swallow his tongue. He stared at his brother for a long moment and then lowered his head and focused on his own feet.

Kabix turned and gave Jeyrra a look that told her he wanted to wrap his hands around her throat and squeeze until she stopped moving for good. She waited, ready to defend herself if need be, but he eventually looked away.

She hid her sigh of relief.

"Okay, that's over. Drulo, you're right. The moment Leyndra escaped, we all became targets of the Guard. Even if we had done nothing to help her, they would still assume otherwise. That means we need to find a new place to stay for a while, one that lets us keep an eye on our territory, but one that no one outside our gang can find."

She looked at her boys one by one. None of them looked happy. She couldn't see any rebellion in their eyes, so at least they weren't focusing their disappointment directly on her.

"Drulo, take a couple of others and find us a safe place. You know what we need. I figure we've got until dusk tomorrow to clear out of here. Leyndra should be able to move by mid-morning. We'll regroup at our new place and decide what the next steps are for all of us."

Jeyrra turned and walked from the room, hoping she had sounded confident enough for her boys. The last thing she wanted was for them to see how worried she was.

*   *   *

LEYNDRA AWOKE JUST AFTER DAWN, AND A FLOOD OF MEMORIES hit her as soon as she opened her eyes. She lay there for a minute, replaying the last dozen hours in her mind. She almost had trouble believing she had done it, had escaped from the Fortress. No doubt the Imperial Guard was scouring the city for her right now.

She lowered the blanket and checked the wound in her side. It was scabbed over and looked as if at least a handful of days had passed since the Guard soldier had managed to stab her with the spear. That had been right before she shoved him over the parapet and off the outer wall. It was very unlikely he had survived the fall.

Leyndra sat up slowly, feeling a few twinges in her side, but otherwise free of any serious pain. She wouldn't be able to do any fighting today, or much running, but she was well enough to move about.

She stood up and found a pair of Jeyrra's pants and a shirt. As she dressed herself, Leyndra listened for any sounds from the rest of the house, but it was completely silent. This surprised her. She assumed that someone was always up and active in this house. It was unlike Jeyrra to run a gang who slept late.

Leyndra moved to the small window and peered out through a slit in the canvas that covered the opening. People were out on the streets, moving on with their lives. It appeared to be a normal morning to most of them. Things would change as the day wore on, however. Every hour that passed would make the Imperial Guard more desperate to recapture her.

She was concerned about how many people would suffer during the Guard's search of the city, but there was nothing she could to do to prevent that, short of turning herself in. And that was the last thing Leyndra would do. She had a score to settle.

The door opened behind her, and she had to stop herself from spinning around and dropping into a fighting stance. Zheemeng entered and bowed to her. She couldn't help noticing that he was a good-looking man. He was handsome in a way that was all rough and rugged, though she knew he had a soft and tender touch. It was a nice combination.

"You are well?" he asked.

She nodded.

"Thank you for tending to my wounds last night. I will find a way to repay your kindness."

He smiled.

"You don't have to. It's what I do for all of us. But if you want to repay me, I won't mind."

Leyndra wasn't sure what he meant by that, and she forcibly stopped her mind from going to the obvious. She was in no condition, and no mental state, to contemplate anything physical with this man. Not right now, anyway.

"Is Jeyrra around? I'd like to speak with her, if she's awake."

Zheemeng continued to smile at her. She suddenly remembered that she had been naked the entire time he tended to her, and she was now glad that she wasn't one to blush.

What has gotten into me? I haven't felt this attracted to anyone in ages.

"Jeyrra's out right now, taking care of some things. She will return soon. Why don't you come downstairs and have something to eat? That is, if you're hungry."

At his words, Leyndra realized she was starving. She followed Zheemeng out of the room and down the stairs and was shocked at the feel of the wooden boards under her feet, the smell of grime and food and sweat and *life* in this house. All her senses seemed to be heightened to their maximum. She wasn't fully healed, yet she felt more alive than she had in ages.

She focused her thoughts and sought out the source of her abilities, and it was suddenly there in her heart and mind, a blazing light that instantly warmed her body and caused her to break out in a sweat. She gasped and saw Zheemeng turn and reach out to steady her.

"No!"

She flinched back and shoved both hands against the wall. In the instant that he had moved to touch her, she had felt the overwhelming desire to lash out with a fatal strike as if he was some kind of threat to her. She tried to push the *virtus* away from her, and with a sudden snap inside her head, it was gone.

Leyndra felt her legs buckle beneath her and she fell to the floor. Zheemeng rushed to her side, but stopped before he touched her.

"I'm...I'm all right. It was...."

How could she explain what was happening to her? She didn't even know what had caused this sudden flow of *virtus*. Even were she somehow able to contact the Guild, she doubted anyone there could provide an answer.

She realized that she was no longer starving, and her senses were back to normal. She looked into Zheemeng's face and knew the...*lust*...she had felt only moments ago had completely faded. Leyndra continued to wonder what it all meant as Zheemeng helped her back to Jeyrra's bed.

"I'll bring you something to eat. You stay here and rest."

He left her alone in the room and went back downstairs.

Leyndra lay on the bed, contemplating what had just happened to her. Truthfully, she should not be able to access her abilities at all. Once a Warden's charge was dead, the power was supposed to be cut off entirely. She didn't want to think about Osho's death at her hands, but she had to face it—she was directly responsible. The branding on her face had declared that to anyone who looked at her.

But now, the situation was even more confusing. The power had healed one side of her face, but left the imprint of the brand on the other side. Her access to *virtus* was fickle at best. And there were times she could almost *feel* Osho standing near her.

It was all beyond her understanding. All she could do was move forward and hope she would gain some measure of control over the situation. In her heart, however, she knew it wasn't going to be as easy as that.

Zheemeng returned a few minutes later with a small basket of bread, cheese, and pickled meats, and a jug of water.

Leyndra took a few bites and felt her hunger return with a vengeance. She was careful not to eat too quickly or consume too much. It would not help the situation to make herself sick.

Zheemeng remained on the second floor—she could hear him moving around—but left her to eat in peace. She was grateful for his consideration. Despite her imprisonment, or perhaps because of it, she felt like being alone while she ate.

By the time she was done, she heard Jeyrra's voice call up from the floor below. Zheemeng went down to speak to her, and Leyndra couldn't make out what they said to each other.

When Jeyrra entered the room, Leyndra took the opportunity to look her friend over. Her duties had kept her from spending time with Jeyrra for most of the last year. She was glad to see not much had changed. Jeyrra still wore her brown hair short, revealing the small scar on her forehead over her left eye. She was still fit, taller and more muscular than Leyndra. And she still carried herself with an economy of movement that demonstrated her long experience of living in Ythis' criminal underworld.

As soon as she entered, Leyndra could see the worry on Jeyrra's face.

"What's wrong?"

Jeyrra closed the door to her room and came to sit on the bed.

"The Guard has announced the reward for your immediate capture."

"Well, we knew that would happen. How safe are we here?"

Jeyrra looked around the room.

"Not very. Everyone knows we're friends. Someone will tip off the Guard pretty quickly, on the chance they can cash in."

Jeyrra looked Leyndra in the eyes.

"They're offering two thousand crowns to anyone who helps them capture you by dusk today."

Leyndra gasped at the price. It was a sizeable fortune to most of the citizens of Ythis.

"I guess they want me pretty badly. I'm sorry for putting you in this position."

Jeyrra shook her head and stood up.

"Don't be. This is what Ythis does to us. I was getting too comfortable and Iathephos decided it was time shake things up."

Both Jeyrra and Leyndra made the sign to ward off the attention of the god. It was a common superstition that the god of Ythis would shake up people's lives with tragedy, adventure, opportunity, or some combination of all three. Only the priests knew if it was true or not, but they were all mad and would never reveal their god's secrets.

"What are you going to do, Jeyrra? You can't stay here."

Jeyrra grabbed a sack and began stuffing clothing into it.

"No, and neither can you. We've already got a backup place. It's secret and secure and no one knows about it but those I fully trust."

Leyndra didn't want to ask, but she couldn't stop herself.

"Jeyrra...your gang. Are there any—"

"You want to know if any of them would betray you for a couple thousand crowns? I'd like to say 'no' but I'm not stupid. That's why I had to change our plans. We were all going to hide together. Now I'm taking you and Zheemeng to a different place the rest don't know about."

She finished packing and slung the bag over her shoulder.

"Every minute we stay here it gets more dangerous. It's time to go."

Leyndra went to the window and took a last glance out.

The street was deserted.

She turned to look at Jeyrra and her friend didn't have to ask what was wrong.

"Zheemeng!" shouted Jeyrra. "They're coming! Let's *MOVE*!"

Chapter Eleven

LEYNDRA AND JEYRRA MET ZHEEMENG AT THE BOTTOM OF the stairs. The street outside was silent.

"Back door?" asked Leyndra.

Jeyrra shook her head and led them to a set of stairs leading down.

"Too late for that. They'll have us completely surrounded by now. The alleys will be blocked off and crossbowmen are probably on the roofs around us."

She proceeded down into a cellar with a dirt floor and wooden walls. She raised her finger to her lips to signal Leyndra and Zheemeng to be quiet. Then she moved over to one wall and pressed her ear to the wood.

A moment later, Jeyrra stepped away and crossed to the opposite wall. She stuck her finger into a knothole and pulled a hinged panel away from the wall to reveal a dark passage. Gesturing silently for them to enter, she waited until they were inside and then pulled the wooden panel closed.

Jeyrra reached out in the dark and grasped Leyndra's hand. Leyndra was grateful for the contact. She waited, but Jeyrra didn't lead them down the passage. It was pitch black in the space, and stuffy, but Leyndra knew enough to trust her friend.

And then there was a crash from within the house and shouting voices as the Imperial Guard launched their assault. An instant later, another crash came from within the cellar as they heard the other concealed door splinter inwards. Booted feet hammered on the stairs as the second wave of soldiers flowed through the cellar and up the stairs into the house.

Under the cover of the noise of the assault, Jeyrra whispered to Zheemeng, who was in the lead.

"Keep your hand on the left wall and move forward slowly. Leyndra, take his right hand and don't let go."

They proceeded along the dark passage step by step. Behind them, the noise of the soldiers searching the house slowly faded.

After about five minutes of traveling, Jeyrra spoke up again.

"Zheemeng, you will come to a sudden turn. Change hands with Leyndra and reach out to the right-hand wall. We'll follow that for the next while."

In the far distance, they heard the crash of the wooden door to this passage being ripped open.

"Keep silent and keep moving," whispered Jeyrra. "It'll take them a while to get this far. There are too many side passages for them to search before they reach this point."

The sounds of the Guard soldiers searching the initial section of this passage made them all tense, but it soon became apparent they didn't have enough lanterns to search all of the various branches the trio had passed in the darkness.

Time continued to pass as they traveled deeper through the tunnel, and the sounds behind them faded away.

Eventually, Leyndra realized she could see the shape of Zheemeng in front of her. She turned back to Jeyrra and her friend whispered for them to stop.

"There should be no light here. I need to check ahead."

Jeyrra squeezed past them in the narrow passage and moved farther down the tunnel. There was enough light for them to see her silhouette and Leyndra figured out that the light was coming from a side passage up ahead. Momentarily, Jeyrra returned to them.

"There's a doorway that shouldn't be there, opening into a larger space that's filled with what looks like glowing fungus. I can't tell if the wall collapsed or if something dug its way through."

Leyndra could feel Zheemeng's grip tighten on her hand.

"Where did this tunnel come from?" he asked in a low voice. "You never told us about it."

"When we were digging the other passage to connect to the building across the alley, I found this one. I don't know what it was used for, but I explored it and found this route that will take us well out of our neighborhood. There are maybe fifteen or twenty side passages that branch off this one. I never explored them all, but the ones I did explore are all just dead ends."

She trailed off, and Zheemeng just looked at her and did not speak.

"I kept it my secret in case I was ever betrayed by someone in my own gang."

Zheemeng took a deep breath and slowly nodded.

"That's what happened back there, isn't it? One of our own betrayed us to the Guard."

Leyndra could see Jeyrra's shoulders slump slightly as she answered.

"Yes. No one but our guys knew about that other passage."

They stood there in silence for another minute, thinking about what that meant. Finally, Zheemeng whispered what was on his mind.

"That means our other supposedly secret place is probably getting raided right now. We have nowhere safe to go, and our gang is in the hands of the Guard."

Jeyrra placed her hand on Zheemeng's shoulder.

"Not if they did what I told them to do. I expected this, Zheemeng. I know who I can trust, and who I can't. The only ones who are going to the new location that Drulo found are those who decided to sell us out. The rest are in hiding and we will collect them once we are settled and safe."

Leyndra couldn't contain her smile. Once again, Jeyrra had outsmarted everyone around her. Part of that was due to her paranoia, but most of it was based on experience and brains.

"Why didn't you tell me?"

Leyndra's smile faded at the anger in Zheemeng's voice.

"Because you were the only one I trusted to stay with Leyndra and protect her while I was out making arrangements. I only had a short time to speak with the others."

Zheemeng looked down at the ground, obviously embarrassed by

Jeyrra's words.

"Sorry, I—"

"Forget about it, my friend. We don't have time for apologies right now anyway. We have to get past that opening, and I'm worried about what might be in there."

That brought Leyndra up short. Like most citizens of Ythis, Leyndra knew the story about the creatures who had built the city's sewer network, and who now lived in the tunnels that ran under Ythis.

"What do you mean? You think those creatures—um, the Tsojim—might have done that?"

Leyndra could see Jeyrra nod.

"That's one possibility. I've heard others. If it's those Tsojim creatures, we should be okay. Otherwise...."

She sighed.

"Either way, we need to get moving."

Jeyrra took Leyndra's hand, and began to move slowly toward the opening. Leyndra grasped Zheemeng's hand and felt his grip tighten as they neared the light.

There was a small pile of broken rocks and dirt in the passage beside the opening.

"Careful," whispered Jeyrra. Leyndra watched where she was placing her feet to avoid the loose rocks. The last thing she wanted was to twist an ankle in this place.

Leyndra glanced up and though the opening right as she reached the point at which she was most exposed. She saw what looked like a long, natural cave. The walls were covered with a fungus glowing a sickly green color. She couldn't see the ends of the cave, and so could not tell if there were other entrances or exits besides this one.

Just as she was about to look back at her feet, something large moved in front of a patch of moss, showing her its outline. She watched as its segmented body—longer than Zheemeng was tall and twice his thickness—flowed over the rock and into another patch of shadows, its dozens of pairs of legs skittering over the uneven floor.

She gasped and clutched at Jeyrra's and Zheemeng's hands.

Jeyrra turned back to look at her and saw the terror on Leyndra's face. She didn't hesitate, but yanked Leyndra from in front of the doorway and pulled both her and Zheemeng down the passage as quickly as she dared in the dim—and rapidly fading—light.

A few moments later Jeyrra slowed and led them in a few twists and turns before stopping. Leyndra heard her friend fumble with what sounded like a latch of some kind, and then a wooden door opened in front of her, leading into a bright cellar.

Zheemeng emerged behind her, and Jeyrra closed and locked the door. Leyndra looked around the cellar and realized there wasn't much light in here, but compared to the pitch blackness of that tunnel, it seemed like daylight.

She located the source of the illumination, a shaft of sunlight coming down between two hinged wooden panels in the wall that led out onto the street.

"What did you see in there, Leyndra?"

Leyndra turned to her friend.

"I couldn't see any details, just its shape. It looked like a centipede, only bigger than a man."

Jeyrra's eyes widened and she shuddered.

"This building belongs to a friend. I'll tell him to permanently wall up that door. I can't see myself ever using those passages again."

Zheemeng had gone to peer through the tiny opening into the street.

"We've come some distance. There's no sign of the Guard."

Jeyrra went to a wooden box in the corner and pried up a lid. Inside there was a jumble of clothing. She began picking through the items.

"There shouldn't be. We're in a different neighborhood now, and we've never spent any time around here. There would be no reason for the Guard to suspect we've come in this direction."

Jeyrra began to hand out items of clothing.

"Put these on. Leyndra, that hood will cover your face. We have to go out on the street to get to where we're going, and we need to look like we belong here. Or at least not attract any attention."

The three dressed in silence before Jeyrra led them to the stairs leading up to the ground floor. She looked at Leyndra.

"Ready?"

Leyndra nodded.

"Okay then, let's go."

*   *   *

MORIT PACED BACK AND FORTH BETWEEN THE TWO COTS, FROM the wall to the door and back again. Hathi lay stretched out on one of the cots, their two children snuggled together on the other.

"Please, Morit, sit down."

Morit stopped and looked down at his wife. She was so calm, as were the children, but Morit couldn't keep himself still. They had been locked in this small room for the past ten days. Only Morit himself had been taken out, but that had been for questioning and the one...visit...to see Leyndra.

He was glad the children were sleeping, at least. There had been such a commotion in the Fortress in the middle of the night, with the horns sounding the alarm and soldiers running about and yelling orders. They could hear that a few Guard soldiers had stationed themselves in the hallway outside this room, and more than once Leyndra's name had been shouted by someone.

Morit could only assume she had tried to escape, and the Guard was hunting her down. They must have thought she might come try to rescue Morit and his family, but he could have told them she wouldn't bother. Leyndra was too busy saving herself to risk her neck for anyone else.

They had told him she was sentenced to death, but not when. Leyndra must have decided it was better to die fighting. Morit had never understood her. Dead was dead—it really didn't matter how it happened.

Things had eventually quieted down somewhat, though the noise continued on until well after dawn. Morit had tried to question the servants when they brought in the food, but as usual they refused to say anything. So, he still didn't know if Leyndra had eventually been recaptured or cut down.

"I can't, Hathi. I'm too wound up."

She looked at him and smiled, and he knew she was trying to take his mind off their problems. They still didn't know how long they'd be kept here. This wasn't a cell like Morit had seen in the depths of the Fortress, but they were still prisoners. He wished for a window, if only for the children to be able to see the sun and the sky.

A key rattled in the door and Morit heard the lock click open. He stepped back as a soldier opened the door. Three more stood in the hallway beyond.

"Morit Jirau, you will come with us."

Morit didn't move.

"What's been going on? Leyndra tried to escape, didn't she? Is she—"

The soldier stepped into the room and took Morit's arm. Hathi had sat up on the cot and was reaching over to the children. The man gave a quick glance down at their sleeping forms and, surprisingly, lowered his voice.

"You will get no answers in here. Come with us. *Now.*"

Morit heard the unspoken threat in the man's final word and complied with the order. Once in the hallway, he turned to tell Hathi to be calm, but the door was closed and locked before he could get any words out. The soldiers fell into place around him.

Morit was led to another, larger windowless room with a single stool in the middle and a lantern hanging from the center of the ceiling. All four soldiers entered the room and placed themselves around him and the one in the lead gestured for him to sit on the stool.

"I've been sitting too much. I'd like to stand."

Without a word, one of the soldiers behind Morit grabbed him by the shoulders and yanked him off balance. He fell onto the stool, and only the soldier's iron grip prevented him from spilling onto the floor. Looking up, he saw the hard looks on the faces of the men around him and an ice-cold fear flooded his belly. These men could kill him without breaking a sweat, and Hathi would never know what had happened to him.

"Okay, okay, I'll do what you want."

He hated the whine that crept into his voice as he spoke.

The hands on his shoulders pulled back and the soldiers stood at attention in the four corners of the room, saying nothing further. Morit wanted to ask them what they were waiting for, but his fear kept his mouth firmly shut.

After what seemed like forever but was probably only ten minutes, the door opened again and another Guard soldier entered. Morit recognized this one as the man who had first questioned him when he was taken into custody ten days ago—Investigator Chamirra. Only he looked very different than the first time they had met.

Chamirra was obviously tired, his face—and especially his eyes—betraying his exhaustion to everyone. He was covered in road dust and sweat, and looked as if he had just been in a battle. He closed the door and stood in front of Morit, staring down at him. Morit couldn't help but fidget on the stool, careful not to give the impression that he was going to stand up.

"Where is she going to go?"

Morit's mouth gaped open, no idea how to respond.

"Sh-she escaped?" he finally asked, stupidly. Of *course* she had escaped. They wouldn't all be acting like this if she was safely back in custody. Or more safely dead.

"We know about Jeyrra. We know where her gang usually holes up, and where they were going to go hide. But they abandoned their building before we got there, and their hideout is empty. Where will Jeyrra take her?"

Morit's thoughts frantically raced around his head.

"I-I-I don't know. I haven't spoken to Jeyrra in years—"

Inspector Chamirra's fist lashed out and slammed into the side of Morit's head. Morit pitched off the stool and hit the floor, hard. Stars swam before his eyes, but he managed to pull himself into a ball to protect his body against the blows he expected to come.

Morit waited, but nothing happened. He blinked back the tears that were threatening to erupt.

"You obviously do not understand your situation," continued Investigator Chamirra, his words slow and measured, a sharp contrast to his sudden attack. "Your sister was convicted of the murder of a nobleman. She is now also responsible for the deaths of multiple Imperial Guard soldiers this morning. You have a single chance to prove that you are not in league with her."

Morit heard the investigator lean down over him.

"You will tell me everything I need to know, or I will hand you over to an Inquisitor. I watched your sister be put to the question. She's far stronger than you, and the Inquisitor broke her will with an ease that shocked me. You won't last nearly as long."

Morit was terrified. He looked up at Chamirra and knew that he would give up Leyndra to avoid being tortured by an Inquisitor. He would give up Hathi, too. He might even give up the children.

"Please," he begged. "I'll tell you everything I know. Please don't torture me."

Investigator Chamirra straightened up and looked down on Morit with obvious distaste.

"Where is your sister going?"

Morit began babbling. He told them everything he knew about Jeyrra, where her gang lived, all about her friendship with Leyndra, anything he could remember that might have been mentioned in passing yet may yield a clue to their whereabouts.

He spouted Leyndra's life story, all he knew about her favorite places in the city, every acquaintance he could think of, every detail that might buy him a way out of being put to the Question. When he couldn't think of anything else, he began offering names of others who might know something—anything—useful about Leyndra.

When Morit finally trailed off, the investigator looked just as grim as when he started. Morit knew, despite everything he had just told them, Chamirra was going to send him to the Inquisitor anyway. He tried to think of a bargain, any bargain, he could make to avoid that fate.

There was a sharp rap on the door and another soldier entered. He handed a rolled-up note to Chamirra, saluted, and left the room. Chamirra unrolled the note and stared at it for a long time. His expression became even grimmer, if that was possible. Morit could tell he was not remotely happy about the contents of the missive.

Finally, Chamirra looked up at the other soldiers.

"We have new orders. We are to return Morit and his family to his home, where they will be kept under house arrest."

Morit didn't register his words at first. They were going...home? Could it be true, or was it all just a trick to get him to admit something?

Chamirra looked down at him.

"You will not be permitted to leave your dwelling for any reason. Two soldiers will remain inside with you at all times. You are being given a chance to prove useful. Fail me and you will regret it severely."

Morit eagerly nodded at Investigator Chamirra.

"I will do whatever you need. Just tell me and I'll do it."

Morit detected the slightest of smiles on the faces of the two soldiers in front of him as Investigator Chamirra answered. There was no humor in either of those expressions.

"Simple," replied Chamirra. "You'll be the bait."

Chapter Twelve

L EAVE HERE AND YOU'LL BE KILLED."
Leyndra looked askance at her friend. Jeyrra was on the
floor at Leyndra's feet, the muscles in her arms flexing as she
pushed herself up and down, over and over.

"I don't think it'll be as easy as that, Jeyrra. It's not like I don't
know how to disguise myself. Besides, I can't let them keep me bot-
tled up like this while they tear the city apart looking for me."

Jeyrra remained silent as she finished another half-dozen push-
ups and then pulled her knees under her and sat up. A sheen of
sweat covered her face and arms. She had been exercising for the
last hour. Leyndra figured it was as much to get rid of stress as it
was to stay in shape.

"I didn't risk my boys and myself just so you could throw that all
away in a useless attempt to get revenge on whoever framed you."

Jeyrra stood up and faced Leyndra eye-to-eye. "You hate losing.
So do I. You want to fight back, and I don't disagree with that. But
there's losing and there's ... what happened to you. The entire Imperial Guard wants your head, and from what you've told me, whoever
set you up must be either a sorcerer or a pretty high-ranking priest.
It's only a matter of time before one of us makes a mistake and then
they all win for good. You're going to make that more likely every
time you go outside."

Leyndra could feel the tension building in her shoulders and
neck. She wanted to lash out at a target, *any* target. She swallowed
her angry retort, though. Jeyrra didn't deserve her anger and frustration.

She turned and leaned against the rough, wooden wall. They were deep in the Warren, a section of Ythis where the most dangerous, destitute, and desperate lived. The area was filled with twisting, narrow streets and tiny alleys. Dilapidated buildings leaned on one another, and many no longer belonged to any one individual. It was the perfect place to hide from the law, and it was where they had been holed up since yesterday morning.

"Jeyrra, if I run away from Ythis, they'll win anyway. And I won't even have given them a fight."

Jeyrra turned and crossed to the pair of cots at the far end of the cellar. She stripped off her damp shirt and used one of the rough blankets to wipe herself down.

"Come on, Leyndra. You know better than that. Didn't you once tell me that the first thing the Guild taught you was that if you had to fight to protect your ward, you had already failed? This isn't any different. There's a whole city waiting to come down on you. If you 'give them a fight' then you'll lose. And so will everyone who's trying to help you."

Leyndra sighed and kicked the wall with her heel. The wood chipped.

"Okay, you want me to leave Ythis. Are you going to come with me?"

A guilty look passed over Jeyrra's face.

"I...hadn't planned on it."

Now Leyndra *was* angry.

"You tell me that I should run away, but you're going to stay here? They're looking for you just as hard as they're looking for me! If you get caught, they'll throw you to an Inquisitor and, believe me, you'll wish they had just killed you."

Jeyrra pulled another shirt over her head.

"Listen, Leyndra. They only want me, or my boys, because we can lead them to *you*. But if we can get you out of the city, well, word can be spread pretty quickly that you're gone. Then it's not worth their effort to come after us. There'll be nothing for us to tell them."

Leyndra could feel the rage boiling up inside her. Jeyrra was supposed to be her *friend*. But all she wanted was for Leyndra to leave so they could be safe again. Jeyrra wasn't helping Leyndra escape, she was just protecting her own skin.

"So, once I'm gone things will just go back to normal for you, then? I'll have to run as far and as fast as I can, because you know they'll come after me. But you, you just wait a bit for things to settle down and it'll be business as usual. If you want to be safe so badly, why don't you just turn me in and make a profit while you're at it?"

Leyndra saw the punch coming and had all the time in the world to block or avoid it. As tough as Jeyrra was, she was no match for a trained Warden. And Leyndra *wanted* this fight. She wanted to have a reason to beat on someone and Jeyrra was pushing her away when she needed friends the most.

And then Jeyrra's fist connected with her cheek and Leyndra's head snapped sideways. She lost her balance and fell against the wall. For an instant there was no pain, but the rush came before she was ready and blossomed across her face.

As much as she had wanted to fight, her body hadn't reacted to the threat. Leyndra's muscles had locked as she saw the fist coming. Jeyrra had really *hit* her.

She looked up at Jeyrra face and saw that her friend was frozen in shock. Jeyrra hadn't expected to connect with the punch, either. Leyndra realized her own expression matched the other woman's.

Leyndra took a deep breath and let out a bellow, and as she did so she threw herself at Jeyrra. All of her fighting skills—honed until they were instinct—were forgotten as she tackled Jeyrra and drove her down into the floor. As the wind was knocked out of the other woman, Leyndra pulled her own arm back and threw a punch at her face.

Jeyrra was no easy target, however. She twisted her head at the last instant and Leyndra punched the floor. Pain exploded in her knuckles, just enough to distract her from Jeyrra's grip on her other arm. With a quick twist, their positions were suddenly reversed, Jeyrra on top and Leyndra pinned under her.

Leyndra continued to lash out and caught Jeyrra across the chin. But Jeyrra dropped her forearm down across Leyndra's throat, pinning her head to the floor and cutting off her air supply. Panicked,

Leyndra tried to claw at the other woman's face, and Jeyrra was forced to let up on her throat to pull back.

Jeyrra twisted and came back with a backhand blow across the other side of Leyndra's face. Stars swam in front of Leyndra's eyes and she tensed for another punch. But suddenly Jeyrra's weight disappeared from Leyndra's chest.

As Leyndra blinked away the stars, she wondered if Jeyrra was about to lay into her with kicks, but no further blows came. Finally, Leyndra looked up and saw Zheemeng holding Jeyrra back. He must have come into the room and pulled Jeyrra off her.

What confused Leyndra was the expression on Jeyrra's face. She was smiling, and burst out laughing as Zheemeng let her go.

All the rage had drained from Leyndra. Her face ached on both sides and she knew she would have a couple of deep bruises for the next few hours. She slowly pulled herself to her feet as Jeyrra leaned against the wall and laughed.

"That...was fantastic!" she gasped in between guffaws.

Leyndra looked at her like she had lost her mind, which caused Jeyrra to burst into fresh laughter. Zheemeng just stood there and stared at the floor, obviously unsure what to do next.

"What is wrong with you?" asked Leyndra. "You think we were having fun?"

Jeyrra calmed down, but her smile never left her face.

"Yeah, you could call it that. You needed a fight, so I gave you one. I was a bit worried at first that you'd break me into little pieces, but you held back from the using the stuff you learned from the Guild, so it worked out okay."

Leyndra didn't feel *okay*. She felt exhausted. The fight had lasted only seconds, but she was completely drained. Her anger was gone, though. She turned to Zheemeng.

"How did you get in here so fast?"

"I didn't," he replied. "I had come to talk to Jeyrra about what to do next and was about to knock on the door when I heard bodies hitting the floor. So I came in without knocking."

Jeyrra chuckled.

"We could have been naked."

Zheemeng gave her a deadpan look.

"Is there someone in this room I haven't *already* seen naked?"

His words caused Leyndra to feel a small pang of jealousy. She shoved it into a corner of her mind—she didn't have time to explore the ramifications of that right now. Besides, he acted as the medic for the whole gang. He had probably seen most of them naked at some point, all part of his duties.

Leyndra was vaguely aware that she *really* wanted that to be the explanation for his remark.

"I ... I'm sorry, Jeyrra. I shouldn't have said—"

Jeyrra waved off her apology.

"You needed a fight, and I gave you one. I don't believe you'd think I'd turn you in, so it was just anger talking, and that's all just noise."

Leyndra nodded at her, and then grabbed her friend in a bear hug.

"Zheemeng's right, though," said Jeyrra as she hugged Leyndra back. "We need to plan out our next steps, whatever they're going to be. The Guard won't stay out of the Warren forever, no matter how hard it'll be for them to come in here."

Leyndra let her go and stepped back. She knew she still hadn't convinced Jeyrra to help her stay in Ythis. Jeyrra spoke before she could say anything further.

"It's going to take some time for me to make arrangements to get you out of the city. The ships are getting searched before they can leave the docks, and every person going through the gates gets checked. I don't want to see you get killed by the Guard, or by whoever framed you. But you're a big girl and it's your choice what you do with yourself."

Leyndra realized that Jeyrra was agreeing with her decision to investigate Osho's death further.

"But if you lead the Guard back to this building, you won't have to worry about them," continued Jeyrra. "I'll kill you myself."

*   *   *

FLASEK REFLEXIVELY PULLED THE HOOD OF HIS CLOAK FURTHER over his face and tried not to hunch his shoulders. It was one thing to look like you didn't want anyone to see your face. It was entirely another to look like you were afraid of any attention. The people who lived in the Warren could tell a predator from a victim with a glance, and Flasek didn't want anyone to think he was the latter.

Besides, he had spent years as a watchman—there was always a chance someone here might recognize him if he caught too much attention. If that happened, he wouldn't be leaving the Warren alive. Even as crooked as the Watch was, it was still considered an enemy to most of the criminals who lived in this part of Ythis.

Flasek concentrated on the directions he had been given. There were no street signs in the Warren, which meant if you didn't know exactly where you needed to go, you could get very, very lost. It was another way to identify those who didn't belong.

He stepped over the legs of a dead man lying in the narrow roadway. The body was naked, three stab wounds in the back displaying the cause of death. Flasek figured the man had been killed no earlier than dusk yesterday, and all his possessions had likely been stripped from him well before the body had cooled.

He continued on without so much as a glance back at the corpse. There was no use getting involved in a murder that would never be solved, and he was here for a purpose. For a moment he wondered if Leyndra Jirau was hiding out in one of these buildings, and figured it was fairly likely. Not that he had any chance of finding her if she was. She had managed to escape in the early hours of the morning three days ago, and it was two days since the Guard had raided the building where someone had told them she was hiding.

Flasek made a last turn and found the stone steps leading down to a basement entrance. He carefully descended and pounded twice on the door, waited, and then pounded three more times. He knew eyes were watching him, and he waited, motionless, for the door to open.

Eventually, he heard bolts being drawn back, and the door creaked open on rusted hinges. A wrinkled face, framed in dark scarves, peered around the edge of the door at him. One of the witch's eyes was completely white, while the other was sharp and piercing. He had the feeling this woman instantly knew who he was, what he was thinking, his entire past.

And then she blinked, and the feeling disappeared. She stepped back and pulled the door open wide enough for him to enter. She gave him a single nod, but said nothing.

Flasek stepped into a short hallway that opened into a small room lit only by three candles on a tiny square table. A stool sat on either side of the table, and a short shelf on the wall held a few small glass jars, a deck of cards, and what looked like a human eyeball.

"Sit on the stool to the left," croaked the witch as she closed the door behind him. The squeal of the rusty hinges matched the pitch of her voice perfectly. She threw the two bolts and followed him into the room.

Flasek sat on the stool and looked around. He could see no other exits, nor was there anywhere for the witch to sleep or do anything else except sit at this table.

"You live here?" he asked.

Again, that sharp look from her one good eye pinned him in place.

"That's not the question you came here to ask."

She lowered herself onto the stool opposite him and peered at his face over the candles. The flames danced slightly as she moved and settled once she went still.

"You're right. It's not. I need to know about . . . some kind of magic."

"Hah!"

Her laugh had no humor in it. Her tone was mocking.

"You want to be a sorcerer, is that it? Think you can become one of the Five?"

He bit back an angry retort. He needed this woman to give him some answers, and he didn't want to make an enemy of her. Witches weren't known for their forgiving natures.

"No, ma'am. I just need to know who might have been able to . . . do something. That's all."

She grinned at him, showing three ragged, brown teeth hanging from blackened gums.

"So polite. But nothing is for free, watchman."

"How do you—?" He stopped. It hadn't been just a feeling. She really did know who he was. For the first time, he fully realized just how dangerous it was to come here. Witches were few—at least as far as he knew—and outlawed in the Empire. They used what they called "gifts" which gave them special powers. Stories about them said that it was neither sorcery nor a connection to one of the Empire's gods. Some speculated they made pacts with other, older entities.

There was no reliable to way to separate fact from fiction, and the witches weren't going to reveal their secrets. Some would, however, provide answers to questions and perform small services in return for payment. They were notoriously hard to find, though, a result of being hunted by both the Church and the Five. Flasek had been lucky to have a contact who could tell him how to reach this woman, and how to pay her properly.

Flasek pulled a small bag of coins from the folds of his cloak and set it on the table. Then, from another pocket, he pulled out a small glass vial. It had cost him a major favor to get this much falcon's blood. He put the vial on the table beside the coins.

The witch's eye never left his face.

"Tell me what happened, and I will tell you what caused it."

Flasek described what Leyndra Jirau had told him. He didn't leave out her name, or the name of the dead nobleman. He figured the witch had already heard about the incident, and probably knew about the huge reward for Leyndra's capture as well. He was careful not to embellish or rephrase the words Leyndra had used.

When he was finished, the witch nodded once and closed her one good eye, leaving the milky-white orb open. She sat motionless, and a slight chill began to fill the air. The candle flames got smaller and smaller until they were two tiny points of light that gave off no illumination. In the darkness, the only thing Flasek could see was that white eyeball, floating in front of his face.

The room was utterly silent—no sound came from the street outside, or from the witch across from him. He could hear only his own breathing, and even that seemed muffled. The darkness started to become a physical thing, pressing down on Flasek with a great weight.

When the witch spoke, Flasek nearly jumped off his stool. He could *feel* the creaking of her voice like rough wood being dragged across his skin. A shudder ran up his spine and he had to force himself to remain motionless.

"Like a beacon, it is. The rituals are tangled in the instant of the nobleman's death, too much power flowing in that room, an accident caused by necromancy. I can see it, a bonfire of conflicting energies, drawing me to the moment of unmaking. The nobleman dies, he flees yet returns again and again, his will unfocused but drawn back to his killer. I see him, chased by shadows. He hides yet returns...hides yet returns..."

Flasek wanted to ask her if she saw his killer, the person who summoned the shadows, but he dared not interrupt her.

"He still has connections. He moves between them, the woman who protected and slew him, and...the other. A dark tunnel it is, full of shadows and necromantic power. I cannot see the figure there in the utter darkness, but I *feel* him. He is unaware of me, but I must take care to remain unseen. I can taste his power and it poisons my blood."

Flasek knew now he was out of his element. Was her reference to necromantic power something that came from the Five, or was it something used by the Church? Was there even a difference? He only hoped she could explain to him what it all meant once her vision was over.

"A shape...I can see his shape and he is a man, yet...something more. Something dead yet alive, a channel through to the utter darkness. Even the abyss recoils from the touch of that darkness, the emptiness, the annihilation of all that is. He whispers and...wait! I move closer to hear his words."

Flasek wanted to tell her to stop. He didn't want her to get closer to whoever it was, didn't want her to listen to the whispers. He leaned forwards, his palms on the table, ready to leap up and stop her, but he couldn't move, couldn't look away from that eye, floating in the darkness.

"I am...too close! He feels me, he turns...AAAAAAHHHHH!"

She screamed and the candles flared back to life, forcing Flasek to shut his eyes. He threw himself backwards off the stool and smacked the back of his head against the wall. When he opened his eyes, the witch was on the floor on the other side of the table, curled up into a fetal position.

She was completely motionless.

Flasek slowly raised himself to his feet and stepped over to her. He couldn't tell if she was breathing, and he wondered if she had been killed by that figure in the darkness. He bent down and reached out to touch her shoulder.

With a snarl, she sat up and grabbed his arm, her nails clawing long furrows in his flesh. Blood streamed from her nose and painted her face and neck. Her eyes opened wide and two completely white orbs stared sightlessly up at him.

Flasek yanked his arm back and staggered against the wall.

"You owe me, Flasek Lumayth!" she growled at him. "Falcon's blood won't restore my sight. I will find you and give you a price, and you will pay it, watchman."

"I—I'm sorry! I didn't want you to—"

"Leave now. I have done my part. I heard the whisper, I have a name. Necromancy, it is. We have a necromancer in Ythis, and his name is Wydo Idaphos."

She slumped back against the wall.

"Leave me, watchman. I will find you when I have a price. Now go."

Flasek ran out of the room and down the hallway. He fumbled with the bolts in his haste, but eventually threw them back and yanked open the door. He stepped out onto the stairway and pulled the door closed behind him.

He stood there for a moment, taking deep breaths to calm himself down and wait for his heartbeat to return to normal.

He had a name, Wydo Idaphos. And he even knew who that was. Wydo was the brother of Osho, the dead nobleman. And he was a necromancer.

Climbing the stairs back onto the street, Flasek wondered what he could possibly do now.

Chapter Thirteen

L EYNDRA CROUCHED, MOTIONLESS, IN THE SHADOWS AT the base of a tree, the hood of her cloak pulled up to cover her head. She waited for any sign she had been spotted approaching the estate, but no one moved on the wide avenue in front of the main gates.

She was taking a huge risk returning to this building. Investigator Chamirra knew she was innocent and would be looking for a way to find whoever had caused Osho's death. It was likely a contingent of Imperial Guard soldiers occupied the grounds of the estate on the chance she would return here for some reason. Chamirra may even be here himself.

Leyndra had considered her options and figured she had no other choice. It was obvious Tyina was involved somehow, and there might be a clue in her chambers that could lead Leyndra in the right direction. She couldn't ignore that chance, no matter the danger.

Keeping to the shadows, she moved off down the length of the stone wall that ran around the estate. Her senses were alert to anything out of place—any shadow, or sound, or movement that might indicate a sentry was watching over this area. Finding nothing amiss, she stopped two-thirds of the way down the length of the wall and waited silently. The only sounds were of a slight breeze and a small animal rustling in the bushes down to her left.

Leyndra slowly scaled the rough stone wall, careful to remain as quiet as possible. She raised her head over the top and quickly scanned the grounds for any signs of activity. She immediately spotted two patrols of the estate guards walking the inside lengths of the walls. Both patrols had dogs with them, a new addition since the night of Osho's death.

This added a new complication. By crossing the ground to the main building, she would leave a scent trail the dogs would pick up as soon as they got close enough. That meant that she would have to get in, find what she needed, and get out again between the passing of the patrols.

She continued to watch the patrols move around the estate, one heading away from her into darkness, the other slowly making its way toward where she clung to the side of the wall. Counting in her head, she tried to estimate how long she would have once the closest patrol passed her before the second group would circle around.

As the approaching patrol got nearer, Leyndra lowered herself back down and crouched once more on the outside base of the wall. By her estimate, she would have from five to ten minutes between patrols. That wasn't nearly enough time to do what she needed to do.

She considered her options. She could attempt to take out the patrol as it passed, but even if she managed to kill three men and a dog without making a sound—or letting any of them raise the alarm—she'd also have to do it to the second patrol when it came around as well. The chances of her doing so successfully were slim.

Leyndra didn't have a way of easily disguising her scent, either. If she could get the clothing from one of the guards, it would likely be enough to mask her own trail from raising the dogs' interest, but there was no way for her to do that from out here.

She could hear the voices of the guards as they approached the other side of the wall where she hid.

Sloppy, she thought. *They're masking any noises an intruder might make.*

It still wasn't enough to help her. And she still didn't know if there were soldiers inside the mansion or not. She continued to ponder the situation as the patrol moved past her and continued along the inside of the wall.

As she tried to figure out another option, another way to find some clue without needing to enter the estate, some small part of her mind kept counting. And then she was suddenly at the moment of truth—the patrol had moved far enough along that she could cross without being seen or heard, and the next patrol was as far away as it could be.

Without giving it another thought, driven purely on instinct, Leyndra rapidly scaled the wall, was over, and landed softly on the damp grass. She hadn't even consciously made the decision to take the risk, but something had pushed her to move and now she was committed. If she turned around now, she wouldn't get another chance—the discovery of an intruder's scent would only increase the alertness and frequency of the patrols.

Crouching low, she glided over the ground toward the main building. There were three entrances to the mansion, but she expected all of them to be guarded, so she angled toward a particular window on the ground floor.

The wooden shutters were all closed and locked, but Leyndra easily undid the catch with the blade of her knife between the slats. She pulled back the shutter and climbed into one of the most unused rooms in the mansion.

Tyina had temporarily become infatuated with the idea of playing music, and so Osho had purchased a beautiful harp and had this room redecorated as her music room. Before the season had changed, Tyina had grown bored of practicing—she had obviously expected to create beautiful music without any actual work—and so the room was abandoned. The servants kept it clean and ready for use, but no one ever came in here anymore.

Leyndra lowered herself into the room and carefully pulled the shutter closed. As she did so, she heard someone let out a snort directly behind her. She whirled around, ready for combat, but no one was there.

The sound came again, and she realized someone was lying at her feet. Her eyes slowly adjusted to the deeper darkness of the enclosed music room, and she made out the sleeping forms of five men scattered across the floor.

Leyndra could have kicked herself. Of course, Tyina had hired additional guards, and the small barracks couldn't possibly hold any more. So, these men were given an unused room on the ground floor of the estate to sleep in when they weren't on duty—the same room Leyndra had figured would be the best place to enter the mansion.

Clenching her jaw, she very slowly and carefully picked her way among the men towards the door. She briefly considered slitting their throats to prevent their interference once the alarm was raised, but decided she wasn't willing to murder men in their sleep. Battle was one thing, but this was different.

She reached the door and hoped the servants were still keeping the room in good condition. A single squeaky hinge could cause Leyndra a huge amount of difficulty right now. But when she pulled the door open just enough to slip into the hallway, it didn't make a sound, and neither did she. The guards slept on, blissfully unaware of the intruder in their midst.

Leyndra moved to the main staircase. The servants' stairs were more sheltered, but were also far busier, even this late at night. She climbed to the third floor and ducked into a shadowed corner. Listening intently, she waited for any sign of servant, guard, or soldier. She forced herself to give it a full minute, though she was acutely aware of how little time she had before the alarm would be raised.

Eventually, she moved out of her hiding place and proceeded down the hallway towards Tyina's chambers. Now came the riskiest part of this evening's tasks. There was little doubt Tyina would be in one of these rooms. The late hour meant she was likely in bed, but Leyndra didn't know how deeply she normally slept.

She would have to remain as quiet as possible while searching these rooms for clues.

She opened the door and was surprised to find the antechamber empty. Leyndra had been prepared to encounter a guard in this room. Something about this didn't feel right to her. This entire affair had been entirely too easy so far. It didn't feel like a trap, though. But it was definitely not right.

Leyndra put her ear to the door to Tyina's bedroom but didn't hear anything. That wasn't unusual. The doors were thick enough to stop the sound of someone sleeping, unless that person snored heavily. She listened at the other door, the one that led into Tyina's sitting room and further to her dressing room and bathroom. Again, no sound could be heard.

Tyina's handmaiden would be in her own, adjoining bedroom on the other side of her mistress' sleeping chamber. Leyndra hoped she was also asleep and not up and about performing chores that could only be done when Tyina wasn't demanding her attention.

Leyndra opened the door to the sitting room and glanced in. The room was dark, but she could see no one was inside. She stepped in and closed the door softly behind her. Her first target was the small writing desk that sat against the wall opposite the window. Leyndra pulled open the first drawer and quickly checked the contents, but it was just paper and writing implements.

She pulled open the second drawer and heard the sound of Tyina's bedchamber door opening. Leyndra had maybe two or three minutes before the second patrol would cross her path and the dog would start barking. She didn't want to stop what she was doing, but the last thing she needed was for Tyina to catch her in here.

In an instant, as she heard the door to Tyina's bedchamber close, she made her decision and leaped across the room to duck behind the heavy drapes on one side of the window.

A second later, the door to this room opened and someone entered, carrying a candle. The light grew brighter as the person lit more candles on the holder above the desk.

And then Leyndra's blood ran cold as she heard Tyina's voice.

"There's no point hiding, Miss Jirau. I knew you would come here sooner rather than later. I think it's time we had a talk."

*   *   *

"YOU'RE NOT LISTENING. IT DOESN'T MATTER HOW MUCH YOU'RE willing to pay. I can't do it."

Jeyrra sat back in the rough wooden chair and crossed her arms.

"I never thought you to be a coward, Kaus."

The captain of the *Titan's Blight* leaned forward across the table. His long, dark hair hung damp and sweaty around his unshaven face. His eyes were in shadow, but Jeyrra knew he was pinning her to the chair with his gaze. She noticed the seams on his shirt stretching as his broad shoulders shifted forward and the muscles in his arms flexed.

"If anyone but you said that to me, Jeyrra, I'd drag them outside and beat them nearly to death," he growled at her. "I've half a mind to give you a good beating anyway, despite our history."

He waited and Jeyrra heaved a sigh.

"You're right. That was over the line and uncalled for. You may be a lot of things, most of them rotten, but you're no coward." She grinned to take the sting out of her words.

He nodded once.

"Fair enough. I'm no courtier, and never claimed to be. But I'm also not ready to throw my life away for a lost cause. Money's no good if you're not alive to spend it."

Jeyrra glanced around the dingy tavern, full of sailors and dock-hands eating, drinking, talking, laughing, swearing, and spitting. She usually felt at home in places like this, but she kept wondering if someone would recognize her and try to collect on Leyndra's bounty.

It was risk she had to take. She couldn't make arrangements to get her friend out of Ythis without visiting her connections. And at least she had the one nearly private table in the place, enclosed by walls on three sides and set far enough back from the other tables to give them some privacy without the risk of being overheard.

Jeyrra wanted to get up and pace, but she forced herself to stay seated. Standing would draw unwanted attention.

"Look, I know it's not easy. But... by the Abyss, you're Kaus Kagunvar! You've never faced a lost cause in your life. When you want to do something, you find a way, never mind the odds. What's different about it this time?"

He smiled, took a huge gulp from his tankard, and wiped his forearm across his mouth.

"Jeyrra, you know most of the stories about me—"

"I know most of 'em are *true*."

"Yah, but the average sailor don't. Even those who sign on with me 'cuz of what they've heard, they don't really believe most of the tales. They think it's all stories that grew and grew with the retellings. Do you have any idea how many times a sailor has tried to slit my throat, or shank me in the back, just for the bounty on my head and bragging rights? A good chunk o' my crew I can trust, but there are enough I can't."

Jeyrra shook her head.

"I don't see what that has to do—"

"Let me finish, woman!"

Jeyrra could see he was starting to get annoyed. She was one of the few people who understood the man, had been there before his exploits created the legend. But she was being dense tonight, a consequence of too little sleep and the constant worry about Leyndra.

For all she knew, her friend had already been captured again, or killed, and this was all for naught. She didn't want to think about what Leyndra was doing tonight, where she had planned to go, because Jeyrra was truly scared.

The feeling was unfamiliar, and she really didn't like it very much.

She realized that her thoughts had drifted away from Kaus again, and she gave a guilty start.

"I'm sorry. I'm listening, Kaus. I really am."

He looked down at the table and gave a slow nod.

"I know you're worried. I'm worried about you, too. If I could take you and your friend onto *Titan's Blight* and make it out of the harbor, I'd do it tonight. And then we'd have an adventure and create a new story, eh?"

The thought brought a smile back to his face, but it quickly faded.

"The problem is, Jeyrra, even the crew members I trust would be sorely tempted by the reward they're offering here. And your friend is an oath-breaker. That matters to the crew I can trust the most. It's another reason for them to justify turning her in for the reward. But even that's not the real problem."

Jeyrra didn't want to hear any more. A terrible feeling was building up in the pit of her stomach, and she had a sense he was going to tell her something that would make it even worse. But she couldn't speak, couldn't move. She just waited for his words to hit her.

"You know I hear a lot of rumors, a lot of nonsense. But I also hear a lot of truth, often before it gets out onto the street. This comes from people who are reliable."

He paused, and she wanted to scream at him to get on with it. Or to tell him to shut up. She couldn't decide which she wanted more, so she sat there, waiting.

"Jeyrra, the Emperor is going to order the Five to track down your friend. You know what that means."

It was like a physical punch in her gut. The size of the bounty on Leyndra's head was bad enough, but at least they had people they could trust. But no one could face down a demon and survive. No one, except....

She looked up sharply.

"No!" he nearly shouted. He glanced around and lowered his voice. No one paid them any mind.

"Okay, I bested a demon once, but I lost most of my crew doing it. I almost lost my ship. I myself barely survived, and still carry the scars of that fight today. I didn't go looking for that battle—we were trying to run away. I'm still alive because I got lucky, really lucky, and luck like that doesn't show up too often. If I ever get myself into a situation where I'm facing a demon again, there's little chance I'm going to crawl away from it a second time. And I'm not going to drag my crew into something like that. They know and accept there are risks to serving under me, but not something like that. Not again."

And there it was. Kaus Kagunvar may have been fearless, but he was also looking out for his crew. To live alongside him through his adventures was exciting, and rewarding, and *dangerous*. He would risk his own life with but a moment's thought. But he wouldn't casually throw away the lives of those he led.

And to take Leyndra on a ship out of Ythis was to doom his crew to almost certain death.

"You know if I thought there was a chance in the Abyss you would leave your friend, I'd offer you a place on my ship."

Jeyrra nodded but remained silent. They both knew she would never take him up on his offer. She was also responsible for others, and would never abandon them to be hunted down by a demon. And she wouldn't just leave her friend, not after all they had been through together.

She raised her eyes to Kaus.

"What would *you* do?"

He blinked at her.

"What d'you mean?"

"I've got a commitment to my boys, and a commitment to my friend. I can't abandon her, but to stick with her will likely mean my death and the death of those who follow me. Once the Emperor asks the Five to track her down, it'll just be a matter of time. So, I ask you, what would you do in my place?"

Kaus pondered that for a moment. He took another long pull on his tankard, let out a belch, and leaned in.

"Change the wind."

"What's that supposed to mean?"

"The wind is blowing your ship where you don't want to go. It's pushing you to a place where you'll lose everything. You can't abandon your ship, but staying on it means you die. You can't change what's in front of you, so you have to change what's at your back. You change the wind."

"So, in order to avoid the impossible, like fighting off a demon, I'm supposed to do the impossible, like changing the wind. Well, that sounds so easy."

Kaus shrugged.

"I never said a word about it bein' easy."

Jeyrra had to give him that. But then, as she thought about Kaus and the stories about his exploits, she realized he had done both of those things.

Maybe it wasn't impossible after all.

Chapter Fourteen

TYINA'S EYES WENT WIDE AS LEYNDRA LUNGED across the room. Before she could move, Leyndra's blade was at her throat and she was bent backwards almost onto the writing table.

"Where are they?" asked Leyndra through gritted teeth.

If Tyina had expected to be in control of this situation, Leyndra could see she was now completely out of her depth. She was trembling in terror and her eyes darted around the room, looking for help or escape or anything to get her out of this position.

"W-who—"

"The Guard! Where are they waiting for me?"

Tears started to form in the corners of Tyina's eyes.

"I-I sent them away yesterday. I knew you w-would come back and I want to t-t-talk to you."

Leyndra yanked Tyina away from the desk, spun her around, and wrapped her arm around the other woman's neck. The blade remained at Tyina's throat, but now Leyndra could use the woman's body as a shield against any archers that might appear.

"I had to d-do it! He made me!"

Leyndra forced Tyina over to the window. She glanced out but neither of the patrols were visible.

"Who forced you?"

"You have to believe me. I didn't want to pin it all on you."

"Yeah, you've been my best friend all along, haven't you?"

"Okay, yes, I hated you. I'm not going to lie about that. I was jealous of you—Osho loved you when he should have loved me."

Leyndra let out a single, sharp laugh.

"If you're going to lie, you need to be more convincing. Osho and I weren't having an affair and you know it. The ritual that bonds a Warden to her charge kills any feelings of lust between them. It's impossible."

"I didn't say anything about lust. I'm talking about *love*. Osho loved you. He never smiled except when you were in the room. He never got tired of you, no matter how many hours you spent together. You were first in his thoughts in all things, and I was a distant second. You didn't *need* to have sex with him. He was under your power anyway."

Leyndra opened her mouth to argue and then snapped it closed. Tyina was obviously trying to delay her, to give time for her guards—and probably the Imperial Guard soldiers—to get into position. Tyina appeared to realize this and changed tact.

"You have to listen to me! If I had wanted this to be a trap, do you really think I'd be here? That I'd come in alone and give you this perfect opportunity to kill me? Do you think I'd do any of this if I had any other choice? I've risked my life to talk to you. This isn't a trap!"

As much as Leyndra didn't want to listen to her, Tyina's words made sense. She knew what Leyndra was capable of doing, and it was monumentally stupid to put herself in harm's way like this.

"Then if you have something to tell me, spit it out. Who is forcing you to lie about me? Who made you plant evidence to make it look like I was hired to kill Osho?"

Tyina hesitated.

"You won't believe me if just tell you. I have to show you."

Leyndra tightened her arm around Tyina's neck and the other woman gasped. She relaxed the pressure slightly.

"I'm tired of your games. Tell me now or I will *make* you tell me."

"It was W-Wydo!"

Again, Leyndra wanted to laugh.

"You forget, I've met Wydo Idaphos. You're insane if you think I'm going to believe he managed to force you to betray his brother."

"But I didn't betray Osho! I had no hand in that. Wydo took care of that himself. He's made some kind of pact with...something. Some creature. It has given him powers and he's after something. He needs Osho's fortune to get it."

"What is he after?"

"I don't know. I don't *want* to know."

Leyndra didn't believe Tyina's story. Wydo was a quiet, unassuming man. He was highly intelligent, though had been much less successful than Osho when it came to expanding the family's fortunes. He collected books and never raised his voice. He couldn't have been the one to summon those shadows.

As if she had heard Leyndra's thoughts, Tyina said, "He told me he had discovered some ancient secrets in a book, and the creature made contact with him in his dreams after he read about some ritual. He said he could send shadows to kill me just like he did to Osho. All he wanted was for me to tell the investigator that you and Osho were having an affair, and to hide the money in your room."

"Don't forget about the note."

Tyina hesitated.

"Yes, I also burned the note in your fireplace. I figured that a burnt note was harmless—I never knew they had a way to read it."

"Now that you've done what he asked, why hasn't he killed you already? You're an awfully big loose end."

"He can't kill me yet. Osho made special arrangements. Wydo had tried to get money from Osho many times, always for stupid ideas. Osho didn't want the family fortune to be wasted away by his brother, not after all the work he had put into it. Osho got the Emperor's seal on a document that gives me control over the family estate, at least until the Emperor decides how the estate will be divided up. Wydo needs me in order to access the fortune."

Despite herself, Leyndra found herself pondering Wydo Idaphos. The story Tyina was telling was preposterous, but Leyndra had to admit that didn't mean it wasn't true. She also didn't want to think that Tyina was a victim in this whole mess.

"Okay, I've listened to your nonsense. Where's this evidence you claim to have?"

"I have it in a hidden compartment in my bedchamber. It's a short letter from Wydo telling me what to do with the money and the note that implicated you. You've seen Wydo's handwriting. You can tell the letter is from him."

Leyndra shook her head.

"A letter? You'll have to do better than that. A letter can be faked too easily for me to go rushing off to kill Wydo on your claim that it came from him."

"Then go to his home! He keeps the book with him at all times, and he's become strange. He always read too much, and now it's turned him into something...terrible. You don't have to believe me. Just check for yourself. It's all I ask. I would run away if I could, but his shadows will track me down and kill me. It's only a matter of time before he figures out a way to get rid of me. But you can do things I can't. Don't let him get away with this!"

Leyndra was reminded of her pleas to Investigator Chamirra to keep investigating Osho's murder after her execution. Tyina had that same desperation in her voice, that need to know that her death wouldn't be the end of the matter.

Leyndra didn't want to believe Tyina's claims, but she found herself wondering if it was all true. She had never considered Tyina to be a threat while Osho was alive. To have Tyina be part of the plot to kill Osho meant that Leyndra had been wrong all along. But she couldn't be sure she wasn't listening to the woman's words just to prove to herself that she had been correct and Tyina was incapable of murdering her husband.

Leyndra realized that the dogs should have found her trail by now, should have started barking. But there was no sound from outside the mansion.

"Where are the patrols? Why haven't they found my scent yet?"

Tyina trembled at the anger in Leyndra's voice.

"They're just for show. The dogs are attack dogs, but they're not trained to hunt by scent. I need to make it look like I'm protecting myself in case you return here, but that I didn't really believe you would. It was the only way to convince the Imperial Guard to leave."

"I suppose you conveniently convinced them to leave Wydo alone, too?"

"No! I keep my distance from him as much as possible. They are probably watching his home in case you go there, though they have no evidence he is involved in this at all. They seem to be focused entirely on you."

"And you certainly did your part to aim them at me, didn't you?"

Leyndra unwrapped her arm from around Tyina's neck and shoved her to the floor. The woman began weeping quietly. She seemed sure Leyndra was going to kill her. Leyndra bent close to Tyina's ear.

"I'm leaving now. If you so much as cause the slightest commotion, I will come back and kill you. I don't care how afraid you are of Wydo. I'm much, much worse."

With that, Leyndra left Tyina on the floor of her sitting room and prepared to leave the estate for what was likely the very last time.

*   *   *

PHIRAL NAJARE SHIVERED UNDER HIS HEAVY CLOAK, THOUGH he should have been overheated. His reaction was partially due to the unnatural chill that surrounded him, and mostly due to his knowledge of what was causing it.

This is ridiculous, he thought. *The man I'm meeting knows who I am. I shouldn't need to be disguised.*

Unfortunately, the necromancer had not agreed. Phiral had argued that the swordsman, Vaysarr, was discrete, but Eothep was concerned other eyes might see the meeting. He demanded Phiral's cooperation, and the nobleman ultimately had no choice but to do the necromancer's bidding.

And now Phiral stood at the end of a short alley in one of the seedier neighborhoods of Ythis, waiting for the arrival of Vaysarr. If that wasn't bad enough, his appearance was cloaked by shadows...living shadows sent by Eothep.

The unnatural chill moved over his skin and, though he could not see them, he knew the necromancer's shadow creatures were wrapped around him. They apparently made it impossible to see under the hood of his cloak. There would be no way for anyone stumbling onto this meeting to identify him.

Phiral was more worried about being mugged by some thug in this neighborhood. The shadow creatures wouldn't protect him if someone decided to take his money purse, or his life. They would simply report his death to Eothep.

He could only hope no one else was using this alley tonight. If he was wrong, Phiral was likely a dead man. He shivered again at the thought of the … things … crawling over his flesh. Once more he wished the final reward would be worth all of this danger.

He heard the sound of booted feet a few seconds before the figure emerged at the other end of the alley. He couldn't tell for sure in the darkness, but he hoped it was Vaysarr. The man's identity was confirmed a second later when the swordsman spoke.

"You'd better tell me who you are before I decide you're a threat."

Great, thought Phiral. *This disguise is worthless if I shout my name out loud.*

"I'm the man who hired you," answered Phiral. "You received my message this morning from a boy with yellow hair."

Vaysarr paused and then seemed to relax. He approached Phiral and tried to peer into the shadows of the nobleman's hood.

"Aren't there better places to do business than a dirty alley?"

"Probably," answered Phiral, annoyed at having to follow Eothep's instructions even when they didn't make any sense to him. "But this is where I asked you to meet me, so this is where it's going to happen."

Vaysarr grinned without opening his mouth, a look that said he considered Phiral to be a rank amateur at this type of work.

"Okay, then. The arrangements for the caravan have been made," said the swordsman. "Now I need you to tell me where we're going."

Phiral hesitated. He wanted to keep the destination a secret as long as possible.

"You'll find out as soon as we're outside the walls of the city."

Vaysarr shook his head. His braid swung back and forth across his back as he did so.

"That's not going to happen, for two reasons. One, the provisions one needs on a trip into the mountains are not the same as for a trip along the coast. Two, I need to make sure the rest of the guards are prepared to handle anything that might threaten the caravan, and each direction has different threats than the others."

Phiral shrugged at him.

"You're being paid to be prepared for all eventualities."

"But I'm not being paid to be stupid. If you want stupid, there are many men in this city who'd be happy to take a smaller share of your money in return for this job. But you'd end up dead somewhere along the route. You're paying me a much higher fee to make sure you get where you're going, and back. That requires information."

Vaysarr crossed his arms and leaned against one wall of the alley. It was obvious to Phiral that the swordsman didn't truly need this job. He was doing it because the money was good and he was looking for adventure, but he wasn't going to walk blindly into danger. Could he really be trusted?

As if he could hear Phiral's thoughts, Vaysarr answered the unspoken question.

"You know my reputation. I didn't get it by sharing my clients' secrets with anyone who asks. I intend to hand-pick the guards for this job, people I trust to be discrete. I'll arrange the right supplies for wherever we're going. And I'll earn my pay with more than just the sword at my belt."

Vaysarr tapped his finger to his temple. "Experience is far more valuable than a quick sword arm. Of course, if we need it, I've got that, too."

Phiral sighed. He knew now he'd have to at least give the man enough information to prepare properly. At this point, he couldn't afford to go looking for someone else to take the job.

"Okay, I'll tell you what you need to know, nothing more."

The swordsman nodded at him, apparently satisfied with that arrangement.

"I've said the journey will be dangerous. We're heading into the Bleak Waste."

Phiral paused, waiting for Vaysarr's reaction. The swordsman raised one eyebrow as he contemplated the challenge of keeping them safe in such a landscape. Then he motioned for Phiral to continue.

"My...patron...must be escorted into the Bleak Waste. He has a map, or he will by the time you leave. That map will show you exactly where he needs to go. Once you reach your destination, you'll guard the camp while he retrieves an item. And then you'll escort him back to Ythis."

"And your patron? What kind of man goes into the Bleak Waste looking for...anything?"

Phiral tried to suppress a shudder, but he could tell Vaysarr noticed. He wondered if that would lead to more questions, but the swordsman merely waited for Phiral to answer the one he had voiced.

"He's someone you'd do best to obey, to leave to himself, and to ensure remains safe on the journey. He will travel in the covered wagon, and it's possible you won't ever get a chance to see his face. Count yourself lucky if that remains true throughout the journey."

Phiral was concerned the swordsman would decide this job was too risky, too full of unknowns. There were few hired blades capable of traveling with Eothep and maintaining their composure for the entire journey. Fewer still who would choose to enter the Bleak Waste with the necromancer.

But Vaysarr didn't look like he was having second thoughts. He looked intrigued.

"The challenge is to find those willing to travel into such a place. I know of one, certainly, but we need at least four besides me. I'll look into it."

"Be careful!" hissed Phiral. "You can't go around telling people you're looking to hire guards for a trip into the Bleak Waste. News might reach the wrong ears, and then you'll have a much larger problem on your hands."

"I already told you, the men I have in mind are discrete. Considering the pay being offered, I can go straight to the best. Well, the best after me, that is."

He's arrogant, thought Phiral. *I hope that's not a problem. Eothep doesn't like arrogance in his servants.*

"Don't get too cocky. Confidence is fine, but remember who you're working for."

Vaysarr didn't respond, so Phiral continued. "Have the caravan ready to go on the date I gave you. I won't be traveling with you, so everything has to be perfect. You can't go pestering...my patron...every time something comes up. I'll contact you again before we leave."

The swordsman uncrossed his arms and pushed himself away from the wall.

"I'll have everything ready as agreed. This isn't the first time I've done something like this, or you wouldn't have come to me. Make sure you have the rest of the money the next time we meet."

Vaysarr turned and strode away, confident in his ability to defend himself from any dangerous inhabitants in these alleys. Phiral had no such assurances. Looking around for any signs of danger, he scurried off down one of the alleys, the shadows still slithering around him like a shroud.

Chapter Fifteen

THE MANOR HOUSE OF WYDO IDAPHOS WAS A FRACTION of the size of the mansion where his brother had lived. It used to be well-kept, but the grounds were now in a state of disarray and the roof of the house needed repair. It no longer looked like the home of someone directly related to one of the noble houses of Ythis.

Leyndra was surprised to see Wydo's home like this. He had always been a meticulously neat man, though she had not seen him in more than a year. This was an unexpected change, and she considered how it related to Tyina's story.

She watched the building from a distance, through a small window in the attic of a manor house situated down the road from Wydo's home. Leyndra had discovered the family who owned this house was away—probably traveling on some business—and the lone servant had already locked up and left for the night. It provided a perfect hiding place for Leyndra to spy on her target.

Leyndra was sure Tyina had been trying to manipulate her last night into doing Tyina's bidding, even if parts of her story were true. Leyndra wasn't about to just walk into a trap. There was a good chance of Wydo's home being watched by a spy of the Imperial Guard. They were getting more desperate every day that passed with Leyndra on the loose.

With such a reward being offered for her capture, many of the poorer citizens of Ythis were reporting their neighbors for any slightly suspicious activity, and the Imperial Guard responded to each report with rapid and overwhelming force. Many families had watched their homes be ransacked by soldiers looking for any evidence of Leyndra's hiding place. She felt sorry for the victims of these search efforts, but she wouldn't let it distract her from her mission.

Now, it was only a matter of time before the Imperial Guard invaded the Warrens. Leyndra was sure it would result in many deaths. The Warrens were filled with wanted criminals and thugs, and the soldiers would find themselves attacked by an enemy they would not be able to engage directly. It would be a long, bloody affair that would change the face of this city.

She hoped to resolve this matter before it came to that, but no one knew when the Guard would decide it was time to move into the Warrens. She was racing against a deadline she couldn't see.

There was no visible movement around Wydo's manor, and so she decided it was time to proceed. Making her way down from the attic, she was careful not to disturb anything that would give away her intrusion into this house. She intended to leave no clues for Investigator Chamirra that might help him track her down.

Leyndra moved into the master bedroom and checked the wardrobes. She found an old dress at the back of one of the wardrobes that had obviously not been worn in some time. In the darkness, it would appear bedraggled enough to pass for something a servant might wear. Leyndra took it and quickly put it on over her normal clothes. She expected this dress would not be missed for weeks, if not longer. It was exactly what she needed.

She left the manor house through the servants' door, careful to lock it behind her. Other than the missing dress, there was nothing to show that anyone had been in this house beyond the one servant today. Leyndra pulled her cloak over her shoulders but left the hood down. In this heat, it would draw unwanted attention if she wore it up.

Earlier in the day, Jeyrra had hacked off most of Leyndra's hair, leaving it short and slightly ragged. The haircut changed the shape of her head, and in the darkness, she should be able to pass by anyone who had never seen her face directly without being immediately recognized. While her mission tonight carried a lot of risk, she had done everything possible to prepare as best she could.

She pulled out the basket that she had brought with her and hung it from one arm, and then proceeded up the road toward Wydo's manor. She walked with a purposeful stride and slowly enough to give the impression of exhaustion. In the early evening like this, most servants heading to their own homes had been working all day and didn't usually have much energy left.

In minutes, she was passing Wydo's house. She kept her head facing straight forward, but her eyes darted back and forth searching for any sign of a watcher in the shadows. She was almost past the house when she spotted him, a figure standing in the shadows of a small tree across the road from Wydo's home. He wasn't being particular careful to hide, but could not easily be seen from the roadway unless one were specifically looking.

Leyndra was careful to keep moving and give no indication she had seen him. Any hesitation on her part would draw his attention. She continued on up the road and kept walking until she was well away from the area. It appeared only the one man was stationed to watch the house, but there was no way to be sure.

Still, unless Tyina had told someone from the Guard the same story she had told Leyndra—an unlikely prospect, she had to admit—there was no real reason for the Guard to expect Leyndra to show up at Wydo's home. They were likely keeping an eye on him only because of his relation to Osho.

Leyndra stopped and considered the situation. She could easily approach the manor from the rear and thus remain out of sight of the watcher, unless a second watcher was stationed to cover the other side of the house. It all depended on whether Investigator Chamirra considered it remotely likely for Leyndra to try to see Wydo. And whether he could spare the two men while the search for her continued.

Finally, Leyndra shrugged to herself and began to backtrack. As much as she didn't trust Tyina, she couldn't ignore the woman's story or how fearful she had appeared the night before. Leyndra would have to try to reach Wydo and see if there was any truth behind Tyina's words.

She also had to be prepared for the possibility that Wydo really was behind Osho's death. If the story was true, Leyndra might have a real fight on her hands. She didn't have a clue how to engage a necromancer who could summon shadow creatures. She would have to rely on her training and abilities and adapt as necessary, and do whatever she could to flee if the situation turned against her.

Partway back to Wydo's estate, Leyndra slipped into the shadows and made her way to the back of another manor house. She listened for any guard dogs, but heard nothing to indicate her presence had been detected. She moved across the grounds towards the back where a wooden fence separated this home from the yard behind Wydo's manor house.

Within a few minutes, she had shed the dress disguise and hidden it in the hollow between the roots of a tree, then scaled the fence and dropped noiselessly into Wydo's yard. She waited and listened and watched until she was sure she was alone.

Heavy curtains covered the windows of Wydo's house, but two small gaps showed light coming from two rooms on the ground floor. One of the lights flickered like the illumination from a fireplace, while the other was stronger and was likely a bunch of candles on a candelabra or chandelier. Leyndra wanted to look into the windows, but then she would be outlined against the side of the house for anyone watching from the outside.

She considered her options and decided to enter the house directly without looking in the window first. At the moment, there was likely more danger from outside the house than inside.

Leyndra quickly crossed the yard and moved to the door in the rear of the house. She tried the handle and found it was unlocked. This caused her to hesitate—it was unusual for minor nobles to leave their doors unlocked when servants and guards were not around. She placed her hand on the hilt of the short sword at her hip and slowly pushed the door open.

A short, dark hallway led from this door into the house. Closed doors framed either side of the hallway, and another closed door at the end of the hallway appeared to lead into one of the lit rooms. Leyndra stepped inside and closed the door behind her.

She listened at both doors on either side of the hallway, but heard nothing, so she continued to the end and listened there. Someone was moving around on the other side of the door, and it sounded as if they were turning pages in a book.

Gripping the hilt of her sword, Leyndra pushed open the door.

*   *   *

MORIT CAME INTO THE SMALL BEDROOM WHERE HATHI WAS watching over their children quietly playing with their small wooden blocks. She looked up at him and tried to smile, but he could see it was forced. Neither of them had slept much over the last few days since they had been returned to their rooms above the cobbler's shop.

With their main room continuously occupied by pairs of soldiers, they spent most of their time in this small space. Morit didn't trust the soldiers to keep their hands off Hathi, and he was terrified of what those men might do to the children if they got in the way.

He hated living like this. It was no better than the small room they had been held in at the Fortress, and he resented the presence of the soldiers. As far as Morit was concerned, this was a fool's game. There was no way Leyndra would bother trying to contact him. She was probably halfway across the Empire by now.

A pounding on the front door made him jump. Hathi gasped in fright. Both children looked up at their parents faces and immediately began to whimper.

"Keep them quiet," he told his wife and stepped out into the main room.

The two soldiers were on their feet, weapons drawn and ready for combat. Morit stopped, his heart pounding at the sight of the bared steel blades. He wanted to hide in the children's bedroom and let the soldiers deal with whoever was at the door. One of them motioned him over, however. He was expected to open the door.

He tried to control his trembling hands as he lifted the latch and pulled the door open. Another soldier of the Imperial Guard stood on the landing, with a man in black robes on the stairs behind him.

"Stand down, soldiers," called the man at his door. The two soldiers relaxed and sheathed their weapons. He pushed Morit back as he stepped inside.

"You have a visitor. This is Brother Tann. He has some questions for you."

As Morit stepped back to let in the new visitors, he realized the second man was a priest from the Church of Iathephos. He stumbled against one of his wooden chairs and fell heavily into it, nearly tipping over. He dumbly noticed the new soldier wink at the two others, who grinned slightly in return.

The priest was tall and thin, with a long-hooked nose set between two piercing green eyes. He was completely bald, and his ears were set flat against the sides of his skull. His thin lips curved upwards in a slight smile at Morit.

"Please, do relax Morit Jirau. I am not here to cause anyone any harm."

His voice was lower than Morit would have expected coming from that face, rich and smooth. He had no doubt there was great power in that voice when the priest wanted it.

The priest turned to the two soldiers who were currently stationed here.

"If you will leave us for a bit, I will get started. Please don't go too far—I do not think I will take up too much of Morit's time today."

The soldiers looked at the man who had escorted the priest, and he nodded once at them. The two soldiers turned and walked out, closing the door behind them. Morit was left alone with the priest and his escort.

"As the good man here told you, I am Brother Athural Tann. You may call me 'Brother' and I will call you Morit. I trust that is acceptable."

It was not a question.

"What—"

Morit's voice came out in a rasp and he had to swallow twice.

"What do you want from me?"

The priest stepped around the table and pulled out another chair. He carefully sat down and folded his arms on the table in front of him.

"Let me set your mind at ease, Morit. I am not here to torture you, or drag you off to the Temple, or anything you might deem...unpleasant. I am merely here to ask a few questions. Most of them will be questions you have already been asked by others, but I have a good mind for these things, and may end up somewhere others have not thought to go. And when I am done, I will bid you a good day and my escort and I will leave you in peace. That is all."

Morit didn't feel particularly comforted by the priest's assurances. He had no guarantees here.

"Please tell me about Jeyrra."

This was not unexpected. Morit had been asked question after question about Jeyrra. Apparently, the Guard had evidence she was helping Leyndra hide out somewhere in the city.

"She's lived on the streets as far back as I can remember. She tried to rob Leyndra once when we were kids, and Leyndra punched her in the face. A couple of months later, I discovered they had become friends when I saw Leyndra and her playing together in one of the back alleys behind our home."

"This was back when your parents were still alive, yes?"

Morit nodded.

"What do you remember about their deaths?"

It was a strange question, and Morit heard something in the priest's voice that set him on edge. Brother Tann seemed...eager...to hear this story.

"Um, I was only ten when it happened. It was during the time of the Harvest...."

He trailed off. It was a subject no one was ever supposed to discuss openly, by decree of the Emperor himself. Brother Tann motioned him to continue.

"You may not know the prohibition about speaking of the Harvest comes, in truth, from the Church, and I can temporarily grant you an exception for the purpose of this interview. Were your parents taken as part of the Harvest?"

"No. They were killed in the riots that happened when the people found out they couldn't leave the city. My father had gone out to try to find food, and he was gone a long time. Someone came and told my mother that he had been injured, and she went to bring him home. A neighbor came over a few hours later and told us that they had both been killed by a gang of looters. They were...."

The priest nodded.

"Taken as food, yes. It was a dark time for Ythis, and we can thank the Emperor and the Church for working together to restore order."

Morit was struck by how casually Brother Tann spoke of the fate of his parents and the weeks of brutality that he simply referred to as "restoring order."

"And Leyndra became the head of your household?"

Morit grimaced.

"Well, she took over, certainly. I wouldn't call her the head of the household, though. She made a lot of bad decisions."

"And she would have been... around thirteen at the time?"

Morit nodded. "Jeyrra was around a lot during that time. She brought us food sometimes, and she and Leyndra became really close. They would sit up and talk late into the night, making plans for when they were older...."

Morit trailed off as Brother Tann suddenly leaned forward, his eyes widening.

"What kind of plans?"

"Honestly, I didn't listen to most of it. I thought it was nonsense anyway. Jeyrra wanted to form her own gang and take over the criminals and street thugs across Ythis. She figured she would run the underworld of Ythis, and everyone would bow down to her. Leyndra wanted to join the Imperial Guard."

"How did Jeyrra think she would accomplish her goals? What did she *say*? Try to think back, focus on something specific she might have said about anything related to her future. See if you can't remember the exact words she used at some point, part of a sentence, anything."

Morit shook his head.

"How could that help you now? They were just dreaming. Jeyrra never made it big, and Leyndra found herself sidetracked into the Guild instead."

The priest's mouth twisted in annoyance.

"I care not about the present. My interest is in the past, and words of the future. It doesn't matter if that future came to be or not. I need the *words*."

Morit didn't understand what the priest was talking about, but he wasn't in any position to argue. He thought back to those nights, sprawled on his hard-sleeping pallet while his sister and Jeyrra lied to each other about their futures. He pictured Jeyrra sitting beside Leyndra with her back to the wall, talking about what she was going to do.

And then a moment formed in his mind. He remembered her telling Leyndra about beating up some boy that had been trying to intimidate her. She was bragging about her skill and how she had pounded on him until he had run away. He couldn't remember her exact words about the boy, but he remembered Leyndra smiling and asking if that was how she was going to build her criminal empire.

He looked up at the priest.

"I remember something she said. She was talking to my sister—"

Brother Tann held up his hand.

"Just her words, please."

"Okay. She said, 'This is how it starts, showing that boy that I'm tougher than he is. And when I've got my gang, they'll follow me because they'll know no one is tougher than Jeyrra.'"

The priest looked over at the soldier and smiled.

"I believe I've just heard what I came here to find," he said. "We can leave now. I've got them."

Chapter Sixteen

THE FLICKERING LIGHT OF THE DANCING FLAMES illuminated the room in fits and starts. Leyndra glanced around but could not immediately see anyone in the shifting shadows. She heard the sound again, of pages turning, and spun to face a small desk. A single book lay open on the desk, and she watched as the pages turned, one by one. She could feel no breeze, and the pages moved rhythmically, not fluttering like they would if they were being blown around.

Leyndra slowly moved towards the desk, her sword in her hand. As she got closer, she could see the book was bound in black leather, and the paper was yellowed with age. A spidery script was scrawled on each page, line after line.

The pages continued to turn.

She reached the desk and looked at the writing in the book, but it was in a language she couldn't identify. She didn't want to touch it—it seemed like it must be some kind of trap for the unwary. She raised her hand and moved it over the book, but felt nothing.

More than half the pages in the book had been turned, and she wondered what would happen when it reached the end. Would the whole process start over, or would something else be triggered? Leyndra wasn't sure she wanted to find out.

A movement in the corner of her eye caused her to spin and drop into a fighting stance, her blade at the ready. She looked around but could see nothing out of the ordinary. She waited, her every sense alert for any threat.

Nothing happened.

Leyndra had decided to move further into the house and search for Wydo when, from out of the murk in one corner, something long and sinuous stretched up the wall. A quick glance behind her told her that the book was three-quarters to the end, so she focused on the new tendril of darkness that rose up in front of her.

It suddenly coalesced into a humanoid shape similar to that of the shadows that had attacked Osho in his room that night. It was joined an instant later by several others that crawled up the walls around her.

Okay, then, she thought. *I guess this confirms it.*

The shadows leapt off the wall toward her. Ignoring them, she spun and brought her sword down on the book, splitting it in half. The pages exploded upward into the air, momentarily blinding her, and she felt ragged claws rip into her back. An unnatural chill burst from the wound and filled her body.

She twisted away from the attack and passed her blade through the neck of one of the shadow creatures. Just like before, it dissipated into nothingness at the touch of her weapon. Leyndra blanked her mind from the pain in her back and let her training take over as she fought the living darkness.

The creatures were fast, but were unable to score another hit as she went on the offensive. Unlike the last time she had faced these creatures, more did not appear as these succumbed to her attacks. In a moment, she was alone in the room once again.

Leyndra felt her back, but her skin was unbroken. Four long welts were raised where the creature had slashed her with its claws, and it seemed as if she had been wounded more than a week ago. She had *felt* the claws enter her body, but she had to admit she knew practically nothing about these shadow creatures.

She hadn't wanted to believe Wydo was capable of murdering his own brother, but it now appeared Tyina had not been lying about his recent corruption. Leyndra's knowledge of necromancy and other sorcerous arts was sadly lacking, and she worried about what else she might face in this house.

She looked down at the pages of the book scattered across the floor. None of them moved. She prodded a couple of the pages with the tip of her sword, but nothing happened. Leyndra wasn't sure if she should try to burn the book or just leave it. She didn't want to handle the pages, but the fireplace was right here, and she may not get another chance.

Using the toe of her boot, she shoved the papers into a small pile. Then she bent down and grabbed a handful, and quickly tossed them into the fire. They burst into flames and curled into ashes in seconds. She returned to the desk and gathered up the rest of the pages before tossing them into the fire as well.

When they had been consumed, Leyndra turned away from the fireplace to explore more of the house. As she reached the door, she heard behind her the crinkle of paper. She turned back to the desk and saw what appeared to be the same book lying open in the same spot where she had first seen it. The book was open to the beginning, and as she watched, the next page turned, and then the next.

Keeping her sword drawn, Leyndra backed farther away from the table. She turned to the door that led further into the house and pushed it open. It led into a short hallway that ended in a pair of double doors. As Leyndra approached the doors, she could hear a faint whisper of chanting that continued without pause.

She waited, listening, but the chanting continued in an unbroken stream, a strange language that made her feel slightly nauseated. Whoever was making that whisper, it didn't need to stop for breath.

Leyndra reached out and grasped one of the door handles. It had a chill on it, though the air in here was quite warm. She slowly turned the knob until she felt it release, and then pushed it open a crack. The room beyond was too dark to see much, and her vantage point didn't provide much of a view.

Gripping her sword in one hand, she pushed open the door until she could step into the room and look around.

A figured was crouched on the floor of the large, sparsely furnished room. A handful of candles placed throughout the room gave off meager light. Piles of open books were scattered in a circle around the figure like cadavers around a sacrificial altar, their yellowed pages reflecting the light from the fireplace. Leyndra couldn't tell if it was Wydo in the center of the circle, and wasn't sure she wanted to get close enough to find out.

The figure appeared not to notice her entrance, and she could still make out that faint whisper, barely heard, that continued without pause. Leyndra quietly drew one of her short swords and stepped fully into the room. As she moved from the shadowed doorway, the figure snapped its head in her direction. She saw it was naked from the waist up, and strange symbols were painted on the skin of its chest and arms. It raised a thin arm to point at her and let out an inhuman howl.

The sound set her teeth on edge and she almost lunged forward to strike with her blade. She forced herself to hold back until she could be sure the figure was a threat. She knew she was taking a risk—she might not have time to act later.

The horrid sound trailed off and the arm slowly dropped. The figure remained crouched over the circle of discarded books, but it began to speak in a harsh, broken voice.

"In the name of Maristasta and Orarash, by the ancient stones of Phaesriru, *I banish thee to the Realm of Shadow*."

*　　　*　　　*

"ARE YOU SURE ABOUT THIS?"

Annoyed, Flasek turned back to Watchman Yaral Beori.

"That's the third time you've asked me that question. What do *you* think?"

Yaral frowned at him.

"I think this is the second time you've had us out to a nobleman's estate in the last two weeks. I think the last time we did this it was an utter waste o'time. I think there's no profit in it, and I don't see why we're here."

Flasek stepped close to the other man and looked down into his face.

"Then it's obvious to me you need to do a lot less thinking and a lot more following of orders. With*out* questions."

As Flasek turned away he heard Yaral mutter "Well, I'm *here*, ain't I?" He knew he was being hard on the man, but Flasek was nervous.

This could all go bad in a great hurry. He turned to the man in his squad he trusted the most.

"Lassim, walk with me."

The other man stepped in beside Flasek and the two moved out of earshot of the rest of the squad. The men continued to check their armor and weapons and prepare for the assault on the house of Wydo Idaphos. Flasek turned to the other man and looked him in the eye.

"You trust me?"

"Of course, Sarge." Once again, Flasek was struck by the man's smooth voice, smooth movements, smooth…everything. He was a sleek hunter among the burly thugs of the Watch. Flasek knew Lassim had another source of income, and wondered if he was an accomplished burglar or safecracker. Not that Flasek ever tried to find out. A man's secrets were his to keep.

"No, Lassim, I need to know for real. You follow me because those are the orders, but do you *trust* me?"

Lassim carefully considered Flasek's question.

"I trust you not to get us into something unless you already have a plan to get us out. I trust you to look out for us. But I trust you to be you."

"What's that supposed to mean?"

"Some men, when they make sergeant, they see themselves as little more than crime bosses. But you don't see things that way, do you Sarge? You do this because you *believe* in it. In some ways, that makes you unpredictable. But I know there's a limit to how much you'll let us get away with while we're on the job. So, I trust you to be you."

Flasek stood silently for moment. The rest of his men were ready. They'd start getting itchy to move things along in another minute.

"What is it, Sarge? What are we here to do?"

Flasek took a deep breath and let it out slowly.

"We're here to take down a corrupt nobleman."

Lassim snorted.

"Isn't that the Guard's job?"

"I'm not talking about normal corruption, Lassim. This man, he's possibly a ... well, a necromancer."

Lassim smiled, waiting for the punch line. Flasek waited him out. Eventually, the smile faltered.

"You're joking, right?"

Flasek shook his head. Lassim stared him in the eye, trying to figure out if he was telling the truth or just having fun at Lassim's expense.

"I'm not joking, Lassim. There's a good chance he's got ... things in there with him. And powers of some kind ... over the dead."

Lassim took a step back and looked at the other men, who were now watching the two of them, waiting for the word. Lassim stepped forward and lowered his voice.

"And why is the Church not out here in force, then? Isn't this the kind of thing they usually handle? Why us?"

Flasek put his hand on Lassim's shoulder.

"Because, one, I don't know if it's true. Two, I can't go to the priests because they'll ask me how I heard and that puts me in a very bad place. And three, this is the brother of the nobleman who was killed by his Warden, that woman who escaped. It's already complicated, and getting the Church involved would only complicate things even more than they are now."

"You realize you're asking these men to face ... what, exactly? The walking dead? Vengeful spirits? What else? You have no idea what might be in there."

Flasek wiped a hand over his face.

"You're right. But this is related to the death of that other nobleman. Listen, when we arrested his Warden, she told me what happened. There's more to this than a simple murder, Lassim. There's something bigger going on in this city, and someone has to get to the bottom of it."

Lassim shook his head.

"Then we come back to my first question. Why us and not the Imperial Guard? I know you hate them, but let's be honest here. They're far better equipped and trained for something like this. Wouldn't an anonymous tip get the same results and be a lot safer? And that's assuming this woman was telling you the truth."

Flasek thought about Leyndra's words that night. And then his thoughts went back to his encounter with the witch and he shuddered.

"It was the truth, all right. I can assure you of that. And that's exactly the problem. If *I* could confirm what Leyndra Jirau told me, then the Imperial Guard must have done that already. But she was convicted and sentenced to death anyway. They're trying to execute her to cover up the truth."

Lassim shrugged.

"And why do we care? I'd bet the Guard cover up the truth about a lot of things."

"*I* care, Lassim. The Imperial Guard is sworn to the Emperor. They don't consider the citizens of Ythis in their decisions, and our safety is not important to them. At all. The nobleman in this house may be a necromancer, but the Imperial Guard won't care unless he becomes a threat to the Emperor himself."

"Are you sure that's it, Sarge? You're just thinking about the people of Ythis?"

Flasek knew Lassim was insinuating he had an alternate motive for going after Wydo Idaphos. Flasek's hatred of the Guard was no secret, and he had to admit to himself that part of the reason he kept pushing forward on this case was his own pride getting in the way.

Investigator Beyus Chamirra had done it to him again. He had gotten help from Flasek and then dropped him from the investigation without another word. Flasek had sworn he would never trust that man a second time, but he had fallen for the same trick twice. He needed to prove his worth, to himself as much as to anyone else.

"Hey, Sarge! Are we gonna move out or wait here all night?"

Yaral, again. Flasek scowled at the man and then turned his back on the squad.

"Listen, Lassim, I value your opinion. I'm in a spot, stuck between doing what's right and doing what's easy. If it was just me, I wouldn't delay this at all. But I'm responsible for my squad, and I'm not going to toss your lives away just to prove that I can. All I can do is tell you this is important. I *know* it. And I just don't trust anyone else to deal with it."

Flasek paused, considering his words.

"The truth is, something's wrong about this whole situation. I don't know exactly what it is, but my gut tells me it's too neat. If that nobleman is truly a necromancer, then he's the one who killed his brother and framed Leyndra Jirau. And for what, his brother's fortune?"

Lassim's expression told Flasek it didn't sound right to Lassim either.

"Necromancy? Just to get money?"

Flasek nodded.

"As I said, it doesn't make sense. As much as it's possible that nobleman is some kind of evil being of power, even though the wit—uh, someone told me he's behind all this, it just doesn't add up. If someone managed to frame the Warden, could they also be framing Osho Idaphos' brother? So, the thing is I can't just let this be—I have to know. But I'm not going to order you to follow me in there."

He waited while Lassim considered his words.

"Sarge, I don't think you're going to get us all killed. But I do think you'll eventually get *yourself* killed. You don't belong in a city like Ythis, and one day this place will be the death of you."

Lassim grinned.

"But not tonight. Not while your squad is with you."

Flasek let out a breath he hadn't been aware he was holding.

"Sarge, if this guy is a necromancer, we can't take him alive. We've got to strike fast and put him down before he can summon whatever he's got in there to protect him."

Flasek put up a hand to protest.

"I just said we don't even know for sure if that's really what he is."

"We also can't give him the chance to use his powers against us. If we go in there, it'll be him or us."

Flasek's mind returned to the words of the witch.

We have a necromancer in Ythis, and his name is Wydo Idaphos.

"Yeah, you're right. Strike fast and put him down...but don't kill him unless you see no other choice."

Lassim smiled.

"And just as I was getting bored with the Watch...."

He walked back to the others before Flasek could ask him what he meant by that. As he approached his squad, the men readied themselves. He looked each of them in the face, one by one. Any one of them might not survive the night. But these were some of the best men in the city. Even Yaral, who liked to complain too much, but who could read a situation like no one else.

They were criminals, the lot of them. But they were also his squad.

"All right, men. I'm going to tell you what this is all about."

He smiled at them.

"And when you're done wetting your pants, it might just be time to make history."

Chapter Seventeen

LEYNDRA WAS MOVING AS SOON AS SHE REALIZED an incantation had begun. She grabbed the sparse hair on top of the figure's head and placed her blade at its throat.

"*Silence*! Another word and I end your life right now!"

She vaguely wondered if it was a hollow threat—the creature might not even *be* alive. She realized she could still hear the whispering. It wasn't coming from whoever she had in her grip. It sounded as if the whisper was coming from everywhere at once.

With the figure's face tilted up at her, there was enough light to see the sunken eyes, gaunt cheekbones, and bared teeth. There was something familiar in its features, and Leyndra thought back to her last meeting with Wydo. There was still enough resemblance for her to recognize him, though he was only a shell of the man she had seen just over a year ago.

He swallowed and spoke again.

"You cannot trick me, shadow!"

Leyndra pressed the blade more firmly against his throat, but didn't slice him open.

"These symbols protect me from your whispers and touches, shadow. Be gone before I summon my power to destroy you!"

Leyndra was confused. He was calling *her* a shadow, which didn't make any sense. Then again, if his mind was twisted by contact with some otherworldly entity, he might be losing his ability to tell real people apart from the very things he summoned.

"You know me, Wydo Idaphos," she answered. "I am Leyndra Jirau. I was the Warden for your brother, Osho. I am here for vengeance."

His eyes widened as he stared at her face, and then his whole body began to tremble.

"Leyndra Jirau is dead, executed by the Imperial Guard. You are just...a shadow, of no substance."

His voice wavered. It was obvious to Leyndra he was trying to convince himself that she wasn't really there.

"Why did you send the shadows, Wydo? Why did you want your brother dead?"

He surprised her by laughing, a crazy laugh that sent a shiver up her spine.

"A spirit of vengeance, are you? You've come for the wrong person, spirit. I didn't send the shadows. They come to *me*, whisper in my ears, torment me in my sleep. I cannot escape them, though I try."

He motioned to the books surrounding him.

"I have been searching for answers."

She continued to look down into his face.

"And?"

He gave his head a tiny shake.

"There is no magic in these books. I tried to find something to protect myself, but it's all just nonsense practiced by ignorant savages. I am lost."

She let go of his hair and he sank back down to his knees. Leyndra took a step back.

"What about the book in that room?" she asked, pointing back through the double doors. "That one seems to have its share of magic."

A shudder ran through Wydo's thin body.

"That book was brought here by the shadows. It almost got me, it did. I looked at it once and right away it began to make sense. A terrible sense!"

"Did you read the book, Wydo?"

"No! I broke away and haven't been in that room since. I cannot go in there, or the book calls to me, and I worry that I won't break free if I see the writing again."

Leyndra didn't know what to believe at this point. Wydo's mind was obviously damaged by whatever was happening in this house. What if he really *had* read the book, and his memory was blocking it now? Was there any way for her to tell?

"The pages are turning on their own, Wydo. What happens when the book gets to the end?"

He looked fearfully at the double doors.

"I don't know. I was in there just the one time and I haven't been back!"

"Then who's been keeping the fire going? Someone must have been in there a few hours ago to lay a new fire."

He shook his head.

"The fire burns all day and night. I have heard no one moving around in there. Maybe the shadows tend the fire. There can be no shadows without the light."

He gave her an appraising look.

"A spirit of vengeance, yet you know so little. What brought you to me, spirit?"

Leyndra was getting nowhere. While she doubted Wydo was, in truth, a necromancer, he had obviously been through *some* ordeal that affected his mind. He appeared to be terrified and desperate, and was likely also being tormented by the same shadows that had attacked Osho. Leyndra sheathed her sword.

"I am not a spirit, Lord Idaphos. I am Leyndra Jirau and I escaped from the Fortress. The Imperial Guard hunts me, but I am still alive."

Wydo continued to stare at her for another moment, and then his face twisted, and he began to sob pitifully. He covered his face with his hands and hunched over onto his knees, all the while repeating Osho's name between the sobs.

Leyndra looked down at the books and quickly took in a few passages and titles. It appeared he had been studying history and books on ancient cults and their practices. One book had a list of protective runes that matched the symbols painted on his arms and chest.

She reached out and put a hand on his shoulder and he flinched away before bursting into fresh sobs.

"Wydo, I'm so very sorry."

"They...they said you killed him...but it was the shadows, wasn't it?"

A rush of relief filled her at his words. He already knew the truth.

"Yes, Wydo, the shadows tricked me. But it's also true that it was my hand that ended the life of your brother. I cannot tell you how sorry I am for failing him. I'm trying to find out who sent the shadows, Wydo. I'm trying to avenge your brother's death."

At her words, Wydo looked up at her.

"I cannot help you. I have no way even to protect myself."

He rubbed at the symbols on his chest, smearing them into unrecognizable messes. She realized they had been painted on with ashes, possibly from the fireplace.

"Wydo, someone told me you were the one responsible for summoning the shadows."

He looked horrified at the thought, but she could see a spark of the man he once had been in his gaze.

"Who would say such a thing?"

Leyndra couldn't help sneering when she said the name.

"Tyina."

A puzzled look came over his face.

"That cannot be. She needs me to give her money until the Emperor decides how to divide up Osho's estate."

A flush of anger rushed through Leyndra's body. Tyina had lied to her—manipulated her—and she had completely fallen for it. It was a huge gamble on the woman's part, but it had paid off.

Leyndra suddenly drew her sword and moved over to one of the windows. At the sight of the bared steel, Wydo cringed backward with a small cry. Leyndra ignored him for a moment. She peered out between the curtains, looking for the trap. It was obvious that Tyina would try to get rid of both her and Wydo at the same time. Leyndra just didn't know if would be through the Imperial Guard or more of the shadow creatures.

She moved to another window, but it was too dark out there to see much. And then she spotted them. The glints of metal on buckles and hilts gave them away. A group of what might be soldiers was surrounding the house.

Leyndra looked back at Wydo. He had been driven crazy by the shadows, the same shadows that killed his brother. And yet he was still alive, most likely because of his temporary control of the Osho estate. Now the soldiers were coming, and Leyndra had to get out before it was too late.

Alone, she could do it. But could she also save Wydo?

*   *   *

JEYRRA CROUCHED IN THE SHADOWS AND KEPT SILENT. ACROSS the hall, Zheemeng was doing the same in another room.

In her mind, Jeyrra cursed this situation. She had no way to co-ordinate with Zheemeng and attack the intruder from different directions at the same time. From the sound of the footsteps, it was a single individual, which did not reassure Jeyrra in the least. People didn't travel alone in this area unless they were a bigger threat than anything they might face.

Jeyrra heard the intruder step back into the hallway and move to the next room in line. By her count, there were two more rooms to check before this one. She heard the door open and heard the slow, measured footsteps proceed inside.

She debated trying to quickly and quietly cross the hall to reach Zheemeng, but knew she shouldn't risk it. She could only hope he was waiting until the intruder reached either his or Jeyrra's door, and then they could both attack and hopefully take whoever it was by surprise.

At least it's not the Imperial Guard, she thought. *They will come in force and make a lot more noise.*

It was unlikely that the intruder was specifically searching for Jeyrra and Leyndra—these abandoned buildings often hid fugitives from one group or another. That didn't make the situation any better, though. Either the intruder might recognize Jeyrra and report back to the Guard, or it was a hired killer who wouldn't want to leave witnesses.

Both options spelled trouble for Jeyrra and Zheemeng.

The footsteps returned to the hallway and moved across to the next room.

Last one, she thought.

She shifted her dagger to her other hand and wiped her sweaty palm on her pants. A thrill of fear was crawling up her spine for some reason she couldn't identify. It wasn't just the danger of a possible fight—she had been in her fair share of those.

No, something felt *wrong* about his situation. Jeyrra was on edge far more than was normal for her. She listened to the footsteps enter the last room and forced herself to control her breathing. She wanted to jump up and flee, and was starting to gasp for breath.

Jeyrra rose and quietly made her way to the wall beside the door. She shifted her dagger back into her good hand and prepared to attack. She could only hope Zheemeng was doing the same on the other side of the hallway.

The footsteps came out of the last room and moved along the hallway until they stopped right outside Jeyrra's door. She tensed, ready to attack. She watched the door handle, waiting for it to turn.

The seconds stretched out and nothing happened. Maybe the intruder had decided to search the room on Zheemeng's side of the hallway first this time. She waited for the sound of the other door opening, her every nerve stretched taut.

Still nothing happened. Jeyrra realized she was holding her breath and almost let it out in a gasp. Whoever was out there was waiting for *her*. Jeyrra knew that now—that she was the target of the search and no one else. She was going to die a horrible, violent death in this dirty room in an abandoned building in the Warrens of Ythis.

She couldn't take it anymore. With a scream of fear and rage—though mostly fear—she grabbed the handle and yanked the door open. Lunging out into the hallway she saw Zheemeng's door open as he leaped out to attack as well.

The hallway was empty.

Both Jeyrra and Zheemeng stood there in the dark hallway, panting for breath, gripping their knives.

And then Jeyrra watched as four white, puckered tentacles reached out of the darkness behind Zheemeng and wrapped themselves around his neck, arms, and waist. Before she could open her mouth to scream, her friend was yanked back into his room and the door slammed shut.

And she did scream, leaping forward and slamming herself into the door in an attempt to force it open.

The door didn't budge.

"I wish to speak with you in private."

The voice was low but cut right through her fear and brought her up short. She snapped her head around to see a figure standing half-way down the hallway. It was tall and thin, but Jeyrra could make out no features in the gloom.

Jeyrra was gasping for breath and straining to hear anything on the other side of the door to Zheemeng's room. It was utterly silent.

"Your friend will not be harmed, but he is not part of our discussion. He will be returned to you when we are done."

Jeyrra leaned against the door as her legs nearly turned to jelly.

"Wh...who are you? What was th...that thing?"

"I am here on behalf of my master. She was able to track you to this building, but not to the specific room. I sent my demon to find you."

The figure paused.

"He likes to toy with mortals when he can," said the figure, apparently by way of explanation. "He feeds on their fear."

"Demon?" she whispered.

This man was a sorcerer. And he had come to speak to Jeyrra.

This time, her legs did give out completely and she slid down the door to land unceremoniously on the floor.

"As I said," continued the figure, a note of irritation creeping into his voice, "your friend will not be harmed."

Almost as an afterthought, he added, "You will also not be harmed."

Jeyrra felt weak. A *demon* had been sent to find her. And it had deliberately frightened her so that it could feed on her fear. As if a demon wasn't frightening enough.

"How did you find us?"

This time, she could hear more than just a note of irritation. This man's patience was rapidly wearing thin.

"I do not intend to repeat myself. It is time for you to *focus*."

He walked closer to Jeyrra and looked down at her. Even at this closer distance, she still couldn't make out his face.

"My master wishes to speak with Leyndra Jirau. I know this is where she stays, and I know she is not here now. When do you expect her to return?"

Jeyrra's mind was furiously trying to catch up.

He's here for Leyndra. Maybe this is the man who summoned the shadows. Or this is the sorcerer who was tasked by the Emperor with finding Leyndra.

"I don't know. She may not be coming back here."

"Do *not* lie to me. Your only value is in connecting Leyndra with my master. If you cannot do that, then I have no further use for you."

Jeyrra had no doubt it was a deadly threat.

"Okay, I will speak to her again tomorrow."

"You will tell Leyndra Jirau that my master is interested in her situation. She wants to know more about what happened to Osho Idaphos. Your friend will come to the Tower of Threads and tell her story to my master at her first opportunity."

Jeyrra didn't say anything, but just nodded, though she had no intention of sending Leyndra to seek her own hunter.

"My master is willing to provide assistance to Leyndra Jirau in return for information. It is in your friend's best interest that she comes to the Tower."

He turned and began walking back down the hallway toward the stairs.

Assistance? This didn't make any sense. He was supposed to be trying to catch Leyndra.

"Wait," called Jeyrra. "Who is your master?"

He turned and looked back at her.

"She is the master of the Tower of Threads. She is one of the Five. She is known as Xeylien."

With that, he stepped into the shadows of the staircase and was gone.

An instant later, the door to Zheemeng's room opened. Jeyrra scrambled on all fours into the room to find Zheemeng unconscious on the floor. He was breathing normally and Jeyrra listened to his heartbeat to make sure nothing was wrong.

She quickly looked around the room, but there was no sign of the demon.

Jeyrra sat in the darkness beside Zheemeng, waiting for him to wake up. She couldn't focus on anything other than the fact that an apprentice of one of the Five had been here looking for Leyndra.

She had difficulty imagining how this situation could possibly get worse.

Chapter Eighteen

WYDO, YOU MUST LISTEN TO ME. TYINA IS TRYING to arrange my capture and your death, so that she can gain control of the estate. I have no doubt now that she was involved in arranging your brother's murder. It was planned too perfectly. She just didn't count on me escaping from the Fortress."

Wydo stared at her in wonder.

"You really escaped from the Fortress?"

She nodded at him.

"I'll tell you the tale another time. We both need to get out of here as quickly as possible. There are soldiers out there, and they're not just coming for me."

Wydo began to shake his head.

"My books—I cannot leave them. It's taken me a lifetime to accumulate my library. I cannot just abandon them all."

Leyndra returned and grabbed Wydo's arm and dragged him to his feet. He cringed away from her, but she held him close and stared into his eyes.

"You don't seem to understand. Your life is in danger here, and so is mine. I won't let Tyina win without a fight, and that's exactly what I'm going to give her. Osho wouldn't want you to just let her have you killed either. She's trying to pin your brother's murder on you, and if you die then there's no one to refute her accusations and the real power behind the shadow creatures will get away."

She let him go and returned to the window.

"That's not going to happen if I can do anything about it. Your books are worthless—you said so yourself. But you've got control of Osho's estate and that gives you a certain amount of power. You can only use that power if you're alive."

Wydo began to pace back and forth, his hands nervously twisting around each other.

"Please tell me what happened to my brother."

Leyndra sighed in exasperation.

"We don't have time for that. You need to grab some clothes and we need to get out of here. We can talk later about what happened that night."

Wydo shook his head.

"I cannot leave. The only protection I have is in this house."

Leyndra turned back to face him.

"What protection?"

He looked at her, confused.

"Osho protects me. He is not always here, but he protects me when he can. If I leave, he may not be able to find me."

Leyndra ground her teeth together. Wydo had obviously been driven crazy by the shadow creatures. What could she possibly do to help him now, other than keeping him alive? She couldn't bring him back to their hideout in the Warrens—he couldn't be trusted not to do anything dangerous.

Still, she didn't want to just leave him to die.

"Wydo, Osho is dead. I wish it wasn't true, but it is. We have enough enemies that time itself is against us. I want to help you, but you must decide to come with me, or stay here and face whatever Tyina is going to throw at you. But if you decide to stay, you'll do so alone."

Wydo looked her in the eyes and she saw pain, fear, and resignation in his face. He shook his head. There was a certain finality in that gesture.

"No. I cannot leave my home. If I run, then it will appear I was guilty of something. I will face the Imperial Guard and they will show respect."

Wydo seemed to transform before her eyes. He straightened up and raised his chin until he was looking down his nose at her.

"I only need a moment to get one of my robes, and then you will see the real Lord Idaphos."

Leyndra looked into his eyes and realized he was mad. His fear of shadows had disappeared to be replaced by a total arrogance, an assumption of the role of nobleman. The Guard wouldn't be impressed.

"You, however, should not be here when they enter the house. Your presence will only confuse matters."

"It's too late for that, Wydo. I'm going to have to fight my way out. They've already surrounded the house."

His mouth twisted in a strange grimace and she realized he was *grinning* at her.

"Follow me."

He led her over to a staircase that rose up to the second floor of the house. He gave a quick push on a section of wall below the staircase and it swung open to reveal a ladder in a hole leading down into the ground.

"There is a tunnel under the house that emerges at the back of the grounds. Go now and I will deal with the Guard."

Leyndra wanted to scream in frustration. He was going to be captured by the Guard and would likely die in their custody. As much as the soldiers appeared to be honorable, there was always a way to get to a prisoner. She knew that better than anyone. But she also knew he wouldn't listen to her, and she couldn't delay any longer.

Wydo turned and went upstairs, most likely to get some clothing. Leyndra stepped under the stairs and lowered herself onto the ladder. She shoved the panel closed and was plunged into utter blackness.

Her mind immediately returned to her flight through the tunnels from Jeyrra's previous home, and the huge...thing...she had seen down there. And now she was back in a pitch-dark tunnel under the ground again. Only this time, there was no one to help her along, no one who knew the way.

Leyndra clenched her jaw and slowly climbed down the ladder until she reached the bottom. When she stepped off the bottom rung, she could tell it was soft dirt under her boots. She felt around and figured she was in a rather narrow tunnel made of packed dirt. There was an opening on only one side, and she hoped there were no branches or intersections. It would not do to get lost down here.

She drew a dagger from her boot—the tunnel was too cramped to use a sword—and proceeded along the tunnel, her left hand in contact with one wall. The tunnel walls were rough and uneven, but the passage seemed fairly straight. It was utterly silent except for the sound of her own breathing and the scuff of her boots on the dirt.

She had no sense of the passage of time, but it seemed not too long before she noticed a faint circle of light up ahead. She moved toward it and found a small hole blocked by iron bars. Looking out, she could see that the exit was past the fence separating Wydo's grounds from his neighbors. Not that it would make any difference if she couldn't get past these bars.

She gripped the bars and pushed, and the entire frame slowly slid out of the hole. Leyndra was careful to minimize any noise in case there were soldiers stationed out here somewhere. She wriggled out of the hole and looked around, but saw no one. Taking a moment to replace the grate, she listened carefully for any sounds from Wydo's manor house, but she could hear nothing unusual.

Leyndra stood and debated her options. She wanted to return to her vantage point in the other house and watch the situation unfold. But she was also in great danger and should get out of this area as quickly as possible.

She knew Jeyrra would be able to find out what had happened to Wydo by mid-day tomorrow, but she didn't really want to wait that long.

And then, from the other side of the wooden fence, men's voices began shouting.

*   *   *

FLASEK'S FOOT HIT THE DOOR JUST BELOW THE LOCK AND THE wood cracked but held on. Cursing under his breath, he planted another kick in the same spot and the bolt ripped free of the frame. The door swung open into a wide, dark hallway.

Flasek heard the faint crash as his men broke through the door in the rear of the house. He led the way forward, followed by Lassim and three of his own squad mates.

He kicked open the first set of double doors on his right and found a large dining room that, by its appearance, had not been used in quite some time. Layers of dust had settled over every surface and, in the light of his lantern, now stirred from the breeze from the swinging doors. Another set of closed double doors at the far end likely led into the kitchen, which would be at the back of the house.

Not seeing anything of import, Flasek motioned his men back to the entry hall. He strode across to the opposite wall, where another set of double doors stood. One kick shattered the handle and burst the doors wide open.

This room was already sparsely lit by a low fire in the fireplace. A pile of open books lay in a semicircle around a lone figure in a long robe, who stood facing the doors that Flasek had just kicked open.

The lantern light illuminated the figure. Flasek saw an older man with sparse, gray hair. He was thin, the robe hanging off his shoulders and showing a bare chest covered in what looked like soot. There was something in the man's eyes that set off warning bells in Flasek's head.

Lassim raised his crossbow and aimed at the figure as Flasek shouted.

"City Watch! Step away from the books and put your hands on your head!"

The man did neither. He planted his feet and crossed his arms in front of his chest.

"How dare you!" he thundered. "Do you have any idea who I am?"

Flasek could feel Lassim tense and he knew his comrade was about to fire. He glanced at Yaral, and the man looked back at him and gave a slight shake of his head.

He doesn't see any threat here.

Flasek had never seen Yaral misread a situation. Of course, Yaral had never encountered a necromancer before, either. Even so, he trusted Yaral's instincts.

Flasek raised his hand and Lassim paused, though the crossbow in his hands never wavered.

The other door to the room slammed open and the rest of the squad charged in. Two more crossbows pointed at the man, who would now be caught in a crossfire if Flasek gave the order to shoot.

The man didn't seem to care.

"This is my *home*," he snarled. "By what right do you break in and threaten me? The Emperor will have your heads!"

Flasek had expected threats, but not like this. The man sounded like a typical noble—invoking the Emperor's name to cause fear—but it was not something he expected a necromancer would need to do. A real necromancer would have other, more immediate, threats to make. Still, Flasek wasn't going to take any chances.

"I order you to step away from the books and put your hands on your head! You will not get another warning!"

This time, the man did step over the pile of books and move toward Flasek. He uncrossed his arms but did not place his hands on his head.

"I am Wydo Idaphos, of House Idaphos."

He looked Flasek up and down.

"How dare you point your weapons at me! You are merely the City Watch. You have no authority here. I don't know what Tyina is paying you to come here and threaten me, but I will have the Imperial Guard arrest every last one of you."

Tyina? Why does he think...?

And then a terrible thought entered Flasek's mind.

Someone else is pulling a whole lot of strings, and it's not Osho's wife, either.

He thought back to the witch and what had happened in her room. Could she have been tricked somehow? Flasek needed to see Wydo's reaction to his next words.

"I don't work for Tyina. I'm here to help *Leyndra*."

Wydo blinked at him and glanced over at the staircase leading up to the second floor. Flasek could tell the look was involuntary, a guilty start.

Is Leyndra in here somewhere? Did he kill her? Or is he helping her hide?

As if Wydo's earlier words had summoned them, Flasek heard booted feet charge into the entry hall behind him. He immediately recognized the voice that called out.

"Imperial Guard! Stand down and move aside!"

Flasek turned to see Investigator Beyus Chamirra stride into the room, accompanied by a half dozen Guard soldiers. They fanned out and aimed more crossbows at Wydo.

Beyus strode past them and planted himself in front of Flasek.

"Wydo Idaphos, by order of the Emperor, you will come with us peacefully."

Wydo looked from Flasek to Beyus and back again, confusion on his face.

And then the walls came alive with shadows.

Flasek saw figures rise up from the darkness and leap off the walls to attack the soldiers and his own men. Valdish screamed as a shadow plunged long claws into the watchman's back. He dropped to the ground, twitching, as Lassim fired his crossbow into the shadow, which dissipated as the bolt passed through it. The members of the Watch and all of the Guard soldiers spun to face their attackers.

All except Beyus Chamirra. The investigator drew his short sword in one fluid movement and planted the blade in the chest of Wydo Idaphos. The nobleman's eyes went wide in shock. Beyus withdrew his sword and swung it down and across Wydo's neck, neatly severing his head from his body.

In an instant, the shadows faded to nothingness.

Flasek raced across the room to Valdish. The man laid face down, still breathing but unconscious. Flasek checked his back, but could find no holes in his leather armor, no blood seeping from underneath his uniform.

Valdish let out a low groan and began to move. Flasek rolled him over onto his back, and Valdish opened his eyes.

"Wh...what stabbed me?"

"You don't want to know. You don't appear to be injured, but lie here and rest."

Flasek stood and walked over to Beyus, who was standing over the pile of books. He grabbed the investigator by the front of his uniform and slammed him against the wall. The Guard soldiers charged over and grabbed Flasek's arms, and his own squad started to intervene.

Someone drew a weapon and, in an instant, steel was once more bared around the room.

"Hold!"

Beyus' shout froze everyone in their tracks.

"Sergeant Flasek and I need to have a discussion. The rest of you have jobs to do."

The soldiers, still facing armed watchmen, all sheathed their swords and began to search the house. Flasek let go of Beyus and turned to his men.

"Wait for me outside."

He could see they wanted to protest, but they sheathed their weapons and left the house. He turned back to Beyus.

"You're a right bastard, you know that?"

"I guess I shouldn't expect you to be grateful to me for saving the lives of your men."

Flasek snorted.

"The nobleman didn't summon those shadow things, and you know it."

"You are out of your depth, Sergeant. You have just taken a difficult, complicated situation and made it worse. You and your men should not be here. You're watchmen. Why don't you act like it?"

Flasek ignored the dig.

"Those shadow creatures looked remarkably like the ones Leyndra described attacking Osho Idaphos, didn't they? Think she was telling the truth, after all?"

Beyus shook his head.

"Once again, you think you are leading an investigation when in fact you are so far behind, you'll never catch up. We already knew someone paid Leyndra Jirau to murder Osho Idaphos. My investigation led me to his brother. And now there is no more mystery to solve. It's unfortunate Wydo will not face trial for his part in his brother's murder, but killing him was the only way to stop him. Once we recapture Leyndra, this case will be closed for good."

Flasek stepped close to Beyus and looked him in the eyes.

"Not for me, it won't be."

Beyus' face was hard as he stared back at Flasek.

"Don't interfere again. There's more at stake here than just your pride, and the Emperor isn't known for his patience."

Flasek clenched his fists, but forced himself to leave before he took a swipe at Beyus. It wouldn't help if he got himself locked up. But he had no intention of letting this go.

Chapter Nineteen

A SINGLE SPIKE OF BLACK OBSIDIAN THRUST INTO THE sky at the end of a narrow street. The low buildings along the street were all empty, their inhabitants long since fled. Leyndra pictured them running away from their homes on the day they discovered their newest neighbor. She wondered if the Tower of Threads had grown out of the ground with a great rumbling, or simply appeared one night in silence.

There were no windows in the Tower, which stretched up taller than a four-story building. There was a single break in its smooth surface, an iron door at ground level with no handle or other visible means of opening from the outside. The walls were highly polished, reflecting the wan lights of the street lanterns behind her.

Jeyrra had been frantic last night when Leyndra returned to their rooms in the Warren. Her blood had gone cold as Jeyrra told her about the visitor. Zheemeng had mostly recovered from his encounter with the demon, though chills still swept through his body every few minutes.

Leyndra had listened in disbelief at Jeyrra's words. It was likely that one of the Five was behind Osho's death. And Jeyrra's friend had told her the Emperor was going to ask the Five for help in tracking her down. If either of those things were true, she would be walking right into a trap.

On the other hand, if the sorcerer was really hunting Leyndra, her friends would not likely have survived the night, and the demon would have been waiting for her when she returned to them this morning. Further, she didn't believe the sorcerers were all united the way the priesthood was. If one of the Five *was* controlling the shadows, perhaps that sorcerer was a rival of Xeylien.

Unfortunately, in that case, Leyndra might find herself being used, caught between two sorcerers of Ythis. That would likely be even more dangerous.

Jeyrra had tried to convince her once again to run away from Ythis. Nothing good could come from a trip to the Tower of Threads. And yet, Leyndra had to admit she was intrigued. The sorcerer's apprentice had said that Leyndra could gain assistance in return for information. She wasn't sure she wanted the assistance of a sorcerer, but it might be worth the trip to find out what Xeylien wanted.

And while Jeyrra believed it was a trap, Leyndra understood that the sorcerer had found out where they were hiding but had not given her up to the Imperial Guard, or sent a demon to kill her. Ultimately, Jeyrra had been angry with her, but Leyndra had decided to go. Zheemeng had stayed out of their argument—he was still shaken up by his own experience.

And so Leyndra now stood in front of the Tower of Threads. For the first time in her life, she was about to meet one of the Five, and she was doing so willingly.

She stepped up to the door and was about to knock when it swung silently open. She peered in and saw a large hall, dimly lit from above. She stepped in and the door closed behind her.

Leyndra stood near one wall and gasped at the sight. The entire Tower of Threads was hollow inside. Strangely glowing fungus spread up the walls toward a pale blue light at the apex of the roof. What appeared to be thick spider webs hung across the width of the Tower, and as she looked at them, she could make out strange patterns in the webs that she felt held important secrets. She stared at one of the web patterns and felt herself becoming weightless and lethargic.

With a great effort, she pulled her gaze from the pattern and snapped back to full consciousness. As she continued to look around the vast room, she saw massive spiders the size of large hunting dogs crawling among the webs. There was something *wrong* about the spiders in addition to their great size, and she realized they were all asymmetrical—they had nine legs instead of eight.

A figure suddenly appeared walking toward her, as if it had just stepped out from behind a curtain. As it neared, she saw a beautiful but strange woman dressed in long, flowing, pale blue robes. The woman's long black hair seemed to move as if she stood in a breeze, and there was something unsettling about her eyes.

"I thank you for coming, Leyndra Jirau."

When the woman spoke, Leyndra saw a flash of another shape where the woman stood—a huge black spider with pale blue markings on its legs and abdomen. The image was gone as quickly as it appeared.

"Who are... I mean, are you Xeylien?"

The woman nodded once.

"Leyndra, I wish to know everything about the night your nobleman died. You will tell me everything—leave out no detail—about what you saw, heard, smelled, and felt. And then I will tell you what you need to know to survive."

Leyndra got another glimpse of the spider again while Xeylien spoke to her. This time, she understood the spider had thirteen legs, though it disappeared long before she could possibly have counted them.

"Can you please tell me why you are interested in the death of Osho Idaphos? I have been found guilty of his murder, and there is a price on my head. I must be careful what I say."

Xeylien frowned and the light at the top of the tower dimmed.

"You misunderstand, Warden. There are greater powers at play here, and you know nothing of what you face. You will give me what information I wish to have, and in return I will reward you with information you need. If you do not choose to give me your memories willingly, I will take them, and there will be no reward."

Leyndra knew she would not leave the Tower alive unless Xeylien willed it. She wondered if the spider that kept appearing in her place was her true form or the form of her demon. Not that it mattered. Either way, Leyndra was here and it seemed her options were rather limited.

"Please forgive me for angering you. I did not wish to do so."

Xeylien waved off her apology and waited expectantly. So Leyndra told her everything, from the moment she awoke with Osho's rapid heartbeat in the palm of her hand to the moment when she returned to the hideout in the Warrens last night. Xeylien did not interrupt to ask any questions, but listened intently to every word.

When she was finished, she closed her mouth and waited to see what the sorceress would do. Xeylien just stood there, staring at her for another minute or two. Finally, after considering everything she had heard, she spoke again.

"The shadows were indeed summoned by a necromancer. And yet, no necromancer would come to this city and face discovery by the Five unless it had no other choice. The necromancer is after something here. There is a reason it caused the death of the nobleman and his brother."

Leyndra felt as if someone had kicked her in the stomach.

"What do you mean? Are you talking about Wydo? What happened?"

Xeylien paused, obviously irritated at being interrupted. She glared at Leyndra, for a moment. To Leyndra's surprise, Xeylien chose to answer her question.

"Wydo Idaphos is dead. The shadows attacked Guard soldiers in his home while they were there to take him into custody. He was slain in the fight."

There was no room for Leyndra to feel any sadness, as rage filled her from head to foot.

"I'm going to kill Tyina for this."

"Then you will die. The necromancer expects you to try to avenge the death of Wydo Idaphos, and you cannot overcome its power on your own. I cannot bring my own full power to bear until I know where in the city the necromancer is hiding. If I reveal myself now, the necromancer will flee the city before I can destroy it."

Leyndra felt hopeless.

"Then what I can do?"

Xeylien pondered this for a moment.

"The death of the second nobleman means the Idaphos estate will be given to another House. You must discover who will receive the estate. That person is the next link to the necromancer."

Xeylien stepped closer to Leyndra.

"You will not engage the necromancer directly. When you know where in the city it is hiding, you will send a message to me. I will eliminate the necromancer."

"And then what?" asked Leyndra. "What happens to me after that?"

"You will have your vengeance on the being responsible for the noblemen's deaths. My only concern is the necromancer. What happens to you after he is eliminated is *your* concern."

*   *   *

"SHE'S NOT GOING TO COME. SHE DOESN'T CARE ABOUT US."

Morit stood in the small room where the children slept. Hathi sat on the floor between them.

"She knows it's a trap, Morit. We'd be in more danger if she came than if she stays away."

Morit shook his head and heaved a great sigh.

"We're trapped here—prisoners—while she's out there somewhere doing...something. Probably finding a way to get out of the city, if she hasn't already. She got me...us...into this situation and now she abandons us. If she's gone for good, who knows how long we'll be kept here, unable to leave on the chance she's still in the city?"

"I don't think it will be much longer, dear. It's obvious the trap isn't going to work, so the Guard will let us go. There's no reason to keep us prisoner if we can't help them catch Leyndra."

Morit wasn't so sure. The Guard was desperate to catch his sister, and they were willing to use whatever methods were necessary to do so. If that meant keeping them here as bait, then that's exactly what would happen for as long as there was a chance it would work.

What Morit hated the most was being stuck here. None of them had been allowed outside since they got here five days ago. The children were getting more restless each day, and Morit wasn't sure how long he could handle being trapped in these rooms. Only Hathi accepted it all without complaint.

Her lack of anger only made Morit feel worse. She just let herself be a victim, let herself get pushed around by others, never fighting back. There were times he felt ashamed of having her as his wife. She was good with the children, sure, but she was weak.

He felt a flush of guilt as he stood there looking down at her. He didn't really have any right to be angry at her. She was holding them all together while they went through this ordeal. And yet, Morit was disappointed in her. He couldn't help himself.

He heard the front door open and the voices of the soldiers in the main room. The two soldiers who had been here for the last three days were getting replaced tonight by others. From what he had overheard, the men considered this job to be some form of punishment. None of them expected Leyndra to show up here, and so now the "protection" of Morit and his family was falling to soldiers who had done something to draw the ire of their commanders.

Morit listened intently as the soldiers in the main room briefed their replacements.

"I should go see who they sent to guard us."

Hathi looked up at him and shrugged.

"What difference does it make? They are not our guests, and we have no choice in the matter."

"Because I'm not a sheep," he snarled at her and stepped out of the small room.

The two soldiers were making themselves comfortable—one laying down on the sleeping pallet and the other sprawling out in a chair—when Morit came out. They turned to look at him.

"What do you want?" asked the larger of the two soldiers.

He looks mean, thought Morit. *Mean and unhappy.*

"I just thought I'd come out to...meet you...," he trailed off.

The soldier on the pallet snickered. The other soldier, the larger one, stood up and looked down his nose at Morit. He was at least half a head taller than Morit was.

"Why d'you think we'd want to meet our prisoners?"

Morit's stomach began to churn.

This one's not like the others. The rest have been—not friendly—

but professional. This one is a bully.

"I-I just thought, since you're in my home, I should—"

"This isn't your home anymore. This place belongs to the Imperial Guard until we say otherwise."

The man stepped up to Morit and leaned down over him.

"Are you going to give us trouble?"

Morit shook his head, unable to speak. He trembled in fear. And then he saw movement out of the corner of his eye and turned his head to see Hathi step out from the children's room.

"I'm sorry, sir. My husband meant no harm. We will remain in the small room and not bother you again."

Morit watched the soldier look Hathi up and down. He turned to the other soldier and flipped his head in her direction. The other soldier stood up and stepped over to where he could see Morit's wife. The two of them grinned at each other, and Morit could see no humor in it.

The larger man sat back down at the table.

"Your husband can stay in the other room, but you will stay out here. I'm hungry and you can prepare something for me to eat."

Morit was frozen in place, but Hathi came over and took his hand. She led him back into the children's room.

"Hathi—"

She put a finger over his lips and leaned close to his ear.

"Wait until they are fed. If they don't seem willing to let me leave, wake the children."

Morit looked at her, confused.

"Make them cry," she whispered. "However you have to, make them cry."

Morit stood there as Hathi left the room and began to prepare a meal for the soldiers. He peeked out past the curtain that covered the doorway but was careful not to be seen. The second soldier joined the first at the table, and the two men watched Hathi moving around the small kitchen.

Morit felt sick. If they decided to...do something...to Hathi, Morit knew he would not be able to stop them. He wasn't strong enough to fight the two soldiers. They were trained killers and he was....

Hathi fed the soldiers and cleaned up after they were done. It was a simple meal of bread and cheese, but they seemed satisfied. Supplies had been brought a few days ago, enough to keep Morit and his family fed while they were stuck here.

Eventually, the men finished the meal and Hathi moved to leave the main room. The larger of the soldiers reached out and grabbed her arm. Morit stepped back from the gap in the curtain as the other one looked in his direction.

"Stay here," he heard the soldier say. "Your husband will be fine without you for a bit."

"I must check on the children."

"That's your husband's job, isn't it?" Morit heard the other soldier snicker at the insult to Morit's manhood.

"Please...," he heard Hathi say.

And then there was no more noise from the main room. The silence was a physical thing, rooting Morit to the spot. He felt tears on his cheeks.

Wake the children.

The thought hit him, and he lurched over to their sleeping pallets.

Make them cry, she had said.

Morit took his son by the shoulders and shook him roughly. He yanked the blanket off the boy's sleeping form and pinched his son's earlobe between his fingers. As Frocho was startled awake, Morit reached over and shook Gita until she woke up as well.

Frocho immediately began to cry, but Gita only whimpered and turned over. So Morit took a handful of his daughter's hair and pulled, hard. The girl let out a cry that drowned out her brother.

Morit moved over to the doorway and heard the big soldier curse loudly.

"I'm sorry, sir. I must—"

"Just shut them up, woman! I don't want to hear crying children all night. Move!"

Hathi swept into the room and shoved Morit to one side. She gathered the children in her arms and soothed them until they were quiet. In a few minutes, both children were sleeping once more.

Morit could see that he had been fast enough to prevent the soldiers from doing anything…harmful…to his wife.

And yet, when Hathi looked up at Morit standing against the wall where she had pushed him, her glare was full of rage.

Chapter Twenty

L EYNDRA WAITED IN THE SHADOWS OF THE ALLEY across the street from The Everfull Tankard, a tavern on the outskirts of the Nobles' District. She had been there for an hour, watching the entrance and waiting for her prey. The place seemed to serve mostly servants of the nobility, at least the ones at the top of the hierarchy.

She had seen Usun enter the place and now waited patiently for him to emerge. Leyndra had to admit to herself this was a long shot, but it was the best one she had. It was possible Usun—as the coachman who drove Tyina about in Ythis—might know if the noblewoman had been secretly meeting another man.

There was no way for Leyndra to reach Usun while he was on the grounds of the estate, but she knew he spent his nights off at this bar. It had been useless information when she first overheard it, nearly a year ago, but the knowledge had now turned out to be most valuable.

Of course, Usun would not want to tell Leyndra anything about his employer. And it was likely he feared for more than his job at this point. Leyndra knew she might have to resort to drastic measures to ensure his cooperation.

With Wydo dead, the Idaphos estate would soon become the property of the Emperor. He would reward another noble house— one that maintained close political ties to him—with the holdings. It was also possible that he would split up the holdings and reward more than one house. Regardless, it was likely that one of the recipients was tied to the necromancer in some way, even if only as another link in the chain.

The problem was that, while the Emperor's decision was most likely already made, knowledge of it might not trickle out to the common people for another week or more. Leyndra didn't believe she had that much time. She had already been found by one of the Five. She didn't know what resources the Imperial Guard could bring to bear, but it was possible they might be narrowing down her location even as she stood here.

She briefly considered ignoring the words of Xeylien and going after Tyina. There was no question the woman was involved, if not directly with the necromancer then at least with whoever might know where the necromancer was hiding. But she couldn't trust anything Tyina told her. She had already lied to Leyndra once and was sure to do it again.

Leyndra realized now that Tyina had expected her to kill Wydo. The woman had tried to use Leyndra to eliminate the next obstacle to her plans. The fact that both the Watch and the Imperial Guard had shown up meant Tyina wanted to permanently remove them both from the situation.

Moreover, if Leyndra went after Tyina now, there was sure to be a trap of some kind. The woman had let Leyndra onto the estate the first time on purpose. But now things would be different. Tyina must know that Leyndra had seen through her lies. The woman would do whatever was necessary to protect herself.

Another hour passed before Usun emerged from the tavern. His gait was mostly steady, but it was obvious he was at least partially intoxicated. Leyndra didn't know if that would help or hurt her interrogation, but there was nothing she could do about it now.

Leyndra followed Usun as he walked back toward the Idaphos estate. He lived in a small room in the servants' quarters, shared with one other servant. Once he reached the grounds, he would be out of her reach. But he wouldn't be returning to the estate until she had what she needed from him.

Knowing his destination gave Leyndra an advantage. She didn't have to follow him. Instead, she slipped into a side alley and moved swiftly down its length. There were many places where Leyndra would have a perfect chance to ambush Usun, but she needed to reach one before he passed them all by.

Within minutes, Leyndra was well ahead of her prey. She came to the opening of another dark alley between a row of storefronts—now closed for the night—and an abandoned building. She knew it was likely full of Ythis' homeless, but as she was already a fugitive she didn't have to worry about witnesses to her crimes as long as she could be gone before the Guard could respond.

Leyndra peered around the corner and saw Usun approaching her location. He was walking more steadily now, the exercise obviously clearing his head somewhat. She moved back into the shadows and waited, listening intently for the sound of his boots on the stones.

An instant after Usun had stepped just past the center of the alley's mouth, Leyndra lunged out. Her forearm found his throat and her other hand covered his mouth before he could react. She yanked him backwards into the alley, pulling him off balance to prevent him from trying to break free.

A quick twist and he fell heavily onto his stomach on the floor of the alley, Leyndra on his back. She released his throat and grabbed a dagger. As he reached for her hand over his mouth, she placed the blade of the dagger in front of his eyes.

"You don't want to struggle, Usun," she whispered.

His eyes went wide as they fixed on the blade a hand span from his face. He immediately let go of her hand and spread his palms wide and placed them on the ground.

"Good boy. In case you're wondering, it's Leyndra Jirau. You know, the woman who killed Osho."

She could feel his body start trembling and knew she had the advantage she wanted.

"I don't *have* to kill you, Usun. You're not my target tonight. But give me trouble and I'll slit your throat and leave you for the rats. Understand?"

He moved his head in a slight nod. Leyndra removed her hand from his mouth.

"Keep it quiet and you'll walk out of here none the worse. I've got some questions for you and you'll tell me exactly the truth. I don't want embellishments or lies. I don't want you trying to tell me what you think I want to hear. I want the truth."

She leaned down close to his ear.

"I won't hurt you for the truth, even if I don't like what you have to say. I *will* hurt you if you lie. And you don't know which of my questions I already know the answer to. Is all that clear?"

Again, he said nothing but just nodded, though she was no longer covering his mouth.

"Good. Tyina has been seeing another nobleman. She started before Osho died. And you took her to her secret meetings."

She paused, waiting to see if he would confirm it for her.

"L-listen," he said in a low voice. "If I tell you anything, she'll have me killed."

She chuckled in his ear.

"It's just you and me in this alley, Usun. Who do you think is the bigger threat right now? If I was willing to murder Osho for money, what makes you think I won't end your sad little life right here? You can run away from Tyina. You won't be running away from me."

He sobbed once and she prepared to cover his mouth again, expecting a cry for help. But he swallowed his emotion and remained quiet.

"Tell me the name of the nobleman she was meeting."

"I-I d-don't know his n-name."

Leyndra almost shouted in joy. She wasn't completely sure Usun would be able to confirm her suspicion, but now she knew there was another conspirator.

"Are you sure Tyina has never mentioned his name, even a first name, in your presence? I want you to think about it carefully, Usun. Think back to all those times you took her to meet him...."

Usun was quiet for a moment, and then answered in a weak voice that sounded like was barely holding back another sob.

"No, she n-never mentioned his name to me. I would take her in the carriage to a spot at the end of an alley in the middle of the city. He would come out of the alley and get in the carriage. I only ever saw his face twice."

An alley? That doesn't sound like a nobleman.

Leyndra considered Usun's answer. The nobleman would likely have had his own carriage bring him to the other end of the alley and then he would walk its length to meet up with Tyina. That way, no one could connect them—the carriages were parked on different streets.

"Describe him to me."

"He wears a big ring, like the house sigil ring Lord Idaphos used to wear. I only got a good look at it once, the last time Tyina saw him. They didn't spend the evening together. I took them to the usual place, but when we arrived the man told me to take him back to the alley. He had his fist clenched, and the ring just . . . stood out."

Leyndra licked her lips.

"What was the sigil, Usun?"

"I couldn't read the writing around the edges, it's too small to see from a distance. But the design in the center was a crescent moon."

Leyndra leaned down and kissed Usun on his scruffy cheek.

"If you see Tyina again," said Leyndra, a great smile on her face, "give her a message for me. Tell her she's next."

*   *   *

PHIRAL KNEW SOMETHING WAS WRONG AS SOON AS HE MOVED down the stairs into the lower level of the crypts. There were no flickering shadows, no whispering voices. It was as if Eothep was no longer there.

Phiral raised the lantern and peered down the passageway into one of the crypts, and then moved to the next in line. There was no sign of the necromancer. He was about to look down the third passageway when he heard the shuffling steps coming from one he had not yet checked.

He turned and waited, his eyes on the floor.

Eothep moved into the main chamber and stopped. Phiral continued to wait for him to speak, but the necromancer said nothing. He risked a glance up near Eothep's face and saw he was being watched.

"I, uh, came to tell you what is happening."

The silence from the necromancer continued. Phiral's uneasiness grew. He knew Eothep liked to toy with him, use his shadows and his powers to frighten the nobleman. There was none of that this time.

"Um, Wydo Idaphos was killed by the Imperial Guard. They bought the story of him being a necromancer and they killed him during the raid on his house. The Emperor will pass control of the estate to Tyina until arrangements can be made to divide up the assets. My contact in the Guard has told me I will receive the bulk of the holdings, as we planned."

Eothep watched him and still remained silent.

"I have been advised the item you are waiting for is scheduled to arrive by ship this week. It will be brought directly to me and I will bring it to you as soon as I have it in my hands. By the end of next week, your expedition will be ready to depart. All is going according to plan—"

"FOOL!"

The power in Eothep's voice nearly knocked Phiral off his feet. He glanced involuntarily up at that horrid face and found it twisted in rage. A terrible fear gripped his body and he felt his bladder release as from nowhere the room was suddenly filled with shifting shadows and a dreadful cold.

"I have given you simple instructions and you have failed me," continued the necromancer in a voice as cold as the grave. "You were to ensure the Warden was used and then executed. You were to ensure the brother was blamed for the murder and also slain. You were to keep my presence secret until I could leave this wretched city."

Phiral tried to protest that all was well—except, perhaps, for the fact that Leyndra Jirau was still out there, somewhere—but he could only blubber and stutter in the face of Eothep's fury.

"You have failed me too many times and now I must fix things myself. You had a chance at immortality, but you would rather know death."

Phiral shook his head and tried to get control of his tongue.

"No!" he squeaked, his voice barely working. "No, it doesn't matter that the Warden is not dead yet. Everything else is in progress! And she will be caught and killed soon!"

Eothep took a step toward Phiral and the cold grew stronger.

"Someone has been asking questions about me. Someone who knew enough to find a witch to help him."

"A w-witch?" repeated Phiral stupidly.

"She was strong, and nearly found me. I had to expend my power to take her sight so she could be sent on a false trail. I was not expecting such a spy and was nearly discovered before I noticed her spirit watching me."

Phiral didn't know anything about witches, other than the children's stories, and found himself confused by the necromancer's words. One thing he did know what that his life had never been in greater danger. He tried to pull himself together. If he could get out of the crypts, he could call for his house guards. They wouldn't be able to stop the shadows, but it might buy him enough time to get off the estate.

The Guard would help him. They would bring in the priests to handle Eothep. Phiral would contact the expedition to help him flee the city if necessary. He just had to make it out of the crypts.

"But the witch was just a distraction," Eothep continued. "You should have handled whoever is trying to find me. But you did not. And now the Five know I am here."

If Phiral wasn't frightened enough, the mention of the Five threw him nearly into a blind panic. Eothep hadn't stated he was hiding from the sorcerers specifically, but Phiral had put the pieces together. Necromancy was forbidden in the Empire, and while it was technically enforced by the Church, the Five were eager to hunt down anyone engaging in the practice.

"B-but...how?" he managed to stammer out.

"I do not know yet, but I expect it is your missing Warden. She is the element of chaos in my plans. An element you were supposed to eliminate!"

Phiral's mind raced. There was no way the Warden could have known about Eothep. It had to be someone else. But who?

"I would not have come to this wretched city," Eothep continued, "but I need a secret known only to one who lived here in the early days of Ythis. It is a secret I can only recover once I find the crypt where he was interred. Your failures may now make that impossible."

Those who knew Phiral often thought he was a coward at heart. And it's true that he was often ruled by his fear. But the secret he kept from most was that his core wasn't made of fear, but of anger. He could be pushed and pulled and prodded and would often give in out of fear of consequences. But he could face only so much before his anger took over and gave him the strength he usually lacked.

Phiral was now at his limit. After everything he had done to help Eothep, the necromancer was now breaking his promise and threatening him with death. Phiral was to be young, immortal, and powerful—rewards he had *earned*. He would not be denied now.

He pulled himself upright and faced the necromancer. He forced himself to look the gaunt figure full in the face.

"I have done what you asked!" he shouted. "I set everything up for you. The Warden was in the depths of the Fortress and was sentenced to death. Do you think I could have kept her in there when the Imperial Guard failed to hold her? Do you think I could have planned for that? The whole city hunts her and no one has found her yet, including *you*!"

He stepped up to Eothep and realized how small the man was. Power or no, Phiral felt he could break the necromancer in half with one blow.

"You worry about the Five hunting you? Then you will stop threatening me this instant! If you think I trusted you—that I didn't make arrangements in case you decided to betray me—then you are the fool! I'm still willing to live up to my end of our deal, and it's in your best interests to live up to yours."

Some part of Phiral's mind couldn't believe the words coming out of his mouth, despite his fury. He was prepared to bolt for the stairs if Eothep refused to see reason.

The necromancer surprised him by lowering his head and looking at the floor. Phiral could barely make out his low voice and leaned in closer.

"Stupid, stupid nobleman dares to threaten me. I chose poorly when I selected you to be my servant. Now you will serve me the way you should have from the beginning."

Eothep raised his head and opened his mouth, exhaling a black fog into Phiral's face. Phiral staggered back, choking on the toxic fumes. Icy claws sliced into the backs of his legs, and he dropped to the floor, unable to scream as his throat swelled from the poison he had breathed in, cutting off his air supply.

Phiral tried to drag himself toward the stairs, but the chamber began to darken, and he heard Eothep step forward to stand over him.

"It is time for you to become the tool I need out in the city. In life you failed me. In death, I own your soul. Your 'arrangements' mean nothing—you will tell me all about them and then will do as I command to ensure my safety."

As Phiral's vision faded, he heard the rasp of the necromancer's voice for the last time as a living being.

"It is time for you to hunt."

Chapter Twenty-One

L EYNDRA CROUCHED IN THE SHADOWS AT THE BASE OF the wall. She was getting tired of sneaking around in the darkness all the time. She wished she could just march onto the estate and have a straight-up fight. She knew, however, she couldn't take the risk that the nobleman would escape while she fought his house guards.

Some distance down the wall stood the large metal gates with the crescent moon insignia of House Najare. Leyndra had recognized the description given by Usun, though she wasn't sure who in the House was involved in the plot. She vaguely remembered the head of the House was named Phiral Najare, but she didn't know if he had any sons or brothers.

Regardless, this was her only lead and she was going to follow it to the end of the trail. She scaled the stone wall and peered over the top at the estate. There was no movement visible anywhere on the grounds, which was not unusual at this time of night. Patrols were often irregular and sloppy unless the House guard had faced threats before.

She slipped over the top of the wall and lowered herself to the ground on the inner side. Light from a couple windows of the mansion told her that someone was awake inside, but there was still no sign of anyone out here. Though she knew it wasn't impossible, something about this situation set her nerves on edge. She could *feel* something was wrong here.

Finding the shortest open distance between the walls and the mansion, she sprinted across the open grass and tucked herself into a pool of shadows below a darkened window. She waited, listening for any sound of alarm or pursuit, but heard nothing but typical night sounds.

Staying below any windows, she moved around to one of the two servant entrances. She listened at the door and then tried the handle. It was unlocked and she opened it slowly, peering into the gloom beyond. An empty hallway greeted her, and she entered the mansion.

Every sense alert, Leyndra moved to the servant staircase. Still, she heard no sounds within the mansion. Even at this late hour, someone should be moving about. If the guards weren't outside, then she would expect at least one or two active in here. Could this be a trap? Usun hadn't had time to alert Tyina and get a message to whichever Najare family member was involved. This couldn't possibly be a trap for her.

Unless Usun was lying. Leyndra dismissed that possibility—he was too afraid to feed her any lines.

Just like Tyina was too afraid to lie.

Leyndra mentally cursed herself. There was no way the coachman was a master manipulator just like Tyina. She just didn't believe it.

She reached the third floor where she expected the family bedrooms to be situated. She stepped out of the servants' staircase onto the main landing and waited in a corner, listening for any sounds up here.

"There's no one left here to catch you."

The man's voice came out of the darkness across the landing. He stepped into the wan light of a lamp hanging on a hook partway down the hallway. He was a dark-haired man of average height, dressed in expensive clothing, with a pale face that shone like the moon in the dusky hallway.

"No one but me, that is."

Leyndra's sword was in her hand without conscious thought.

"And you are?" she asked.

The man gave a courtly bow and took a step toward her as he straightened.

"I am Phiral Najare, head of House Najare."

He took another step forward and Leyndra raised her blade. A dozen paces now separated them.

"At your service," he added, and he grinned. His teeth were dark, as if most were rotten. Or perhaps he had been eating or drinking something that stained them. She couldn't tell in the low light.

"Is that how you usually greet armed intruders in your home? I would think you'd be more...concerned."

Phiral shrugged.

"You're no stranger, Leyndra Jirau. I feel as if I already know you. And I certainly know why you're here. I'm interested in hearing how you found out about me."

His smile disappeared as a thought occurred to him.

"And Tyina? I really hope you didn't do anything rash and harm her in some way."

Now Leyndra smiled.

"Not yet. I'm saving her for last."

She stepped away from the wall and angled closer to the main staircase. The point of her blade never wavered. Now that Phiral was in front of her, she wasn't sure how to proceed to get him to talk. He was too confident, especially if no one else was in the mansion. Was he the necromancer? Her smile faded.

"Tell me this was about more than just money. Tell me that Osho died for something bigger than your greed."

"Oh, much bigger. Of that you can be assured, Leyndra. May I call you Leyndra, or do you prefer Miss Jirau?"

"I'd prefer it if you didn't say my name at all."

He laughed.

"I would have preferred you to go your execution quietly, Leyndra, but we don't always get what we want. Although sometimes, we get something greater. Something we didn't even know was possible."

He took another step toward her and now the point of her blade was only a hand's span from his chest. Leyndra had reached the head of the main stairs. She didn't like having the drop at her back, but it was better than being trapped against a wall.

"You want to know about the necromancer, no doubt. Well, I

must apologize, but he has no interest in meeting you. He really just wants you dead, and he's sent me to handle that."

Leyndra could feel the flow of *virtus* just out of her reach. She pictured Osho's face, and a slight trickle made it through to her, but she couldn't concentrate enough to open it up. She was too focused on Phiral Najare.

She was about to answer him, to try to get him to tell her any other details about the conspiracy or the necromancer, when he dove at her.

Without warning, he crouched and sidestepped, her sword going over his left shoulder as he lunged forward, his hands curved into claws. Leyndra tried to backpedal and felt the edge of the top step at her heel. Phiral's palms slammed into her midsection, his nails gouging chunks out of her leather armor.

Leyndra would have been thrown backward down the stairs with the force of the blow, but she twisted at the last second and brought the hilt of her sword down on Phiral's head. Grabbing one of his wrists, she used his momentum to shove him forward toward the banister. Impossibly, the wood splintered when his body slammed into it, and she realized too late that she had killed him.

With a yell, he plunged over the edge and dropped three stories to the marble floor below. Leyndra heard the stone crack when he hit, and knew there was no way he could have survived the fall. Her best lead had just died.

Leyndra looked over the edge and saw his body sprawled out on the cracked marble flagstones. And then she gasped as he pushed himself up into a sitting position. She couldn't believe he was still alive.

Phiral climbed to his feet and looked up at her.

"That was...interesting. I'm still getting used to my new abilities. It turns out a three-story fall doesn't hurt me. I know what you just saw is shocking. You stay where you are."

Leyndra watched as his arms and legs elongated, his spine curving and his shoulders suddenly expanding and ripping through his shirt. She was struck speechless by his transformation into some kind of alien beast. His face stretched as his mouth widened, his teeth growing longer and the ends narrowing into points.

"I'll be right up."

*   *   *

CROUCHING ON ALL FOURS, PHIRAL TOOK THE STAIRS AT A RUN, like some misshapen hound bounding up toward Leyndra. She snapped out of her shock as soon as he began moving, and she bolted down the hallway toward one of the bedrooms. She didn't know what kind of creature Phiral Najare was, but his survival from the three-story fall made her doubt her blade would be any more effective.

She kicked open the bedroom door and entered the room, ready to fight anyone who might try to bar her way. A quick glance told her someone was on the bed with the blankets thrown back. The outer wall was pierced by a curtained doorway that likely led out onto a balcony.

Leyndra moved towards the doorway and took a better look at the bed. She realized the inhabitant of the room was not going to give her any trouble, as the young woman was dead, her torso ripped open, blood soaking the bed.

Leyndra flashed back to Phiral's smile, the stained teeth.

By the Abyss, Phiral Najare did this! No wonder I didn't see anyone. That creature has killed them all!

Leyndra flung the curtain aside and stepped out onto the narrow balcony. There weren't many options out here. The rough stone walls could be climbed, but she would have to sheath her sword, making her completely vulnerable if he caught her on the wall. She knew she would have only a few seconds longer before he reached the third-floor landing, so she made a snap decision.

Jumping up and catching the stone frame above the doorway, Leyndra pulled herself up onto the roof. If she could make it up over the apex before Phiral emerged onto the balcony, she might be able to hide from him. It wasn't much of a chance, but it was the only one she had at this point.

The slate roof was smooth and did not give her much purchase for climbing. Leyndra moved slowly, knowing that if she tried to scramble up the slope, she would likely slide off the edge and fall to her death. She realized she wouldn't make it in time before she was halfway to the top.

Phiral emerged onto the balcony and looked around. He spotted her immediately and climbed up onto the roof behind her.

"You can't escape me, Leyndra. I will feast on your flesh and drink your blood, and then I'll make you beg me to let you die."

His voice was rough, and he had difficulty pronouncing the words through his distended mouth. Phiral moved toward her slowly, not because he found the slate to be difficult to climb, but because he was stalking her.

He's enjoying this, she thought.

Holding onto the roof with one hand, she drew her sword with the other. But there was no way for her to fight up here—one swing of the weapon would likely dislodge her from her perch. Still, she refused to give up.

Phiral climbed up to one side of her and smiled with his huge, misshapen jaws. He was just out of reach of her sword. She wouldn't be able to kill him like this. She didn't even know if her weapon would harm him.

Leyndra let go of the roof and threw herself backward. She tumbled down the slope as Phiral watched, too shocked to chase her. She let go of her weapon and tried to time it so that she could catch the edge of the roof and swing onto the balcony.

She missed.

Her hands flailing for anything to grab, she rolled over the edge and plunged down just beside the balcony. She caught the railing with one hand for an instant, just long enough to slow her descent, but the sudden yank wrenched her arm and shook loose her grip.

She fell another story and barely managed to catch herself on the railing of the lower balcony with both hands. A scream tore itself from her throat as agony flared in her arm. A matching howl of rage came from the rooftop where Phiral still perched. He would be coming for her, and this time he wouldn't take his time playing.

Desperation gave her the strength she needed to pull herself over the railing onto the balcony. She didn't look up to see whether he had reached the edge of the roof, but plunged through the doorway. Scenes of carnage flashed by her as she fled through the rooms of the mansion, but she reached the main stairway without further incident.

A quick glance upward didn't show her the nobleman—or whatever he was now—coming down at her. Taking the stairs three at a time, she fled toward the main entrance, hoping that he hadn't just thrown himself off the roof and was waiting for her at the bottom.

She flung one of the doors open and bolted out onto the grounds. She glanced around as she ran and didn't see him anywhere, but a snarl from behind her caused her to look back over her shoulder.

Phiral was clinging to the outer wall of the mansion and had climbed down face-first more than halfway to the ground. As she looked, he leaped out from the wall and plunged to the ground. Leyndra turned her head back in the direction she was running and put on a burst of speed. She had seen how fast he could move, and the fall wouldn't slow him down at all.

And suddenly, *virtus* was flowing through her and she began running even more quickly. The ache in her arm faded away and her breathing remained normal, though she was running flat-out as fast as a human body was capable.

In a moment, she was at the wall surrounding the grounds. With her momentum, she practically ran up the wall and, using only her good arm, she vaulted over the top and landed on the other side. And just as suddenly as it had come, the *virtus* left her. She staggered a step or two and then forced herself to keep moving.

The ache in her arm came back, though greatly diminished, and she figured her power had healed some part of whatever damage she had sustained in arresting her fall from the roof. But she could no longer run tirelessly and found herself breathing hard shortly after moving again.

Leyndra needed a place to hide. Phiral Najare would still be chasing her, and was probably moving faster than she was now that the *virtus* had left her. She likely had only seconds to get into some kind of cover.

She immediately focused on a sewer grate on one side of the street that ran past the main gate of the Najare estate. She yanked up the grate and slid into the hole, careful to lower the metal cover back quietly and not give away her hiding place.

The tube was barely large enough for her to fit, but the rough stones gave her a place to wedge her feet to prevent sliding down into the main tunnel. Leyndra waited quietly, hoping that Phiral didn't have some way of tracking her, by scent or by other, supernatural means.

One of the stones was putting pressure on her injured arm, and she tried to shift slightly to relieve the pain. She didn't realize the stones were slick from the effluvium that passed through this tube, and her feet slipped off their perch as she moved.

Leyndra barely managed to bite back a yell as she slid down into the sewer.

Chapter Twenty-Two

L EYNDRA DROPPED INTO THE DARKNESS, UNABLE TO stop her descent on the slippery stones. An instant later, she emerged from the tube and plunged into the thick, viscous contents of the horizontal sewer channel. Her feet hit the bottom of the channel before the liquid—if it could be called that—surged up past the middle of her chest.

For a moment Leyndra felt her feet sliding on the floor and was in danger of losing her balance and plunging further into the horrid mess. She desperately fought to keep her footing, and keep her face above the surface. The last thing she wanted was to go under—the thought of her head in the sewage was too horrible to contemplate.

She regained her balance and steadied herself. The tunnel was nearly pitch dark, only a small bit of moonlight coming down from the tube where she had entered. She saw that the roof of this tunnel was quite low—she could reach up and touch it with her hand. There was no way back up the vertical tube, however, not without a ladder or a grappling hook and some rope.

The stench in the tunnel was nearly overpowering. The air was thick with noxious odors, and Leyndra's stomach churned at the thought of being immersed in such slime.

Leyndra stood very still and listened for any sounds from above. She couldn't be sure she had lost Phiral Najare. He might at this moment be searching around for her, may find the sewer grate and figure out this was the only place she could have gone. Her descent had not caused much of a splash in this sludge, but she didn't know how keen his senses were.

She slowly and carefully moved to one side of the channel to brace herself against one wall. Only then did she lift one foot high enough to draw the dagger from the sheath in her boot. She had lost her sword, but that did not leave her weaponless. Leyndra had at least three more blades secreted in her clothing.

Now what do I do? she asked herself silently. *I've got no light source, but I can't go back the way I came in.*

Leyndra knew her options were limited. She couldn't stay here in the sewers expecting any kind of rescue—her friends didn't know where she was. There were no visible exits in the area she could see. It was still a few hours before daybreak, and she didn't want to wait around in this muck any longer than she must. While she doubted anything lived in this toxic slime, she didn't want to meet any creature that could.

And I sure don't want to end up poisoning myself by staying in this stuff.

She tried to get her bearings and managed to figure out which direction led toward the center of the city. That direction would bring her to larger tunnels and more access hatches. Unfortunately, those tunnels would likely be darker as well, as the buildings would block the moonlight. She could only hope enough light came down here by which she could see where she was going.

Leyndra moved off down the tunnel, keeping one hand on the right-hand wall. Her left arm continued to ache, and she wondered if she had dislocated it in her desperate effort to arrest her plunge from the roof of the mansion. Which made her think about the flow of *virtus* she had managed to touch while fleeing across the grounds. It had come and gone so quickly, seemingly without reason.

She hadn't been thinking about Osho when the power reached out to her. And yet, it had suddenly been there, giving her the one chance she needed to escape from Phiral Najare. And then, as soon as she was off the grounds of the estate, the *virtus* had just disappeared like a flaming candle suddenly drenched in water.

She continued onwards into the darkness, her eyes slowly adjusting to the lack of illumination. The darkness was pierced here and there by a dim shaft of light from a sewer grate at the top of a vertical tube, which gave her just enough light to make out the walls and ceiling of the tunnel.

Leyndra had been walking for some minutes when she heard a strange hissing sound from up ahead. She stopped and switched her dagger to her good right hand.

Could that be a snake of some kind? Living in the sewers?

She waited a few minutes but heard nothing else. She took another few steps forward and stopped once more. The hissing noise, when it came this time, was directly behind her.

She tried to spin around but the thick fluid surrounding her prevented the sudden movement. She nearly lost her footing and had to reach out to steady herself on the wall. In the dimness, she could barely make out someone's head rising from the slime.

At first, Leyndra thought Phiral Najare had followed her down in the sewers and had managed to catch up with her. What little she could make out of the creature's head was misshapen in a way that suggested it was not fully human, and she thought of Phiral's distended jaws and elongated teeth.

And then the eyes opened and, despite the lack of light, she could see them clearly. They were not the eyes that had looked up at her from the bottom of the staircase in the Najare mansion. They were fully human eyes, and while they gave off no light of their own, they were somehow illuminated in this dark tunnel.

The hissing noise came again, combined with strange whistles, and Leyndra realized the creature was speaking to her in an unfamiliar language. She pondered whether this creature was one of the Tsojim and remembered Jeyrra's words about them in the passage.

'If it's those Tsojim creatures, we should be okay. Otherwise....'

She wondered if Jeyrra knew how to speak to these things.

"Um, my name is Leyndra and I fell into the sewers. If I'm trespassing in your territory, I apologize. I'm just trying to find a way out."

The creature watched her and then began hissing and whistling again. It seemed more urgent this time, and she could see the creature becoming agitated.

Leyndra made sure she had a firm grip on her dagger.

"Listen, if you don't want me to go any farther, I can turn back the way I came. But I need to find a way out. Can you help me?"

A second hissing began to her left and she saw another creature emerge from the sewage, and then a third beyond it. Leyndra backed up a step, and the creatures lunged.

They cut through the sludge with ease, and as they approached, Leyndra saw them change shape. Jagged spikes emerged from their head and torso and the liquid around them began to bubble as if it was boiling.

Leyndra doubted her ability to get out of this situation, armed only with a dagger and with her mobility dramatically reduced in the slime. As the first of the creatures reached her, she prepared to stab her dagger into the one part of it that might be vulnerable—its eyes.

At the last second, Leyndra stopped her dagger thrust as the creature charged past her and leaped nearly out of the sewage to land on a huge shape behind her. She looked over her shoulder to see a long, sinuous silhouette begin flailing as the Tsojim landed on its carapace.

The other two creatures moved past Leyndra and joined the fight, which became a mad, thrashing melee in the midst of the muck. She backed away from the flailing limbs and lashing spikes and managed to get a few glimpses of the monster with which they were battling. As its front half reared out of the sewage, she saw a human head at the top of a giant centipede's body. Curved tusks extended from either side of its mouth, and it used these to bite down on the head of one of the Tsojim.

Leyndra screamed, unable to contain the horror she felt at seeing this monstrous creature, more terrible than anything out of her worst nightmares. Her shriek attracted the notice of one of the Tsojim, who turned to her and dived under the surface of the sludge. She had no time to move as some kind of tentacle wrapped around each of her legs.

Reversing her grip on the dagger, Leyndra was about to bring the point down on the head of the Tsojim when it heaved up out of the muck, lifting her clear and shoving her up into one of the tubes that led to the street above. She dropped the dagger and clung desperately to the rough stones, ignoring the pain in her left arm and shoulder.

The Tsojim's tentacles unwrapped from her legs and shoved at her feet from below. Leyndra was thrown upwards and managed to get a grip on the metal grate at street level. Terror gripping her, she braced herself as well as she could in the tube and shoved the grate away from the opening.

She clawed her way up out of the tube and rolled away from the opening. A part of her mind wanted her to pull the grate back over the hole, but she knew it wouldn't make any difference if that huge creature came up after her. The Tsojim had saved her life, and she could even now hear the faint sounds of battle continuing down below.

Leyndra dragged herself to her feet. She had to get off the street before someone saw her. She was in no condition to lose any pursuit or fight off any attackers. Stealth was her only option at this point.

As she staggered away from the hole in the street, the sounds from below rapidly faded away. Leyndra would probably never know which side had won the fight. She only knew she owed the Tsojim her life.

Now she just had to make it home.

*   *   *

JEYRRA PACED BACK AND FORTH IN THE SMALL ROOM AS THE SUN rose above the roofs of Ythis.

"Something bad has happened to her. I just know it."

Zheemeng was seated on the floor against one wall.

"You of all people should never underestimate your friend, Jeyrra. She fought her way out of the Fortress only eight nights ago."

Jeyrra noted the tone of admiration in Zheemeng's voice whenever he spoke of Leyndra.

Don't get your hopes up, my poor man. This whole mess won't end well for any of us.

She couldn't say that to him, of course. It wouldn't make any difference, other than to give him the wrong impression. Men were too quick to jump to conclusions, especially when it came to women.

And isn't that exactly what I'm doing? I'm ready to declare Leyndra lost just because she didn't return this morning.

Of course, this was a completely different situation. With the knowledge that they could be tracked by the sorcerers if they stayed in one place too long, the three of them had kept on the move, never spending more than a single night in any one place. But that meant they had to find their new hideout together.

Jeyrra and Zheemeng were stuck here until Leyndra returned, and this was the first time she had not come back before dawn. Which meant Jeyrra couldn't even guess when she might show.

Assuming she can *come back.*

Jeyrra tried to shut down that line of thought, but she couldn't help herself. There were too many things that could go wrong.

Zheemeng stood up and grabbed his cloak.

"I'm going to find our next home. I'll come back once I've got a good place."

Jeyrra stepped in front of the door.

"We shouldn't split up. If something happens, we may not be able to find each other again."

Zheemeng looked at her impassively and said nothing.

"Look, we've got a whole city hunting for us. Leyndra may have found herself in a position where she couldn't make it back to us today. If we leave, she won't be able to find us again, and we'll never find *her.*"

Zheemeng shrugged.

"Jeyrra, we cannot stay here. You know this. I can find us our next place and come back. We'll wait for her here, and as soon as she shows up, we all head over to the new location together. But we can't wait until tonight, possibly, to go looking for someplace safe to stay. That's just as dangerous as spending another night here."

Jeyrra frowned but found herself stepping away from the door.

"Don't delay, Zheemeng. As soon as you have the next location, you get back here."

He nodded at her and left.

Jeyrra swore and kicked the wall. Zheemeng was a good man, skilled and reliable, loyal. But there was a limit to how much of this he could take. Jeyrra knew he still wasn't over the encounter with the demon three nights ago. She heard him moaning in his sleep last night, saw the look on his face this morning.

Jeyrra paced for a few minutes and then decided to sit down. She had just crossed her legs when the door to the room was kicked open.

She leaped to her feet as three Imperial Guard soldiers barreled into the room and tackled her. She went down under their combined weight and was pinned to the floor. She twisted and clawed but the men were wearing armor and helms and she couldn't get in any solid strikes.

In less than a minute she found herself overpowered, her arms and legs manacled. She saw only these three soldiers. Surely, they would have sent more men if they thought Leyndra was here.

And then it hit Jeyrra like a punch to the stomach. They must already have Leyndra, or had killed her sometime last night.

Zheemeng! Did he get away or do they have him outside?

And then Jeyrra's blood ran cold as a priest stepped into the room. His bald head glistened in the light from the boarded-up window and with his hooked nose Jeyrra thought he looked like some strange bird of prey. The priest stepped up to Jeyrra's side and gazed down at her.

"I am Brother Athural Tann, Jeyrra. I am the man who found you. Did you really think you could hide? You might have had a chance if you ran, but Ythis belongs to the Church."

Jeyrra licked her lips and had to clear her throat to make any sound come out.

"What have you done with Leyndra?"

The priest smiled with his lips pressed tightly together. Jeyrra felt like he was drilling into her head with his eyes.

"Nothing yet, Jeyrra. I do so hope they take her alive, however. I have so many questions for her the Imperial Inquisitor neglected to ask."

Hope swelled in Jeyrra's heart. They hadn't captured Leyndra, after all. And Jeyrra couldn't be forced to betray her friend because she had no idea where Leyndra had gone.

Brother Tann crouched down beside Jeyrra.

"But Leyndra can wait a moment. I am here to talk to *you*, Jeyrra. I have many questions for you about a great many things. Leyndra is only one part of that. These fine soldiers will bring you back to the Temple and we will spend some time together, just you and me. I'm sure your mind holds some wonderful secrets and I would love to hear all of them."

Terror gripped Jeyrra. The last thing in the world she wanted was to enter the Temple. She knew once she crossed that threshold she would never emerge.

"Y-you don't need to take me to the Temple. I can answer your questions right here."

The priest shook his head slowly, his eyes never leaving Jeyrra's face.

"These fine men are too busy to wait around while we talk. And I believe you have secrets they are not supposed to hear. No, at the Temple, our discussions will be private, and uninterrupted."

"Leyndra isn't coming back here. We decided to split up. It wasn't safe with us together. I-I was going to collect my gang and wait this whole thing out."

"Of course, she will come back here, Jeyrra. She is just delayed. And when she returns, I will get my chance to talk to her. There is no need for you to lie. I can see through your lies so easily."

Jeyrra forced herself to laugh.

"She fought her way out of the Fortress. What makes you think you and these three will be able to capture her?"

Brother Tann stood up and moved over to the window. He peered through a crack between two wooden boards.

"The Imperial Guard soldiers are skilled fighters, Jeyrra, brave and honorable. But I have gifts they do not have. You have no doubt heard stories about the things my brethren and I can do. They are not exaggerations."

He turned back to Jeyrra.

"I did not bring these soldiers to protect *me*. I brought them so that you would survive your capture. If I were to take a direct hand, things would get messy."

Jeyrra could see a gleam in his eye as he thought about what he could do to her with his 'gifts.' She knew, as did everyone, that the priests were all insane to one degree or another. But many of them were masters at wearing masks to hide their twisted psyches. Brother Tann's mask had just slipped.

"Men, please escort Jeyrra to the Temple, and then return here. I will await the arrival of Leyndra Jirau, personally."

The soldiers hauled Jeyrra to her feet and forced her to shuffle toward the door, the chains binding her ankles preventing her from walking normally.

"I will see you at the Temple, Jeyrra. Do not worry. I shall not be long."

Chapter Twenty-Three

L EYNDRA STOOD IN THE RECESSED DOORWAY OF A SMALL, stone building less than a block away from the decrepit tenement where Jeyrra and Zheemeng had spent last night. This building had once been an outpost of the Ythis Watch, before they abandoned this section of the city to the desperate and dangerous. Leyndra was pretty sure it now housed the headquarters of one of the major gangs in Ythis. She was idly concerned that the door would open while she used the doorway as shelter, but this was the only place of concealment that allowed her watch the entrance of the tenement.

She had arrived on the street just in time to watch a priest and three Imperial Guard soldiers enter the tenement. Panic had nearly taken Leyndra and she considered running away from here as quickly as she could, but her training had taken over before she could call any attention to herself. She had scanned the area for any signs of more soldiers or priests, but the streets seemed to be fairly normal—except, perhaps, a bit quiet as people had moved away from the sighting of the priest.

Leyndra wasn't sure what to do. There was no doubt in her mind that the men were there because of her, but it didn't make sense that only three soldiers had shown up. Were multiple squads on their way right now? There was no question Leyndra would be able to take down three soldiers without difficulty, and they knew it.

The priest was another matter. Leyndra didn't know enough to be able to separate stories from reality when it came to the abilities of the Church brotherhood. Were they really as hard to kill as she had heard? Was that why there were only three Guard soldiers?

And then another thought hit her—if the Church was now involved in the hunt, it meant the Emperor was no longer worried they had been behind the attack on Osho. And since Xeylien had confirmed that the Five had not created those shadows, but that a necromancer had come to Ythis, it meant that her name should now be clear of the murder charges.

But the price on her head had not been rescinded. She knew the Imperial Guard would not stand for the hunt to be called off. She had killed their soldiers in her escape from the Fortress, and they would pursue her until she was captured or dead.

She still didn't understand, though, why the Church had been brought in to aid in the hunt for her. Shouldn't they be focusing instead on the real necromancer?

And, thought Leyndra, *whatever it is that Phiral Najare has become.*

She had to consider the possibility the priest and the soldiers were in that building to find someone else who was hiding in the tenement. That it was just a coincidence they were in the same place at the same time. She had no way to know if Jeyrra and Zheemeng were fighting for their lives inside right now.

Or perhaps they had already left. The three of them were changing hiding places each night now, and it was possible her friends had moved on when Leyndra didn't return before dawn. They might have thought she was captured.

Leyndra would have to move soon. If she remained in this doorway too long, she would start to draw attention to herself, which would only make matters worse. But she couldn't very well leave without knowing whether or not her friends were safe.

At that moment, the three soldiers emerged from the doorway of the crumbling tenement. They surrounded a figure Leyndra immediately recognized—Jeyrra. Her friend was chained and could barely walk, and two of the soldiers held onto her arms, one on either side. The third walked ahead, scanning the road for any signs of trouble.

Where is the priest?

And then a terrible thought hit Leyndra. Zheemeng was most likely still inside, perhaps injured, while the priest questioned him. He would wait there for her, while Jeyrra was taken to the Fortress. And this time there would be no escape.

Leyndra wasn't in the best condition to fight off three trained men. She had an injured shoulder, and retained only a pair of daggers, while they were fully armed and armored. A straight-up fight could quite possibly get her killed or captured along with her friends.

And yet, she couldn't just let them take Jeyrra to the Fortress. She couldn't leave Zheemeng to the ministrations of the priest. It took her only a scant moment to make up her mind and figure out a plan of attack.

Pulling up her hood to hide her face, she staggered out of the doorway into the road, limping heavily and weaving side to side. She was filthy from her adventure in the sewers, and a malodorous stench surrounded her, along with a slowly growing cloud of flies.

The lead soldier saw her coming and waved her away, but didn't draw his weapon. He obviously saw her as some homeless beggar, certainly disgusting but no threat to him. Leyndra continued to stagger in his direction.

"Please," she croaked at him. "Some help for a poor woman who needs to eat."

The soldier continued leading the trio behind him, but held out one arm, his finger pointing at Leyndra.

"Stay back, woman, we have nothing for you. This is Imperial business."

In the folds of her cloak, Leyndra held both daggers in one hand, while the other clutched at her hood and held it low. As she got closer, the lead soldier rested his hand on the pommel of his sword.

"Move away or you will feel my blade. This is your last warning."

He was still too confident, sure that he could cut down this harmless beggar with a single swipe and continue on without further interruption. He didn't even stop to set himself up for an attack.

Leyndra came to within about twenty paces and stopped, close enough for her purpose, yet far enough that the soldier thought he had scared her off. As he moved past her, one of the other soldiers proved more alert and slowed. This proved beneficial to Leyndra as the other soldier holding Jeyrra continued to move at normal speed, and so took a couple of extra steps, which spread them out and turned Jeyrra to face Leyndra.

Jeyrra's eyes widened as she realized the identity of the beggar.

"Corporal," said the alert soldier, in an attempt to warn his fellow ahead.

It was too late.

Leyndra whipped back her cloak to free her weapons, and shifted one dagger to her good hand. She was moving forward toward the unprotected flank of the lead man as she threw one of the two daggers at the third soldier, who was caught unprepared for her sudden attack.

The blade flashed through the air and embedded itself in his throat.

One down, she thought, knowing she was fortunate to have made such a perfect throw while on the move.

The Corporal began to turn as she lunged at him. His training took over and he swung his arm out in a backhand as he turned, forcing her to duck or retreat. Instead, she dove to the ground and slammed the second blade home through his boot. He howled in pain as she ripped the dagger out and rose inside his guard.

He didn't have room to draw his sword and tried to backpedal, but the wound in his foot caused him to stumble and he gave Leyndra a perfect opening. She slammed the dagger up under his chin and his head snapped back.

The man fell, yanking the blade from Leyndra's hand and leaving her weaponless.

"Leyndra!"

Jeyrra's warning came just in time.

At the sound of her friend's voice, Leyndra tucked and rolled to avoid the sword thrust of the third soldier. Pain exploded in her shoulder as she hit the ground in a somersault, and she sprawled out in the road. The last soldier stepped over to where she lay and raised his blade for a killing blow.

*   *   *

FLASEK KNEW SOMETHING WAS WRONG AS SOON AS HE entered the Watchhouse. His entrance drew a bunch of looks, a mess of whispers, and a few frowns. Considering that he was—as were most sergeants—mostly ignored when he came on shift until he started yelling, Flasek made himself ready for trouble.

When the lieutenant stepped out onto the second-floor balcony and motioned to Flasek to come upstairs, Flasek started to sweat. The officers of the Watch didn't usually care what their men got up to, as long as it didn't directly affect their own lives. The summons meant Flasek had brought trouble to the upper echelons of the Watch, and he was well aware of how quickly shit rolled downhill.

Flasek was heading for the Duty desk to relieve the nightshift sergeant, but he changed direction and made for the stairs. This earned him a scowl from the sergeant-on-duty, but there wasn't anything Flasek could do about it—you didn't ignore a summons from upstairs.

When he reached the top of the staircase, Flasek swore under his breath. An Imperial Guard soldier stood on either side of the door to the lieutenant's office. He knew what this meant.

As he moved along the balcony overlooking the main floor, he eyed the two soldiers. They stood at attention, all business, staring directly ahead. Flasek stepped up to the door and paused, but they ignored him. Evidently, they knew he was the watchman the lieutenant had waved up.

Flasek rapped twice on the door, and it was opened by a wide-eyed cadet. Flasek understood the young man's nervousness—it was a rare sight to see Guard soldiers in the Watchhouse, and Flasek expected the visitor in the office had also made quite an impression. The cadet stepped aside and Flasek entered the room.

As the door closed behind him, the cadet stepping out into the hallway, Flasek took in the figures seated in the room. The office was not large, though it was well-appointed with a nice desk and a handful of chairs. The lieutenant was seated behind his desk, and Investigator Beyus Chamirra sat tall in one of the other chairs.

The investigator was in full official regalia, his breastplate gleaming, his red cloak brushed and dirt-free, and his polished helm—placed on the edge of the lieutenant's desk—reflecting the sunlight coming through the window behind the desk. Beyus played the part of an Imperial official with a commanding presence that impressed everyone who saw him.

Even Flasek had to admit to himself he wished the Watch could look like that sometimes.

Beyus watched him without expression, but the lieutenant was frowning. Flasek stood at attention and said nothing. He knew better than to speak first. Silence was often used by the officers to make the watchmen nervous and encourage them to fill the void with words, words which often gave away whatever transgression they had made. Flasek felt no such need to talk. He was no fresh-faced cadet. He had long ago learned that whatever was going to happen, *would* happen.

After almost a full minute of silence, the lieutenant sat back in his chair and opened his mouth.

"Sergeant Lumayth, I believe you know Investigator Chamirra."

"Yes, sir."

"Tell me what you were doing at the house of Wydo Idaphos three nights ago."

"All the details are in my report, sir."

Flasek had stayed up through the rest of that night filing a complete report on the incident. Well, not *exactly* complete—he left out the identity of the 'confidential informant' who had given him the tip about Wydo. But the rest of the report had been comprehensive, and completely true.

He honestly hadn't expected the lieutenant to read it. He was just covering his own ass in case there was trouble down the line. Now he was glad he had put in the time.

The lieutenant frowned and looked down at the surface of his desk, bare of any papers. Flasek knew his superior was wondering if Flasek was bluffing about the report—keeping good records had never been a requirement in the Watch. He glanced back up at Flasek's face and nodded grimly. He understood the game.

"Yes, I've read your report in detail, Sergeant," the lieutenant lied. "But I want you to tell us in your own words about the incident, from the beginning."

Beyus continued to sit there, watching Flasek impassively. Flasek didn't care. He wasn't afraid of the investigator and he certainly wasn't going to let the other man see him sweat.

"Yes, sir. Six days ago, I received a request to meet from one of my confidential informants. The informant told me that he...or she...had witnessed strange goings on at the manor house of Wydo Idaphos. The informant could be no more specific, other than to say that strange shadows, chanting, and flickering lights were coming from the manor house. The only reason the informant bothered to tell me was he...or she...was aware of the murder of Wydo's brother, and the bounty on the head of Leyndra Jirau. He...or she...hoped that the tip would lead to the capture of Leyndra and therefore the reward."

For the first time, Beyus spoke up.

"Who is this informant?"

Flasek said nothing, but looked at the lieutenant. The officer shifted uncomfortably in his seat, but answered Beyus' question.

"Investigator Chamirra, the Watch has many informants among the people of this city. They agree to help us on the condition their identity is never revealed—"

"I don't care, lieutenant," interrupted Beyus. "This informant is a witness to the necromancy performed by Wydo Idaphos—"

Flasek barked out a laugh, interrupting the investigator in turn. Both men glared at him, and he forced his own mouth shut.

"Investigator Beyus," continued the lieutenant. "Why don't we hear out the sergeant's complete story, and then we can discuss the particulars?"

Beyus gave a curt nod, and the lieutenant turned back to Flasek, motioning him to continue.

"Well, I don't know anything about necromancy, but I had heard the story that someone had hired Leyndra Jirau to murder Osho Idaphos. I decided to conduct a raid on the manor house and take Wydo into custody."

Again, Beyus broke in.

"That was something you had no right to do. The Imperial Guard is tasked with handling matters involving the nobility, *Sergeant*. Why didn't you report your informant's information to me?"

Again, Flasek turned to the lieutenant, and again his superior was forced to intercede on his behalf.

"Actually, investigator, Wydo Idaphos was part of the lower nobility. He did not directly belong to one of the noble Houses. The sergeant was well within his rights to conduct his operation."

Flasek could see Beyus' frustration mounting. He had expected the lieutenant to throw Flasek to the wolves, but it wasn't turning out that way. Flasek knew if he continued to cause trouble for the officers of the Watch, that's exactly what would happen, but the first inclination of watchmen was to stick together.

Especially against the Imperial Guard.

"That doesn't justify what the sergeant did the night of Osho Idaphos' murder! He should never have responded to the original call!"

Beyus was beginning to raise his voice, and lose his cool. This was not something Flasek had ever seen before. He barely managed to keep a grin from spreading across his face.

"That is a different matter," replied the lieutenant. "You are correct in that Sergeant Lumayth should not have responded to that call. He has been disciplined for that mistake."

Flasek hadn't truly received any trouble from the Watch captain over his violation of regulations that night, but from the look on the lieutenant's face, Flasek knew he certainly would *now*.

"Sergeant, wrap up your account."

Beyus didn't speak up again, so Flasek continued.

"My squad executed the raid on Wydo Idaphos' manor house. We found Wydo in his main room, surrounded by books. He appeared mentally unbalanced, but harmless. I was about to take him into custody for questioning when Investigator Chamirra marched in and threatened my men."

"Don't you mean to say that I saved them from being slaughtered by a necromancer? Or do you think he wasn't responsible for the living shadows that leapt off the walls and attacked everyone in the room? Who do you think *was* responsible, Sergeant? What piece of information do you have that the rest of us lack?"

Flasek had no answer for that. He just knew, somehow, that Wydo had been a victim, not the perpetrator. But he couldn't talk about *how* he knew, couldn't prove he was right and Beyus Chamirra was wrong.

"I—nothing, investigator. I don't have anything else."

Beyus gave him a searching look and said nothing. The lieutenant cleared his throat.

"That is all Sergeant. Return to your post and begin your shift. Investigator Chamirra and I will discuss this further, and I will come to a decision on how to proceed."

Flasek looked at Beyus and saw the man was angry. He would likely try to get Flasek fired from the Watch, and would be even more angry when he failed. The Watch needed men like Flasek, and the lieutenant knew it. Even so, there was a limit as to how far Flasek could push things. But for now, he considered himself safe enough.

Flasek nodded and left the lieutenant's office. He would have to be more careful in his future investigations. Investigator Beyus Chamirra wasn't finished with Flasek. Not by a long shot.

Chapter Twenty-Four

THE IMPERIAL GUARDSMAN SWUNG HIS SWORD DOWN at Leyndra's head. She tried to roll away from the strike, knowing she would be too slow.

As the blade arced down, someone tackled the man from the side. The edge of the sword missed Leyndra's head by a finger-length as the soldier stumbled away. Another blade—a short sword—clattered to the road beside her.

Grabbing the hilt of the short sword, Leyndra forced herself to her feet as the soldier struggled with his assailant. She turned to see it was Zheemeng who had attacked the soldier and saved her life. But he was no match for the trained soldier.

The man brought a knee up into Zheemeng's gut, doubling him over. An armored elbow crashed down onto the back of his neck, and Zheemeng dropped to the ground. Leyndra lunged forward before the man could raise his own sword again, and the soldier was forced to give ground to Leyndra's ferocious attack.

Despite her wounded shoulder, Leyndra managed to stay close to her opponent and continue her assault, preventing him from bringing his larger weapon into play. Unable to get away from Leyndra, with his own, longer, sword a liability in this close combat, the soldier saw the inevitable conclusion to this fight.

"I yield!" he shouted, as he dropped his sword and continued to backpedal.

His eyes widened as Leyndra stayed with him and forced him against the wall of the crumbling tenement where Jeyrra had been captured. He tried to plead with Leyndra one last time, but she drove the point of her short sword into his side between the front and back plates of his armor.

He shuddered once as she withdrew her blade, and then slid to the ground and was still. She looked down at the man's face, but the remorse she had felt over killing the soldier in the Fortress on the night of her escape didn't return to her. It was one more thing she had lost in the last few days.

Zheemeng slowly staggered to his feet as Leyndra went over to him. He was dazed but seemed otherwise uninjured, and she grabbed his arm and led him over to where Jeyrra still stood beside the corpse of one of the other watchmen.

Jeyrra motioned to the manacles around her ankles.

"I'm not doing any running until we get these off."

"I'll carry you," answered Zheemeng.

Jeyrra scowled, but Leyndra interrupted before she could make any comment.

"We need to get off the street, *now*. The priest is still in there, and the bounty on my head will make people stupid. I'm in no condition to fight off a whole gang or three, and that's what we'll have here in a few minutes. Zheemeng, are you sure you're able to carry Jeyrra? You look like you're barely able to walk."

Zheemeng nodded.

"That bastard gave me one serious knock, but I'll be okay. You're right—we can't stay here and argue."

Jeyrra resigned herself to being carried, and Zheemeng threw her over his shoulder. It was rather undignified, but she didn't have any other choice.

The three of them entered the alley beside the tenement just as the priest emerged from the front of the building.

"Leyndra Jirau," he called to her.

A third of the way down the alley, Leyndra turned. She motioned for Zheemeng and Jeyrra to continue.

"Run!" said Zheemeng.

"You go. I'll be right behind you," she answered.

"No!" replied Jeyrra, but Zheemeng gave a growl of frustration and continued down the alley. The priest continued to walk slowly toward them.

"Leyndra Jirau, you cannot escape me. There is nowhere you can hide that I cannot find you. Come with me now and spare yourself—and your friends—further unpleasantness."

Leyndra faced the priest, but kept moving backward, her short sword at the ready.

"The Church has joined the hunt, has it?"

The priest gave a thin-lipped smile.

"We are less concerned with the part you played, Leyndra, and more concerned with the *circumstances* of the death of Osho Idaphos. I have been assigned to find out more about these shadows, and their summoner. I am considered an expert on matters such as these."

Leyndra was past the halfway point now, and the priest was perhaps a third of the way down the alley. She didn't know what the priest could do, what abilities he could bring to bear against her, but she had to stall him long enough for Zheemeng and Jeyrra to get a good head start. Once a chase began in earnest, they would need every advantage they had.

"So, you just want me to tell you my story, is that it? I thought the Emperor was too worried that it was the Church behind Osho's murder to get you involved. That's why I had to die, wasn't it?"

The priest continued to smile at her as he approached, and she backed away.

"Our Emperor sometimes worries overmuch. The Church has no intention of working against him. We are his most loyal subjects. That is why there are those in his court, and in the Imperial Guard, who make sure we know about important events like these. So that we can help the Emperor when he needs it."

Leyndra laughed.

"So, there's no longer a bounty on my head? I'm a free woman now?"

The priest gave her a pitying look and shook his head.

"I'm afraid there's the unfortunate matter of your escape from the Fortress. And now today's incident. You have a habit of killing Imperial Guards, and they are not overly fond of you. No, your execution will come one way or another. But your friends don't have to die with you."

The hairs on the back of her neck tingled. She could *feel* him drawing some kind of power around himself, preparing an attack against her. She had made it two-thirds of the way down the alley, while he was in the middle. Leyndra figured it was about time to make a run for it.

"Do not be foolish Leyndra. I found your friend. I found *you*. Do you not think I can do it again?"

Leyndra shrugged.

"Maybe next time you'll be more successful."

She was about to bolt when the priest opened his mouth and uttered a terrible sound. She realized he had said a word, but of no language belonging in this world. The sky above them dimmed slightly and the priest spat out a bright red gob of blood.

Leyndra was already moving as a pulse of energy burst from the priest's body in all directions, like some huge, expanding bubble. The surge ploughed into the walls on either side of the alley, ripping wood and splitting beams. Leyndra felt it coming and threw herself to the ground.

Most of the energy passed over her prone form, but she was still picked up as if by an invisible hand and flung down the alley. The wind was knocked out of her as she landed, and she gasped from the renewed pain in her shoulder.

Everything went silent, and she forced herself to roll over onto her stomach. She raised her head to see the priest still standing in the middle of the alley, surrounded on all sides by debris from the tenements that framed the alley. He took another step toward her and a terrible groan echoed around them.

Leyndra was in no shape to withstand another attack like the one that had just happened. But the look on the priest's face transformed from smugness to concern. He looked around as the groan rose in volume, made louder by a series of cracks and pops that joined the chorus. He began to run as Leyndra finally understood what was happening.

She scrambled on all fours away from the mouth of the alley as the tenement where Jeyrra and Zheemeng had spent the night suddenly collapsed in a rising cloud of dust and splinters. Three floors of building tumbled into the alley onto the running priest, and Leyndra saw the look of terror on his face as he ran, before he was obscured by the pile of timbers and debris.

Zheemeng and Jeyrra waited for her half a block away. Leyndra pulled herself to her feet and staggered over to them, still trying to regain her normal breathing.

"I think he overestimated the strength of the buildings around here," she said to her friends as she joined them. "The Warrens are more dangerous than people realize."

*　　　　　*　　　　　*

PHIRAL NAJARE HAD NEVER FELT SO POWERFUL. HE MOVED through the shadows of Ythis unseen and unheard, but not *unfelt*. People on the streets this evening shivered as he passed them by, a feeling of death stalking among them. A palpable fear followed him, sweeping over those he passed, leaving them eying the shadows nervously, many deciding this was not a night to be out and about.

Phiral loved every minute of it, knowing he could easily end the life of anyone whose path he crossed. Though his heart no longer beat, and no blood flowed through his veins, he reveled in his newfound power. He was the ultimate predator, among so very many helpless prey.

But hunting wasn't on his mind tonight. Despite the changes wrought to him by the necromancer, despite Eothep now having complete control over his actions whenever the ancient being exerted his will, Phiral still maintained one obsession.

And tonight, he was going to see her.

The grounds of the Idaphos estate were quiet, but well-lit by bonfires spaced evenly around the mansion in the center. House guards patrolled around that circle of light in four teams of three, each with a pair of dogs looking for any scent of an intruder. Phiral expected additional guards were stationed inside.

Tyina was obviously worried about a return visit by Leyndra Jirau. She had good reason to fear. That damned Warden had managed to escape Phiral last night, while he was still getting used to his new form. She was far more resourceful than anyone had anticipated, and if she came after Tyina, Phiral's love would likely die at her hands.

No, thought Phiral. *Tyina belongs to* me.

Phiral peered over the outer wall at the ring of bonfires and patrolling dogs, and smiled. He easily vaulted over the wall and flitted from shadow to shadow until he was as close to the mansion as he could get without exposing himself.

He watched the dogs sniffing around and concentrated on them. He could feel his dark energies pushing out from him in waves. The closest hounds picked it up almost immediately and began whining. The trio of guards looked around nervously as they were affected by his aura. The dogs began pulling at their leads, taking the guards away from Phiral's hidden presence.

Though he was still some distance away, Phiral could clearly hear the guards asking the dogs if they had picked up some scent. But it was obvious they were not chasing anything—they were trying to get away from the source of their fear. The guards, if they had given it any thought, would have realized this and turned back in Phiral's direction, but their own uneasiness made them follow the dogs away from his path.

He pushed out further and another patrol, just approaching this direction, reacted similarly. The other two patrols heard the yipping and whining of these hounds, and all four teams converged near the front entrance to the house to examine the dogs and discuss what might be wrong.

Phiral moved quickly between the bonfires and settled into the shadows at the base of the mansion. Long claws sprouted from his fingers and he scaled the wall like some horrid spider. In less than a minute, he hung beside a window on the top floor, directly outside of Tyina's bedchamber. The guards below him peered out into the darkness beyond the fires, too afraid to pass beyond their protective ring of light.

He inserted one claw into the small gap between the wooden shutters and flicked the latch. Then he pulled open the panels and climbed into the bedroom.

Tyina had not yet retired for the night, and he could hear her in her sitting room beyond. Her chambermaid moved back and forth, tidying the rooms and bringing her Lady whatever she needed. For the first time tonight, Phiral felt the hunt take him, and he knew he would consume the chambermaid before leaving. The thought brought a smile to his face, and he could feel his teeth begin to extend in anticipation.

He forced himself to calm down—there was business to be done before he could indulge. He waited until the chambermaid moved off into Tyina's powder room, and then he silently opened the door and moved up behind the target of his obsession. She shuddered as he approached her back, and he knew she would turn around and scream, bringing guards running to defend their employer.

Swiftly, he slapped a hand over her mouth and lifted her bodily from her chair. His newfound strength allowed him to carry her out of the room without effort. He took her into her bedroom and stood her against the wall behind the door. Her eyes were saucers and he could feel the terror coming off her like a sweet perfume. Her fear was only partially due to the sudden abduction—his very touch sent dread surging through her mind and body.

Her eyes focused on him and she realized it was not Leyndra Jirau who had appeared from nowhere. She still shivered at his touch, but he could see she recognized who it was and understood that her death was not imminent.

Phiral stepped back and pulled his hand from her mouth. She opened it as if to speak, but she couldn't seem to find any words to say.

"My Lady?" called the chambermaid, who had returned to the sitting room to discover Tyina's absence.

Phiral shook his head at Tyina, and she remained silent. The chambermaid approached the bedroom door, assuming her mistress was inside. The darkness inside the room caused the chambermaid to pause at the threshold—she no doubt felt uneasy at the unseen presence of Phiral—and he thought she might run and call for the guards. But she stepped into the room and her fate was sealed.

Phiral shoved the door closed behind the chambermaid and grabbed her around the neck, cutting off her air and silencing her scream before it could begin. He felt the change come over his body and he pushed out the waves of dark energy inside him, filling both Tyina and the chambermaid with stark terror.

Tyina was so overcome with dread she could not move, could not make a sound. Phiral had hoped for such a result, as he could hold off no longer. Still holding the chambermaid by the neck, he threw her onto the bed and thrust his face into her chest. As he ripped into her flesh, seeking her fluttering heart, he saw out of the corner of his eye Tyina sinking to her knees against the wall, unable to fully comprehend what she was seeing.

The chambermaid's struggles abruptly ceased. Phiral continued to gorge himself on her heart and other organs for another minute or two before he was able to pull himself away. He climbed off the bed, slick with gore, and turned to Tyina.

Tears rolled down her cheeks as she looked up at him, her breath coming in shallow gasps. He enjoyed seeing her like this, submissive to him. She was such a strong woman—one of the reasons he was so taken with her—but this was a new perspective and he decided he liked it even better. He would be her master, now, just as Eothep was his.

What fun they would have together.

"Tyina," he rasped at her, his voice altered by his inhuman form. "I've found immortality, of a sort. It wasn't what I wanted, at first, but now I realize this is far better than anything I had imagined."

He crouched down in front of her and she flinched back from him.

"Don't worry, my love," he said to her, reaching out one clawed hand to gently caress her hair. "You'll come to enjoy it, too."

Chapter Twenty-Five

ZHEEMENG WAS HUNCHED OVER JEYRRA'S ANKLE, working away at the manacle's lock. He had already removed the ones around her wrists, and had tightly bound Leyndra's shoulder with strips of torn cloth—after she had shed the soiled clothing she had ruined in the sewers of Ythis. The pressure eased the ache she felt whenever she moved it.

She watched his fingers manipulating the small, metal picks.

He's good with his hands, she thought, and forcefully kept her mind from going further down that path. She couldn't deny she found him attractive, and not just physically. But the last thing she needed right now was another complication, and that's exactly what anything between them would be.

"You saved my life," she said out loud.

He looked up at her and gave her a smile.

"I really just gave you a couple of seconds to pull yourself together. You did the rest."

Jeyrra snorted.

"If Zheemeng hadn't been there, you'd be dead, Leyndra. You're wounded and yet you still decided to take on three armored Imperial Guard soldiers with nothing but a pair of daggers."

Leyndra looked her friend in the eyes.

"Would you have preferred I let them take you to the Temple?"

Jeyrra had told them what the priest planned for her. The Fortress was bad enough, but the Temple…Leyndra didn't want to think about it. But Jeyrra wasn't going to be deterred.

"If trying to rescue me meant your death, then yes, I *would* have preferred to go to the Temple. Don't think I don't appreciate what you did for me today. But everything I've done for you—everything *we've* done for you—becomes pointless if you throw your life away."

Leyndra didn't want to have this discussion yet again. She did what she felt she had to do. Protecting others was in her nature, and she would lay down her life for Jeyrra without a second thought, just as she had been willing to sacrifice herself to protect Osho when she was his Warden.

Morit resented her for taking control of their situation when their parents were killed. But the truth was—and deep down he knew it—Morit couldn't have done it, couldn't have kept them alive and safe the way Leyndra had. He was full of fear, and he let it control him. Leyndra knew what fear was, but she had mastered it, learned to use it instead of letting it take her over.

She wondered how he was doing, kept prisoner in his own home by the Imperial Guard. She had easily discovered his whereabouts, and had deliberately kept away from him. It was a trap—a painfully obvious one—and she knew Morit would have less trouble from everyone if she acted like she had abandoned him after their argument in the bowels of the Fortress.

"Jeyrra, I'm... well I'm *not* sorry I rescued you. And I'm not going to lie to you and tell you I'll be more careful in the future, because that's not who I am."

Jeyrra opened her mouth to interrupt but Leyndra held up her hand and she stopped.

"What I will say is that you're right, to a point. I shouldn't have tried to fight those guards today. I threw myself into a bad situation while not at my best, and I should have waited and tried to find a better way to take you from them. When I saw the priest I just... I feared the worst."

Zheemeng popped the lock on the manacle and pulled it from Jeyrra's leg.

"Last one," he said as he bent over her other leg. "Do you think that priest was killed?"

Leyndra almost shrugged, but she remembered her sore shoulder at the last second, and he wasn't looking at her anyway.

"I hope so, but who knows what he may be able to survive? I certainly wasn't expecting him to be able to do what he did. My bigger concern is that the Church has gotten involved in the hunt for me. If the priest is dead, they'll throw everything they have into finding me."

She looked at Jeyrra and Zheemeng in turn.

"The priest said he was able to track me. If so, being near me puts the two of you into even greater danger than before. It's one thing to be wanted by the Imperial Guard. It's entirely another to be hunted by the Church."

"We'll be executed by whoever finds us," replied Jeyrra. "I don't think the manner of our death makes much difference at that point."

Leyndra knew Jeyrra was bluffing. The Church had many ways to kill a person, ways that were unavailable to the Guard. And some of those ways meant the torture didn't end at the moment of death. Leyndra would take a headsman's axe or a hanging over whatever the Church could dream up any day.

Zheemeng looked up from Jeyrra's manacle.

"It looks to me like we can't hide as easily as we thought. The sorcerer found us. The Church found us. How can we hide when they can track us with sorcery or the power of a god? I think our time has almost run out. The next time the Church comes for us, they'll have an entire company of Guard soldiers with them, and more than just one priest. I think we've got another night or two, at most."

No one argued. Leyndra figured whatever method the Church used to track her took some time. Otherwise, they would have been found again sometime during the day. But the sun had now set, and they were still free. As soon as the last manacle was off, they'd move again to a new location. They couldn't afford to stay in one place more than a few hours, now.

There was one other thing she needed to bring up with Jeyrra and Zheemeng, and she had been delaying it as long as she could. But she needed to tell them.

"I'm going to go back and meet with Xeylien again."

She watched her friends look at her at the same time, the same expression of concern on their faces.

"Listen, I know it's dangerous, but I'm not sure I can beat Phiral Najare on my own, not unless I know more about what he's become. I don't know if a sword through the belly will kill him, and it's questionable if I can even accomplish that much against him. He's inhumanly strong and fast. And he's also hunting me."

Jeyrra shook her head.

"Still, Leyndra, you're talking about asking one of the Five for help. Don't you think Xeylien will want something in return?"

"What other option do you think I have, Jeyrra?"

"Leave Ythis," interrupted Zheemeng. "Let's be honest, this is far bigger than you could have imagined. Think about it—you've gone from being a Warden protecting a single nobleman to being hunted by the Church and the Imperial Guard, consorting with a sorcerer, and fighting some inhuman creature who works for a necromancer. Don't you think this has gotten far more complicated—and dangerous—than any of us guessed at the beginning?"

Jeyrra said nothing, but just nodded at Zheemeng's words.

"Leyndra, I know you want to see this through," he continued. "And we will help you to the end, whatever that may be. All I ask is that you consider the possibility that the forces arrayed against us are no longer beatable. Consider letting the Church, and the Five, and the necromancer fight it out themselves. No one will think less of you if you decide to move on."

She thought about what he was saying. She felt she owed it to Osho to pursue this to the bitter end, but it wouldn't change the fact that she had failed to protect him in the first place. He would still be dead—at her own hand—and she would still be an Oath-breaker. Throwing her life away to avenge Osho wasn't the same as sacrificing herself to save him. She knew that.

And yet, she didn't feel she could just run from this. She had been accused, beaten, tortured, and hunted. She had been manipulated into taking the life of the man she was sworn to protect. She couldn't just let go of that and leave the city.

"I will think about everything you just said," she replied. "Truly, I will consider it carefully. But ultimately, I have to do what's right for me. I appreciate everything the two of you have done for me, and I wish I could have spared you the trouble I've brought to your lives. But I'm not sure I can let this go."

Zheemeng nodded and Jeyrra looked angry. Leyndra only hoped she could accomplish something before the whole city came down on her.

*   *   *

MORIT WOKE IN A COLD SWEAT, HIS FISTS CLENCHED AND his breathing ragged. He sat up, and Hathi stirred at his side, a low moan escaping her lips. He looked down to see her frowning in her sleep.

She's having a nightmare, too, he thought.

He tried to calm himself down, but a cold dread had settled in his belly and his heart continued to race. Hathi moaned again. He placed a hand on her shoulder and she started awake. His son cried out, once, and was silent.

Hathi looked at Morit and then at the children. They were both restless, twisting and turning on their small pallets.

"Something is wrong," his wife whispered to him as she tended to their daughter.

Morit didn't understand. Nightmares had visited them all tonight, but it was bound to happen. They were all under so much stress. Hathi was forced to feed and serve the soldiers all the time now— at least they hadn't tried anything further with her after that first night—and Morit had to take care of the children. It was something he didn't enjoy doing, and they were all out of sorts because of it.

Hathi gave Morit a look, and he reluctantly moved over to his son to see what was wrong. The boy was sweating and Morit could see his eyes flicking back and forth under his eyelids. He was afraid to touch his son, terrified of what might happen.

"We need to get out of here!" Hathi hissed at him. "Don't you feel it?"

Morit could hear the low murmuring of the men in the other room. Anxiety filled him from head to foot. Hathi appeared to be on the edge of losing her control. He had never seen her like this, her eyes wide, hair plastered to the sides of her face with sweat, her breathing shallow. It increased his apprehension and his hands began to shake.

One of the soldiers came to the doorway and yanked the curtain to one side. His sword was in his hand, and his eyes darted around the room, looking for a threat. He looked as terrified as Morit felt.

"Get up, all of you. Keep the brats quiet."

He stepped back from the doorway and stood looking around the larger room, searching for some sign of attack. Morit couldn't see his partner, though he could hear the other soldier moving around.

Morit picked up his son, who shuddered and tried to twist away, but Morit held the boy to his chest and that seemed to sooth him slightly. It did nothing to combat Morit's terror, which grew by the second.

Hathi woke their daughter and cradled the girl on her lap. Morit stared at his wife, willing her to get to her feet. The soldiers obviously felt the fear as well, and Morit was worried they might do something nasty if they felt their orders were being ignored. He didn't want to say anything to his wife out loud, however, for fear of drawing attention to her.

They all startled—Hathi even let out a small yelp—as someone knocked on the front door. Morit saw the soldier in their bedroom doorway nod to his fellow, and then he moved out of sight toward the front door.

Hathi stood and stepped to the small window that overlooked the alley behind their tenement.

"Morit, climb down there right now, and I'll drop the children to you. Then I'll come behind."

Her face as she whispered to him was pale and drawn. He wanted to argue, wanted to say he was too afraid to move, but the look in her eye told him that she—and the children—were going out that window *right now*, and if he didn't help he would probably never see any of them again.

The silence from the outer room was shattered with a huge crash as the front door was knocked inward by a great force. The soldiers yelled out in alarm and then another crash sounded as one of their bodies hit the floor.

Morit handed his son to his wife and climbed out the window. The walls were very rough, the wooden beams uneven, and it was fairly easy to find places to put his hands and feet even though he was by no means an accomplished climber. Morit heard one of the soldiers scream in terror and a horrible tearing and ripping noise erupted from the outer room.

Morit climbed down far enough to drop to the floor of the alley below. Hathi lifted his son over the window's threshold, and he saw she had her hand over the boy's mouth to prevent his own screams from alerting whoever was in the room beyond.

He knew with absolute certainty it wasn't Leyndra who had come to rescue him from the Imperial Guard. Something horrid had invaded his home, and only the presence of the soldiers was delaying it from coming for him and his family.

Hathi let go of their son and the boy dropped down to land in Morit's arms. He yelled as he fell, a piercing shriek that echoed down the alley. He saw Hathi look back over her shoulder once, and then she grabbed their daughter and flung her bodily out the window.

As Morit moved to catch the girl, he saw a pair of hands with long, twisted claws reach out of the darkness behind Hathi and grab either side of his wife's head. Morit caught his daughter as his wife was yanked back from the window, a terrible scream ripping from her throat.

Morit felt his bladder release as he was choked with terror. He wanted to flee from that sight, never mind the children. Let them be taken, if only to delay whatever had killed his wife from coming for him.

Some small part of him knew he couldn't do that. His wife had just sacrificed herself to save their children, and he couldn't just abandon them, no matter how afraid he felt. He picked up his son in one arm and his daughter in the other, and bolted down the alley away from the tenement.

A single howl of pain and anguish rose from his wife to follow him down the alley, and was suddenly cut short.

Chapter Twenty-Six

L EYNDRA STOOD OVER THE SLEEPING FORM OF SERGEANT Flasek Lumayth and drew her sword. He hadn't stirred a whisker when she climbed in his window, the sky behind her beginning to pale as dawn approached. Now, she prepared to wake him up.

It was time they talked.

She wanted to take the pitcher of water from the small table and dump it on his head, but she knew he'd probably make enough noise to wake the dead, and there was enough of that going on right now. So, she prodded the back of his hand with the point of her sword.

"Sergeant," she said in a low voice. "Wake up."

Flasek grumbled in his sleep and tried to swat away her weapon as if it was a biting insect. She sighed and poked him again.

"Sergeant, wake up. It's Leyndra—I need to talk to you."

She gave him one last poke and his eyes snapped open. He was alert in an instant, and moved a lot faster than she expected.

He batted away the flat of her blade with one hand while the other emerged from under the thin blanket clutching a dagger. Instead of rolling away from her to get distance, he threw himself toward her, trying to get inside her guard with his own short blade.

Leyndra's training took over. She stepped back and drew up her weapon, angling the point down to stop inches from Flasek's face. He checked his lunge and froze.

"Drop the knife, Sergeant. If I was here to kill you, you'd already be dead."

He considered her words for a second and sat back down. She saw him, surprisingly, *relax*. He tossed the dagger back on his pillow and crossed his big arms over his chest.

"You play a dangerous game, woman, waking me up like that. You're the not the first to come at me in my sleep, so I've got long experience waking at the first sign of a threat."

Leyndra couldn't hide her smile. Flasek glanced around the room and finally realized he hadn't caught her as she came in. She could easily have killed him in his sleep.

"By the Abyss, what a way to wake up. You here to bring me more trouble?"

Leyndra nodded.

"Most likely. I heard you kept asking around about me, kept trying to investigate my story, after the Imperial Guard took me away from you. I heard you were even there when Wydo was killed and you nearly got into a fight with Investigator Chamirra."

"You hear a lot, lady. How d'you know all this? Who's been talking?"

She shrugged and sheathed her sword. She had decided to trust him, and threatening him with a weapon wasn't a good way to start off.

"Word gets around, and people talk. I overhear a lot, especially when they don't know I'm listening. Why did you keep investigating? What's your interest in all this?"

Flasek laughed out loud.

"My interest is in you."

She looked at him askance and he waved her off.

"Not like that. You know what I mean. You kill a nobleman, even though you're a Warden. You tell me some crazy story about how you were tricked into doing it by living shadows. Then you escape from the Fortress. Next thing I know, the nobleman's brother is accused of necromancy and killed in a raid by the Imperial Guard. Except, I also know—and I bet you do, too—he was no necromancer."

Flasek uncrossed his arms and climbed off the bed. Grabbing the pitcher of water from the table, he poured a glass and drank it down in one long guzzle.

"And now you ask me why I'm still interested? Would you have dropped this whole matter at the first sign of trouble?"

Leyndra didn't bother to answer. He already knew what she would say.

"So, what brought you here to wake me up a good hour before I had to? What story are you going to tell me *now*?"

Again, Leyndra had to fight her smile. She couldn't help liking this big man. He was tough, and honest, and *real*. He genuinely wanted to investigate, solve crimes, and help people. She knew his type were a dying breed in Ythis—such inclinations were usually beaten out of most people at a young age.

"This one is a bit of a shocker, Sergeant."

He snorted and sat back down on his bed, waiting for her to continue.

"You're right in that Wydo Idaphos was not the necromancer. That creature is still out there, somewhere in the city. It has a servant that's hunting me."

"What kind of monster serves a necromancer?"

"His name is Phiral Najare."

"The nobleman?" he asked, surprised.

Leyndra nodded. "At least, he used to be the head of House Najare. Now everyone on the grounds is dead—or it appeared so when I was there the night before last. And Phiral Najare has turned into some kind of inhuman creature. He's very strong, very fast, with teeth and claws that put your dagger there to shame."

Flasek wiped a hand across his eyes and heaved a great sigh.

"And Najare serves the necromancer?"

"Yes," she replied. "But I don't know where the necromancer is hiding. I figured he was probably somewhere on the Najare estate, but with everyone now dead, someone is going to notice very soon and then the Imperial Guard will be all over that place. So, he must have moved by now."

"Okay, Leyndra. I think I've heard enough for the moment. It's a bit much to take in all at once. So, answer a different question for me. Why are you here, telling all of this to me? There's not much I can do to help you with this. Or do you want me to go to the Imperial Guard with it?"

"No, that will only make things worse. I think I might be able to kill whatever it is Phiral Najare has turned into. But that won't necessarily get me the location of the necromancer. And it won't tell my why he came to Ythis in the first place, what he's trying to accomplish."

"Why does he need a reason?" asked Flasek. "Couldn't he have come just to visit our fair city?"

This time, Leyndra didn't smile. She was thinking about Xeylien, and the visit she'd have to make tonight.

"No necromancer will come to this city without an objective. The Five will go after anyone practicing such arts with all the power they have, and so will the Church. He has to be here for a reason. He wants something, and I bet Phiral Najare promised to give it to him."

"And you want me to find out what he's looking for, why he's here."

"Exactly, Sergeant. It might just give me an idea where he's hiding."

Flasek sat there for minute, considering everything she had told him. She knew better than to press him at this point. It was a lot to take in all at once. Finally, he looked back up at her.

"You know, I could just forget everything you just told me and bring you in for the reward. I'd be a rich man."

"You'd have to somehow subdue me first. If a fortress full of soldiers couldn't do it, what makes you think you could?"

He grinned at her.

"You've never seen me fight. One of me is worth a whole battalion of them."

He sat there staring at her face for almost half a minute before he pulled himself out of his reverie.

"Ah, screw it. I'd be bored out of my skull with all that money, anyway. I'll do it, and I'll start at the House Najare estate this morning, before someone discovers the corpses."

"Be careful," she warned him. "If Phiral Najare is still there, you probably won't be able to kill him. It could be dangerous."

"Yeah?" he said to her, and she realized by his expression that he would do it anyway, because it was their best chance at getting a lead. Apparently, he was just as single-minded as she was.

"I'll be in touch," she said as she climbed back out the window. It was time to get back to her friends.

*   *   *

FLASEK GAVE A FEW COINS TO A BOY TO RUN A MESSAGE TO the Watchhouse, telling them he was off on an investigation and probably wouldn't be in today. He hoped Lassim had come in, so his second-in-command could relieve the sergeant who had been there all night. Flasek didn't want to start making enemies among the other sergeants.

Dressed in his watchman's uniform, he paid a carriage to get him up to the Nobles' District much faster than he could have walked. He asked the driver to drop him off well away from the House Najare estate, and he walked the rest of the way. As he approached the main gate, he saw a large, enclosed wagon stopped out front. A man was peering between the bars of the gate, which was closed.

Flasek came up behind the man.

"Sir, please step away from the gate." The commanding tone in Flasek's voice immediately brought the man's head around and he complied with the instruction in haste.

"I was just looking for someone to open the gate," the man explained. "I'm supposed to make my delivery, but the gate is locked, and no one is around. How am I supposed to deliver all this food?"

Flasek peered over the man's shoulder at the grounds of the estate, the mansion in the distance rising above the trees near the outer wall.

"If the gate is closed, then House Najare is not accepting deliveries today. You'll have to move along."

It was a silly statement—the estates were always open in the daytime to accept deliveries of the supplies a house of that size needed to run—but Flasek hoped his commanding tone would override any inclination of the deliveryman to argue. It seemed to work.

"It doesn't make any sense. Some of this food will spoil if I can't deliver it today."

He moved around to the front of his wagon and climbed aboard.

"What am I going to do?"

Flasek shrugged.

"If they aren't taking deliveries, then you're not getting in. Come back tomorrow."

Shaking his head and muttering, the driver flicked the reigns and the wagon rolled away. Flasek turned back to the gate and gave it an experimental push, knowing the deliveryman had probably already done this. The gate was locked.

There was too much traffic on the road—mostly servants on their way to run errands for the nobles who lived in this part of the city—for Flasek to scale the wall here, so he moved off down the street. When he came to the spot where the stone wall angled away from the road, Flasek took a quick glance to see if anyone was watching him, and then ducked down between the bushes lining the wall.

Hunched low, he moved down the wall until he was sure no one from the road would easily spot him as he climbed. A minute later he was over the wall and hoping none of the dogs were still alive, or on strong leashes if they were.

Flasek moved between the trees to the edge of the brush and stared across the expanse of open ground at the Najare mansion. He felt sweat running down his back under his leather armor and cursed the heat. He could tell the day was going to be particularly hot and muggy, not the best time to be doing a bunch of physical exertion.

What am I complaining about? he asked himself. *I need the exercise.*

He could see no movement on the grounds, or in the windows of the mansion. There was no way to approach any of the entrances to the building without being seen, so he moved out from the trees and strode purposefully straight toward the front door. Anyone spotting him would see a watchman openly approaching as if he had every right to be there, never mind that he was walking across the grass from one side of the estate rather than up the road from the front gate.

Flasek reached the front door without incident. Something was definitely not right here. And then it struck him—he hadn't heard any birds in the trees on the grounds of the estate. It was unnaturally quiet, as if all the animals and insects had left this area along with anyone who might live here.

Deciding he'd had enough, Flasek pulled out his truncheon and tried the front door without knocking. He was surprised when the door opened easily. He had expected another locked portal. He peered into the entry hall, lit by sunlight streaming down through a skylight far above. There was no sound from inside. The smell, however, was a palpable thing.

Flasek had encountered countless dead bodies in his time as a watchman in Ythis. He knew this smell, knew from the strength of it that he was going to find more than one or two corpses in this building.

Breathing shallowly, he stepped across the threshold and looked around. The Najare noble House was obviously wealthy, and their home was well decorated, though not ostentatiously so. He moved further into the hall and noticed a patch of brown on the floor just this side of a pair of double doors.

Flasek walked closer and could tell immediately it was dried blood, probably a few days old. The stench grew almost unbearable as he approached the double doors. But there was something wrong about this situation, something missing he couldn't quite identify. He steeled himself and opened the doors.

At least a dozen corpses—all of them torn open, their torsos nearly shredded—were scattered around the dining hall. Some were draped across the dining table like macabre meals. Others lay in the corners as if they had been tossed there by some giant hand. Flasek's eyes darted back and forth, taking in details. It was a scene he would remember to his dying day.

And then he realized what was missing. No clouds of flies rose up at his approach, no maggots feasted on the dead flesh. The room, like the rest of the grounds, was unnaturally still. He noticed one of the windows was open, and yet no insects had come in here to feed.

He left the room and shut the doors, barely able to breathe. Returning to the entry hall, he noticed the marble floor was cracked at the center of the circular main staircase that led to the upper levels of the mansion. It was time to find the office of Phiral Najare and see what he could discover.

The hairs on the back of his neck tingled as he ascended the stairs. He knew he would find more victims on the floors above, and wasn't looking forward to searching the rooms for the office he sought. He wished he had brought along his squad, but this was something that needed to remain a secret. He couldn't take the chance that one of his men might speak out of turn and alert the wrong people to what he was doing.

Flasek reached the second floor and moved down the hallway. The smell of death wasn't as strong on this floor, though it was still present. Most of the doors lining the hallway were open, and he found a gallery, sitting rooms, a music room, and a library. At the very end, a locked door barred his path.

He threw his shoulder into the door a few times and the wooden frame splintered. Stepping into the room, he saw an expensive desk, a few cabinets, and a painting of what was likely an early Najare scion hanging on the wall.

Flasek moved around behind the desk and started searching. He hoped he could find what he needed and get out of here before anyone else started investigating the terribly quiet House Najare estate.

Chapter Twenty-Seven

L EYNDRA STOOD AT THE END OF THE STREET, STARING down the empty row at the Tower of Threads. The black rock of the tower walls seemed to absorb all light, making it look like a black hole in the wall of reality. Only the single, iron door at the base of the tower reflected the wan moonlight, a portal to another world.

It was a world of which Leyndra wanted no part. And yet, here she was once again, this time voluntarily. This time, she was ready to ask for help from one of the Five.

She had felt her first visit was necessary because of the implicit threat to Jeyrra by Xeylien's apprentice. Leyndra needed to know what Xeylien wanted of her, why the sorcerer had tracked her down. And the sorcerer had offered...not help exactly. No, it was a deal that benefited Leyndra only by default.

What would Xeylien want from her in return for providing assistance against Phiral Najare? Leyndra didn't want to ask Xeylien for help, but was concerned she might not be able to defeat Phiral Najare without at least knowing more about what he had become. He was faster than she was, stronger, and able to shrug off damage that would have killed her. He had become something other than human, and she wasn't sure a simple blade would be enough to slay him.

And, Leyndra didn't just have to slay the nobleman. If that was all that was required, she would have tried to do it alone. She would have used her brain, and her skills, and would have found some way to accomplish her goal. The issue wasn't that she couldn't defeat him.

Leyndra had to somehow defeat him in such a way that she could still question him. She needed to know where the necromancer was hiding, and Najare was most likely the only being in Ythis who knew the location. But she couldn't scare Phiral Najare, couldn't intimidate him, couldn't beat him into submission and force him to talk.

I could track him, follow him back to his master.

It was not the first time this thought had crept into her mind. But could she really do it? She had no idea how difficult it would be to find him without him also finding her. And then to follow him, unseen, for however long it took for him to return to where the necromancer was hiding, assuming he ever did. And she had to do all this while the whole city hunted for her.

Leyndra strode forward, along the abandoned street, toward that iron door. And then, after a few steps, she stopped herself.

How could she possibly accomplish her goal without supernatural help? She was alone in this. Sure, Jeyrra and Zheemeng were ready to give her whatever help they could, but Leyndra refused to put their lives on the line, especially when the situation was so perilous. It was one thing for her friends to hold a safe haven for her, a place to which she could return morning after morning. It was another thing entirely to ask them to face a creature like Phiral Najare.

But the 'safe haven' is no longer safe, she thought.

Leyndra didn't like that idea, but she had to admit to herself it was true. Their location had been found twice, first by Xeylien and then by the priest. They could no longer stay in the same spot for more than half a day before needing to move again. And the two 'visitors' had been just as dangerous, if not more so, than the head of House Najare.

In truth, Leyndra was doing a lousy job of keeping her friends out of danger. Just being near her put them in more danger than they had ever faced before.

Leyndra started walking toward the Tower of Threads once more. She had to do whatever was necessary to end this quickly, before people she cared about were permanently harmed.

Again, she faltered after a few steps. The Tower stood there, a deeper darkness at the end of the gloomy street, the door seeming to beckon her forward. She resisted the urge.

Leyndra was not quite ready to enter that portal again.

Anger flushed through her. What was wrong with her? She had people to protect, a mission to accomplish. It was time to do what was necessary.

Is this really *necessary?*

On the tail of that thought, another came unbidden.

I'm afraid.

Leyndra had learned long ago not to be ashamed of her fear. Fear could be useful. It could empower rather than cripple, if one accepted it and used it to drive considered action. Admitting her fear to herself was no revelation. It was a simple reality.

And yet she continued to stand on this street, neither moving forward nor away, caught in her choices like an insect caught in one of those huge webs hanging inside the Tower.

The problem wasn't that Leyndra was afraid. The problem was that she was *terrified*.

Living in Ythis, both the Church and the Five were realities one had to accept if one was to survive, never mind prosper. A living god dwelt in the bowels of the Temple, driving its own worship through madness and sacrifice. Demons stalked the streets of the city, controlled by the whims of a handful of powerful beings who had given up their humanity for power. The plots and machinations of these two groups pulled innocent people from their lives, changing them forever, and always for the worse.

This was life in Ythis, and every citizen had to learn to accept it or leave the city for good. And Leyndra *had* accepted it, even after her parents had died during one of the darkest times in the city's history. She had taken over keeping Morit and herself alive in the days that followed. She fed them, found them a place to live, made friends with people like Jeyrra who helped them survive.

Protecting others was just something Leyndra accepted as part of herself. It was what led her to the Guild, to becoming a Warden.

It was what led her to this street, on this night.

Because Leyndra was trying to protect Jeyrra and Zheemeng. She was trying to protect the rest of Jeyrra's gang, scattered and in hiding across the city. She was still trying to protect Morit, by keeping her distance from him.

But who is protecting me?

That thought brought the rising heat of anger. Leyndra didn't *need* anyone to protect her. She had already done the impossible; had escaped from the Fortress, had managed to elude the Imperial Guard for ten days now. She knew how to take care of herself. She knew how to take care of others.

Then why am I here?

Leyndra tried to dismiss that thought. She was here because Xeylien could help her defeat Phiral Najare and get the information she needed....

She stopped that line of thinking. Leyndra forced herself to acknowledge the truth. She was terrified of whatever the nobleman had become. She was terrified of the thought of her friends ending up in the clutches of the Church. She was terrified of losing everything she wanted so much to protect.

Leyndra had been using her fear to drive her, to give her energy to keep fighting. But she finally realized her fear was pushing her in the wrong direction.

Xeylien wouldn't protect her. The sorcerer would pull Leyndra into her webs, use her, and leave a withered husk behind. If Leyndra was going to go after Phiral Najare, she would have to master her terror. She would have to think, carefully plan, and be decisive when it came time to act.

Leyndra didn't belong in the Tower of Threads. She turned her back on the iron door and walked away.

*　　　*　　　*

JEYRRA DUCKED INTO THE SMALL ALCOVE AND SHOVED THE DOOR open. The scent of stale beer, vomit, and body odor threatened to overwhelm her senses. A quick glance around the main room of the Cellar showed her less than a handful of patrons sprawled around the five small tables, all too drunk—or perhaps in a drugged haze—to notice her arrival. She kept the hood of her cloak up in case other eyes were watching from hidden vantage points.

Guilo, the owner, stood behind the short bar, wiping a filthy mug with an oily cloth. He looked up at Jeyrra and winked at her, a sign that all was well. She did not let down her guard. Guilo was helpful, but far from trustworthy. Honor was hard to come by in the Warrens.

She stepped up to the bar and he set down the mug and reached for a bottle.

"Not right now," she said in a low voice. She wasn't sure which was the bigger risk; the chance that Guilo might drug her and call in the Guard, or the chance she'd catch something nasty from the mug itself.

Guilo leaned across the bar toward her and she realized he was a major contributor to the horrible stench that filled the establishment.

"You've caused a lot of trouble around here," he slurred. She noticed the pupils of his eyes were dilated and wondered what drug he was currently riding.

"We've been trying to keep it quiet, but sometimes trouble comes looking for you."

He grinned at her. The few teeth remaining in his mouth were ragged and rotten.

"I'm happy you came to see me. I've got a message for you."

Jeyrra tensed up at his words, expecting a sudden ambush. But Guilo kept talking.

"Word came earlier today from the Wolf's boys. About your friend's brother. I was told to pass the message if you came by."

Jeyrra was taken aback. Could Guilo be referring to Morit? It was pure coincidence that had brought Jeyrra to Guilo's bar tonight. She was going to pay him to get a message out through the Wolf's network for her boys to pick up. Jeyrra hadn't expected any message to be waiting for her.

"What's the message, Guilo?"

He put his hand on the bar, palm up, and licked his lips. His tongue was nearly as black as his remaining teeth. Jeyrra shook her head.

"You're already getting paid by the Wolf if the message reaches me. You don't get paid twice for the same service."

"You're not paying me for the message. You're paying me not to talk to anyone about your visit."

Jeyrra was surprised by the overt threat. But she realized Guilo knew he held all the cards. If she wanted the message, she'd have to hand over some money. She dumped a few coins in his palm and his arm slid off the top of the bar like some pasty, white snake looking for somewhere to hide.

"The Wolf's boys found your friend's brother wandering in some back alleys very early in the morning. He's got his kids with him. They brought him to the Wolf, and the Wolf put out the word to pass along the message if anyone saw you."

"Where is he? At the Wolf's Den?"

Guilo shook his head.

"Too dangerous. He's being kept somewhere here in the Warrens. In case your friend wanted to see him."

Jeyrra considered the situation.

"Wait—you said Leyndra's brother and his kids. What about his wife?"

"No wife in the message," Guilo replied, shrugging.

Jeyrra had a feeling something terrible had happened. She couldn't wait for Leyndra to return from her trip to the Tower of Threads. This was something that had to be dealt with quickly.

"Okay, how soon can I see Morit?"

"I'll send a boy to tell my contact. He'll come back with a location for you. Go away for an hour—I don't want anyone finding you here. You bring too much trouble with you."

"You don't know the half of it," she replied.

Jeyrra didn't go far. She found a place to watch the entrance to the Cellar, in case Guilo decided to betray her. She saw the boy leave a few minutes after she did, and waited to see what might happen. Perhaps half an hour later, the boy returned to the Cellar. Jeyrra continued to wait. If she was being set up, she wanted as much warning as she could get.

She was surprised to see no further activity. Of course, there was probably a back entrance that led in through the kitchen area. The entire bar could be filled end-to-end with Imperial Guard soldiers by now, and she wouldn't know until she walked back in.

She didn't feel she had much of an option, though. She hadn't seen Morit in years, but she remembered the frightened little boy she had helped care for when Leyndra's parents were killed. From what Leyndra had told her, he hadn't changed very much as he grew up. He was still that same fearful child he had been back then.

Still, Jeyrra would do what she could to help him. They had heard he was being held prisoner in his own home by the Imperial Guard, as bait for Leyndra. It was possible, though unlikely, he had been released as part of some trick. Jeyrra doubted it, though. The Guard wouldn't be able to keep him under control if they let him go.

Jeyrra waited until the hour was up and then returned to the Cellar. She pushed the door open, a dagger in each hand, her body tensed for either a fight or a rapid retreat.

Neither option was required.

Guilo stood behind the bar, and there was no sign of the boy. The same grubby patrons still occupied the tables, a few having shifted position since her last visit, but not by much.

She moved up the bar, still ready for a fight.

"Where is he?"

Guilo put his hand out on the bar again. Before he could react, the tip of Jeyrra's dagger was pushing against the skin of his palm, ready to pin his hand to the surface. He gaped at her, his mouth working wordlessly.

"I'm not going to ask again, Guilo. You've been paid twice. The third time I pay you with steel."

"Okay, okay! You don't need to threaten me, woman. I'm just trying to make a living."

Jeyrra glared at him and said nothing.

"Fine, go outside and head left. Turn right at the fifth cross street. He's in the third building on the right-hand side. There are two of the Wolf's men with him. They're keeping an eye out for you, and will let you in when you get there."

He moved his hand slightly, trying to pull it away from Jeyrra's dagger, but the point just dug into his flesh. He hissed and held his palm still. Jeyrra held his gaze, and the threat there was clear. If this was a trap, he'd have to worry about more than just his hand.

He looked back at her and nodded, understanding, but said nothing.

Jeyrra removed the dagger from his hand and left the Cellar. She would not be returning to the dingy bar, probably for good.

She followed Guilo's directions and was shortly approaching the small building where Morit was hiding. As she moved toward the door, it opened and a man in leather armor, a short sword strapped to his side, motioned her inside with his head. His hand never left the pommel of his weapon.

Jeyrra appraised the man as she entered. He was more than hired muscle. This kind of man tended to work for the Wolf as a skilled bodyguard and assassin. He was no thug.

Jeyrra saw a second man like the first in the door at the end of the hallway. He stepped aside as she approached. She looked into the room and saw Morit sitting on a pile of old blankets, his son and daughter clinging to each other in his lap. Both children were awake, but neither paid any notice to Jeyrra as she entered. They just stared off into the distance at something she could not see.

"Morit," she said, kneeling down in front of him and the children. "What happened to you?"

Morit looked into her face and began to sob.

Chapter Twenty-Eight

AND WHAT, EXACTLY, DOES THE WOLF WANT IN RETURN for all this help?"

Leyndra stood in the hallway outside the room where her brother rested with his children. Jeyrra had brought her and Zheemeng back here as soon as Leyndra returned from her aborted visit to the Tower of Threads. Now she questioned the two hired swords who stood guard at the front door.

"That's between you and him," replied the bigger of the two men. "Our orders were to keep your brother hidden and wait for you to make contact."

"So, what happens now?" asked Jeyrra.

"You take him and the kids with you into hiding. Or, for a price, we can arrange for them to get out of the city. Whatever killed the soldiers who were holding him, along with his wife, has got the Imperial Guard riled up something fierce. They weren't ready to deal with something like that. They'll be disorganized in their searches for a short bit, but they'll recover soon enough. So, the chance for escape isn't going to last very long, but we can move quickly and get them out of Ythis if you've got the money."

Leyndra considered her options. She couldn't see any advantage to keeping him close to her. The lives of Morit and his children were in terrible danger already. Things would likely get worse before they got better, and there was no guarantee they *would* get better. Leyndra knew she would probably have to get them out of the city for good eventually.

The question was whether or not he was ready to leave Ythis.

Leyndra was honestly unsure if Morit could provide for his family if he ran away from the city. He had relied on Hathi to take care of the kids, and Morit himself had few skills of value. Once he was gone, Leyndra would be unable to help him any longer.

The children were too young to leave alone while he worked. And that was based on the assumption he would find a job wherever they ended up settling. Could he do it, or would the children end up in an orphanage? Leyndra barely knew the kids—she had not spent any time with Morit's family since he'd married Hathi. Still, she felt responsible for them, knowing her brother's limitations.

"Okay, back to the Wolf. He's done me a huge service. Does he expect me to meet with him somewhere? Give him money?"

The swordsman shrugged.

"The Wolf is the Wolf. He doesn't tell us his reasons, just what he needs us to do. But this isn't the first time he's helped someone out who desperately needed it. And your brother in there really needs someone to help him."

Jeyrra snorted. "Are you saying the Wolf is helping Morit out of the goodness of his heart?"

The soldier shook his head. "Not really. But sometimes he'll help someone first and then figure out payment later."

He turned to Leyndra. "I guess he figures you'll be around for a while. Maybe you can do something for him in the future. But I'm not in a position to negotiate that with you. You know how to get a message back to him if you want to talk."

Leyndra didn't like the situation. Now she owed a crime boss for rescuing her brother and his children from the streets of Ythis, and she hadn't been given any choice in the matter.

Don't be silly, she thought. *You know you wouldn't have turned down help for Morit.*

"Let me talk to my brother."

She moved to the door and quietly opened it. Zheemeng had managed to get the children to lie down on the blankets, and sat there rubbing their heads to keep away the nightmares as they slept.

Morit saw Leyndra and stood up. His face was drawn and haggard, and he nearly staggered as he led her back into the hallway and pulled the door closed.

"Morit, I'm so sorry about Hathi."

"You should be. It's all your fault."

She saw his fists were clenched, and his eyes blazed with anger. She couldn't deny the truth of the matter. Phiral Najare was most likely responsible for the attack on Morit's family, and it was all because Leyndra had not gone quietly to her own execution. The nobleman was trying to hurt her through her family and friends.

And he had succeeded. Morit would always blame Leyndra for Hathi's death. He would never forgive her for dragging him into this mess. What ties were left between them were now well and truly severed.

Leyndra understood this, and understood her responsibility. It didn't matter if Morit hated her, she was responsible for making sure he was safe. She had stayed away from him in the hope that he would not face any further difficulties, but it was her absence that had resulted in Hathi's death.

Leyndra should have assaulted the soldiers holding Morit and his family prisoner and taken them into hiding with her. If she had kept them close, Hathi would still be alive.

She realized she couldn't send Morit and the children out of Ythis. Morit didn't have the strength to protect himself or his family. He needed her, even if he resented everything she did for him.

"You're right, Morit. I should have protected you. I tried to keep you away to be safe, but it was the wrong decision. It's a mistake I will not make again."

Morit was confused.

"What's that supposed to mean? What you can you possibly do to protect me? The whole city is looking for you. You're a convicted murderer of the head of a noble house. One of the Wolf's men said the Church has officially decided to help the Imperial Guard track you down. You can't hide forever, and you can't protect anyone, including yourself!"

His voice was rising as he spoke, and Leyndra put her hand on his arm to calm him down, in case he woke the children.

"Morit—"

"Don't touch me! You killed my wife! Her blood is on your hands!"

"Morit, you need to be quiet."

But Morit didn't hear her. He was losing control of himself and in another minute would likely start screaming. Leyndra couldn't afford to let him explode like this. There was too much danger of the sound carrying out into the street, and they didn't need any attention right now.

"Who do you think you are? You dragged me into this and then hid while I had to face the Imperial Guard alone! I hate you, Leyndra! I—"

His volume had increased to the point where Leyndra couldn't let him go on any longer. She brought her fist up and hammered him in the stomach, doubling him over. His words were cut off as he gasped for breath. Leyndra wrapped her arm around his neck and squeezed, cutting off the supply of blood to his brain.

Jeyrra ran down the hallway to Leyndra as Morit rapidly lost consciousness. In seconds, he was limp in her arms. She let go of his neck and lowered him down to the floor.

"Leyndra, what in the Abyss are you doing?"

"I had to shut him up. He's in shock and was being too loud. He'll be fine."

Jeyrra looked at Leyndra as if she was crazy.

"But—"

"Jeyrra, I'm sorry, but I just don't want to hear it. I'm trying to keep everybody safe, and I don't have time to be delicate."

She pushed past her friend to return to the two hired swordsmen standing at the front door.

"I've made my decision," she told them. "Morit and the children will be staying here with me."

*   *   *

PHIRAL NAJARE PUSHED OPEN THE LARGE MARBLE DOOR, A low grating noise echoing across the grounds of the Forgotten City, the largest cemetery in Ythis. Tyina looked around nervously.

"What if someone hears us?"

Phiral let go of the stone slab once the opening was wide enough for them to pass through, and turned to her.

"Then they'll probably flee to the other side of the city. No one is going to investigate strange noises coming from the middle of this cemetery at this hour of night."

Tyina continued to scan the grounds, looking for any signs of trouble. As much as she had embraced her newfound abilities, had reveled in the slaughter at the home of Leyndra's brother—though Phiral was disappointed the children had managed to escape with their father—she was still worried about her future. Phiral expected her to move past that feeling soon enough.

She was about to meet Eothep for the first time, to feel the power in their master, to be given new purpose. Phiral looked forward to being near the necromancer once again, but he understood Tyina's reluctance. She would understand shortly what it was to bask in the presence of someone who had power over life and death.

"Come," he told her, and entered the mausoleum.

She followed him in, and he pushed the door back into its closed position. This was something he never would have been able to do when fully alive, and he was thrilled at the power flowing through his body. The changes in Tyina were not as profound yet, as Phiral hadn't been able to transform her into the same creature he had become. She was...lesser...somehow.

He believed Eothep would be able to correct that.

The inside of the mausoleum was pitch dark, but both Phiral and Tyina could now see perfectly in such gloom, and they made their way through the entry chamber to the balcony overlooking the crypt itself. Four stone sarcophagi lay in a line on the floor below, all white marble covered in ornate carvings.

This crypt belonged to some rich merchant family, one with money to rival a few of the noble Houses. They were not permitted to maintain a family mausoleum on their own grounds—a privilege reserved for the nobility only—so they had built an ostentatious display of their wealth here in the public cemetery.

It was *just* good enough for the necromancer.

Eothep stood in the center of the room below, motionless, his spirit no doubt off performing some task vital to the expedition on which he would soon depart. Phiral led Tyina down the stairs that curved around one side of the circular room. He waited there, Tyina beside him, until he could be summoned into the presence of his master.

Moments later, Eothep's body shuddered, and he turned to Phiral. A wave of power swept through the nobleman, and he felt his teeth and claws lengthening as he basked in the glory of it.

"Approach," the necromancer commanded, and Phiral obeyed. Tyina followed him, one step behind.

"Master, I have brought you an offering," he told his master. "This is Tyina, the woman I desired. I have brought her across the threshold of death, so that she may serve you as I do."

He turned to look at Tyina, and saw her own face was disfigured by the changes wrought in her, brought forth by her proximity to Eothep.

The necromancer turned to regard her, and she shivered under that gaze. Slowly, she dropped to her knees before her new master, finally understanding the power held by the figure standing before her.

Eothep continued to look at Tyina, but when he spoke, it was to Phiral.

"You have failed me *again*."

It took a moment for the words to sink in, for Phiral to realize what his master had said.

Failed? How could I have failed?

And then Tyina screamed.

Thrown onto her back by the sudden power directed at her, she twisted and writhed on the floor of the crypt, agony coursing through her body. Phiral watched, unable to move, as Eothep focused his will on the woman Phiral had desired above all else, and slowly began to destroy her.

Her howls of pain filled the crypt, waves of sound that battered at Phiral's senses. He watched as her bones began to shatter, and smoke drifted from her as if she was burning from the inside.

He wanted to plead with Eothep, to beg the necromancer to accept Tyina as his servant, but Phiral could not move a muscle. He was as much under Eothep's control as Tyina, and he could only stand by helplessly as Tyina faced a horrid, final death.

After what seemed an eternity of torture, her cries died away and her body stopped twitching. Phiral was filled with despair. He had wanted nothing more than to share his undeath with her as he had once wanted to share his life. And now she was gone forever.

But Eothep wasn't finished.

A shadow covered Tyina's body, and pulled itself up from her corpse. Phiral realized she had become one of the creatures that constantly flitted around the necromancer in the darkness. Phiral's master, however, had decided to make an example of her.

The shadow body began to ripple as wisps of shadow stuff appeared to boil away into the air around them. The form diminished, and a chill wind blew through the crypt as Tyina's spirit tried to hold onto what little remained of herself. But Eothep's power was overwhelming, and her spirit was torn apart and dissipated just as her body had been crushed of its unlife.

Phiral could barely believe she was truly gone. All he had done to possess Tyina was swept away in that moment. It had all been for nothing. In the end, death had taken her from him, death in the form of the necromancer. The master of death had destroyed the one thing Phiral had wanted most.

And now Eothep turned his full attention on Phiral.

"I would crush your will, all of your thoughts, and turn you into another tool under my complete control. But then you would be little better than my shadow servants. No, I still have need of your independence for now."

Pain exploded across all of Phiral's senses. He dropped to his knees in front of the necromancer.

"But you must learn discretion. Your actions have gained too much attention for yourself, and therefore for me. The slaughter of so many has brought me no closer to my goal, and increased the risk of attack upon me."

Despite the waves of agony coursing through Phiral's body, the necromancer's words cut through it all and cemented themselves in

Phiral's mind and soul.

"You have only two goals, my servant. Two things you must accomplish beyond all else. First, you will find the Warden and slay her. I do not care how, but you will ensure her body—or at least her head—is recognizable. Leave it to be found by the Imperial Guard. With her dead, the Guard will have no need to examine everyone leaving the city."

Phiral howled as a terrible heat filled his body, and he felt as if he was cooking from the inside. His muscles contracted with great force, bending his bones almost to the breaking point.

"And then you will attend to the matter of my expedition," the necromancer continued. "Ensure all is ready. As soon as my last item arrives, retrieve it and bring it to me. We will depart Ythis and leave them all to their petty squabbling. When I return, I will have the power to crush them and turn this city into a haven of death, under my control."

Phiral writhed on the floor of the crypt as the necromancer finished his instructions. But the pain didn't cease. If anything, it became more intense.

"You may not leave yet, however. First, you must be punished."

The inhuman screams of Phiral Najare continued for quite some time.

Chapter Twenty-Nine

FLASEK OPENED ONE EYE AND LOOKED UP AT LEYNDRA.
"You've become a real pain in my arse, woman."
She looked down at him and shrugged.

"You could have walked away when you had the chance. Instead, you chose to be involved."

Flasek heaved a huge sigh and opened his other eye. In contrast to the first time she had awoken him, this time he slowly pushed himself up into a sitting position and blearily looked around his room.

"What time is it?"

"Almost dawn," she replied. "I've had quite a night, and I need to get back. Tell me what you found."

To her surprise, he didn't ask what she meant by 'quite a night.' Not that she wanted to get into those details. Morit's presence was a serious complication, but not something that would affect the sergeant.

Flasek climbed up off his sleeping pallet and stretched. He wasn't wearing a shirt, and she noticed many scars across his torso and arms. Most looked like knife wounds, though there were small burn scars in a couple of spots. Despite being overweight, she could see the muscles moving beneath his skin as he stretched—he would still be a formidable opponent in a physical confrontation.

She wondered why he had let himself go like this. But then she pushed that thought out of her mind. The sergeant's past was his own, and she had no time to pry into his private life.

"I found bodies, Leyndra. Lots of 'em. That whole place stinks like you wouldn't believe. This nobleman of yours must have killed every single person on the grounds of the estate. Looks like he enjoyed it, too."

Leyndra imagined Phiral hunting the servants through the house, across the grounds, as they tried to escape or hide. One by one, he had slain them all. She forced herself to shut down the anger and pity welling up in her.

"I figured as much. Anything useful to me?"

"Nothing that'll tell you where the necromancer is hiding. But I did discover this."

Flasek went over to where his Watch uniform hung on a peg and pulled a few rolled papers from one pocket. He handed them to Leyndra, and she glanced through them. They appeared to be documents outlining plans to hire a number of laborers, wagon drivers, and sell swords, including a list of provisions. She looked back up at Flasek, confused.

"This looks like plans for a trip somewhere. What does that have to do with anything?"

Flasek grinned at her and took the papers out of her hand.

"It's not the 'what' but the 'who,'" he replied. "I know a few of these men named in here. They're known for being discreet—in fact, they'd be pretty pissed to find their names recorded on a list like this. You don't hire these guys to guard a normal caravan or a trade delegation. You hire these guys when you want the whole trip to remain secret."

Leyndra still didn't understand what he was trying to say.

"So Najare was involved in shady dealings. This isn't exactly a revelation, Flasek."

He grabbed a shirt and began pulling it over his head. She heard him mutter "civilians" as the cloth passed over his face. She chose not to challenge his comment—he *was* helping her out despite the danger and for no discernible reward.

"Okay, Sergeant. Walk me through whatever I'm missing here."

"You have to take a step back and look at the whole thing at once. That's the only way to see whatever patterns might be hidden in these events. They all look unrelated one-by-one, but there are links here, I'm sure of it."

He tossed the roll of papers on his small table and began to pace, counting off the points on his fingers.

"One, we know a necromancer has come to Ythis. This is a huge risk, and you know he's after something specific, otherwise he would never have come. Two, he manages to get the head of House Najare to give him sanctuary. Three, that same nobleman, coincidentally, arranges some kind of secret expedition somewhere. Four, the nobleman again, is having an affair with the wife of Lord Idaphos, who gets killed using shadows summoned by the necromancer. Those same shadows manage to trick the Imperial Guard into killing Wydo Idaphos as well, leaving Tyina in charge of the estate."

"Temporarily," interrupted Leyndra. "And I don't see what she could accomplish before the Emperor split up the Idaphos family holdings amongst the other nobles."

"I don't know that yet, either," Flasek admitted. "But the other facts may give us a hint. Moving on, we have number seven, the fact that the necromancer went to the trouble to frame you for the murder of Osho. Since you have no history with the necromancer, I'm going to assume he did it to throw any investigators off his own trail. And it probably would have worked, if you hadn't managed to escape from the Fortress."

Leyndra considered Flasek's comments.

"Okay, everything you say seems to be correct. The necromancer convinces Phiral Najare to help him. He's looking for something in Ythis. When he gets it, he plans to leave the city and go somewhere else, maybe to look for the next item he wants. Phiral makes the arrangements for this expedition while the necromancer searches. All that makes sense. But where's the connection to Osho? Why did *he* have to die?"

Flasek was silent for a full minute, considering her questions.

"You know," he said at last. "In my experience with the Watch, most crimes come down to money, connections, or women. We know Najare was having an affair with Tyina, so there's the woman. There's got to be more to it than that, though. I can't see the necromancer setting up Osho's murder and your frame job just so Najare gets Tyina. Add in Wydo's death, and you've got him manipulating things so that Tyina has control of the holdings."

Leyndra motioned to the roll of papers on the table.

"Najare's got all the underworld connections he needs to outfit this expedition, so that can't be it."

"Which leaves only money," said Flasek.

"But Phiral Najare is head of a noble House. Wouldn't he have lots of money?"

Flasek shook his head.

"Not really. Nobility and wealth are not the same things. Sure, they often go hand-in-hand, but being a noble doesn't make you rich. Or *keep* you rich. These men he hired are costing him an arm and a leg."

"So, he needs the money from Osho's estate," Leyndra speculated.

"Which Tyina can give him while she's temporarily in charge," finished Flasek. "It doesn't matter if the executors of the estate appointed by the Emperor find all the money missing when they begin to divide everything up. Tyina doesn't have to stay around for them to find her."

Leyndra nodded. It all added up.

"What do you think Phiral was getting from the necromancer in return for his help? It couldn't be money—the necromancer doesn't seem to have any."

Flasek laughed.

"What do you get from a necromancer? What do you get from someone with the power over death?"

"Are you saying Phiral *planned* to become that creature I fought the other night?"

"Probably not," answered Flasek. "That was probably a reaction by the necromancer to his plans beginning to unravel from all your meddling. But what if his power over death meant he could make sure it didn't happen to you?"

"Immortality?" Leyndra asked, shocked at the idea.

"Really, I'm just guessing now," replied Flasek. "We'll probably never know the truth. But it doesn't matter. The big question is what we're going to do now."

Leyndra went to the window.

"We need to figure out what the necromancer is looking for. And also find a way to stop Tyina from transferring the Idaphos money into the hands of Phiral Najare. I can't do much about the second part, but there's always a chance I can find out the first."

"Where are you going now?" asked Flasek. "It'll be dawn soon."

"I've got to return to my friends before the streets get busy. But tonight, I'll try to track down a lead."

She climbed out and stood for a moment on the windowsill, leaning down to look at Flasek.

"Tonight, I'm going hunting for Phiral Najare."

*   *   *

FOR THE FIRST TIME, FLASEK SHOWED UP EARLY FOR HIS SHIFT. The on-duty sergeant gave him a double-take when Flasek walked in, and immediately started gathering his things from the Duty Desk overlooking the hall where a small handful of watchmen worked, finishing their tasks and waiting for their shifts to end.

Flasek was tired—he had been unable to go back to sleep when Leyndra left, and he was missing almost two hours of rest. He hoped the day would be quiet. He had too much to think about, and no energy to deal with the city's many crises.

"Anything going on?" he asked his nightshift counterpart.

"Nothing out there," responded the other sergeant, nodding toward the front doors. "In here? Something's happening upstairs."

Flasek glanced up at the balcony that ran around the perimeter of the room.

"The lieutenant causing trouble?" he asked.

His fellow watchman shook his head.

"Worse. Word is, the captain showed up an hour ago with a couple of visitors. Came in the back way and used the private stairs. The lieutenant showed up a few minutes later and went right up with a word to no one."

That explained the lack of watchmen lazing around the hall, waiting to end their shifts and hand it over to the next crew. He watched the other man grab his truncheon and hop down from the platform where the Duty Desk stood.

"Since you were late the day before yesterday, you can start early today," he said to Flasek as he brushed past.

Flasek didn't bother to argue. He didn't know what else to do with himself, so he might as well start working. It was a bad precedent, but he didn't have the energy to fight.

"Sergeant Lumayth!" called a voice from the balcony above. He saw the other sergeant put on extra speed toward the front door, and looked up to see the lieutenant standing at the railing.

"Sergeant Lumayth, come up here now."

There was a note of apprehension in the lieutenant's voice. The man whistled, a shrill piercing note that cut across the hall and brought every head up instantly. The man Flasek had relieved had almost made it to the doors, but even he stopped and turned.

His mistake, thought Flasek. *He should have kept going and pretended not to hear.*

The lieutenant pointed at the other sergeant and motioned for him to return to the Duty Desk.

"The upper level is off limits to all watchmen of any rank below mine until I say otherwise! Pass this on to the next shift when they start arriving."

No grumbling greeted this pronouncement. Most of the watchmen avoided the balcony anyway—they usually only had business up there when they were in trouble.

The lieutenant watched as Flasek climbed down from the Duty Desk. The sergeant who had almost gotten out the door early glared at Flasek as he headed for the stairs.

"I tried," he said to the other man. "Maybe next time."

If there is a next time, he thought to himself. He knew he was in serious trouble if the captain was here. He wondered what crazy accusation Beyus had brought against him this morning.

The lieutenant wordlessly led Flasek to the meeting room down the hall from his office, which was too small to hold a meeting with multiple participants. When Flasek entered the larger room, he saw Beyus Chamirra seated on one side of the long table. The investigator seemed nervous, and then Flasek realized why.

The man seated beside Beyus was a priest, though he appeared to be one who had undergone quite an ordeal recently. The man's bald head was covered in small cuts and bruises, and one of his eyes above his hawk nose was almost swollen shut.

Someone has done a number on him, thought Flasek. *I hope they're not going to try pinning this on me.*

The captain sat on the other side of the table, across from Beyus. The lieutenant closed the door and went to sit beside the captain. Flasek was not invited—or ordered—to sit, and so he stood near the door, his hands clasped behind his back.

"Sergeant Flasek," said the lieutenant. "This is Brother Tann from the Church of Iathephos. Both Brother Tann and Investigator Chamirra have some questions for you. The captain undoubtedly will have further questions when they are done."

The priest looked Flasek over carefully, taking in every element of his appearance. Flasek felt as if he was being laid bare in that gaze, every secret he had revealed to the man in black robes. When Brother Tann spoke, his voice was weak, as if he was in pain just sitting there.

"Sergeant Flasek, what do you know about the deaths on the estate of House Najare?"

Flasek barely held himself back from being visibly startled by the question. A cold shiver ran up his spine, and he held himself rigid, refusing to let the men in this room see his sudden fear.

He wasn't sure how to answer that question without incriminating himself. Did they know he had been at the estate yesterday morning, or did they just suspect he was still investigating? Flasek didn't know what the priest might be capable of discovering. This might just be a test to see if Flasek was willing to cooperate.

On the other hand, they might just be guessing. But would Beyus Chamirra bring a priest to the Watchhouse to meet with the captain on a hunch? The man was too careful to make a mistake like that. The risk was too great it might make him look the fool if Flasek managed to convince his own superiors he was never on the grounds.

He didn't really have time think this out—he had to answer the question.

"I know the gates were locked up tight yesterday, and no guards were there to deal with visitors."

Brother Tann waited for more, but Beyus couldn't remain patient enough to give Flasek room to hang himself.

"How do you know that? What were you doing there?"

Flasek stepped carefully into his answer.

"I spoke to a deliveryman yesterday morning. He told me that he had a shipment of food for House Najare, but the gates were closed, and no one was there to tell him what to do with the delivery. I told him that if the gates were closed, he would have to come back another day. It seemed strange to me that the estate grounds were closed off to visitors, but I don't really understand nobility very well."

Brother Tann smiled, his thin lips pressed together, the very ends of his mouth curling just slightly.

"You haven't answered my question, or the questions of Investigator Chamirra, Sergeant Flasek. Please address my inquiry first. I will repeat it, so you are clear what I wish to know. What do you know about the deaths on the estate of House Najare? I am not interested in deliverymen, nor locked gates. I am interested in the terrible slaughter which occurred on the grounds, and I wish to know everything you know about it."

Flasek was well and truly screwed. He wouldn't be able to manipulate the priest into anger the way he could with Beyus. This man couldn't be led astray by a careful twisting of the answers. But Flasek also couldn't tell the priest the whole truth. He would have to carefully mix the facts with some creativity.

"I know that something killed everyone on the grounds of the House Najare estate. From what I saw, the killings appeared to have been done by natural weapons—claws, teeth, and such—of some creature."

The priest leaned forward and, though he tried to hide it, winced at the discomfort his movement caused.

"What do you know about the creature that did the killing?"

Flasek took a breath before answering.

"I was told it was Phiral Najare himself, turned into something no longer human."

The looks on the faces of the captain and the lieutenant told Flasek he had opened the door on more than just a room full of trouble. They were both shocked at what he said, but he could tell they were just as surprised he knew anything at all.

"And how did you know to go to the House Najare estate? How do you know about Phiral Najare?"

"I—I've been getting messages. They're anonymous, though I can guess who's sending them. They told me about the slaughter at the estate, and who was responsible. I didn't believe the message at first, but then decided to check for myself. I went to the estate and discovered the bodies."

Beyus was livid.

"And you kept this to yourself? A whole noble family murdered, and you didn't think to tell anyone in the Imperial Guard? As far as I'm concerned, you keeping this a secret makes you an accomplice!"

At that, the captain frowned. He might be ready to punish Flasek a hundred different ways for bringing this trouble to the Watch-house, but he still disliked the Imperial Guard on principle. The Watch took care of their own, both in protecting and punishing those who wore the uniform. They didn't like outsiders barging in and taking over.

Brother Tann placed a hand on Beyus' arm, and the investigator startled at his touch. Beyus' face flushed in embarrassment and he became even angrier at his display of nerves in front of the other men. It had the intended effect, though. He did stop yelling.

"Sergeant Flasek," continued the priest. "The messages are from Leyndra Jirau, aren't they?"

"I think they are, yes."

Beyus opened his mouth again to start yelling, but glanced sideways at the priest and held himself in check. Barely.

"And why did you not tell anyone about these messages? Or what you found?"

Flasek licked his lips and prepared to lie directly to the priest.

"I wasn't sure anyone would care about some anonymous messages, so I didn't bother to report them. When I found the bodies, I figured I'd better tell my superior in the Watch. But it was late by the time I was done looking around, so I decided to report the incident this morning."

He turned to the lieutenant.

"It was why I came in early today, sir. I didn't want to make any decision without letting you know first, this time."

He could by the look on Beyus' face that the investigator knew what Flasek was doing. His story was perfect. He really had come in early for his shift—something that watchmen just didn't do. And by bringing up that he had gone off on his own before, the night of the murder of Osho Idaphos, he was acknowledging to his superiors that he had learned his lesson and was trying not to cause further trouble for them.

Brother Tann was considering Flasek's story. When he spoke, Flasek knew he had made a terrible mistake.

"Sergeant, I understand your hesitance to contact the Guard directly. However, now that the truth is out, there is no longer any reason to hold anything back."

Flasek nodded, but said nothing else.

"But there's something I would most like to see," continued the priest. "Please give me these anonymous messages you received."

Flasek's heart dropped into his stomach. He tried to keep the stammer out of his voice as he answered.

"I don't have them with me, uh, sir. I can go get them for you, but it'll take a bit of time."

"I'll go with you," spoke up Beyus. "I think you're lying. You've been in contact with Leyndra Jirau directly—you're trying to help her."

But Flasek was saved, ironically, by the priest.

"Investigator Chamirra, you will accompany me back to the estate. There is further work to be done there, and your presence is required."

He turned back to Flasek.

"You will bring the messages directly to the Temple yourself. Give them to Brother Voziart, no one else. He will be expecting you."

The priest slowly pushed himself to his feet, leaning heavily on the table. Beyus Chamirra stood also and moved out of his way as Brother Tann walked with slow, careful steps to the door of the meeting room. As Beyus opened the door for him, glaring at Flasek with a look of pure rage, the priest paused.

"Do not tarry, Sergeant. I do not wish to come looking for you."

The look in the priest's eyes told Flasek he didn't want Brother Tann to come looking for him, either.

Chapter Thirty

LEYNDRA STOOD IN THE SHADOWS WELL DOWN THE street from the front gates of the Najare estate. She could see the glow of the large bonfires spaced evenly across the grounds, surrounding the mansion and illuminating the estate. A full contingent of Imperial Guard was stationed on the grounds, and they were slowly working their way through the mansion recovering bodies.

Leyndra knew she would no longer find Phiral Najare here. Every room in the mansion, every blade of grass outside, would be examined in detail. She had even seen a few priests entering through the main gates. One could only imagine the rumors that would flood the streets of Ythis by morning.

She turned and walked away from the Najare estate. If Phiral Najare wasn't here, then she knew where he'd likely be waiting for her. She wondered if Tyina knew yet about the changes her lover had undergone.

And then she realized Tyina might not even be alive by now. Somehow, Leyndra didn't think Phiral's new existence would engender much sentimentality in him. He might see Tyina as just another meal.

Leyndra hoped Tyina was still alive. She wanted to kill the woman herself.

Less than 30 minutes later, Leyndra stood outside the wall around the Idaphos estate. Peering over the top of the wall, she saw the grounds were quiet, and no light escaped from the windows of the mansion. A terrible foreboding swept through her. No guards patrolled the grounds, no dogs barked, only a terrible silence hung over the area.

Leyndra realized that not even crickets were chirping in the darkness.

She climbed over the wall and dropped into the shadows on the other side. She knew, even before she approached the mansion, that nothing living waited for her inside. Leyndra didn't bother to hide, but walked out of the shadows and directly across the grounds toward the building.

No one challenged her. No light shone from any window. No movement could be seen.

She reached the front door and tried the handle. It was unlocked and opened easily. As soon as the door opened, the smell of death assaulted her senses. She reeled back, gagging. If Phiral had been waiting for her inside, she would have been defenseless in that moment.

Leyndra moved away from the doors and regained her composure. Another massacre of a noble family and all their servants—this situation kept getting larger and more difficult. The Emperor was going to want answers from the Imperial Guard and the Church. The other noble families were likely to flee the city or turn their estates into heavily armed fortresses until the situation could be resolved.

And time was running out for Leyndra to discover the location of the necromancer. Once he acquired whatever it was he had come to Ythis to find, he would leave the city. The hunt for Leyndra by the Guard would likely continue, even while they and the rest of the city tried to find out who had murdered every person on the two noble estates.

Leyndra's first instinct was to leave the estate immediately. There was nothing left alive in the mansion, and she doubted Phiral was waiting here for her. It was too risky for someone to notice something was wrong and that would summon the Guard in force. No, he was probably hunting her—just as she was hunting him—but he was no longer here.

Morbid curiosity stopped her from leaving. She had a perverse desire to confirm that Tyina was dead. Leyndra didn't know she was capable of hating someone the way she realized she hated Tyina. The woman had destroyed Leyndra's life. Leyndra wanted to know Tyina had gotten what she deserved.

Leyndra breathed deeply of the warm night air and prepared herself for the gruesome ordeal ahead of her. She figured she would check Tyina's rooms first, and then work her way back down if the woman's body wasn't immediately visible.

She didn't draw her weapon—there was no threat here, except perhaps to her own mental state.

She returned to the front door and stopped on the threshold once again. The open doors had let some fresh air into the mansion, and the stench was slightly weaker because of it. It was barely enough to make a difference, but every little bit helped. She stepped inside and looked around.

Leyndra was intimately familiar with this house, the way she had not been in Phiral Najare's home. She made directly for the stairs and proceeded up, trying not to breathe through her nose. By the time she reached the top floor, the fetor had lessened further, which told her there were fewer bodies up here.

She moved directly down the hallway toward Tyina's rooms, but found herself stopping at the door leading to Osho's bedchamber. Her heart gave a lurch and she felt her eyes water. She hadn't come this way when she had been here to question Tyina—this was the first time she had returned to the scene of Osho's death.

Leyndra reached out and put her hand on the doorknob.

What am I doing? she asked herself. *This is pointless.*

Regardless, she turned the knob and opened the door. The small chamber that led into Osho's bedroom proper was exactly as she had last seen it, that dark night. She stepped in and noticed the door to her own room was wide open. She could see the bed and the small chest of drawers that had once held her possessions.

Now she had nothing but what she kept on her person.

Tyina did this to me. I should go make sure she's dead.

But Leyndra turned to the other door and pushed it open. The room was tidy, and the rug on which Osho died had been removed.

Leyndra had expected a worse reaction at seeing the place where she had killed the man she had sworn to protect, but the tears that had threatened to spill a moment before were now gone.

Leyndra felt nothing but anger.

She turned and stalked out of the room, heading for Tyina's door.

When she reached it, Leyndra saw that it had been ripped nearly in half, chunks of heavy, brown wood on the floor in the hallway. She couldn't tell if Phiral had done it on the way in or out. It didn't matter. What mattered was what was on the other side.

She entered the room and the smell told her someone had died in Tyina's bedroom. Leyndra entered, prepared to see her foe beyond the reach of Leyndra's vengeance. But she knew immediately it wasn't Tyina who lay gutted and rotting on the bed. The shreds of a maid's uniform still clung to the cadaver.

Leyndra stepped back out to get away from the smell, but it seemed to have filled her head. She moved over to one of the windows and shoved the wooden shutter open, hoping for a breeze to take the stench away, but the air was completely still. If anything, the smell was getting stronger.

She had had her fill of this place. She turned and strode back to the hallway, but as she reached the broken door a movement on the other side caught her eye. In an instant, without conscious thought, Leyndra drew her blade and dropped into a fighting stance.

Someone was moving slowly toward the door to these chambers, but in the darkness, Leyndra couldn't tell who it was. She readied herself for Phiral Najare to enter. When the door opened, however, her first thought was that this was worse.

The uniform of the Idaphos House Guard was torn open at the front, but the figure shuffling toward her was past caring about the state of his clothing. Rotting entrails hung from his torso, and his eyes were black pits of nothingness. Behind him, Leyndra could make out more figures, filling the hallway, all moving in that same shuffling gait.

And then cold, dead hands grabbed her by one arm and Leyndra turned to see the corpse of the maid from Tyina's bedchamber lunging toward her face with open jaws.

*　　　　*　　　　*

WITH A QUICK TWIST, LEYNDRA AVOIDED THE CLUMSY BITE. She tried to yank her arm out of the corpse's grasp, but the grip was too strong and she only broke free of one fist. She quickly transferred her blade to her free hand and hacked down on the wrist of the dead maid, severing the hand from the cadaver's arm.

Thankfully, the grasping claw fell away, twitching, as the maid stumbled after Leyndra. The guard—along with a number of other dead servants—had filled up the space around the door, preventing Leyndra from escaping in that direction. In moments she would be surrounded and overwhelmed by sheer numbers.

Leyndra reversed direction and slashed her blade across the neck of the maid. The cut almost beheaded the creature, but the sword lodged in its spine and stuck there. Cursing, Leyndra gave it a single yank, but when it didn't budge, she used it to throw the dead woman off balance. That gave her the opening she needed to retreat through the only available entrance—Tyina's bath chamber—and slam the door shut in the faces of the remaining creatures.

She noticed immediately there was no lock on the door, and knew she would not be able to hold it against the strength of the animated cadavers outside. Leyndra quickly glanced around the room and realized that the only furniture large enough to hold them out for any length of time was too far from the door for her to use before they breached the room.

She flung herself away from the door as the creatures fumbled at the knob, and kicked open the shutters over the only window. She knew there were no balconies on this side of the mansion, but a small ledge the width of a few fingers ran the length of the building. She doubted any of the corpses would be able to climb out onto the narrow ledge after her.

The door to the room was shoved roughly open as Leyndra stepped up onto the windowsill. The creatures stumbled forward, pushed by those behind. Leyndra saw the maid, the sword still stuck in her neck, trying to get through the bottleneck at the door. As the first of the dead things focused on her and moved towards the window, Leyndra climbed out onto the ledge that ran the length of the exterior wall.

Clinging to the bricks, she shuffled sideways out of the reach of the grasping hands that reached for her. One false step and she would plummet to her death, and this time there was no balcony railing on which to catch herself.

Leyndra uttered another string of curses. She had come here expecting an encounter with Phiral Najare—had been *looking* for him—and now was stuck on the side of the mansion surrounded by the unquiet dead. She knew if she could reach the ground before being surrounded by the creatures, she could easily outrun them.

But getting down safely would take time, and she had no idea if these corpses could anticipate her likely direction. Not that she had any real choice. She couldn't stay here and be found by the Imperial Guard in the morning, and she certainly couldn't climb back in the window and fight her way down to the foyer.

She began feeling around for other foot- and handholds on the rough stone wall. The tiny ledges were spaced below each ring of windows, which put them too far apart to just lower herself from one to the next. Leyndra would have to climb down, inch by inch. She couldn't lean back far enough to get a good look at the wall, so it would all have to be done by touch.

It took her a good couple of minutes to find suitable grips and she lowered her feet carefully over the tiny ledge. She was forced to drag her boots back and forth against the wall in an attempt to find some place that would allow her to rest her weight long enough to shift her hands to a new position. She felt her grip slipping on her left hand, but she couldn't find anywhere to place her feet.

The ledge was at her waist now. Just before her hand would have slipped off, she let go of both hands in a controlled drop, catching the ledge with her fingers. She hung there for a moment, taking a deep breath. She realized there was no way she would be able to climb the entire distance to the ground—the wall was just not rough enough to provide her with an adequate climbing surface.

Leyndra knew she would have to move fast now if her only other option was going to work. Hanging by her fingers, she began to slide one hand and then the other back toward the window. The dead servants continued to grasp for her, but they couldn't reach down quite far enough to grab her hands.

Leyndra had no intention of climbing back up to that window. Instead, she decided to gamble on the room below. She was grateful the shutters on this window were already open. She didn't know how she would have gotten past them hanging by her fingers.

The top of the window was at her waist, and her legs dangled in the opening. Leyndra took another deep breath and prepared to drop into the room. She straightened her legs and aimed her feet at the windowsill below, and then let go of the ledge.

Leyndra was relying entirely on the quickness of her reflexes, honed by years of training. As she fell, she thrust her arms forward and out to the sides. Her feet hit the windowsill with a crash, and she began to fall backward away from the building. But she was just quick enough to catch the sides of the window frame with her hands and prevent her fall. She pulled herself forward and jumped into the room.

She had re-entered the mansion in a small sitting room. A fireplace filled one wall, with a small loveseat and two expensive chairs facing it. Leyndra didn't recall this room ever being used by Osho, and wondered if Tyina had spent any time in here either. It didn't matter. Leyndra moved to the door and listened.

She could hear no sounds from the hallway on the other side, so she opened the door and peered out. It appeared to be clear of the walking dead. She moved quickly down the hallway to the main staircase, but stopped before stepping out of the shadows.

A grotesque parade of corpses was filing down from the top floor toward the foyer and the front doors. As she watched, one stumbled and rolled down a flight of stairs, knocking over two others. She heard bone crunch, and when the cadaver picked itself up, its head was twisted at an odd angle. It didn't seem to affect the creature, which continued to proceed down.

I definitely can't get out this way. I only hope the servants' stairs are empty.

All at once, the shuffling creatures stopped moving, and the ones on the landing closest to Leyndra turned their heads to look right at where she was hiding. She didn't wait to see what might happen—she bolted back down the hallway toward the back stairs.

As she slammed open the door to the stairwell, she caught a glimpse of the creatures stumbling down the hallway toward her.

Taking the stairs three at a time, Leyndra reached the ground floor without incident. She opened the door to the hallway leading to the kitchen—and an exit from the mansion—and found a dead guard standing in front of her.

Leyndra reacted to his presence before the dead thing realized she was in front of him. She planted a kick in the middle of the creature's chest, and her foot sank into the rotting flesh. But her boot connected with the guard's rib cage, shattering bone and shoving it backwards. It gave her the opening she needed as more corpses entered the hallway from the foyer.

She ran to the exit and thrust it open, bolting out onto the stone walkway that ran around the building. A group of walking dead came around the far corner, and Leyndra ran in the opposite direction. In less than a minute, she was at the outer wall and scaling the stones.

As she reached the top, she looked back at the horde of corpses emerging out onto the front lawn. Like a puppet with its strings cut, the bodies suddenly all collapsed into motionless heaps. Whatever had been animating them left, or was withdrawn, and they became nothing but rotting bodies once more.

Leyndra took a last long look at the mansion. She knew she would never be returning here again. With a heavy heart, she jumped off the wall and walked away.

Chapter Thirty-One

FLASEK WALKED TOWARD THE SMALL BUILDING WHERE he rented a couple of rooms. It wasn't much, and he didn't even really consider it his home. It was just the place he kept some of his possessions, and where he often slept. But as much as Ythis was where Flasek belonged, he really never felt as if he *fit* anywhere in particular. The Watch was where he had ended up, and these rooms were where he stayed when he wasn't working or drinking.

The alley that ran beside and behind his building was narrow and dark. He had walked past it hundreds of times, and no threat had ever emerged from that darkness to threaten him.

Tonight was different.

Some sound, some change in the nature of the gloom in between the buildings, caught his senses and he realized something was wrong just as he stepped in front of the mouth of the alley. He was already reaching for his truncheon as four figures barreled out of the darkness and ploughed into him, driving him to the ground.

Flasek gave up on trying to draw the weapon and jabbed his rigid fingers into the throat of one of his assailants, even while he kicked upwards and felt his boot connect with an unprotected limb. But the figures attacking him were also large, strong, and trained in combat tactics. He felt hands grab his arms and twist, locking his elbow and wrist joints.

The man he had jabbed in the throat dropped a forearm across Flasek's own throat and pushed hard, cutting of the supply of air. He knew he had only seconds before he would black out, and tried even harder to break free. But it was no use—he couldn't overcome his four well-prepared attackers.

As darkness began to swim at the corners of Flasek's vision, the man released the pressure on his throat. He tried to gasp in a lungful of air, but the man drove a knee down into his stomach, knocking what little wind he had out of him. The leather on his chest absorbed some of the impact, but not enough to ignore the weight of the man dropping on him. Flasek felt as if he was drowning, unable to get a breath back into his body.

The men surrounding him pulled him to his feet and twisted his arms behind his back, preventing any movement. He was yanked into the darkness of the alley, away from any witnesses, and pushed along toward the junction where another, wider alley split off and ran in a different direction.

One of the men pulled a knife—a short, sharp thing designed for close-in fighting—and held it in front of Flasek's face. The blade caught a glimmer of moonlight and Flasek knew this little, ugly weapon would end his life tonight. He would be left to bleed out on the floor of this alley, just another victim in a city full of victims.

"So, the Imperial Guard is reduced to using knives in alleys," he said in a low voice. It wasn't a guess—he had known these were soldiers as soon as the fight had started. "Well you can tell your commander I didn't keep Lord Najare's records to myself. Kill me and they'll still find their way into the wrong hands."

The man put the knife against Flasek's throat.

"Tell me where you hid the papers," he demanded. "They're not in your rooms. Where are they?"

"Cut my throat and I won't be telling you anything, will I?"

One of his arms was wrenched in its socket and he bit down on a yell. Much more of that pressure and it would pop. Not that a few dislocated joints would matter once he was dead.

"Okay," he said through gritted teeth. "I gave the papers to someone for safekeeping."

"Who did you give them to? Where are the papers *now*?"

"Leyndra Jirau. I don't know where she is, any more than you lot do."

"I'm right here."

Leyndra's voice cut through the darkness from behind Flasek. An instant later, one of the soldiers holding his arms screamed and let go. Flasek tried to twist away from the knife as it flashed toward his face. He felt the blade nick his ear as it scored a hit, but he was grateful it had managed to miss his eyes.

The other man holding him let go, probably to turn his full attention on Leyndra. The fourth man had drawn a knife as well but couldn't see well enough in the dark alley to aid his fellows.

Flasek's attacker came at him again with the knife, but this time Flasek was ready and unhampered. He stepped into the slash and the blade skittered across the surface of the leather armor on his chest. Before the soldier could recover, Flasek swung a fist at the man's face.

The punch missed, but it forced the soldier back into the path of the other knife-wielding man, preventing them from coming at him together. It also gave Flasek the chance to draw his truncheon. He would have gone for his sword, but it had been taken from him when the men dragged him into the alley. They had ignored the stick, though. That was a mistake.

Flasek wanted to turn and check on Leyndra—he hated having a combat taking place at his back—but he couldn't take his eyes off his own opponent. The soldier came at him again, a quick thrust with the knife this time rather than a wide swing. Flasek was just as quick, and he brought his truncheon down on the other man's hand. Flasek's weapon connected with both blade and knuckles, and the knife dropped to the ground.

The other man facing Flasek called out "Withdraw!" and began to back away. The soldier who had just been disarmed moved into an unarmed fighting stance, prepared to defend against Flasek's expected attack.

"Tell Beyus he's a coward and a traitor!" shouted Flasek. "He doesn't have the guts to come for me himself!"

The two men turned and ran, and he didn't bother chasing them.

He looked over his shoulder to see the other two men fleeing out the end of the alley, one of them practically carrying the other, who seemed to have only one working leg. Leyndra was standing with her back to Flasek, daggers in both of her hands.

"Thanks for the help," he said to her. "I didn't expect to walk out of here alive."

She turned to him, and he couldn't see her face in the darkness. But when she spoke, her voice was full of rage.

"Those men were Imperial Guard. They came here to kill you."

"Yeah."

"And Investigator Chamirra was behind it?"

"Yeah."

Leyndra swore, long and creatively. Flasek was impressed.

"I thought they were supposed to be professionals," she said to him.

"*Everything's* corrupt in this city," he replied. "Some just hide it better than others."

"I came to tell you what happened tonight, but now they know you've been helping me. They'll come in force to arrest you, now. They'll make it official, and then you'll die in the cells under the Fortress."

Flasek shook his head.

"Nah, they can't make it official. They can't afford the scrutiny. The Watch knows Beyus is after me, and the captain would ask too many questions if they arrested me. That's why they tried to take me out like this. It would be just another knifing in an alley."

Leyndra considered his words.

"I don't have the papers. You didn't give them me."

Flasek chuckled.

"I lied. I've got them on me. I figured someone might ransack my room to find them, and I don't have any other hiding place. They would have found the papers if they had searched me."

He chuckled again. "Sloppy work. Beyus would be pissed if he knew. Of course, he'd also be pissed if he knew I'd made a copy earlier today."

Leyndra gave him a questioning look.

"I had to go to a forger I know to get him to fake some messages from you for the Church. I figured I'd get a copy made of the papers while I was there."

"You're full of surprises, Flasek," she said in an admiring tone. "Don't you think they'll try to kill you again?"

"Yeah, they'll try again. But I'm not the kind of man to run and hide. No, tomorrow I'm going to have a private little meeting with Beyus Chamirra. It's a talk that's long overdue."

*   *   *

LEYNDRA, HAVING TOLD FLASEK ABOUT HER ENCOUNTER WITH the walking dead at the Idaphos estate, decided to pay another visit this evening. One of Jeyrra's contacts had provided information on where some of the hired men from the caravan could be found. Leyndra had questions for them which needed answers.

The Rolling Keg tavern was near the Wolf's Den and, rumor had it, was owned by the Wolf himself. It was a place to meet professionals, hard men and women who had earned reputations as the best at what they did. The patrons of the Rolling Keg were discreet, and understood the value of honest dealings with their clients, regardless of the nature of the services they offered.

Leyndra knew she was taking a huge risk entering this establishment. The bounty on her head was incentive for anyone who recognized her to try to capture her, kill her, or report her location to the Imperial Guard. She knew there was a chance that, professional or not, at least one or more of the patrons here tonight would decide the money was worth whatever honor they might lose.

However, at this very late hour, she figured the tavern would be mostly empty. She also felt she didn't have much choice. This was the only place she knew of—besides the Wolf's Den itself—that was considered neutral territory by the criminal element of Ythis. If she was going to make contact with the swordsman Vaysarr, the Rolling Keg was her best chance to do safely.

Regardless, Leyndra drew her hood up over her head, keeping her face in shadows. She had been given a description of Vaysarr and figured she would recognize him when she saw him.

Leyndra pulled the door open and stepped into the dimly lit

main room of the tavern. She smelled the sawdust spread on the floor, mixed with the scent of wine. The tavern was clean, tables spread across the main room with a good distance separating them. A man on a stool in one corner played a melody on a short stringed instrument unfamiliar to Leyndra, the sound helping to mask the low conversations taking place among the patrons.

She saw only six customers, two pairs and two lone individuals. She had guessed correctly that the Rolling Keg wouldn't be too busy this late at night. The bartender looked up, took in her cloaked and hooded appearance, and waved her over to the bar.

He leaned in as she stepped forward, and spoke in a low voice.

"You here for someone in particular, or just shopping around?"

Leyndra saw he didn't try to peer at her shadowed face, but kept his eyes focused on her shoulder. She appreciated his discretion and knew it was one of the reasons the Rolling Keg was a successful place where people understood they could conduct business with a reasonable expectation of privacy.

"I'm here to see Vaysarr," she replied, gesturing toward her quarry, one of the men seated at a table by himself.

The bartender nodded.

"Drink?"

"Wine, please. Whatever's open."

He nodded again and quickly poured her a cup. She handed him a few coins and took her drink in hand. Turning to the table where Vaysarr sat, she steeled herself for the discussion she expected to take place. Getting information from this man wasn't going to be easy.

The swordsman himself was tall and thin, with long blond hair in a braid down his back. His face was narrow and not unattractive, with a strong chin and high cheekbones. He kept his expression neutral as Leyndra approached his table. She couldn't see him tense up, but noted that one of his hands was hidden beneath the table. She wondered if a small crossbow was aimed at her legs.

"Vaysarr," she said in a low voice as she reached the table. "I would like to discuss a business arrangement with you, if you have a few moments."

He gestured for her to sit across from him with his visible hand, but said nothing. Leyndra put the cup of wine on the table in front of her, and placed both hands on the table where he could see them. She could tell he was sizing her up, evaluating her as both a potential threat and a potential customer.

"I'm not an assassin," he said as she opened her mouth to speak. His voice was low and melodic—an unusual sound from someone in his line of work.

Leyndra was confused.

"I'm sorry, I don't—"

"I don't just kill for money. If that's why you're here—if someone has wronged you and you want blood—then it's best you just leave now. You won't find what you're looking for in this place."

"That—that's not why I'm here."

Leyndra was thrown off balance by his remarks and found herself trying to regain her footing. He watched her and nodded for her to proceed. She had to be careful—it would be easy for her to say the wrong thing and cause him to leave. She needed to explain how she knew about the expedition, and what was going to happen.

"There is a trip, an expedition, leaving Ythis soon. The person who arranged this trip has not been discrete. Fortunately, I have taken steps to ensure the details do not become widely known."

He did not outwardly appear to react to her words, but she was sure he was now listening intently.

"I believe you may be aware of this trip. I believe you were not given all the details—details which might change your intentions and any agreement you may have entered into."

Vaysarr leaned forward and rested one hand on the table. His other remained hidden.

"Even if I knew what you were talking about, I'd never tell you a thing," he said, his voice low and pitched only for her ears. "An agreement with me is binding. If someone pays me for a service, that's between that person and me."

A thought came to Leyndra, one that was unexpected and sudden, and she wondered if she would be able to truly do it.

"Then let me give you some information, Vaysarr, and we'll leave it at that. Lord Najare wrote down many details about this expedition, including your name and the names of a few of your fellows. He left this record where it could be found—"

"If you're threatening me," he interrupted, scowling at her, "trying to extort money or services from me, then you've made a deadly mis—"

"Don't be a fool," she interrupted back. "You were betrayed, and it wasn't me who did it. Now I'm offering you information as favor, not as a threat. You can choose to repay my favor, or you can ignore it. It makes no difference to me what you do."

"And you're doing this out of the goodness of your heart, are you?"

"No, I'm doing this because Phiral Najare is my enemy, and I'm going to destroy him. He tried to make me his victim, and he failed. Now I'm making sure he doesn't do the same to anyone else. You were incidental to my goals, though now I realize we may be able to help each other. Assuming you're agreeable."

"What if I'm not agreeable?"

She sighed and shrugged her shoulders at him.

"Then I'll leave and find some other way to accomplish my task. You'll get no trouble from me, but the reality is that your patron won't be around to pay you, and the expedition won't happen."

Vaysarr sat there for a moment, contemplating her words. Finally, he sat back, visibly relaxing.

"Then what are you looking for here? What do you want from me?"

Leyndra hadn't come into the Rolling Keg with this in mind, but now she knew it was the right decision. It was only a matter of getting Vaysarr and his fellow hired blades to agree.

"I want you to stick to your agreement, with one change. You won't be working for Phiral Najare—you'll be working for me. I'm going to lead the expedition."

Her words didn't appear to surprise Vaysarr, and when he spoke, it was to address his only concern.

"And the rest of my payment?"

Leyndra didn't know how she would get the rest of the money

from Phiral and Tyina, but she knew she'd have to if she wanted this to work.

"I'll make sure you get your money, as outlined in your original agreement with Lord Najare."

Vaysarr paused, and then nodded at her.

"Whatever is going on between you and Lord Najare is none of my business. But I'll keep to the agreement if you want to take over his part of it. And I'm sure the rest of my colleagues will as well. A guaranteed payment is better than nothing."

Leyndra stood up.

"Thank you for being a professional. I--"

"You took a real risk coming in here, you know," he said, interrupting her again. It was his admission that he knew who she was. She forced herself to remain calm.

"Yes, well, I was counting on your reputation and the reputation of this place."

"You got lucky," he replied. "Not everyone here has the same sense of pride that I do. Reputation or not, some of the men you'd meet here would have tried to collect that price on your head, and never mind the consequences."

Leyndra smiled at him.

"Then you got lucky, too. Because those men you're talking about? They'd now be dead."

She turned her back on a grinning Vaysarr and left the tavern.

Chapter Thirty-Two

JEYRRA STOPPED OUTSIDE THE DOOR AND LISTENED. SHE could hear Morit speaking quietly to the children, and she hesitated. She felt as if she was intruding whenever she needed to speak to Morit, but some things had to be done.

She knocked softly on the door and he bid her to enter. Opening the door, the first thing she saw was Morit's daughter sitting on the floor facing the narrow window. The girl's straw-colored hair was disheveled and her face was pale, her eyes round and vacant. Jeyrra doubted the child would ever recover from the violent death of her mother.

Jeyrra realized Morit was watching her, not bothering to hide his dislike. While he blamed Leyndra directly for Hathi's death, he also felt Jeyrra was partly responsible for the sequence of events that had led to such an occurrence. If she was being honest with herself, Jeyrra had to admit she didn't really care what Morit thought of her.

The truth was that Jeyrra found Morit to be a self-absorbed coward. She figured his anger at Leyndra was based in part on him being stuck with two children, children he didn't particularly want to care for directly. Morit had relied on Hathi to keep the family healthy and happy, and now he had to face his responsibilities directly. Jeyrra pitied the children.

"What do you want?" he asked her, his voice flat. His son lay on the floor beside him, sleeping peacefully. Morit had one hand on the boy's shoulder to comfort him—they couldn't afford to have the child wake up screaming again in case the wrong people heard the noise.

"We'll have to leave as soon as Leyndra comes back—move to

another building."

Morit looked at her and said nothing. Jeyrra didn't like the way he stared, and idly wondered if he had become unhinged by what had happened to Hathi.

No, he's just full of rage, she thought. *Not that it will do him any good.*

"I'll tell you when she's back, but we won't have much time."

Jeyrra turned to leave when Morit spoke again.

"Do you think it makes a difference?"

The raw pain in his voice was difficult to hear. Jeyrra didn't want to feel sorry for Morit. She didn't like him, and she wanted to keep it that way. But she turned back to look at him and saw the tears silently running down his cheeks.

"Do I think *what* makes a difference?" she asked in as soft a voice as she could manage.

"Moving around like this—do you think it keeps you safe? They found you before, they'll find you again. It won't matter where you go or how often you change where you stay. Either the Church will come, or the creatures to who m-murdered—"

He stopped and swallowed back a sob.

"We have to try," she answered. "If we stay here, they'll find us for sure. Since Leyndra killed that priest, they haven't caught up with us again. It takes them time to track us down."

Jeyrra saw Morit's gaze harden when she said Leyndra's name. Even though she was protecting Morit and keeping him and his children safe, he wasn't going to forgive his sister for what he saw as her fault. Jeyrra understood he was grieving, but his children need-ed him to have a clear head if they were going to survive this ordeal.

"And we're supposed to do this forever? Hide in one abandoned building after another? Eat only the scraps that you're able to scrounge up for us a couple of times a day? Live in fear that any minute we could all be torn apart by one of those...things?"

Jeyrra felt her anger rising. She knew it would only make things worse if she fought with Morit, but she had been living on the edge just as long as he had.

"Leyndra will take care of it. Do you think she's out there drinking and having fun? No, she's doing whatever she can to end this, to make it okay for us to go back to our lives."

Morit barked a laugh and his son gave a low moan in his sleep. Morit looked down at the child and there was no tenderness in his expression. Jeyrra could see by his face that he saw only a burden in that small form. He returned his gaze to Jeyrra.

"You're a fool. Leyndra doesn't care about anyone but herself. Oh, she enjoys being in charge, ordering others around, taking what she calls *responsibility* for everyone else. But Leyndra really just looks out for Leyndra. If you're lucky, she won't get you killed. Don't expect anything more than that."

"Morit, if it wasn't for your sister—and *me*—you'd have died long ago. We took care of you when you were just a rotten little kid, and we're still taking care of you now that you're a rotten adult. You've been jealous of Leyndra all your life—"

"Shut up!" he yelled. "I'm *not* jealous of Leyndra!"

His son woke and immediately began to cry. Morit glared daggers at Jeyrra and then tended to his son. He had no skill dealing with his children and it took him several minutes to quiet the child. Jeyrra wanted to leave him to it, but she couldn't just walk away. If they were going to protect Morit and his family, if he was going to hide with them for however long it took, then Jeyrra had to make sure he would cooperate.

Jeyrra watched Morit's daughter. The girl didn't react to the sound of her brother crying, but just continued to stare off into space. She hadn't said a word since Hathi was killed.

Finally, Morit turned back to Jeyrra.

"Why are you still here?"

"Because I'm not done with you yet. You blame Leyndra for everything—including your parents' death. That's not fair to her. She's done everything to take care of you, protect you, and you hate her for it."

Morit opened his mouth but no words came out. He clenched his teeth and forced himself to take a breath before speaking again.

"You don't even know how wrong you are. I have never blamed Leyndra for the death of my parents. I *do* blame her for controlling me from the moment she found out we were orphans. She always thought she knew what was best, even when we were both kids. *She* made the choice for us to live like we did, and I was never given a say in anything. And then, after limiting me for so long, she abandoned me for the Guild. Left me on my own for the first time, after spending years making sure I wouldn't be ready for it."

He paused for breath and Jeyrra tried to interject, but he cut her off.

"And then she kills a nobleman and drags me and my family into her problems. Hathi is dead because of Leyndra, you can't deny that. I had finally found a life of my own, and she ruined it. And now she's controlling me again. I don't want to be here with her, or you. I want to go home, but I can't because I'll probably be killed. And I'm right back to having her make my decisions for me."

"Do you really think you'd be better off on your own?"

He looked down at his two children.

"I'm not 'on my own,' am I? And whatever happens to me, wherever I end up when this is over—assuming I'm still alive—will be Leyndra's choice, not mine. And if I make my own decision, if I leave, then I probably die. So, I'm right back to being a child, under the control of my big sister."

He sat there in silence, and Jeyrra couldn't think of anything else to say. She knew now that he would follow them, do what they needed him to do, because he had given up his own free will so that he could continue to blame Leyndra. As she turned to leave the room, he spoke up once more.

"And you know what's funny? That you think *you're* in control of your fate. You're exactly where I am, only I *know* it."

Jeyrra wanted to turn back, pick him up, and slam her fist into his face. Instead, she forced herself to walk away.

* * *

SHE HAD ALMOST MISSED HIM. LOOKED AT ANOTHER WAY, he had almost caught *her.*

Leyndra had left the Rolling Keg and immediately ducked into a dark alley in case anyone chose to follow her. She had quickly climbed up onto the roof of a small shop and scanned the streets around her for any signs of pursuit. After a few minutes, it was clear that no one was waiting for her to leave the tavern, and she had turned away from the street to return to the alley.

But something had caught her eye, some movement in the shadows across the street at just that moment, and she glanced back over her shoulder.

Phiral Najare walked out of the shadows, across the street, and up to the entrance to the Rolling Keg.

Her pulse pounded in her ears as she ducked down to peer over the edge of the roof. She couldn't see him clearly on the poorly lit street, but it seemed to her that he moved with an unnatural grace. He pulled open the door to the tavern and entered.

Leyndra wasn't sure what to do. No doubt Phiral had come here to finalize the plans for the expedition. Perhaps he was making the final payment to Vaysarr for his services. If that was the case, then Leyndra wouldn't have to worry about somehow getting the money from him and Tyina.

On the other hand, Leyndra didn't know if Vaysarr might tell Phiral about her visit. She didn't think he would do so, but she wasn't used to dealing with the criminal underworld. She didn't know the rules. Vaysarr seemed like he wouldn't say anything, but she had no way to know for sure.

More important than the expedition was Phiral's presence. She had been hunting him for the last couple of nights and had made no progress. As much as she wanted to destroy him, she had to track him back to his master. It was no use killing Phiral if the necromancer managed to escape.

Leyndra waited on the rooftop for perhaps a quarter of an hour before Phiral emerged from the tavern. He stopped just outside the door and looked around, sniffing the air. Leyndra held her own breath and remained motionless, hoping he wouldn't detect her on the roof of the very next building. He stopped sniffing and just stood for a moment, and then turned and moved toward the same alley she had entered when she left the Rolling Keg.

Had he detected her presence? Was he coming for her? She expected to hear his claws against the rough wall of the store as he hauled himself up to the roof, but no sound came from the alley.

She waited another half minute. If he hadn't detected her—if he had just been using the alley to go back in the direction of his master—she might already have lost him. But if he was still close, listening, she would give herself away if she checked.

Either way, she was taking a risk, but she wasn't one to stay still and let events happen *to* her. She pulled herself to her feet and quietly approached the edge of the roof facing the alley. A quick glance told her the alley was empty. Phiral wasn't waiting for her, but had moved on.

She sprinted across the roof and leapt from one to the next, hoping she could keep her footing and not make too much noise. Another quick glance and she realized he had gotten far ahead of her. If she had lost him, she might not get another chance before the necromancer was ready to leave the city.

Leyndra reached the next street over and scanned the area for any signs of movement. She caught a glimpse of a figure in the shadows between two buildings on the next block. There was no way she could leap across the street, so she lowered herself down over the edge of the roof and dropped to the street.

It occurred to her that Phiral might be leading her into an ambush. Leyndra's only chance to beat him in a fight would come if she had full freedom of movement and a chance to prepare her attack. If he caught her by surprise, she would most likely die at his hand.

It was chance she had to take. She couldn't let this opportunity go, no matter the risk to herself. Everything hinged on her finding out where the necromancer was hiding.

Her pursuit of Phiral Najare became, over the next two hours, a terrifying game of cat and mouse. Even though she was the cat, she knew how quickly the tables would turn if he noticed her. Leyndra had to keep on the fine line of staying far enough away that he didn't know she was following him, but close enough that she didn't lose him. It was chase that could end, at any moment, in her death.

On more than one occasion, Leyndra lost sight of her quarry and had to force herself to stay calm and focus on picking up his trail again. In each instance, she had quickly scaled a wall to the rooftop of a building and discovered him proceeding down a path she had overlooked.

At other times, she found the going easy, and she began to suspect he knew she was behind her. It was maddening, not knowing if she was the hunter or the prey.

When she finally realized his destination, she almost laughed out loud. A cemetery, even the Forgotten City, was too obvious a place for the necromancer to be hiding. Phiral had been playing with her after all. He was going to duck behind a tombstone and attack her as she passed. There would be no witnesses to their fight, no one to interfere.

Leyndra was both disappointed and yet excited. She still was not completely sure she could kill Phiral in his new form. On the other hand, he had so much to pay for, and she could feel the power of her gifts boiling beneath her skin. She might die tonight, but she didn't think it would work out that way.

Perhaps she could get Phiral to give away a clue before she destroyed him. Then again, this fight would be difficult enough without being distracted by a secondary goal. No, she had failed in her attempt to find the necromancer, and would have to settle for Phiral Najare. She wasn't terribly disappointed. She needed this fight.

But as she followed him into the cemetery, scaling the stone walls that were supposed to keep out unwanted visitors, she saw that he didn't attempt to hide from her. She was able to follow him deep onto the grounds before he stopped at the door to an ornate mausoleum. He reached out and pulled the heavy stone slab to one side, and then entered and dragged the door back into place.

Leyndra approached close enough to determine the name on the family mausoleum. Could this really be it? Could the necromancer be hiding in Ythis' largest cemetery? It seemed so obvious, and yet she knew that it was still a great hiding place. The crypts scattered across the grounds provided dozens of locations where the necromancer might make his lair, surrounded by the raw materials he used in his dark arts.

This was both a well-hidden, and rather defensible location.

Leyndra couldn't quite believe she had done it. Once she gave the location to Xeylien, the necromancer would no longer be a threat. Leyndra could focus on destroying Phiral Najare, and then leave the city.

She smiled at the mausoleum before turning back and heading for the Warrens.

Chapter Thirty-Three

SEATED ON THE FLOOR, MORIT COULD SEE A SMALL PATCH of sky through the narrow window that faced the wall of another building an arm's length away. It was beginning to shift from black to gray, and he felt grit under his eyelids as he leaned against the rough wooden wall of the small room he shared with his children.

He looked at his daughter, who had eventually fallen asleep. She had been sitting up as her eyes closed, and he had helped her lie down and get as comfortable as possible on the floor. She still hadn't spoken since Hathi's death, and he wasn't sure if that was a blessing or a curse. Maybe retreating into her own mind was keeping her from the terror of the real world.

Morit's son continued to sleep, the occasional whimper coming from him. The boy was aware of his surroundings, and so very needy. Morit wasn't used to dealing with that—it was something Hathi had always handled. He didn't know what to do with the boy.

He was left to care for children he hadn't truly wanted. They were something he had given to Hathi to make her happy, but now he was forced to take care of them.

If it was just up to him, he would leave them at an orphanage and walk away. He told himself they would be safer there than with him—nothing would hunt them the way whatever it was that had killed Hathi was no doubt still looking for Leyndra and whoever was with her.

A tiny voice in his head admitted that he believed he would be better off without them as well. He didn't have a problem with that—it was Leyndra who would never let him do it. She would stop him, force him to keep the children close, and probably end up watching them die.

As if summoned by his thoughts, he heard Leyndra's voice as she returned. He cursed silently. This meant they would have to leave this room soon and find someplace new to hide. They would expect him to wake his children, deal with their cries, and settle them down again in whatever pit they found next. He ground the heels of his hands into his eyes.

He was so tired, but sleep wouldn't come. Morit wasn't sure how much longer he could go on like this.

The door to the room opened and Jeyrra stepped in. She saw the sleeping children and motioned for him to come out of the room.

"What now?" he whispered at her.

"Leyndra needs to talk to us," she replied in a low voice. She retreated back into the hallway.

Morit pushed himself to his feet, his legs aching from the hours spent sitting on the hard floor. He shuffled over to the door and looked into the hallway, seeing Leyndra standing just inside the door of the other room. Clenching his fists, he forced himself to walk over to her.

Jeyrra and Zheemeng were already in the room. When he joined them, Leyndra spoke.

"Okay, the situation is about to change. I've found the necromancer."

Morit felt the blood drain from his face.

"Necromancer? That's what killed Hathi, a *necromancer*?"

"In a manner of speaking, Morit, and please keep your voice down. I didn't tell you because there was no reason to make you worry even more than you already were. But as I said, we're almost out of this."

Morit looked back and forth between Leyndra and Jeyrra. At least the other woman had the good sense to look concerned.

"What are we going to do?" Jeyrra asked.

"Well, I'm going to be honest with you. There's a strong possibility I may not survive the final confrontation. The sorceress intends to deal with the necromancer, but I don't believe for a second that Xeylien is concerned about my wellbeing. Being near them when they fight isn't exactly safe."

Morit felt lost. This was all too much for him to deal with. He stood and watched the others discuss the situation.

"Do you really need to be there?" asked Jeyrra.

"That's what Xeylien told me. I think I need to summon her once I get near the necromancer. And besides, that's where Phiral Najare will be, and he's *my* problem."

"Okay," replied Zheemeng. "But as Jeyrra asked, what are *we* going to be doing?"

"You're going to wait for me to return."

"By the Abyss I will!" said Jeyrra. "If you think I'm going to sit here and do nothing while you fight for your life, you're mad!"

"Jeyrra, I need someone to take care of Morit and the children. Once Phiral and the necromancer are destroyed, I'm going to be leaving Ythis. I'm taking over Phiral's expedition. I'm going to find whatever it was he was searching for, so it can't fall into the wrong hands."

Morit had heard enough.

"And you'll just leave us to deal with the consequences of your actions, is that it? You can run away, but the Church and the Imperial Guard will still be looking for us. How long do you think we can stay hidden, Leyndra?"

His sister glared at him, and he was glad he had made her angry.

"You won't be staying in Ythis either, Morit. The Wolf's people will smuggle you and the children out of the city. Jeyrra knows who to trust."

Leyndra turned to her friend.

"I need you to take Morit to the Wolf and make sure he gets out safely. You should leave Ythis too, Jeyrra. Morit is right about the fact the Church and Imperial Guard will keep hunting us."

Jeyrra snorted.

"And where, exactly, am I supposed to go?"

"I've got enough money to pay the Wolf to get you and Zheemeng out of Ythis as well. There are other cities both in and outside the

Empire. You'll be running another gang within a year."

"What about my boys here in Ythis? What am I supposed to do about them?"

Leyndra hesitated, and Morit knew she hadn't given a thought to the rest of Jeyrra's gang. They had been hiding out across the city, too. There was no way she would leave them, and no way they would all be able to escape Ythis together.

"I'm sorry, Jeyrra, but that's the best I can do. Get the word out to them to leave the city, to meet you in some village between here and wherever you're going, and take them with you. But if you stay, you'll probably die."

"What about me?" asked Zheemeng.

"I figured you would go with Jeyrra—"

"No, I'm asking what my part is in this final battle. I'm not just the guy who keeps all of you healthy."

Morit saw the expression on Leyndra's face as she looked at Zheemeng. He realized there was something going on between them. Morit couldn't help but grimace. They were all living in fear for their lives, and Leyndra was taking a lover.

"I need you to come with me, Zheemeng, but you cannot fight."

Zheemeng bristled at her words.

"What do you mean? I'm as good with a blade as any man you know."

"No, it's not that. I need you stay back and watch, because if I die, someone needs to know what happened. You can get word to Jeyrra and the rest that I didn't survive."

"*I'll* come and watch," said Jeyrra.

"No, if you come, you'll end up jumping into the fight. I love you Jeyrra, but you have no restraint. Zheemeng, I need you to do this, and I need to know you'll stay safe. If you try to save me and get killed too, then you'll have failed. I need you to be a witness, and nothing else."

Morit watched Zheemeng as he considered her request. He was obviously not happy about it. Morit could tell he was hurt by Leyndra's request to possibly watch her die and do nothing.

Grimly, Zheemeng said "Fine, I'll do what you want," and pushed past them and left the room.

Leyndra looked after him with a longing expression, but then shook her head and got back to business.

"We need to leave here and find a new place to stay right now. The last thing we need is a fight today. One way or another, this ends tonight."

*   *   *

THIS TIME, WHEN LEYNDRA REACHED THE SHORT STREET where the Tower of Threads stood, she did not hesitate. Striding up to the door, she reached out to knock but the portal opened in front of her. She stepped across the threshold and looked around.

Instead of the vast hollow interior of the tower, the door had opened into a small room with walls, floor, and ceiling of black obsidian. A short pedestal of dark gray stone stood in the center of the chamber, a fat candle burning on its top. A lone figure, tall and thin, stood on the opposite side of the pedestal, and despite the candle being directly in front of it, the figure's face remained in shadows.

Leyndra had not expected this and faltered. The door swung closed behind her with a thud. Had she walked into some kind of trap?

As if reading her thoughts, the figure spoke.

"Xeylien is my master. You may speak to me, Leyndra Jirau, and I will deal with your situation."

So, this was Xeylien's apprentice. Leyndra remembered Jeyrra's description of him, how she had never managed to see his face directly during their encounter. And she remembered how he had let his demon toy with her friends before speaking to Jeyrra.

"Is there a reason your master has sent you instead of seeing me herself?"

The figure paused, and when he spoke, she could hear the irritation in his voice.

"Do not overestimate your importance, Leyndra Jirau. My master does not have time for trivialities, and neither do I. Tell me what brings you to the Tower, and be direct in your answer."

Leyndra was about to snap back at him, but held her tongue. She needed the sorcerer's help if she was going to successfully defeat Phiral Najare and his necromantic master, and also help her friends deal with the aftermath of this series of events.

"I've discovered where the necromancer is hiding in the city. Xeylien wanted me to return when I found him. But time is running out. Once he gets whatever he's waiting for, he'll leave the city and your master's chance to confront him will disappear."

The apprentice considered her words.

"Where is the necromancer?"

"He's hiding out in a mausoleum in the Forgotten City. His servant, Phiral Najare, led me to him. I can take Xeylien to the specific crypt. I assume she only wants the necromancer, but that's fine. I want to kill Phiral myself."

"Xeylien will not accompany you to face the necromancer."

It took a few seconds for Leyndra to realize what the apprentice had just said.

"What do you mean? She told me she wanted to destroy the necromancer a week ago when I was here. Why would she not come now?"

"My master will destroy the necromancer. But if she comes by normal means, he will sense her long before she gets close. He has ways to escape that cannot be easily countered."

This was a shock to Leyndra. She had assumed Xeylien was so much more powerful than the necromancer, and it was simply a matter of finding him. She thought the actual battle would have been a foregone conclusion.

"Then how can she catch him? Why did she want to know where he was if she can't get near him?"

Another hesitation by the apprentice, and this time she could hear a smile in his voice when he spoke.

He's enjoying this, she thought. *This one likes to spread fear and uncertainty in his wake.*

"That is why my master sought you out. You will face the necromancer, and you will bring Xeylien into the battle at the right moment. But the creature of death must not know, must not suspect, what you intend. Otherwise, he will flee and all will be for naught."

"You want *me* to fight the necromancer? Is that even possible? Besides, how am I possibly going to bring Xeylien into the battle if she's not there?"

"You will *summon* her."

Leyndra looked at his shadowed face, unable to see any features or even the glint of the candlelight in his eyes. She was unable to imagine what he meant by her 'summoning' Xeylien.

"I don't have any ability to summon anyone or anything. I can fight, sure, though I don't know what good my sword is going to be against something that has mastery over death. But how do you expect me to summon your master into a crypt in the middle of the Forgotten City?"

"My master has made arrangements. A sigil will be placed on your flesh, one that ties you to her. When the time is right, you will activate the sigil, and Xeylien will be brought into your presence."

Leyndra's blood went cold. The last thing she wanted was to be permanently linked to any member of the Five. This was completely outside of anything she had expected.

Of course the sorcerer wants to put her mark on you. Then you'll become her pawn, to use as she sees fit.

"With all due respect, I didn't agree to take on Xeylien's mark. I don't intend to remain in Ythis once the necromancer is dead. Perhaps we can find another way to—"

"Xeylien has decided how you will serve her, and you would be well advised to heed her instructions. Your survival thus far—against the Imperial Guard, against the Church, against the necromancer's creature—has been as much by chance as it has been by skill. But your time is running out."

Leyndra shook her head.

"What does that mean?"

"If you wish to live to see the necromancer defeated before you die, you will do as you are bidden. Otherwise, you will fall, and your friends will fall along with you."

Leyndra considered the apprentice's words. She was responsible for the danger in which her friends found themselves. She was responsible for Morit and his children. If she submitted to the sorcerer's mark, then she would be saving them from continued danger at the hands of their enemies.

Leyndra had embraced her responsibilities all her life. She was always ready to make the sacrifice for everyone else, always ready to put herself last. Her friends needed her to end this horrific ordeal, no matter the cost to her own self.

But was this the only way? If she submitted to the sorcerer's demand, who knew what she might be ordered to do in the future? She wasn't ready to become a plaything for one of the Five, not if there was any reasonable alternative.

She looked up at the shadowed face and said "No."

"You misunderstand," said the apprentice. "There is no element of choice here. It was not a request."

"And I'm sure you could just kill me, or have your demon do it for you. I'm sure you could force me to get this mark placed on me. But I will fight you every step of the way. I will do everything in my power to defy you and your master. I will ensure that the cost is so high, you will regret forcing me to do anything."

The sorcerer's apprentice stood there, saying nothing, letting Leyndra's anger spill out without responding.

"I came here to help you destroy the necromancer because it's something you seem to want as much as I do. But I will not be anyone's tool, to be used and then tossed aside. If the only way to get Xeylien's help is to submit to her mark, then I'll find a way to destroy the necromancer *without* her help. I'm either your ally, or your enemy. I'm not your servant."

Leyndra managed to reign in her anger, but she knew it was probably too late. She expected the apprentice, or his demon, to attack her and force her to submit. With a sudden flash of heat across her skin, her Warden gifts opened up to her and she felt the flow of *virtus* within her. She didn't know if she could fight off a demon, but anything attacking her now would pay a terrible price.

"You are... unsuitable."

Leyndra was wary, not knowing what he meant by those words.

"There are many who would sacrifice much to serve Xeylien directly, many who understand real power."

"I already have power," she replied.

"A pittance compared to what you might gain. But you will not submit to us because you have deluded yourself into believing you can make a difference on your own. Our kind of power comes with a price, one that must be paid willingly. Your power comes freely, and is all the weaker for it."

Leyndra let him have his insults. She was sure she didn't want to escalate this into a real confrontation.

"You may leave. We will find another way, one with a better chance of success. You will die at the hands of the necromancer and all your struggles will have been for naught."

The door behind Leyndra swung open. She glanced over her shoulder to make sure it was clear, and backed away from the apprentice.

"Do not return to the Tower again," he told her.

She stepped out across the threshold and found herself staring at a blank wall where the doorway had been a second before.

There was no help coming from Xeylien. Leyndra would have to face the necromancer alone.

And she had no idea how she could possibly defeat him.

Chapter Thirty-Four

PHIRAL STEPPED BACK AND ADMIRED HIS HANDIWORK. HE was sure Leyndra was hiding out somewhere in the Warrens, and expected news of this to reach her in a matter of a few hours at most. He looked around at the few figures still visible in the square.

He stood at the Warren's Heart, a junction where multiple streets and alleys converged, leaving the most open space in the entire neighborhood. This area was usually busy with a great deal of foot traffic, but when Phiral had unwrapped his grisly prize, most of the onlookers had rapidly found somewhere else to be.

He smiled, his teeth aching as they slid out of his blackened gums. Loping off into the darkness of a nearby alley, he again reveled in the strength coursing through his body.

He wanted to kill again, but he had other matters that required his attention first. The agony of two nights ago still haunted his thoughts, though there was little permanent damage done to his physical form. He knew Eothep could have destroyed him the same way he had eliminated Tyina, and Phiral was not eager to disappoint his master again.

Earlier today, word had come that his shipment had finally reached Ythis. Now, Phiral would collect the item and return to the necromancer. With everything in place, they would depart the city tomorrow at dusk with the caravan he had paid for out of Tyina's riches. By the time any curious parties figured out what had happened, the expedition would be well out of reach of the city's inhabitants.

In the farthest reaches of the Bleak Wastes, Eothep would find the legendary object he sought. And when they returned to Ythis, it would be at the head of an army of the dead. Eothep's dark power would tear down the Five, the Church, and the Emperor himself.

Phiral shuddered in anticipation of that day—the day of reckoning when death would flow through the streets, swelling in power as the living were consumed in an orgy of blood and darkness.

It wasn't long before Phiral reached the docks. He kept to the shadows, creeping between the warehouses and the low row of shops that catered to the sea-traders. Scaling a wall like some grotesque lizard, he gained the roof of a warehouse and scanned the area with eyes that saw through darkness as if it was mid-day.

There was no sign of Leyndra, or Guard soldiers, or anyone who might want to interfere in tonight's business. Still, Phiral forced himself to go slow and take extra care. It would not do to get so close to the item only to lose it through his own impatience. This was the only reason Eothep had come to Ythis—to acquire this last piece of the puzzle that would show him the way to nearly infinite power.

He spotted the broken sign over the door to the tavern where he would meet his contact. Keeping a tight rein on his impulses, he crawled down the wall back to ground level and stepped out of the shadows to approach the door.

Pushing it open, he stepped into a dingy tavern that smelled of dampness and mold. He flung the door shut behind him as he surveyed the room. The tavern was small, only a handful of tables scattered around and one long bench along the front wall, facing the bar. Four drunkards sat at the nearest table, only one still conscious and searching the pockets of his oblivious companions. A lone figure sat at a table to one side, facing the door.

The bartender eyed Phiral suspiciously, but Phiral ignored him. He had more important things to occupy his attention now.

Phiral walked to the table and grabbed a chair. He sat down and leaned forward, staring intently at the woman who sat across from him. Spreading his arms, he smiled and said, "I'm here."

The woman scowled at him.

"Is that your idea of discrete? I thought you didn't want attention."

Her voice had a slight accent, a mixture of the Southlands and something more exotic. Phiral found her words and expression amusing. He chuckled softly.

"I guess you're right, captain. I'm just very, very happy to see you at last."

She narrowed her eyes at him, and he knew she was wondering what had happened since the last time they had met, two months ago. He was obviously a changed man, though she had no idea *how* changed.

"You have it with you?"

She nodded once and then asked the expected question. "You have the money?"

He smiled again. "Of course. I take it you had few difficulties on your journey. The directions from my...employer...seemed extensive."

The captain was obviously uncomfortable with this conversation. She wanted to get paid and be gone from here as quickly as possible. Phiral knew she had figured out that what she was bringing into the city would garner attention from the worst possible quarters. Few people had the guts to conduct this kind of business under the noses of the Five. Those who did still didn't want to waste time with small talk.

"I lost some of my men to creatures living in the ruins. It was...," she trailed off, and shuddered. "Your payment will go some way towards making sure the rest of them don't jump ship in Ythis."

"Yes, of course. Let me see it."

Phiral licked his lips and saw her eyes focus on his blackened tongue as it slipped back inside his mouth. She didn't visibly react, but he could feel her pulse quicken. She could probably feel the *wrongness* of him, like a herd animal when a hidden predator comes near.

She reached down and pulled something out of her boot. When she straightened, she held a small bone tube with a golden seal at one end.

"I'd like to see the money."

Phiral could hear the fear in her voice, and his body ached to taste her flesh.

"Well, captain, things have changed. I thought I would have access to a great deal of money by this point, but in fact I had to scramble to take enough to pay for the expedition. There just isn't anything left to pay you."

Before he even finished his sentence, she leaped up, knocking her chair backwards. Drawing her sword, she pointed it at Phiral's face. The bartender froze, his eyes wide. The men at the table near the door were all snoring now, even the pickpocket.

"You should know better than to threaten me. My reputation comes from deeds, not words."

Phiral stood slowly, his arms out either side. "Who made a threat, captain? I was merely explaining why you won't be getting paid for that case in your hand."

"If I'm not getting paid, then you're not getting the case. I'm going to walk out of here and if you don't want to die tonight, you'll stay out of my way."

"Oh, you've overplayed your hand, captain. Threats of death don't scare me."

"You don't believe I'll kill you?" Her blade never wavered, inches from his neck.

Phiral felt his teeth and claws stretching out, sharpening into points with an edge finer than the woman's sword.

"It's not that you *won't* kill me. It's that you *can't*."

Minutes later, Phiral exited the tavern. He wanted to stay longer and feast on the flesh of his victims, but he knew it was too risky. Now that he had the case containing the ancient scroll Eothep needed, it was folly to delay his return to the crypt.

The inside of the tavern was an abattoir, and Phiral was slightly concerned the city's response would hamper their efforts to leave tomorrow night. But then he remembered Eothep's power and dismissed those thoughts.

By this time tomorrow, they would be free of Ythis and on their way to the Bleak Wastes.

*　　　　*　　　　*

WHEN LEYNDRA SAW THE LOOK ON HER FRIEND'S FACE, SHE knew something bad had happened. Jeyrra stood and came over as soon as Leyndra stepped through the door. Leyndra looked around for Morit and the children, but they always stayed in a separate room when one could be found. Morit didn't like to be near Leyndra.

"That son of a bitch left a message for you," snarled Jeyrra.

Leyndra's first thought was that Xeylien's apprentice had managed to beat her here and do something to one of her friends. But Jeyrra was in a rage—there was no fear there. There had been no immediate threat to them.

"What? Who—"

"The nobleman...Najare. He left a message for you in the Warren's Heart."

"How did he know I was in the Warrens? What message?"

Jeyrra took a deep breath and tried to calm herself. When she had regained control of her temper, she explained.

"I went out to scrounge up some food for Morit and the kids. I spoke to one of my trusted contacts, who told me the whole story."

Jeyrra motioned for Leyndra to sit, but she was too wound up from her own encounter with Xeylien's apprentice, and was now on edge waiting to hear what had riled up Jeyrra.

"Najare went into the Warren's Heart. He was carrying a spear— well, a sharpened stick. He went right out into the middle of the intersection and jammed the stick into the ground, and he was strong enough to drive it in a good couple of feet."

Leyndra knew the road was packed so hard from centuries of use that such a feat would require the strength of many men.

"Then he unwrapped a bundle he had been carrying in his other hand, and put it on the top of the spike. Most people took off at that point—who'd want to get involved in that? But my contact stayed to see Najare wander off down an alley, all proud of himself."

"What did he put on the spike?"

Jeyrra grimaced as she answered.

"Hathi's head. He must have kept it from when he killed her.

Three days he's kept it and now he puts it on a spike in the middle of the Warren's Heart."

Leyndra realized her hands had balled into fists. Rage filled her.

"He's challenging me to come fight him."

"Yeah. He knows you're hunting him, and he's trying to tell you he's not scared."

"He should be," answered Leyndra, but the words sounded hollow to her. She was intending to go fight both Phiral and the necromancer tonight, but she had no idea how she was going to survive, never mind win. Phiral she was sure could be beaten. Even if she had to cut him to pieces, she would destroy him once and for all.

But the necromancer was another matter entirely.

Leyndra paced the room, trying not to show Jeyrra how worried she was about what might happen to all of them if she failed. She tried to draw strength from her anger.

"You didn't tell Morit, did you?"

"No, of course I—"

"Tell me what?"

Leyndra's head snapped around to see Morit standing in the doorway, his face pale in the flickering candlelight. Jeyrra gave a guilty start and turned away from him, hiding her face.

"Leyndra, what now? What new thing is coming to kill us all, or torture us, or...?"

He looked at her, his face raw with despair, and she wanted to protect him. But she couldn't lie to him now. He'd see right through it and it would start another battle she didn't have the energy to fight.

"Morit, my enemies are trying to provoke me. They want me to react, to get angry or scared, so that I'm not thinking straight."

"So, what does that have to do with me, with my family? What did Jeyrra not tell me?"

Leyndra took a deep breath.

"They...did something to...Hathi's body. Earlier tonight."

Morit stood there, staring at her.

"I'm not going to tell you what they did, because it doesn't matter. Hathi's spirit has moved on, and her body is just an empty shell now. And I will take vengeance on them, for what they did to Hathi, to you and your children, to me, to everyone I care about."

"You will take care of it for us." Morit's voice was a hoarse whisper. Leyndra didn't know if he was doubting her words, or accusing her of taking control again, or what.

"Yes, Morit. I will end this."

Morit looked down at the floor and then turned and slowly left the room. Leyndra waited until he had gone back into the room he shared with his children, and then turned back to Jeyrra.

"I'm sorry, I shouldn't have asked—"

"It's done, Leyndra. You know he can't take any more of this. If he isn't already broken, he will be if anything else happens."

"I know. I'm taking care of it tonight." That reminded her of her other companion. "Where's Zheemeng?"

Again, a guilty look passed across Jeyrra's face.

"He's getting ready."

Leyndra didn't know what Jeyrra meant, but then Zheemeng stepped into the room, and she understood. He was fully outfitted for a fight. A leather coat covered his torso down to just above his knees. Metal rivets had been attached to the armor, to better protect against sword blows. He wore a sword on his back, and long knives hung on either side of his waist.

He didn't look awkward—the opposite in fact. He moved as if he was more than passing familiar with this kind of weaponry.

"Where did you get all of that?"

"I have a lot of contacts," replied Jeyrra before Zheemeng could speak. "We needed to be prepared for whatever happens tonight, so a friend provided me with a bunch of weapons and the one leather coat."

"You've worn that before," Leyndra said to Zheemeng. He nodded at her.

"I haven't always been a member of a street gang. I learned my healing skills in army training."

Leyndra considered what she knew of the army, and Zheemeng's apparent age.

"Wouldn't you still be—"

"I'm a deserter," he said, his voice flat as if expecting this admission to affect how Leyndra saw him. "There are things a man cannot do and remain human. I chose not to participate in the slaughter of innocents."

Leyndra moved over to him and looked at his face, his dark eyes once again drawing her in.

"Then you made the right decision. Killing is easy. Not killing is much harder."

He relaxed at her words, and she realized he had been afraid she would think less of him for running away from the army. In her eyes, it only made him seem stronger.

"You realize, though, that you're not supposed to get into a fight tonight."

"I know. But considering where we're going, what you're going to be facing, I figure our enemies might not let me be an impartial observer. If the fight comes to me, I know how to handle myself."

Leyndra looked at Jeyrra, and then back to Zheemeng. She wasn't entirely sure she could trust them to stay out of harm's way tonight. But there was also nothing she could do about it. She had her mission, and though she feared it was all going to come to naught, she knew she would have to let her friends make their own choices.

She realized, as she stood there, that she had never done that before. She had never given up control and hoped that others would do what she needed them to do. This was the first time she could remember since her parents died where everything was such chaos, and she had to *rely* on others instead of protecting them.

"Okay," she said around the unexpected lump in her throat. "It's time to end this once and for all."

Jeyrra looked at her, and Leyndra knew her friend could see the emotion she was holding back.

"I suppose I'm still just babysitting Morit and the kids, then?"

"Actually, no," replied Leyndra. "Once you escort my brother and his children to the Wolf, there's someone else I want you to check on. Bring a weapon, though. You'll probably be walking into a fight."

Jeyrra smiled.

"That's the best thing I've heard all day."

Chapter Thirty-Five

B EYUS CHAMIRRA WALKED THROUGH THE MAIN GATE AND shoved it closed behind him. Flasek, standing on the third floor of the now-empty Najare mansion, watched through a window as the Imperial Investigator left the chain hanging open and walked up the road toward the main entrance to the building. Flasek turned and made his way down to the entry hall.

Beyus reached the front door, which Flasek had left wide open. He hesitated, seeing Flasek standing at the base of the main staircase. Flasek watched Beyus look around carefully before entering. The man was worried about an ambush. He should have known better. That wasn't Flasek's style.

"You shouldn't be in here," said Beyus as he entered the foyer.

Flasek shrugged.

"I wanted to talk to you, and I knew this would bring you out of the Fortress."

Beyus stopped just inside the main door.

"Just talk? You're not going to try to kill me?"

Flasek could hear the disdain in the other man's voice. He was a cocky son of a bitch. Flasek hoped at least part of it was overconfidence. He was relying on Beyus underestimating his opponent.

"We'll start with talking, and then see how things go from there."

Beyus nodded once, curtly.

"So, what do you want to say to me?"

"I'm confused about a few things, Investigator Chamirra." Flasek sneered as he said Beyus' title. "I want some clarification."

"What makes you think I'm going to answer your questions?

You're just a watchman. You have no authority over me. I came because I was curious, nothing more. If you're wasting my time, then there's no reason for me to stay."

Flasek laughed out loud.

"You came because you know I've figured out who you really are. And you're worried that I've found something that proves it. Well, let me set your mind at ease. Not only have I found proof of your bloodline, but your uncle was careless with other information your superiors would be eager to know."

Beyus just stood there, saying nothing. He wasn't going to confirm any of Flasek's suspicions, on the chance the sergeant was just guessing, was lying about having proof.

"Were you in on the whole thing? Or was it just the part about framing Leyndra Jirau for the murder?"

Beyus smiled.

"I don't know what you're talking about. I am an upstanding member of the Imperial Guard. I'm an Imperial investigator, and Leyndra Jirau was found guilty by the Magistrates."

"Your lies don't impress me, Beyus. You don't seem to get that you've been used just as much as you used Leyndra. Do you really think your uncle cares about you? You're just his brother's bastard son from a pox-ridden whore."

Beyus took a step forward, no longer smiling. He stopped himself with a visible effort and took a deep breath.

"You'd do well to avoid that line of attack, Flasek. My patience with you is at its end."

Good, thought Flasek. *I'm getting to you just like I wanted.*

"So, I guess I'm not far from the truth, then, am I? Some of the details may be off, but I've got the basic idea, don't I?"

Beyus remained silent. Flasek pulled out a roll of papers that were tucked in his belt.

"Because your uncle confirms the most important part of it right here. You know, your uncle *Phiral Najare.*"

It was Beyus' turn to shrug.

"Is that all you have? You think my superiors don't know Phiral Najare is my uncle? Who do you think has been my patron in the

Guard? Who do you think has used his political connections to pull strings for me? I'm the youngest Imperial investigator in the history of the organization, Flasek. Do you think that's an accident?"

"So much for the vaunted Imperial honor," replied Flasek.

Beyus waved his hand, dismissing Flasek's barb.

"If you think anyone in this city, in this Empire, puts honor above personal gain, then you're more foolish than I thought. The Guard talks a great deal about honor, and try to show that face to anyone outside the organization, but we're just the same as everyone else. Better trained, better equipped, sure. But honorable? There is no honor in Ythis."

"What does your uncle get out of this patronage?"

"I'm going to be the Lord Commander of the Imperial Guard one day, Flasek. From your lowly perch in the Watch, I know it's hard to see that high. But my uncle can make it happen. Do you have any idea how valuable it is, to have a close ally as one of the most powerful men in the Empire?"

Beyus shook his head.

"Of course you don't."

"Well, you certainly fell flat dealing with Leyndra Jirau," Flasek quipped.

Beyus glowered at him but said nothing.

"That's what I don't get, Beyus. Why did you send her to the Inquisitor when you knew she'd tell the truth? Wouldn't it have been easier to have her executed if everyone thought she was lying?"

"I don't know what you're talking about."

Flasek held up the papers.

"Ah, that's the part your superiors *would* care about, wouldn't they?"

Flasek flung the roll of papers across the room. They came to rest at Beyus' feet.

"Go ahead, look at them. I had a local scribe make that copy, so you can keep it. The originals are safe somewhere else."

Beyus bent down and picked up the papers. He flipped through them and saw his name and the monetary amounts recorded in multiple places.

"This proves nothing about Leyndra Jirau."

"Oh, come on! He paid you to make sure she wouldn't leave the Fortress alive. But you really bungled that up, didn't you?"

Beyus tossed the papers at his feet and sighed.

"Yes, I suppose I did."

Flasek was momentarily taken aback. Had Beyus just admitted he was involved? Flasek hadn't been sure it was true—the ledger really didn't prove his direct involvement. But now Beyus seemed to be resigned to his confession.

"The Inquisitor was part of the plan. You have no idea how paranoid the Emperor is, how much he fears the Church and the Five. As long as they continually struggle against each other, he wields the most power in the Empire. But he has to be careful with them, in case he drives them to unite against him."

Flasek kept silent, not wanting to interrupt Beyus' admission of guilt.

"Of course, he believed one group or the other was responsible for the death of Osho Idaphos. He didn't know there was another power in Ythis that could summon the shadow creatures—and it's not like he has any experts who can tell him what sorcerers or priests are able to do. So, the Inquisitor's report forced the Emperor to avoid bringing in either the Church or the Five to get to the truth, because he figured it was one of them behind the murder. That was supposed to give my uncle enough time to do whatever it was he needed to do. At least, that was before Leyndra escaped from the Fortress. Then the priests *forced* their way into the hunt, and the Emperor knew they weren't involved in the murder."

It all came back to Leyndra. Her escape from the Fortress had derailed the entire plan.

"So, if she hadn't escaped...?"

"She would have been executed on schedule," answer Beyus. "There'd be no reason for the other groups to get involved. Wydo would be killed during his arrest, and the whole matter would be laid to rest."

Beyus drew his sword.

"But it's all gone wrong because of that woman. You've been little more than a nuisance, Flasek, which is why you were supposed to die in that alley last night. Just another random killing in Ythis. But I've lost my uncle, and Leyndra is still out there somewhere, and now I'm on my own."

Flasek drew his own short sword. He knew it had to come to this. There would be no quarter given, no mercy. One of them was going to die tonight.

"You can't beat me, Flasek. You know I'm younger than you, I'm faster, I've had training you can't imagine. Why make it harder on yourself?"

"Do you really think I'm going to just give up?"

Beyus smiled sadly.

"No. That just wouldn't be you."

*   *   *

LEYNDRA CROUCHED BEHIND A MARBLE TOMBSTONE, A square pillar topped with a bust of a stern-looking man's head and shoulders. She assumed the bust was supposed to resemble whoever rested in the coffin below.

If so, I bet he was a real charmer, she thought sarcastically.

Zheemeng crouched behind the next tombstone, a low white rectangle with words carved in large block letters. He held a long knife in one hand, and he scanned the area constantly for any signs of their enemies. Leyndra expected the necromancer and Phiral Najare to be waiting for her in the crypt.

She shook off her expectations. That kind of thinking could dull her sensibilities. She couldn't be sure exactly *where* Phiral might wait for her. He might have set up multiple traps to injure or hamper her, giving him the opportunity to attack when she was vulnerable.

Zheemeng looked at Leyndra and gave a quick shake of his head. He hadn't spotted anything unusual in the darkness around them.

The Forgotten City was a vast, sprawling area that hugged the northwest side of Ythis. Low hills provided ample room for the thousands of bodies buried here over the centuries. Originally, only the nobles were allowed to bury their dead—all others had to be burned. But then the wealthiest merchants petitioned the Emperor for the right to have a cemetery where they could place their own family crypts. Marble tombstones and ornate mausoleums sprang up like weeds.

Over the decades that followed, burials replaced burning for anyone who could afford it. Eventually, even the poor tried to bury their loved ones, though they had to do all the work themselves. Simple wooden markers stood in uneven rows along the northern flank of the Forgotten City, an area that became a massive mud pit when the rains came.

The wealthy could afford to bury their deceased in a deep hole. The graves of the poor were shallow, and their bones were often unceremoniously revealed in the churned-up mud. Leyndra wondered how long her own body would lay in the mausoleum before it would be found by the family caretakers, should she fall tonight.

Zheemeng moved to her side.

"Okay, we're here. Now what?"

She looked at him evenly.

"You wait out here for me."

He raised one eyebrow and shook his head.

"Once you go in there, I don't have any way of knowing if you're alive or not. You brought me here to as an extra pair of eyes in case you lose. But if I'm out here, I won't be able to see anything."

Leyndra sighed. She knew Zheemeng wanted to back her up, to help her in this fight. But the creatures she was about to face were too powerful, too deadly, to let him get close to them.

"If you come into the mausoleum, you'll be in real danger, and that will distract me. I'll need every last bit of my concentration to win this battle. I can't afford to let you in there."

Despite the darkness of the cemetery, she could see him frowning at her.

"Listen, Zheemeng. This isn't going to be a long, drawn-out fight. I've got to kill Phiral and then face the necromancer. I don't see us sparring for any real length of time here. Either I will reach him first and he dies, or I don't reach him before he uses his power on me, and *I* die. If an hour passes after I go in there and you don't see me come out, then I've lost, and you've got to bolt."

He obviously didn't like it, but he didn't argue, either. Leyndra put her hand on his shoulder, a friendly gesture like one did with a comrade or a fellow soldier. It didn't feel right. She slid her hand down onto his chest. The leather breastplate he wore was warm from his body heat and the city's stale air.

He looked down at her hand and then back up to her face. She had a nearly overwhelming desire to kiss him, but forced herself to hold back. That would only make this situation worse. If she gave him anything, any clue how much she wanted him, he wouldn't let her go into the mausoleum alone.

"This is what I need you to do," she whispered. "Someone has to take care of the others if I fail."

She knew her own eyes were giving her away, and he leaned forward to kiss her. She turned her face away and he stopped.

"Please," she said. "Don't make this more difficult than it already is."

He leaned back and looked around, scanning the darkness once more for threats, and she let her hand drop. When he spoke, his voice was carefully neutral.

"Do you think they know you're coming?"

Leyndra looked at the entrance to the mausoleum.

"Phiral left Hathi's head as a message for me. He knows I'm coming. But he doesn't really know what I can do. Most people don't realize...."

She didn't want to explain how deadly she could be when the *virtus* flowed through her and she was able to use her gifts to their fullest.

Of course, everything hinged on her being able to touch that power once she was inside the mausoleum. Without her gifts, she was still highly skilled—but she knew it wouldn't be enough.

Leyndra still didn't know why she was able to feel the *virtus* inside her, why it came and went without warning. She didn't like relying on something that was so unpredictable. But that was the way of things. This was her fight, and this was the time. She had to trust herself, her abilities, her training.

"Zheemeng...."

She didn't want to ask this of him, but she needed the reassurance. She looked at his face and saw she had his undivided attention.

"I need you to promise me, to swear to me, that no matter what you hear—even if my screams reach you as I lay dying—you won't try to rescue me. I know you were a soldier, but if I cannot overcome the threat in there, you will be throwing your own life away to try to help me. I need to know you'll do what I ask."

He looked away, obviously uncomfortable. She knew he was a man of his word. If he swore to do what she asked, then he would do it. He would hate himself for the rest of his life, but she knew he would run away and be safe.

Zheemeng looked back at her and she could see the pain in his face. Again, she forced herself not to respond. She crouched behind the tombstone, looking at him impassively, not letting any emotion loose on her own face.

Finally, he nodded.

"I swear to do as you ask. Though I may think it's a terrible mistake, I don't want you to worry about me. I want you to be able to focus on the task at hand. So, I will keep myself safe, for you."

"Thank you," she whispered, not wanting him to hear the tremble in her voice.

She stood up fully and checked her weapons one last time. And then, with a deep breath, she moved toward the mausoleum.

Chapter Thirty-Six

MORIT HELD THE HANDS OF HIS TWO CHILDREN AS THEY followed Jeyrra along the alley toward a wooden door at the far end. He continued to glance nervously over his shoulder, terrified they would stumble into the territory of some violent street gang. He had somehow survived being kept prisoner by the Imperial Guard, questioning by a priest, and the attack of some supernatural creature.

Now watch us all die on the knives of some destitute gang of thugs, he thought to himself.

But they reached the door without incident and Jeyrra knocked softly. The door opened outward and they stood facing a huge, muscular man wearing a deep scowl on his face. He said nothing, but took in their appearance and waved them forward.

Jeyrra stepped into the dark doorway first and Morit hesitated, ready to bolt if Jeyrra should cry out from some unexpected attack. But only silence greeted him, and so he pushed the children forward and entered the blackness beyond.

They entered a dark hallway, only a single candle visible on a shelf at the far end. A door at the very end opened and light spilled out, illuminating the hallway. A figure stood in the doorway, features obscured by the light behind him or her. As Jeyrra reached the door, the figure stepped aside and motioned her to enter.

Morit and the children followed and entered a small room with four sleeping pallets, a small wooden table covered in nicks and scratches, and two rickety chairs. Morit looked at the man who now closed the door. His face was young, perhaps barely out of his teens, though he had a quiet grace that spoke of experience beyond his years. His brown hair was cropped short, and Morit noticed the bottom half of one ear was missing, as if sliced off. He wore a short sword at his waist, and carried a long knife strapped to one thigh.

"I'm Koral Creyss—I work directly for the Wolf."

Jeyrra nodded and introduced herself and Morit. Koral didn't shake hands, merely nodding his greeting.

He motioned for them to sit down, and Morit told the children to sit quietly on one of the sleeping pallets before grabbing one of the chairs himself.

"Are you the man who'll get us out of the city?" he asked.

Koral leaned against the wall and crossed his arms.

"Yes, that's the arrangement we made. Just you and the two kids."

He turned to Jeyrra.

"The Wolf is looking forward to meeting you in person. He feels you'll make a valuable addition to his organization."

Jeyrra frowned. Morit knew that she preferred to remain independent. She had always been on friendly terms with the Wolf's people, but had never wanted to work directly for the crime boss. She was giving up a lot for this.

Koral misread the expression on her face.

"Don't worry, the Wolf intends for you to lie low until the heat from the Imperial Guard has gone away. You won't be running any rackets or gang activity until your name is clear. He's already got an idea on how to take care of that. But to us, your reputation speaks for itself, and the Wolf respects your abilities, so he sees this as an investment."

"What about me?" asked Morit. "Where am I going?"

"It's a village about ten days ride from here. Far enough to be outside of the range of regular Ythis patrols, but not outside the range of the Wolf's activities. There is a warehouse there where caravans sometimes make stops to exchange contraband items. You'll work in the warehouse, and have a small cabin in the village for yourself and the children."

"A warehouse? What will I be doing?"

Koral shrugged. "Warehouse stuff. You'll report to the guy in charge there—he'll tell you what to do. You'll get enough wages to feed your family, but it'll take some time to pay off your debt to the Wolf, so don't expect anything special."

So Morit was being sent off to work for a criminal in some backwater village where he would be expected to scrape out a living for the rest of his days. He knew better than to think he'd ever be able to pay off his debt to the Wolf. They would keep him under their thumb forever, little better than a slave.

And, of course, Leyndra hadn't even asked him whether he'd be okay with that. No, she had made these arrangements and expected him to meekly follow wherever she led.

"What if I don't like it there? What if I want to go somewhere else?"

Jeyrra let out a laugh that was little more than a bark. Morit looked at her and she had the good grace to turn away and wipe the smile off her face.

Koral cleared his throat before answering. Morit took that as a sign of bad news.

"I'm not sure where else you think you'd like to go. Getting you out of the city won't be easy, and you don't have any skills that would give you more…lucrative…prospects. You're too old to be an apprentice, and with the Guard hunting you, there's not much hope you'll get far without help."

He looked at the children and seemed to see them for the first time.

"Besides, traveling with children makes everything so much harder, and slower. I figured you'd want something quiet and safe for your family."

"But that means I owe my life to the Wolf, is that it?"

Morit realized his voice was getting shrill and he tried to calm himself down. Koral shrugged again, as if he really didn't care about Morit. He had praised Jeyrra and her reputation, but Morit was just dead weight. Once again, he was just Leyndra's little brother.

"Listen, if you don't want our help then I'm not going to force it on you. But we can get you out of the city and set you up in a quiet place where you don't have to worry about someone coming to capture you, where you don't have to look over your shoulder every day for the rest of your life. That comes with a price, yes. But it's far better than doing it on your own and risking your life and the lives of your kids."

He stood up, opened the door, and said something in a low voice to the big man in the hallway. Then he closed the door and turned back to Morit.

"If you're not going to accept our help, then you need to tell us now. Once we set things in motion, we'll expect you to pay us back for our efforts. Do you want our help or not?"

Morit sat there, cursing silently. Leyndra had done it to him again. Once more he was in an untenable situation. He looked at his kids, and knew Koral was right. There was no way he could travel with them without some kind of help. But what kind of life would they have in that little village anyway?

He wondered if it wouldn't be kinder to leave them in one of Ythis' orphanages. Those places were run by people who *wanted* to care for children, something Morit had never wanted to do. Wouldn't they be happier there?

And then he thought of his own childhood, his parents dead, only Leyndra to take care of him. Look how that had turned out. And he could already see how his daughter tried to boss around her little brother. Would his children just become another version of Morit and Leyndra?

And could Morit really survive on the run? Could he really do it?

But even as he considered the question, he already knew the answer. He wasn't cut out for that kind of life. He was terrified of what might happen to him on the road, without someone to watch over him and keep him safe. He didn't want to die alone, starving, or murdered by some pack of outlaws.

He looked up at Koral and took a deep breath.

"We'll go to the village. You're right, that's the best choice for my children."

Koral nodded and shared a glance with Jeyrra. There was almost amusement in that glance, and Morit wanted to confront them. But it wasn't worth it—it was a fight he couldn't win.

"Okay," said Koral. "We leave Ythis in four hours. I suggest you force the children to take a nap, and you'll want to rest for a couple of hours, too. It'll be a long night of traveling."

Koral opened the door and motioned for Jeyrra to come along. She stood and turned to Morit.

"Goodbye, Morit. Have a good life. Be safe."

He looked up at her and saw her eyes were empty of emotion. She didn't really feel anything about this parting. It was just words to her. Morit turned his back to her and knelt down in front of his children.

"Goodbye, Jeyrra," he said without looking at her. She stood there a moment, as if waiting for him to say something else—to thank her, perhaps. Eventually, she left the room and closed the door behind her.

*   *   *

LEYNDRA STOOD BEFORE THE DOOR OF THE MAUSOLEUM AND examined the portal carefully. The door itself was a large marble slab, presumably on some sort of hinge or pivot point to allow access. An ornately carved metal ring hung above a large, dark keyhole.

If this is locked, thought Leyndra, *my night may be over before it's begun.*

She grabbed the metal ring and pulled. The door budged...barely.

This is going to take some muscle.

She was loath to sheath her sword in order to use both hands to open the door. It would be the perfect opportunity for Phiral Najare to ambush her, and she didn't want to give him any advantage. She glanced over her shoulder and debated asking Zheemeng to assist.

That, of course, would put him in the open and potentially in reach of Phiral, defeating her attempt to keep him as safe as possible. She glanced around and then settled on a solution.

Zheemeng stood as she retreated back down the four steps to the grassy hill. She motioned for him to remain where he was, and he obeyed. Leyndra stabbed her sword down into the dirt so that it stood upright. Then she returned to the metal ring.

Should Phiral lunge out of the darkness as she pulled open the door, Leyndra would leap into a diving roll and come up beside her sword. It would hopefully give her the instant she needed to ready her weapon before the undead nobleman was upon her.

Leyndra grabbed the ring with both hands, planted her feet, and pulled. Slowly, the marble slab began to move. As the door opened wide enough for someone to slip through, she prepared to leap away, but nothing came out of the darkness.

She closed her eyes and concentrated on the flow of *virtus*. It was barely a trickle, but enough for her to activate one of her abilities. When she opened her eyes, pale blue light outlined everything, illuminating the darkest corners in a twilight glow. For the next while, she could see in the dark well enough to make her way into the crypt without needing a lantern.

Leyndra hoped that trickle would turn into a flood if she really needed it. Right now, she knew her best abilities were out of her reach unless something changed. She was relying on her faith that the *virtus* would come to her once she was in immediate danger, the way it had the first time she had fought Phiral.

She returned to her sword and drew it from the ground, and then faced the open portal. Stepping up to the dark entryway, she could see the small antechamber beyond, and the stairs leading down to the crypt. Nothing appeared out of the ordinary, though she knew appearances could be deceiving.

She entered the mausoleum and looked up, but the carved ceiling hid no ambush. She moved carefully over to the stairs and looked down. The crypt was a large pit with two ornately carved sarcophagi resting on the bottom, the antechamber little more than a balcony overlooking the crypt's occupants. Alcoves in the walls of the pit held the remains of other family members.

There was no sign of Phiral Najare, nor the necromancer.

Leyndra cursed silently. Was it possible they had moved somewhere else? Could they even now be taking the caravan toward one of the city gates, the necromancer's prize in his hand at last?

She was about to turn and leave but at the last second, she stopped herself. It wasn't like her to give up so easily, and she knew the necromancer had ways to deceive the senses. She decided to check the crypt thoroughly before leaving.

It occurred to her that Phiral and the necromancer might be resting beneath the stone slabs of the two sarcophagi. Perhaps it was a requirement of their existence to repose as one already dead for some portion of each day. She stepped onto the first stair and tested her weight, but it was made of stone and didn't give. Leyndra proceeded downwards.

At the bottom, she moved over to the first of the large stone boxes and began to examine it for signs the lid had been moved recently. She could see nothing that indicated it had been used by anyone but its original occupant.

"I'll do you a favor," said a voice from above. Leyndra looked up to see Phiral Najare standing at the top of the stairs. "When I kill you, I'll put your remains in one of those so you can spend eternity surrounded by wealth."

Leyndra felt her heart speed up. She hadn't been wrong about Phiral, after all.

"Where's the necromancer?"

Phiral crossed his arms and leaned casually against the wall.

"Oh, here and there. He's too busy right now to kill you himself, so I get to do it. It's only fitting, seeing as you were the one who caused me so much trouble."

Leyndra focused herself and melted into her combat trance. She was calm, prepared, and ready to fight. She lightly brushed the power inside her, but it was still barely there. She let it be for now. She wasn't hopeless even without her Warden gifts.

Phiral frowned at her and uncrossed his arms.

"What, no banter? You're here for Eothep and you think you can just ignore me? I'm going to make you regret everything you've done since you were arrested by the Imperial Guard. Your sword can't hurt me, did you know that? You've lost before you even began."

Leyndra looked up at him and smiled, but said nothing. For all his newfound powers, he wasn't entirely sure he could beat her. She could tell from his threats—he was trying to convince himself almost as much as he was trying to frighten her.

But now that the moment had come, Leyndra was no longer frightened.

"Well, if you're not going to talk to me, I guess I might as well just kill you now. I asked Eothep if he wanted me to make you into another servant, but he'd just prefer you to die. Don't think he's being merciful, though. I was told to take my time, punish you for your interference, and make you beg for your death. I've heard you *like* to beg."

Leyndra's mind instantly went back to the Inquisitor and her time spent strapped to his table. She had begged him to believe her, had begged him not to cause any more pain. And of course, Phiral had heard about it from his ally, her torture just another tool for him to use against her.

Rage filled her and she felt herself losing focus. She wanted to attack Phiral and cut him down, slice him into pieces and burn the remains. She wanted....

And then she realized it was a trick. He had been trying to push her off balance, trying to play mind games so that he could take her by surprise. It had almost worked.

She came to this realization as Phiral lunged at her, leaping over the balustrade and diving toward her from near the top of the staircase. Leyndra knew his weight would take her sword out of her hands if she tried to use it against him, and she flung herself sideways to avoid his outstretched claws.

She felt something sharp snag the back of her shirt as she tumbled away and knew he had almost caught her. He hit the stone floor of the crypt with a solid thud, and she spun to face him as she regained her feet. She was horrified to see how fast he leaped back up from the ground and charged her.

She sidestepped him and thrust her sword into his torso. The blade went between his ribs and ripped through the skin of his back. He swung his clawed hand and she was forced to let go of her sword to avoid losing her own head. She tumbled backward and he stood there, looking down at the hilt of her sword sticking out of his chest.

When he spoke, she could tell she had punctured one of his lungs.

"See?" he wheezed, smiling at her and revealing jagged fangs. "Now you're without a weapon, and I've barely gotten started."

Chapter Thirty-Seven

BEYUS LUNGED AND FLASEK USED HIS TRUNCHEON TO knock away the point of the other man's blade just enough to avoid the thrust. He stabbed with his own sword, but Beyus twisted and took the hit on his metal breastplate. Flasek's sword skittered across the armor and he forced himself to backpedal to avoid another short, quick slash that followed the thrust.

Flasek had hoped that his fighting style, something he had developed himself, would catch Beyus by surprise. Watchmen tended to use their truncheons to inflict non-lethal beatings, and use their swords when the situation became serious. Flasek had practiced for years using his sword in one hand, and the truncheon in the other.

His second weapon was little more than a stout stick wrapped in leather, and wouldn't be able to block someone swinging a larger sword. But it was strong enough to deflect the thrusts from a short sword, which was the more common weapon on the crowded streets of Ythis. Most fights took place in narrow alleys or inside buildings, where there simply wasn't room to swing a large weapon. And that gave Flasek's fighting style an advantage.

At least, it *should* have given him an advantage. But Beyus was good, better than Flasek had seen in quite some time. Though the younger man fought only with his single weapon, he had taken the offensive from the beginning and seemed to have no intention of giving it up.

Flasek had managed to score a couple of hits, but the heavier armor worn by his opponent had prevented any strikes from getting through to injure the man. Flasek was beginning to think he wouldn't win this fight. And that meant he was going to be dead before the end of the night.

Beyus didn't give Flasek any time to rest. The soldier kept close to Flasek, thrusting and slashing at any opening. Flasek continued to give ground, noticing he had circled the foyer twice already and was now on his third circuit. At some point, he was going to miss a block, and then the fight would rapidly be over.

Changing tact, he saw another thrust coming and used his own sword to parry the strike. This time, he swung the truncheon in an overhand arc and tried to bring it down on the wrist of Beyus. But Beyus reacted with skill and speed. As the stick came down, Beyus pulled back his wrist and swiped the blade upwards. The edge of his sword caught the middle of the truncheon and Flasek's extra weapon broke in half.

Before Flasek could react, Beyus brought his knee up and drove it into Flasek's abdomen. His leather armor absorbed most of the shock, but the strike knocked him off balance and he flailed his arms as he stumbled backward. He hadn't let go of the broken truncheon, and that saved his life.

As Beyus drew back his blade in preparation for another thrust, he failed to notice that while the truncheon had broken in half, the leather wrapping had not been severed. As Flasek wind-milled his arm, the leather began to unravel, turning the broken stick into a rather effective flail.

The broken end of the truncheon caught Beyus in the cheek and snapped his head sideways. Temporarily stunned by the unexpected blow, Beyus was unable to take advantage of the opening he had created and was forced to retreat and try to regain his senses.

Flasek got his feet back under him just in time to realize he had missed his own chance to end the fight. Beyus pointed his sword at Flasek and felt his own face with his free hand. A large gash bled profusely from under Beyus' right eye.

Flasek used the break to try to catch his breath. He looked down at his broken truncheon—the top half had come almost completely unwrapped. As much as he was happy that it had worked as a flail once, he didn't expect it to hold together long enough to use it again. Flasek tossed it into a corner.

"Down to just a sword now," Beyus said between deep breaths. "You couldn't beat me with two, how do you think you'll do with just one?"

"I'm not the one bleeding," replied Flasek. Beyus grimaced and prepared to engage again.

Flasek knew he couldn't outlast Beyus, and it was obvious he couldn't outfight him in this kind of confrontation. He needed a way to change the circumstances of their conflict. If he let Beyus take the lead again, Flasek would die.

Beyus stepped forward and thrust his sword at Flasek. Flasek stepped into the thrust, turning at the last second to avoid a deadly wound. But the point of the sword drove into his leather armor, pierced it, and continued on into his flesh. He felt the blade scrape across his ribs as he grabbed Beyus' sword hand and yanked him forward.

Flasek lowered his forehead and drove himself toward Beyus' face, hoping to break the other man's nose. But Beyus saw it coming and twisted his own head to avoid the crushing blow. Flasek pounded his forehead into the same cheek he had cut with the truncheon moments before, and Beyus let out a grunt of pain.

Flasek intended to keep driving forward and knock the other man off his feet. He felt Beyus going backward and then Flasek found his own feet leaving the ground as his opponent lifted him up and over, using Flasek's own momentum against himself. Flasek was flipped over and landed on his back, Beyus above him.

The impact of hitting the floor knocked the wind out of Flasek and he knew he had made a terrible mistake. Beyus tried to draw his sword out of Flasek's side, but Flasek hung on with all his strength. He knew if that blade came back into play, it was all over.

He could tell his wound was minor, but it robbed him of some of his strength. Beyus tried to choke Flasek with his free hand and Flasek barely managed to tuck his chin down in time. He didn't have the reach to hit Beyus while the man crouched above him, pulling on the sword and pushing on Flasek's neck.

Suddenly, Beyus let go of the sword hilt and twisted his hand out of Flasek's grasp. Flasek knew he was going for one of his other knives, perhaps one in his boot. With only an instant to react, Flasek hit the wrist at his neck with one hand while pounding his fist into Beyus's shoulder with the other.

Slightly off balance while going for his knife, Beyus was thrown sideways and fell beside Flasek. Flasek held onto the wrist and raised his other fist, bringing it down on the side of Beyus' head.

Beyus tried to twist away, but Flasek used all his remaining strength—driven by his desperate fight to survive—to pound Beyus again and again in the head. He continued long after he felt a couple of his own knuckles break under the onslaught.

When he finally stopped, Beyus lay in a growing pool of blood, his sightless eyes staring into Flasek's face.

Flasek slowly rolled away and pulled himself to his knees. The wound in his side ached, but he could tell it was not life-threatening. It would certainly need stitches, but the scar that would result wasn't his first, and certainly wouldn't be his last.

Behind him, he heard booted feet coming up the front steps to the mansion. He needed a few minutes to rest—he didn't have the strength to stand up just yet.

Looking over his shoulder, he saw four Guard soldiers step into the foyer. He recognized two of them as the men who had attacked him last night. Beyus' personal enforcers.

Their eyes wide with disbelief, they looked from the corpse of Beyus to Flasek.

"Well isn't that just like the Imperial Guard?" he said with a weary sigh. "Always late to the party."

*　　　　*　　　　*

LEYNDRA RAISED HERSELF TO HER FEET, READY TO LEAP AWAY if Phiral so much as twitched in her direction.

"There's more to me than just a sword," she replied.

"I know there is, Leyndra. I'm curious about something, though. Before you die, indulge me for a moment. Tell me how you escaped from the Fortress."

Leyndra watched him carefully. She figured he was trying to distract her, and she didn't intend to fall for it.

"No?" he asked. "Not going to reveal your secrets? You were ready to blurt out everything when the Imperial Guard had you, but you won't tell *me* anything."

"Tell you what," said Phiral. "I'll share a secret with you, if you'll share one with me. I'll even go first."

He was taunting her, trying to get her to show some emotion or lower her guard. He hadn't moved and she wondered if he was secretly in pain from being impaled on her sword. Perhaps she *had* done some damage and he was stalling for time.

"Beyus Chamirra is my nephew. Everything that happened from the moment he took you into custody was done under *my* orders. Everything, that is, until you escaped."

If Phiral was hoping for some kind of reaction, he didn't get what he wanted. Flasek had already broken the news to Leyndra the night before. She had to admit to herself she was disappointed. She had taken Beyus for an honest man, someone who believed in the Empire. That he was willing to commit heinous acts—like having her tortured—didn't change her opinion of his *honesty*. He was her enemy, and yet she had retained some small measure of respect for him. It had been misplaced.

"My escape from the Fortress is the least of your nephew's problems tonight. You were sloppy with your records, and now my friends know all about him. While I'm dealing with you, they're out there, dealing with him."

Phiral stood there, his face expressionless. She could tell he was struggling with the idea she might be telling the truth.

"My nephew is a trained soldier," he replied. "I'm sure he'll deal with the rabble easily enough."

Leyndra just smiled at him. She saw him force himself to remain calm. When he spoke, surprisingly, his voice wavered.

"So, tell me, please, how you managed to get out of the Fortress."

"An ally opened the door," she replied. "I did the rest."

And now Phiral smiled at her again. He had gotten her to speak twice, and now figured she was about ready to open up to him.

"Surely that wasn't the only help you received, was it? No weapon, or clothing, or...."

He paused, waiting for her to fill in the blanks, but she remained silent, watching him. She wanted to reach out to the flow of *virtus* again, but was worried it would be no stronger than when she had tried earlier.

Phiral was getting impatient again. He didn't like that she refused to talk. He wanted to prolong this, but Leyndra just wanted it over. It was no longer about vengeance for her. She just wanted the problem to go away, and Phiral's destruction would bring her closer to that end.

"Did you like the present I left you?" he wheezed. "I kept it just for you."

Again, Leyndra refused to answer.

"I've got another one outside. He died quickly and quietly, not like the woman, your sister-in-law I believe. She screamed over and over, before I ripped out her throat. But your lover, he just shuddered as I gutted him."

Leyndra had to fight the surge of emotion threatening to overwhelm her calm. Phiral had to be lying—Zheemeng couldn't be dead.

"I took him by surprise and covered his mouth so he wouldn't call out and bring you running. I held him like a baby, and he died in my arms. I watched the light fade from his eyes, and it was exquisite."

Phiral *had* come into the mausoleum behind her. He must have been outside when she entered. He knew Zheemeng was out there. Could it be true? Could he have killed Zheemeng while she was exploring the crypt?

She knew Phiral could move fast, but surely Zheemeng would have made some sound. He wouldn't have died for nothing.

Leyndra wanted to believe it was a lie, but couldn't quite convince herself that Zheemeng was still alive. She felt her control slipping and fought to hold onto it. If Zheemeng *was* dead, she wasn't going to let his death cause her to become careless. She wasn't going to let Phiral kill her too.

"I can smell the fear on you, Leyndra. I can smell your despair.

You'll die tonight, just like your friends, your fam—"

Leyndra was moving before Phiral realized it. As fast as he was, she still managed to take him by surprise. He tried to lash out with his claws, but she dove into a roll and drove her foot into the side of one of his knees. She was rewarded with the sound of bones breaking and he was thrown off balance.

Leyndra rose and grabbed for the sword sticking out of Phiral's chest, but he had anticipated her goal. He grabbed her arm and swung her into the wall, hard. Her breath was driven from her body, and Phiral yanked her close. The smell of rotten meat and old blood on his breath made her gag.

"Fight's over, Leyndra. Let's see how you taste."

Chapter Thirty-Eight

JEYRRA LEAPED SIDEWAYS AS THE FRONT DOOR HAMMERED open and a body flung itself toward her. She barely avoided the man in full Imperial Guard armor as he tumbled backwards down the stone steps. An instant later, Flasek Lumayth came barreling out after him, three more Guardsmen on his heels.

Leyndra had asked Jeyrra to look in on the sergeant once she had seen Morit safely into the Wolf's possession. The thought of entering these grounds, where such a slaughter had taken place only days before, had sent a chill down Jeyrra's spine. But Leyndra had told her this was where Flasek was going to confront Beyus Chamirra, and the man likely wouldn't come alone.

Jeyrra was looking forward to hurting a few soldiers and meeting the sergeant of the Watch. He had been an ally to Leyndra, and as far as Jeyrra was concerned, that made him worth knowing. But now wasn't the time for introductions.

Jeyrra drew a pair of long knives as the three soldiers bolted past her.

She saw Flasek suddenly stop, right at the top of the stone steps, and spin around with his huge fists flying. The man right behind him caught the first punch on his temple, and the second on his nose. The soldier's short sword skittered across the surface of Flasek's leather armor but didn't have enough force behind it to penetrate.

The soldier stumbled to the side and dropped to his hands and knees on the landing. The second man managed to stop just out of reach of Flasek's swinging arms. He readied his sword and Jeyrra realized Flasek was weaponless.

As the third soldier noticed Jeyrra and turned toward her, she flung one of her long knives at the back of the man menacing Flasek. It clanged off his metal armor but drew his attention enough to buy Flasek another couple of seconds. The sergeant flung himself down the steps to the walkway and grabbed the sword that lay beside the groaning soldier who had been first through the door and who had gone down the same steps the hard way.

Jeyrra now faced a trained Imperial Guard soldier and only had one knife in her hand. She widened her eyes and took a step backward, toward the edge of the landing. The soldier smiled and lunged toward her, his blade pointed at her heart.

It was exactly what she had hoped he would do, underestimating the poor, nearly defenseless woman. She spun as his sword thrust at her chest, avoiding the point by a finger-width. Her own knife stabbed toward the man's eye, but he twisted his head away and the blade glanced off his helm.

The soldier recovered from his missed thrust quickly and Jeyrra cursed out loud. Her one advantage was gone, and she had missed. The man was faster than he looked. This was going to be a real fight.

The other soldier was slowly moving down the steps toward Flasek, giving his companion on the landing more time to recover from the blows he had just taken to his face. They obviously intended to surround Flasek and cut him down like an animal. And then Jeyrra would be next.

At least, that's what she figured they planned to do. But she knew plans have a way of changing without warning. She focused on the man in front of her, moving slowly, looking for an opening. He did the same, now realizing she was a serious threat. But all he had to do was keep her occupied, prevent her from going to Flasek's aid, and his two companions would murder Flasek in moments.

He didn't know Jeyrra hadn't come alone. As she moved and feinted, keeping clear of the man's longer reach and heavier blade, Koral Creyss came out of the shadows at the base of the mansion's front entryway. The soldier who had taken Flasek's punches slowly regained his feet, but didn't notice the additional figure on the landing.

Koral stepped forward and drove his own, thin, sword into the back of the soldier. The point punched a hole in the man's armor and slid through his body into his heart. He let out a gasp and dropped his own sword, which caught the attention of the last two standing soldiers.

In an instant, the odds had shifted dramatically. Now the Guard members were outnumbered, if one didn't count the battered soldier still moaning at the base of the steps. Jeyrra smiled as the expression changed on the man in front of her. She watched his confidence dissipate like smoke on the wind.

"Who wants to die first?" asked Jeyrra.

Koral stood between the two soldiers, preventing them from linking up and covering each other's backs. Jeyrra saw the thought in her opponent's eyes as he formed it, and was moving even as he tried to backpedal away from her.

"He's running!" she yelled as the man turned from her and bolted in the only direction not blocked—back into the mansion.

Without thinking, Jeyrra pursued him into the building, right at his back. But many doors led out of the foyer, and this man was not familiar with the layout of the mansion. He hesitated for a second, trying to turn around and defend himself from Jeyrra.

She pinned his sword arm as he spun and drove her knife into the man's throat. His eyes went wide, and she twisted the blade, making sure he felt his own death coming for him.

"This is for Leyndra," she snarled into his face and shoved him backwards. He fell onto his back, dropping his sword, and grabbed at the hilt of the knife sticking out of his neck. But his grip was already lessening as his blood pooled under him.

Jeyrra turned and walked outside, leaving the knife. Koral and Flasek stood over the bodies of the other soldiers. Their fight had been as short as hers.

Flasek looked from Jeyrra to Koral and back again.

"Thanks for the help. I want to think I could have taken them all, but...." He looked down at his side and Jeyrra noticed he was bleeding.

"Shit. Koral we need to—"

"I'm okay, it's not deep. I need stitches and some rest, though. I don't think I'm up for any more fighting tonight."

He turned to Jeyrra.

"I'm Flasek, in case you don't already know that."

She smiled at him.

"I'm Jeyrra and this is Koral. Leyndra sent me."

Flasek reached out and clasped her hand, and then Koral's.

"Any word from our mutual friend?"

Jeyrra shook her head. "Not yet. She'll meet us at the Wolf's Den when she's done."

Flasek heaved a huge sigh.

"I hope so, Jeyrra. I really hope so."

*   *   *

PHIRAL GRABBED FOR LEYNDRA'S OTHER ARM, BUT SHE WHIPPED it forward and slammed it into the sword hilt sticking out of his chest. This time, he grunted in pain, and Leyndra used that instant of distraction to spin and twist, breaking his grip.

He recovered quickly, but she leaped up and rolled across the closest sarcophagus, putting distance between them. As she landed, she drew two long knives from her boot sheaths. She could feel her movements were faster than normal, her reactions quicker and more precise. Leyndra had opened herself to the trickle of *virtus* automatically, and it was just enough to keep pace with Phiral.

But was it enough to beat him?

She expected Phiral to lunge over the top of the stone slab, but he held back. Again, Leyndra wondered how much damage her sword had done.

"Knives, Leyndra?" he wheezed. "If your sword didn't kill me, what are you going to do with those?"

He moved around one side of the sarcophagus as he spoke, and she remained still, waiting for him to come into range of her strikes. He stumbled once on his broken leg, but it held together well enough for him to put his full weight on it.

Phiral suddenly bolted forward, claws outstretched. This time, as he neared her, he swept his arms downward to catch her as she tumbled. But she didn't duck. Instead she leaped up and to one side, swiping forward with her knife as the tumbled over the top of the second sarcophagus.

When Leyndra landed on the other side, she spun to face Phiral and was shocked to see a river of black ichor oozing from the wound she had just opened in his neck. It didn't seem to bother him, though. He kept moving toward her.

"Just little cuts and scrapes," he said to her, his wheeze now sounding as if it came from underwater.

Leyndra knew she couldn't keep this up indefinitely. She was fast, but so was Phiral, and if he got both hands on her, her quickness wouldn't matter anymore. There were only so many times he would fall for her tricks and tumbles.

He lunged at her again and she reversed her grip on the knives. As he swept his arms toward her, she parried with her own fists, and the blades impaled both of his palms. But he was so much stronger than she was, and he began to force his claws toward her head as she tried to hold him at bay.

At the right moment, just as he shifted his weight forward, Leyndra suddenly rolled backward, pulling his hands forward. Her back hit the floor and she planted her feet into his belly and pushed, flipping him up and over her head. As he flew over her, she yanked down on the knives, and sliced through his hands. Phiral landed on his back on the stone staircase.

She heard another bone break and felt a moment of hope that his spine had snapped. But he rolled over and pulled himself to his feet, and she didn't see any outward sign of a new injury. His hands were a mess, though. She had managed to slice a finger off from each hand and the black ichor flowed from these wounds as well.

Phiral held up his hands in front of his face and grinned savagely at the damage.

"You think this matters? Look here. *This* is what your attacks really do to me."

He lifted one leg and flexed his knee. It was the one she had broken moments before. Already, the wound in his neck seemed to be smaller.

"You can't kill someone who is already dead, Leyndra."

She gritted her teeth and tried to figure out a new approach. She knew he was right—she wasn't going to kill him by bits and pieces. She needed to inflict heavy damage all at once.

She needed that sword. But perhaps she could pull together a minor advantage first. Leyndra slowly moved forward, ready for Phiral's attack. He closed with her, prepared to grab whatever came within range of his claws. She knew he wanted to pin her, to stop her from moving. Then the advantage would be all his. Or so he thought.

Without warning, he lunged again and this time she didn't dodge. Instead, she stepped into him and, as she let him sweep his arms around her, she plunged both daggers toward his open eyes. Her right blade found its mark and sunk in all the way to the hilt. The other knife hit his cheekbone, and the blade tore a furrow in his face as it was deflected away from his eye.

But the one strike was enough. Phiral screamed and let go of Leyndra to grab the knife buried in his eye. She knew it wasn't enough to kill him, but Phiral still had many of the reactions of a living man. Over time, he would overcome those tendencies, but right now Leyndra took full advantage of his momentary weakness.

While he was distracted by the pain in his head, she grabbed the hilt of the sword and yanked. The act of withdrawing the sword from his body pulled him off balance and he stumbled away from her.

With a speed borne of desperation and what little power she could draw into her, Leyndra leaped forward and swung the sword at his head. With his good eye, he saw the blow coming and managed to awkwardly flinch at the last instant. The blade hacked across the top of his head and his scalp was ripped off as the sword glanced off his skull.

Screaming in rage, Phiral leapt at her. She spun to the side and brought the sword down across his forearm and severed the limb. His momentum took him past her, and as he turned to face her, she brought the weapon up in a slash across his face. Again, he flinched away, and it gave her the moment she needed to recover her stance.

As Leyndra flowed into a devastating attack routine, she saw Phiral's one good eye staring into her face. Rage no longer dwelt behind his eyes. For the first time, Leyndra saw Phiral show fear.

He raised one clawed hand to ward off her blow and she twisted her sword and took it off at the wrist. Before he had a chance to recover from this new wound, Leyndra spun and brought the blade across her body in an arcing swing.

Phiral's head separated from his body and tumbled across the floor of the crypt.

"Recover from that!" shouted Leyndra.

Phiral's body hit the floor like a wet sack of grain. A foul wind suddenly blew through the crypt, and Leyndra saw black smoke begin to issue from the stump of his neck. A black, shadowy hand reached out of the severed hole, followed by another, and Leyndra watched as Phiral's neck gave birth to a shadow creature that dragged itself from his corpse.

The creature raised itself from the body and turned to her. Leyndra could see nothing of Phiral Najare in the creature's shape, but then what shape was a person's spirit supposed to have? She didn't have an answer.

The shadow creature leaped up onto the wall and faded into the darkness.

Leyndra stepped over to Phiral's body and drew forth a small bone tube that was sticking out of his belt pouch. She tucked it into a small pocket inside her boot to investigate later.

"I chose poorly."

The voice rose behind Leyndra and she felt a thousand spiders crawling on her flesh, worms feasting on her corpse as she lay rotting under the ground.

She turned to face Phiral's master. Eothep looked into her eyes and she felt his will crush all thought, all resistance.

"I still need a servant," she faintly heard him hiss at her. "You will do nicely."

Chapter Thirty-Nine

D ARKNESS BEGAN TO DESCEND AROUND LEYNDRA AS her own mind slipped away from her. She fought to hold onto thought, onto her sense of self, but a deep lethargy filled her. A small part of her mind screamed at her to fight, but the peaceful rest of the dead called to her even more strongly.

As her eyelids began to droop, her vision cleared, just for an instant, and she saw the necromancer's face. He had the visage of death incarnate, the uncaring wave of darkness that swept over every living thing eventually. But this was more than just death—it was the perversion of a natural death, a twisted mockery of what should be the end, but an end that would never come.

Eothep took that which was dead and turned it into an abomination, a needle that pierced the skin of reality and drew forth the substance of unlife. Not the Abyss, the roiling chaos where demons were born from the nightmares of gods. No, this was a never-ending pool of dark energy, a bottomless pit of entropy that nonetheless reached out to touch this world.

The shock of looking upon that face, seeing the reality behind those eyes, snapped Leyndra out of her lethargy. She raised one hand and ran it down the edge of her sword. The pain of the blade biting into her palm cleared her mind and she stumbled backward, away from the necromancer.

A hissing sound above her brought her head up and she saw the walls and ceiling of the crypt crawling with the same shadow creatures she had faced the night Osho died.

Osho....

She tried to focus on his name, on his face, but without warning the creatures began to pull themselves from the walls and ceiling and drop toward her, shadowy claws outstretched. She spun her sword and lashed out desperately, causing the creatures to dissolve into nothingness as her strikes found them.

Leyndra needed to focus, to find her rhythm, to flow into that calm place where her movements were fluid and unhurried, and the sword was an extension of her own body. But she couldn't reach that place. She couldn't feel the *virtus* anymore.

It was completely gone.

A shadowy claw made it past her guard and slashed at her arm. Her skin turned grey where the creature touched her, and she felt a pain in her chest, like her heart had stopped for an instant and then restarted.

"Serve me and you will survive this night. Defy me and you will see the true power of death."

Eothep's voice sent a shiver down Leyndra's spine and her elbow joint creaked as she swung her sword and swiped away two more shadow creatures.

Can he turn me into an old woman with just his voice?

"There is no victory for you. Only the reward of bowing to my command, or suffering under my power like you have never imagined. Lay down your sword and become something more than you are."

Leyndra's knees began to ache, and her knuckles swelled under skin that began to loosen on her frame. How long had she been fighting here, in this crypt? An hour? A year?

Maybe she had been fighting here for eternity. Perhaps she was just a ghost, going through the same battle over and over again, experiencing the moments of her death as punishment for choosing not to serve Eothep. Was it too late to take his offer?

Or had it been made centuries ago?

She felt the sword grow heavy in her hands and she could no longer keep the point up, could no longer swing it with speed or precision.

Again and again, the claws of the shadow creatures slipped into her skin and her heart hammered heavy in her chest as grey marks spread across her flesh. Leyndra's vision became cloudy and she could see the crypt only as a blur while she tried to keep fighting.

She heard a clang and realized she had dropped the sword. Her clothing hung on her shriveled frame and the shadows closed in around her, no longer clawing at her, but reaching out to caress her, to take her into their embrace.

"I...will...not...serve...you," she managed to gasp, and her voice was old and weak. A strand of hair hung down over her face and she was not shocked to see it was white.

"No, you are too strong, too stubborn for that. You will fight me to the end, and you will lose."

She realized the shadows had parted to let Eothep approach her. Her head hung heavy on her neck and she couldn't raise her head to look him in the face this time.

"So, I will punish you. And then I will trap you here for eternity. When I come back and take this city, when I bring forth death and fill the world with the void, I will leave this crypt for you. And you will stay here, without even the comfort of madness to which you may escape."

Leyndra felt herself sink to her knees, and the touch of the cold stone floor sent pain up her legs into her groin. She gasped and fell to her side, her elbow driven into her own ribs as she landed. She could feel the bone just beneath her skin, all other flesh shriveled and gone.

Just bone and skin...bone and skin...and soon not even that.

*   *   *

LEYNDRA WANTED TO CRY, BUT KNEW NO TEARS WOULD COME. She was dried out, a husk, an empty shell for her spirit that would stay here forever.

Zheemeng was dead, another corpse in a vast garden of corpses, unaware of how easily he had been slain.

Jeyrra would remain in Ythis to see the fall of the city when Eothep returned. She would join the ranks of the dead, to spread across the world like a dark cloud, blotting out all light and hope.

Flasek had probably been slain by Beyus earlier. If not, the Imperial Guard would end his life in some back alley soon enough. He would feel his blood leaking out into the gutter and wonder why he had fought so hard.

Morit would spend his days hating his life. And when the armies of the dead marched out from Ythis, he would rail against its ending as if he had valued it all along.

These were people Leyndra had promised herself she would protect. She had taken responsibility for them, for their safety, and had failed them all. Just as she had failed Osho. Her friends, everyone in Ythis, would pay the price for her failure.

She had a chance to give herself to the sorcerer, Xeylien, and change all of this. But she had taken it all upon herself instead.

Why didn't I take that help? Why didn't I sacrifice my freedom to protect everyone else?

The question made her uncomfortable.

You know why you didn't do it.

No, she didn't want to think about that. She had responsibilities, just like Jeyrra had been responsible for the gang members who followed her.

Jeyrra sent them on their way when she could no longer protect them.

But that was Jeyrra. Leyndra couldn't do that. She had taken responsibility for Morit when he was just a child. When they were *both* children. She had protected him, kept him safe, sheltered him from the worst this city could throw at him.

And he resented you for it. Because you were never ready for him to grow up. You were never ready for him to stop needing you.

But he did need Leyndra, even if he didn't realize it. She had saved him from so many bad decisions, so many dangerous people. She had taken away some of his freedom, but it had been for his own good.

And now he blames everyone else for his own shortcomings. You protected him from everyone, even himself, and he never learned how to deal with the world. So, he doesn't know any happiness.

Fine, if Leyndra had to take responsibility for Morit's unhappiness, then she would do that too. She would—

But another thought intruded. If she was responsible for his unhappiness, it was the result of everything she had done for him. And wasn't that responsibility more important?

What about your responsibility for yourself?

But Leyndra *did* take care of herself. She had pursued a career as a Warden, one that she enjoyed and allowed her to protect Osho—

And that was the failure that precipitated all others.

Osho, the man she had sworn to protect. Her first oath, severed by her own hand. She had watched the light in his eyes fade away, her sword in his chest.

Osho would forgive you. You need to forgive yourself.

A pain ripped through Leyndra's chest and she felt her heart stutter. She was going to die here, now.

Osho has forgiven you.

But that didn't make any sense. Osho was dead. He didn't have a chance to forgive her for her failure. Once you were dead, there was no way back....

Leyndra thought of Phiral. She thought of the walking dead who had attacked her when she had gone back for Tyina. But that was different—they had bodies to inhabit. Osho would be just a spirit...

... moving through the world, looking for justice...

... looking for Leyndra...

... looking for a way to help....

As Leyndra felt herself dying, she took her final breath and pushed it out, trying to speak one last time. Her lips were barely able to move.

"Osho," she whispered. "Help me."

A gentle hand touched her shoulder as she felt her consciousness slip away.

Chapter Forty

L EYNDRA'S EYES SNAPPED OPEN AS HER BODY CONVULSED. Agony shot through every inch of her, and she arched her back and let out a scream that echoed through the crypt. She felt her muscles contract violently and then snap loose again, and the back of her head smacked off the stone floor.

Every one of her senses was overwhelmed as the *virtus* flowed back into her, drowning her in its exquisite and terrible force. The sensations were too much, and she felt her mind try to black out to avoid the overload, but the power kept her awake and aware, all too aware as her body rejuvenated itself, every nerve ending ablaze.

She could see the surface of the ceiling in the darkness far above her, the blemishes in the stone, minute cracks, the finest threads of abandoned spider webs still clinging to the corners. She could smell the stone, the earth surrounding the crypt, the dust of the necromancer, the bones within the sarcophagus an arm's reach from her. She heard the hissing of the shadow creatures, the sweep of Eothep's robes on the floor as he turned to face her. She could feel the hard stone under her, every thread of her clothing, the rough texture of her leather vest on her skin.

Her throat raw, Leyndra's scream died as she drew in a ragged breath, her first in this new life. She had died at the feet of the necromancer, and she was born anew from the swell of *virtus*—the power that had returned to her when she realized the truth.

Osho was here with her. He still needed her to keep him from the grasp of Eothep, just as she needed his help to bring forth her gifts. He had saved her life, and she must now save his spirit.

With a thought Leyndra was on her feet, her sword in her hands. The blade blazed with light as she poured her power into it. The shadow creatures reeled back from that blade, but the necromancer wasn't done yet.

"Slay her!" he commanded, and the creatures closed on her once more. Time seemed to slow as she opened herself to her Warden gifts. She let her instincts guide her movements and when the blade touched the shadows, they didn't dissipate and reform somewhere else. They burned up in a flash, like a sheet of dry parchment held over a candle flame.

They tried to claw at her, but her sword destroyed them as she dodged and weaved. Leyndra was a gust of wind among them, and they like leaves tossed about and ripped apart by something they couldn't touch.

With a final swipe, Leyndra dispatched the last shadows. She turned to look for the necromancer and gasped. She could *see* Osho standing at her side, a faint glimmer in the darkness. Leyndra could just make out his features, and she smiled at him.

"Enough!" shouted Eothep. "You have occupied too much of my time already, and I cannot spare any more to make you suffer. Your precious nobleman's spirit evaded my grasp, but he could not break free entirely, and now you think his help will be enough to defeat me? You're both fools. Now you will simply die."

The necromancer opened his mouth, his jaw stretching down to make a vast, black hole from which issued a writhing tendril of dark smoke. It reached out toward Leyndra as a second emerged from the same orifice.

Leyndra could feel Osho's fear at her side. This smoke was the pure stuff of death, the entropic energy made real. As the first tendril snapped toward her, Leyndra parried with her blade and managed to knock it away. But its touch left a black scar on the sword, and she could feel the energy she was feeding into the blade recoil from the contact.

A third and fourth tendril emerged from Eothep's distended mouth, and the necromancer held his arms out in front of his chest and clenched his fists. Wrinkles in the fabric of reality spread out from his clenched hands as he grabbed time and space itself as one might grab a hanging curtain.

He slowly began to move his hands apart, and Leyndra could see the air between them rippling as existence itself began to fray. She figured if Eothep managed to open a hole to the yawning void, she would be torn apart, along with much of the surrounding area.

Two of the tendrils reached for her, while two reached for Osho. The *virtus* was a living thing inside of her body, powered by her will to protect her charge from further harm. She batted away the tendrils, each strike leaving another mark on her sword, a dead space which no longer accepted her power flowing into it.

She heard a terrible ripping noise, and felt her ears pop. A rush of blood came from her nose and with a thought she stopped the bleeding. But the necromancer had ripped a tiny hole in the air between his clenched fists. It wasn't merely a hole, but a tunnel into another realm that shone with a terrible sucking darkness. And at the far end of that tunnel waited an ancient, unknowable nothingness, a conscious entity that was the void from which Eothep received his power.

Leyndra knew she had an instant to react. She dropped her sword and, ducking under a thrusting tendril, charged at the necromancer. At the last second, she thrust with her legs and made an impossible leap up and over the tear and its creator.

Leyndra landed lightly behind Eothep and drove herself into the back of the necromancer with such force that he was thrown forward across the hole. The tendrils blew apart into clouds of black dust as Eothep's chest crossed into the space occupied by the intrusion of the void. The power of that alien realm instantly spread across the necromancer's entire body, turning it into ash before Eothep could even scream.

The necromancer blew apart into flakes of ashes and dust in the power of the cold wind coming from the hole. The wrinkled essence of reality was released and snapped back into place, and the hole sealed up with a sucking silence so profound that Leyndra's eardrums trembled at the sudden, utter absence of sound.

Leyndra staggered from the abrupt cessation of the terrible wind. An instant later, her hearing returned to her with a rush and the sound of her own breathing was suddenly loud in her ears. Osho moved toward Leyndra, and she heard his voice as if from a great distance.

"Leyndra, thank you for saving me. For avenging me."

Leyndra could feel tears on her face.

"You saved *me*, Osho. Without you, I would have died. I should have realized you were near me all this time, trying to communicate with me."

"The barriers...were too great...only here...in this place of death...."

He was fading, become fainter and fainter each passing moment.

"...and now...I am free...."

Osho faded away and was gone. The *virtus* inside her slowed to a trickle. And then it, too, disappeared.

Her gifts would not be coming back this time. Leyndra was no longer a Warden.

She didn't want to spend another moment inside this crypt. She left her sword on the ground and dragged herself up the stone steps to the landing. At the top she hesitated, but pushed herself forward without looking back.

Leyndra stumbled out into the night and took a look around. She jumped as a figure rose from behind a nearby tombstone.

Zheemeng. He was alive.

He came around the tombstone and approached her cautiously. She couldn't help but laugh at the concerned expression on his face.

"Leyndra, you did it." His words weren't quite a question, but they weren't exactly a statement, either.

"Yeah, it's done."

"There was a man on top of the mausoleum. He crawled down the wall like an insect and came in behind you. I wanted to yell, to warn you...."

Leyndra held up her hand.

"You're alive because you didn't. That's all that matters."

"What...?"

He wanted to ask her what had happened inside the crypt, but he wasn't sure what state she was in.

"Let's go meet the others. I'll tell you when we're all together. For now, let's just walk in silence, okay?"

Zheemeng nodded and fell into step beside her.

She had a lot to think about while they walked to the Wolf's Den. And some big decisions to make.

*   *   *

JEYRRA LOOKED UP AS THE DOOR OPENED AND HER HEART hammered in her chest. And then Leyndra stepped through the door, followed by Zheemeng. Jeyrra leaped to her feet and threw herself at Leyndra, wrapping the other woman in an embrace that nearly knocked Leyndra off her feet. Zheemeng was forced to grab Leyndra's shoulders to prevent her from falling right back out the door.

Jeyrra clutched her friend, not wanting to let go. She also didn't want anyone to see the tears running down her face—she wasn't one to cry in front of anyone. Never mind that, she wasn't one to cry, period.

But deep down Jeyrra hadn't expected to ever see her friend again. She had felt Leyndra was going to her own death when she left them early in the evening, and Jeyrra needed to make sure her friend was really here, really alive.

Leyndra hugged her back and the two of them stood there, not speaking, just holding each other. Jeyrra was aware of Zheemeng moving away into the room to introduce himself to Flasek and the Wolf's man Koral Creyss.

"I did it," Leyndra whispered in her ear. "Osho was there and he saved me."

Emotion overwhelmed her and she couldn't speak anymore, so Jeyrra just held her tightly. She wanted to hear all the details, but now was not the time, so she kept quiet. She could hear Zheemeng and Flasek exchanging notes about Phiral Najare, the necromancer, and Investigator Beyus Chamirra.

Let them talk, she thought. *My friend needs me.*

"I'm so sorry," Leyndra whispered. "I tried so hard to do it all myself, and I should have kept you closer to me."

Jeyrra released her hold enough so that she could look her friend in the face.

"Enough. You did it. *We* did it. We're all here, we all survived...."

She saw the look in Leyndra's eyes and, with a guilty start, she realized Leyndra was thinking about Hathi.

"I'm sorry. I meant...."

"It's okay," replied Leyndra. "I understand what you meant. And you're right."

She gave Jeyrra another quick hug and then stepped back. Jeyrra moved to one side so that Leyndra could finally speak to Flasek. The big man stood but then suddenly seemed self-conscious. Leyndra stepped forward and wrapped her arms around his chest. He winced in pain, but hid it from Leyndra as he gave her a hug in return.

After introductions were made with Koral Creyss, Jeyrra couldn't wait any longer.

"What happens now?" she asked.

Leyndra looked at the floor.

"I leave with the caravan at first light, as planned."

Jeyrra looked at Zheemeng and saw the disappointment written across his face. He glanced over and met Jeyrra's gaze. She nodded toward Leyndra, but he gave a small shake of his head and looked away.

Jeyrra wondered if anything had happened between the two of them. There was obviously an attraction there, but she doubted it had gone past mutual admiration. Leyndra was too focused.

Her friend turned back to Flasek as Jeyrra moved to stand beside Zheemeng.

"What about you, Sergeant? Do you think the Imperial Guard will come after you for the death of the investigator?"

Flasek shrugged.

"Who knows? There are no witnesses to his death, and we cleaned out any evidence that might point to me. His personal lackeys are all dead, too. I figure the Guard leadership will blame it all on you. And once the Wolf's men start spreading the rumors that you've escaped from the city...."

Jeyrra spoke in a low voice pitched so that only Zheemeng could hear her.

"You going with her?"

"I don't think so," he replied in a whisper. "I'm needed here."

"That's horseshit, Zheemeng. You'll always have a place in my gang, and you're more valuable than you'll ever realize, but Leyndra needs you more than I do."

Zheemeng shrugged.

"She hasn't asked me to go with her."

"Leyndra's not the asking type. I'd think you'd have figured that out by now. But I won't watch the two of you make a stupid mistake just because she's too proud and you're too scared."

Zheemeng frowned at her and stepped away. She gave him one of her looks that said she expected her advice to be heeded.

Flasek was still talking to Leyndra. "Do you really think you'll make it past the gate?"

Leyndra nodded.

"Phiral made preparations to get himself and the necromancer past the soldiers at the gate. I'm going to rely on those preparations."

"And what if it doesn't work?"

"Then I fight my way out of the city. One way or another, I won't be in Ythis past dawn."

Flasek grinned at her.

"This city won't be the same without you. Who's going to cause all the excitement now?"

"I thought I was a pain in your arse," said Leyndra archly.

"Hah! That you are, young woman. But I supposed a bit of pain in my arse is better than me just sitting on it all day long, every day."

Leyndra looked around the room and heaved a weary sigh.

"As much as I'd love to spend even more time with all of you, I must go meet up with Vaysarr and make the final preparations."

Jeyrra noticed Zheemeng frown at the mention of the hired swordsman, and felt her anger rise. The man was being a fool, but she knew how to give him the right push. She stepped in front of Leyndra just as her friend was moving to speak to Zheemeng.

"You take care of yourself. I know you can't tell me when you're coming back, but I'll still be here when you do. When you return, stop at the village where Morit will be staying and send me a message from there. I'll let you know if it's safe for you to enter the city."

Leyndra nodded. She looked past Jeyrra at Zheemeng.

"You have to go, Leyndra. You can't miss your chance to get out of Ythis."

Leyndra looked back at Jeyrra and smiled sadly.

"You're right. I really have to leave now."

She looked around the room one last time and then turned and walked out the door.

Chapter Forty-One

Y OU *CAN'T QUIT.*"

Flasek stood in front of his lieutenant in the man's office at the Watch headquarters. It was barely dawn, and his superior hadn't been too keen to meet with him this early in the morning. But Flasek wanted this to be over before the new day had really begun.

He had waited long enough.

"With respect, sir, there's nothing to prevent me from quitting. I'm not the first."

The lieutenant sat back, stunned.

"Maybe not the first watchman, Lumayth, but sergeants sure don't quit the Watch. Making sergeant is pretty much a guarantee a man will *never* leave."

"I'm not that kind of sergeant."

The lieutenant stared at him in amazement for a moment, and then snorted with laughter.

"No, I suppose you're not, are you? You were a real troublemaker when you were just a watchman—always getting into things that didn't concern you. Did you ever wonder why we even promoted you to sergeant?"

Flasek shrugged.

"To teach me how to lead?"

The lieutenant laughed again.

"By the Abyss, no! We figured two things would happen. One, you'd get used to the perks of the job and stop caring so much about every little thing. And two, you'd still be around if we needed someone who could handle a difficult case that we couldn't pass off to the Guard."

"It worked for a bit, sir."

"Yeah, Sergeant, it did. You calmed down a fair bit, gained some weight, stopped charging into the middle of every bad situation. At least, until that nobleman was murdered. What happened?"

Flasek thought about his answer. His first inclination was to blame it on his hatred of the Guard, his desire to make them look bad. But that wasn't really the truth—it was just a convenient excuse.

He finally understood the truth.

"I got tired of not caring."

The lieutenant looked him over for another moment. Then he sighed and nodded.

"I don't understand it, but it seems right coming from you. What are you going to do now? Go work for the Wolf or one of the gangs?"

Flasek tried not to be insulted by the lieutenant's suggestion. Most watchmen left the Watch to do exactly that—accept a better offer from the criminal element in the city.

But Flasek wasn't most watchmen.

"No, sir. I'm going into business for myself. To help people."

The lieutenant was confused.

"Help people? How can you make a living *helping* people? Or are you giving up all your possessions, too, and will beg for handouts on the street in your spare time?"

Now it was Flasek's turn to laugh.

"Sir, I'm good at solving problems. You know that. I don't belong in the Watch. But I can still have a job helping people solve their problems."

The lieutenant obviously felt that was a dubious way to make money, but he didn't seem to want to argue.

"Okay, then. If that's what you want, I won't stop you. I'll need your badge, truncheon, and sword."

Flasek took his badge and placed it on the lieutenant's desk. He stared at it for a moment, waiting for it to hit him that he was leaving the Watch, but he felt only relief. He undid his scabbard and placed his weapon on the desk beside the badge.

"Um, I can't give you the truncheon. I broke it."

"How?"

Flasek just gave the lieutenant a blank look, and eventually the other man understood.

"Oh. Did you arrest the perpetrator, or just leave him in a gutter?"

"I just left him, sir. He was just some garbage that needed to be taught a lesson."

"Okay. Normally I would dock your pay for that, but I'm going to let it go as a favor to you. This will be the last favor you'll get from the Watch—you know that? You won't be one of us anymore. You'll be just another citizen of Ythis."

"I'm okay with that, sir."

Flasek held out his hand and the lieutenant gave it a shake.

"Go collect your final pay, Ser—uh, Lumayth and then get out of my building. I've got work to do."

Flasek left the lieutenant's office and descended the stairs to the main floor. The on-duty sergeant looked at him in surprise.

"You coming to relieve me early, finally?"

"Nope," said Flasek without pausing and continued walking out of the building.

He stepped outside and looked at the lightening sky. Dawn was about to break. Leyndra would be leaving the city in the next few minutes.

Flasek realized he would have to find his men later and say goodbye in person. Regardless of what the lieutenant said, he knew Lassim would remain an ally. He figured Yaral would also help him out if he needed it, though the man would complain the whole time he was doing so.

He was taking a big risk, leaving the Watch like this. He might be forced to end up exactly as the lieutenant had thought, working for one of the gangs or for The Wolf. There was no guarantee anyone would want to pay him for his help solving their problems.

He should feel nervous about what he had just done. But as he walked along the streets of Ythis, heading for home, he just felt free.

*   *   *

THE WHITE POWDER ON LEYNDRA'S FACE MADE HER SKIN itch, but she forced herself to ignore it and pulled the black cloak tighter at her chin. The manacle around her left wrist was heavy, and the chain clinked as she moved. Before the caravan would head for the city gate, the other end of that chain would be securely attached to one of the wagons laden with supplies.

Leyndra really didn't want to be chained to the wagon, but the soldiers at the gate might check to see if it was secure. She was supposed to be insane, and no one wanted someone touched directly by the god Iathephos wandering loose in the city. She had asked Vaysarr if this was a necessary disguise, and he explained that posing as a Bride of Iathephos meant that no one would want to get too close to her.

All she had to do was roll her eyes, mumble to herself, and generally act like she was crazy, and everyone would keep their distance.

Still, if anything went wrong, she was tethered to a big, slow vehicle. Not an ideal way to sneak out of Ythis.

Her caravan consisted of four wagons with two horses each, and four hired guards on their own horses. Each wagon had a driver and a porter, all hard men with weather-beaten skin and the occasional knife scar. She figured she would end up having to lay a beating on at least one, perhaps two of those men if they got any ideas about her while they traveled.

Leyndra had examined the small bone tube she had taken from Phiral's corpse. It contained an ancient parchment with a map of the Bleak Wastes, marking a route to something called the Ruins of Shujesh. This map must have been what the necromancer was looking for, which meant it led to something powerful and potentially of great evil.

Leyndra wondered if she was making a mistake going there herself. Maybe she would be better off giving the parchment to Xeylien and letting the sorcerer handle whatever was hidden in those ruins.

But she knew she wasn't going to do that. It wasn't in her nature. She needed to get out of the city for a few months at the least, and this gave her a chance to do something important. As long as these men were willing to follow her lead, she was going to take them into the Bleak Wastes.

A figure stepped around the corner at the mouth of the alley and stopped. Vaysarr loosened his blade in its scabbard and approached whoever it was. They spoke for a moment, and then the swordsman led the figure back toward Leyndra. When they got close enough, she saw it was Zheemeng. She realized with a guilty start that she hadn't said goodbye to him.

As he stood there, looking at her, she suddenly didn't know what to say. She took a breath, but then he opened his mouth and she decided to let him go first.

"Leyndra, I...you could use a friend on this journey. Jeyrra thinks I should go with you."

Leyndra was taken aback by his words. Had Jeyrra ordered Zheemeng to leave Ythis to keep her company? Jeyrra knew Leyndra better than that.

"Well, you're not her servant, or her slave. I know this expedition will be dangerous, but I think I can handle it. You're not obligated to come along just because Jeyrra told you to."

Zheemeng looked down at the ground and growled under his breath before speaking again.

"No, that came out wrong. Let me try again. I think you *could* use a friend on this journey, and I want to come with you. I know you don't need my help, but I'm useful in a fight, and my healing skills...."

He paused.

"I want to come with you. If you don't want me to travel with you, if you want me to stay here, I will. I'm not going to demand you let me join the expedition. But, if you'd like me to come, to help out where I can—well, that's what I want, too."

Leyndra didn't know what to say. She wasn't sure if he really was just trying to help, or if he was looking for something more. It was a nice thought, but she still wasn't in any kind of situation where she had the freedom to start a relationship.

It still wasn't time.

"Listen, Zheemeng, as much as I'd like you to travel with me, we can't become more than—"

"I know," he interrupted. "I'm not looking for that, at least not right now. But I also don't want you to walk out of my life, and maybe never come back."

She knew it would end up complicating things if he came along. She wasn't sure she could continue to spend time with him and not want to start something more. And yet, she also didn't want to walk out of his life. Not now that he was standing here in front of her, asking her to let him join the expedition.

"It will be dangerous," she said, and immediately felt foolish. Like they hadn't been in a terribly dangerous situation for the last two weeks. Zheemeng just smiled.

"I figured as much," he replied.

Leyndra turned and called Vaysarr back over.

"Vaysarr, this is Zheemeng. He will be joining the expedition."

The swordsman gave Zheemeng an appraising look and then turned to Leyndra.

"We'll need to get more supplies to feed another mouth."

"We can do that at the first village we pass through," she answered.

"Is he any good with a sword?"

"I will vouch for his skill. Plus, he's a healer."

Vaysarr paused to consider this.

"That's good. Him coming along isn't going to complicate matters, is it?"

Leyndra knew what Vaysarr was asking. There would be no opportunities for Leyndra and Zheemeng to spend time alone with each other. Any outward displays of affection between them would put similar ideas into the heads of the other men. Vaysarr didn't want to deal with rivalries and fights over her.

"You have my word, Vaysarr, that we will conduct ourselves in a manner that causes no additional difficulties."

She could tell he didn't really like the idea, but he nodded anyway and returned to his horse.

"Now what?" asked Zheemeng.

"Now we disguise you as just another porter until we're outside of the city. We'll figure out the rest once we're safely away from Ythis."

Vaysarr gave a low whistle that traveled the length of the alley and got the attention of everyone.

Dawn was breaking. It was time to leave.

*   *   *

THE GUARD SOLDIER EXAMINED THE PAPER VAYSARR HAD handed him and looked over the wagons and other horsemen. He stopped when his eyes alighted on Leyndra.

"Is that a—"

"Bride of Iathephos, yes. There's a village about four days ride in the direction we're going. The local priest there has earned a ... reward."

The soldier tried to suppress it, but Leyndra could see him shiver. She started singing in a low, gravelly voice, a song of nothing but random words. The man turned away from her and back to Vaysarr.

"I don't envy you, traveling with something like that. But I can't let you leave."

Leyndra almost stopped singing, but forced herself to keep going. The soldier didn't seem to notice her slight pause.

"Why can't we leave?" asked Vaysarr. "I've got the writ from the merchant house. What's the problem?"

"*She's* the problem. No woman can leave the city unless she's checked over to make sure it isn't the wanted criminal we've been searching for. We also need to search the wagons in case you've got someone hiding among your cargo."

Vaysarr shook his head and chuckled.

"If you want to examine the Bride, be my guest. Be careful, though. She bites ... seriously."

The soldier looked at Leyndra but didn't approach the wagon where she was tethered.

"Don't you have any letter from the Church?"

Vaysarr shook his head again.

"Can you get a priest to come down here and vouch for her?"

"Maybe, but that'll delay us for hours. I can tell you two of the priests chained her to the wagon themselves. So, I don't think it's possible she's the wanted criminal you're looking for."

"Still, I—"

"Soldier," said a voice from behind Leyndra. She almost turned, but forced herself to go back to mumbling and rolling her eyes around. She knew that voice, and a chill ran down her spine.

The person who had spoken stepped up past Leyndra's wagon and she saw it was Xeylien's apprentice. Once again, his face was shadowed by his wide-brimmed hat. Leyndra wondered why he had turned up here. Could he intend to betray her to the Imperial Guard for her refusal to cooperate?

But Leyndra knew that didn't make sense. If he had wanted to capture her and turn her in, he could have sent his demon to follow her when she left the Tower of Threads on her last visit.

The Guard soldier apparently knew who the apprentice was as well, since he visibly tensed when he saw who had addressed him. All of the expedition's horses became nervous and began whinnying and sidestepping as the dark figure strode along the line of wagons. Xeylien's apprentice stopped before the Guard soldier and Leyndra noted he towered over the soldier, though the soldier was not a small man.

"This caravan will be let through the gates immediately. They cannot be delayed on their travels."

The soldier looked from the apprentice to Vaysarr and back, obviously concerned about having to confront an apprentice of one of the Five.

"S-sir, I cannot do that. I have strict orders—"

"My master has need of this caravan to arrive at its final destination on time. Perhaps you would prefer to return with me to the Tower of Threads and explain your refusal to cooperate to her directly."

The soldier appeared well and truly trapped.

"But I can't let the woman leave. I'd face court-martial."

Xeylien's apprentice leaned in toward the man and spoke slowly and with great enunciation.

"I. Do. Not. Care."

The soldier looked at his three fellows who guarded the gate, but none of them were interested in stepping forward to join the argument. He gave a pleading look to Vaysarr, but the swordsman merely crossed his arms and leaned on the pommel of his saddle, waiting patiently as if none of this really mattered to him.

The soldier opened his mouth to argue further, but then he seemed to deflate suddenly. Leyndra could tell he finally understood he wasn't going to risk losing his life over losing his job. He turned to the other soldiers and motioned them to open the gate.

They looked at him dumbfounded for a moment, and then realized he wasn't going to argue with Xeylien's apprentice any further. The Imperial Guard was giving in.

As the soldiers opened the gates, the apprentice began to walk back along the line of wagons. His voice easily reached Leyndra's ears, despite him not speaking to her directly.

"My master appreciates what you did last night. She felt the destruction of the necromancer echo across the city. My assistance here today removes any debt she might have owed you."

Leyndra kept up her act in case any of the soldiers looked her way, but she whispered "thank you" to the apprentice.

"Xeylien is also interested in whatever the necromancer was searching for. Should you discover an item of power, do not attempt to handle it yourself. If you can transport it safely back to Ythis, my master will accept it and dispose of it appropriately."

Leyndra gave a curt nod and continued her performance.

The apprentice turned and walked back into the city.

The gates were now open, and Vaysarr led the caravan under the stone arch and out of Ythis. Once outside the high walls, Leyndra took a deep breath. The landscape was not beautiful, just ragged scrub leading to broken hills in the distance, but to Leyndra it represented a freedom she had been unsure she would ever have again.

The horsemen spread out from the wagons to better respond to any potential threat and they all continued to travel along the road that would lead, eventually, to a small village near the edge of the Bleak Wastes. Leyndra wasn't sure what would happen there, but she was ready to face it head on.

To her right, the sun continued its rise into the sky.

~ End ~

**More books in the Tales of the Undying Empire series
are available in print or ebook at Amazon.**

Thank you for reading The Severed Oath. If you enjoyed this book, please tell others about it. Honest reviews are also greatly appreciated and are the best way to help other readers discover new authors.

About Andrew J. Luther

Andrew J. Luther lives in Burlington, Ontario with his wife and son. He currently works as a communications professional in his day-job, but spends his spare time playing tabletop roleplaying games and writing.

You can keep up-to-date with Andew by joining his mailing list at www.andrewjluther.com or on Twitter @andrewjluther.